"That's not Ricky Wolfe."

It was a flat statement.

Broghman felt his gun in his palm slip like a frightened animal. His breath hissed in his nostrils. In the silence that followed, he stopped dead still and there was only the sound of Julie's high heels tacking along the wooden floor and slowly, with a kind of frozen dread, coming to a halt, too.

Broghman turned. Out of the shadow a guy slipped who was too well-dressed for his own good. With a long white horse-face and red-rimmed, tired eyes and sweat on his cheeks.

Broghman pulled his gun, and while the darkness got darker, and there was only Merritt in front of him, and the others waiting, he swore, tightened up and fired three shots.

Merritt folded over the bullets, taking them into him with curious, pushing, helpful fingers. He fell flat down on his head, choking...

KILLER, Come Back to Me

THE CRIME STORIES OF
Ray Bradbury

A HARD CASE   CRIME BOOK

A HARD CASE CRIME BOOK
(HCC-S08)
First Hard Case Crime edition: August 2020

Published by

Titan Books
A division of Titan Publishing Group Ltd
144 Southwark Street
London SE1 0UP

in collaboration with Winterfall LLC

*This book is a work of fiction. Names, characters, places, and
incidents either are the products of the author's imagination or
are used fictitiously, and any resemblance to actual events or
persons, living or dead, is entirely coincidental.*

Print edition ISBN 978-1-78909-665-1
E-book ISBN 978-1-78909-540-1

Design direction by Max Phillips
www.maxphillips.net

Typeset by Swordsmith Productions

Printed and bound by CPI (UK) Ltd, Croydon CR0 4YY

Visit us on the web at www.HardCaseCrime.com

KILLER, COME BACK TO ME

Contents

The Talking Box:
Ray Bradbury's Crime Fiction
by Jonathan R. Eller

"I...took all these pages and put them in my talking box. That was the box I kept by my typewriter where my ideas lay and spoke to me early mornings...so my stories got written." In the early 1980s, Ray Bradbury used his imaginary talking box to compose *Death Is a Lonely Business*, an experiment in auto-biography that emerged from decades of suspense crime stories told through unexpected plot twists and vividly dark metaphors. If you want to know how Ray Bradbury developed the power to write this late-life novel and its sequels, you must read through the tales gathered here in *Killer, Come Back to Me*.

As we look back from the vantage point of Bradbury's 2020 centennial year, the significance of these sinister tales is un-mistakable. They are as important to the first twenty years of his career—his most prolific decades as a story writer—as the fantasy and science fiction that he brought into the literary mainstream. In fact, his special off-trail brand of crime fiction found wide popularity in the detective pulps while he was still developing the mastery of science fiction that he would achieve in the postwar genre magazines.

Bradbury's crime pathologies also spilled over into the pages of *Weird Tales*, where by 1944 he would appear in all six bi-monthly issues. "The Smiling People," from the May 1946 issue of *Weird Tales*, is just such an example, but by then Bradbury had already fully established himself in the stable of detective

pulps flourishing within the Popular Publications syndicate.
There was just enough "grue" in some of his crime tales to place
five stories in *Dime Mystery*, one of Popular's "shudder pulps"
modeled on the Grand Guignol tradition of visualized terror.
These include the haunting "Dead Men Rise Up Never," "Corpse
Carnival," and the shocking consequences of birth trauma found
in "The Small Assassin," all featured in this volume.

Popular's subeditors Mike Tilden and Ryerson Johnson
quickly warmed to Bradbury's unusual style and the emotional
fire of his prose and accepted a total of eight stories in the less
gruesome Popular pulps *Detective Tales* and *New Detective*.
The range of these stories is represented in the collection by
"Killer, Come Back to Me!," "The Trunk Lady," and " 'I'm Not
So Dumb!' " Popular's editor-in-chief Alden Norton was frustrated by Bradbury's insistence on letting his characters tell
their own stories, but he nonetheless took "Yesterday I Lived!"
for *Flynn's Detective Fiction* just before wartime paper rationing
killed off that well-respected genre magazine. Although Bradbury never submitted to the logical conventions of crime fiction,
his early mastery of the form is evident in two of his earliest
1944 sales—"The Trunk Lady" and "Yesterday I Lived!," stories highly regarded by Bradbury's mentors Leigh Brackett and
Henry Kuttner.

By the early 1950s, Bradbury's newer crime and suspense
ideas radiated out into the science fiction stories he described as
his "marionette" tales. Two of these, "Marionettes, Inc." and
"Punishment Without Crime," are paired in the second half of
this collection. By this time Bradbury was well-established in the
major market magazines, where he would take his murderers
out of noir settings and into the small-town Midwestern life he
remembered from childhood. "The Whole Town's Sleeping,"
perhaps Bradbury's most famous suspense tale, prompted *Ellery*

Queen's Frederic Dannay to solicit the sequel, "At Midnight, in the Month of June"; both tales are paired here, surrounded by other experiments in crime fiction originating in the 1950s and early 1960s, but often not published until years later.

It didn't really matter when these stories were published; in his mind, they already formed a great part of the foundation that had made him one of the best-known storytellers of our time—a masterful explorer of the dark fantastic; a universally recognized guardian of freedom of the imagination; an abiding presence in Hollywood; and a visionary of the Space Age. But Bradbury was, above all, an explorer of the things that make us human, and his probing creativity reached deepest into the darker regions of the human mind. Perhaps more than any other aspect of his work, Bradbury's crime suspense fiction reveals what Damon Knight called Bradbury's prime area of interest: "the fundamental prerational fears and longings and desires: the rage at being born; the will to be loved; the longing to communicate; the hatred of parents and siblings, the fear of things that are not the self."

Selecting the stories for this collection proved to be a challenge eagerly embraced. An earlier collection, aptly titled *A Memory of Murder*, gathered a number of the stories from Bradbury's Popular Publications magazine sales of the mid-1940s. Hard Case Crime publisher Charles Ardai, Bradbury's long-time literary agent Michael Congdon, and I eventually reached across a far broader span of time to bring together the best early stories with the later tales that document Bradbury's best crime suspense efforts written in the 1950s and early 1960s. In the process, we harvested three of Bradbury's noir-era tales that had evaded the earlier collection entirely: "The Fruit at the Bottom of the Bowl"; our title story, "Killer, Come Back to Me!"; and "Where Everything Ends," the long-unpublished source text for Bradbury's milestone 1985 detective novel, *Death Is a Lonely Business*.

The imaginary talking box of that novel, representing mysterious and unpredictable upwellings from the writer's deep subconscious, is as close as we'll ever get to the enigmatic source of Ray Bradbury's ideas. He viewed life as a long rope that "goes back to the time we were born and extends on out ahead to the time of our death." The moments in between became stories that probe the past or perhaps catch a glimpse of the future. *Killer, Come Back to Me* opens with "A Touch of Petulance," the story of a possible dark future; the second tale, "The Screaming Woman," pivots on a crucial memory from the past. Present, past or future, this new collection of Ray Bradbury's crime stories beckons. You are invited to follow his lead.

Jonathan R. Eller is a Chancellor's Professor of English and director of the Center for Ray Bradbury Studies at Indiana University's School of Liberal Arts. His books on Bradbury's life and career include the trilogy Becoming Ray Bradbury, Ray Bradbury Unbound, *and* Bradbury Beyond Apollo.

A Touch of Petulance

On an otherwise ordinary evening in May, a week before his twenty-ninth birthday, Jonathan Hughes met his fate, commuting from another time, another year, another life.

His fate was unrecognizable at first, of course, and boarded the train at the same hour, in Pennsylvania Station, and sat with Hughes for the dinnertime journey across Long Island. It was the newspaper held by this fate disguised as an older man that caused Jonathan Hughes to stare and finally say:

"Sir, pardon me, your *New York Times* seems different from mine. The typeface on your front page seems more modern. Is that a later edition?"

"No!" The older man stopped, swallowed hard, and at last managed to say, "Yes. A very late edition."

Hughes glanced around. "Excuse me, but—all the other editions look the same. Is yours a trial copy for a future change?"

"Future?" The older man's mouth barely moved. His entire body seemed to wither in his clothes, as if he had lost weight with a single exhalation. "Indeed," he whispered. "Future change. God, what a joke."

Jonathan Hughes blinked at the newspaper's dateline:

May 2, 1999.

"Now, see here—" he protested, and then his eyes moved down to find a small story, minus picture, in the upper-left-hand corner of the front page:

WOMAN MURDERED

POLICE SEEK HUSBAND

Body of Mrs. Alice Hughes found shot to death—

The train thundered over a bridge. Outside the window, a billion trees rose up, flourished their green branches in convulsions of wind, then fell as if chopped to earth.

The train rolled into a station as if nothing at all in the world had happened.

In the silence, the young man's eyes returned to the text:

Jonathan Hughes, certified public accountant,
of 112 Plandome Avenue, Plandome —

"My God!" he cried. "Get away!"

But he himself rose and ran a few steps back before the older man could move. The train jolted and threw him into an empty seat where he stared wildly out at a river of green light that rushed past the windows.

Christ, he thought, who would *do* such a thing? Who'd try to hurt us—*us*? What kind of joke? To mock a new marriage with a fine wife? Damn! And again, trembling, Damn, oh, damn!

The train rounded a curve and all but threw him to his feet. Like a man drunk with traveling, gravity, and simple rage, he swung about and lurched back to confront the old man, bent now into his newspaper, gone to earth, hiding in print. Hughes brushed the paper out of the way, and clutched the old man's shoulder. The old man, startled, glanced up, tears running from his eyes. They were both held in a long moment of thunderous traveling. Hughes felt his soul rise to leave his body.

"Who are you?"

Someone must have shouted that.

The train rocked as if it might derail.

The old man stood up as if shot in the heart, blindly crammed something in Jonathan Hughes's hand, and blundered away down the aisle and into the next car.

The younger man opened his fist and turned a card over and read a few words that moved him heavily down to sit and read the words again:

JONATHAN HUGHES, CPA
679-4990. PLANDOME.

"No!" someone shouted.

Me, thought the young man. Why, that old man is...*me*.

There was a conspiracy, no, several conspiracies. Someone had contrived a joke about murder and played it on him. The train roared on with five hundred commuters who all rode, swaying like a team of drunken intellectuals behind their masking books and papers, while the old man, as if pursued by demons, fled off away from car to car. By the time Jonathan Hughes had rampaged his blood and completely thrown his sanity off balance, the old man had plunged, as if falling, to the farthest end of the commuter's special.

The two men met again in the last car, which was almost empty. Jonathan Hughes came and stood over the old man, who refused to look up. He was crying so hard now that conversation would have been impossible.

Who, thought the young man, who is he crying for? Stop, please, stop.

The old man, as if commanded, sat up, wiped his eyes, blew his nose, and began to speak in a frail voice that drew Jonathan Hughes near and finally caused him to sit and listen to the whispers:

"We were born—"

"We?" cried the young man.

"We," whispered the old man, looking out at the gathering dusk that traveled like smokes and burnings past the window, "we, yes, we, the two of us, we were born in Quincy in nineteen fifty, August twenty-second—"

Yes, thought Hughes.

"—and lived at Forty-nine Washington Street and went to Central School and walked to that school all through first grade with Isabel Perry—"

Isabel, thought the young man.

"We…" murmured the old man. "Our" whispered the old man. "Us." And went on and on with it:

"Our woodshop teacher, Mr. Bisbee. History teacher, Miss Monks. We broke our right ankle, age ten, ice-skating. Almost drowned, age eleven; Father saved us. Fell in love, age twelve, Impi Johnson—"

Seventh grade, lovely lady, long since dead, Jesus God, thought the young man, growing old.

And that's what happened. In the next minute, two minutes, three, the old man talked and talked and gradually became younger with talking, so his cheeks glowed and his eyes brightened, while the young man, weighted with old knowledge given, sank lower in his seat and grew pale so that both almost met in mid-talking, mid-listening, and became twins in passing. There was a moment when Jonathan Hughes knew for an absolute insane certainty, that if he dared glance up he would see identical twins in the mirrored window of a night-rushing world.

He did not look up.

The old man finished, his frame erect now, his head somehow driven high by the talking out, the long-lost revelations.

"That's the past," he said.

I should hit him, thought Hughes. Accuse him. Shout at him. Why aren't I hitting, accusing, shouting?

Because….

The old man sensed the question and said, "You know I'm

who I say I am. I know everything there is to know about us. Now—the future?"

"Mine?"

"Ours," said the old man.

Jonathan Hughes nodded, staring at the newspaper clutched in the old man's right hand. The old man folded it and put it away.

"Your business will slowly become less than good. For what reasons, who can say? A child will be born and die. A mistress will be taken and lost. A wife will become less than good. And at last, oh believe it, yes, do, very slowly, you will come to—how shall I say it—hate her living presence. There, I see I've upset you. I'll shut up."

They rode in silence for a long while, and the old man grew old again, and the young man along with him. When he had aged just the proper amount, the young man nodded the talk to continue, not looking at the other who now said:

"Impossible, yes, you've been married only a year, a great year, the best. Hard to think that a single drop of ink could color a whole pitcher of clear fresh water. But color it could and color it did. And at last the entire world changed, not just our wife, not just the beautiful woman, the fine dream."

"You—" Jonathan Hughes started and stopped. "You—killed her?"

"We did. Both of us. But if I have my way, if I can convince you, neither of us will, she will live, and you will grow old to become a happier, finer me. I pray for that. I weep for that. There's still time. Across the years, I intend to shake you up, change your blood, shape your mind. God, if people knew what murder is. So silly, so stupid, so—ugly. But there is hope, for I have somehow got here, touched you, begun the change that will save our souls. Now, listen. You do admit, do you not, that we are one and the same, that the twins of time ride this train this hour this night?"

The train whistled ahead of them, clearing the track of an encumbrance of years.

The young man nodded the most infinitely microscopic of nods. The old man needed no more.

"I ran away. I ran to you. That's all I can say. She's been dead only a day, and I ran. Where to go? Nowhere to hide, save Time. No one to plead with, no judge, no jury, no proper witnesses save—you. Only you can wash the blood away, do you see? You *drew* me, then. Your youngness, your innocence, your good hours, your fine life still untouched, was the machine that seized me down the track. All of my sanity lies in you. If you turn away, great God, I'm lost, no, *we* are lost. We'll share a grave and never rise and be buried forever in misery. Shall I tell you what you must do?"

The young man rose.

"Plandome," a voice cried. "Plandome."

And they were out on the platform with the old man running after, the young man blundering into walls, into people, feeling as if his limbs might fly apart.

"Wait!" cried the old man. "Oh, please."

The young man kept moving.

"Don't you see, we're in this together, we must think of it together, solve it together, so you won't become me and I won't have to come impossibly in search of you, oh, it's all mad, insane, I know, I know, but listen!"

The young man stopped at the edge of the platform where cars were pulling in, with joyful cries or muted greetings, brief honkings, gunnings of motors, lights vanishing away. The old man grasped the young man's elbow.

"Good God, your wife, mine, will be here in a moment, there's so much to tell, you *can't* know what I know, there's twenty years of unfound information lost between which we must trade and understand! Are you listening? God, you *don't* believe!"

Jonathan Hughes was watching the street. A long way off a final car was approaching. He said: "What happened in the attic at my grandmother's house in the summer of nineteen fifty-eight? No one knows that but me. Well?"

The old man's shoulders slumped. He breathed more easily, and as if reciting from a promptboard said. "We hid ourselves there for two days, alone. No one ever knew where we hid. Everyone thought we had run away to drown in the lake or fall in the river. But all the time, crying, not feeling wanted, we hid up above and…listened to the wind and wanted to die."

The young man turned at last to stare fixedly at his older self, tears in his eyes. "*You* love me, then?"

"I had better," said the old man. "I'm all you have."

The car was pulling up at the station. A young woman smiled and waved behind the glass.

"Quick," said the old man, quietly. "Let me come home, watch, show you, teach you, find where things went wrong, correct them now, maybe hand you a fine life forever, let me—"

The car horn sounded, the car stopped, the young woman leaned out.

"Hello, lovely man!" she cried.

Jonathan Hughes exploded a laugh and burst into a manic run. "Lovely lady, hi—"

"Wait."

He stopped and turned to look at the old man with the newspaper, trembling there on the station platform. The old man raised one hand, questioningly.

"Haven't you forgotten something?"

Silence. At last: "You," said Jonathan Hughes. "You."

❀

The car rounded a turn in the night. The woman, the old man, the young, swayed with the motion.

"What did you say your name was?" the young woman said, above the rush and run of country and road.

"He didn't say," said Jonathan Hughes quickly.

"Weldon," said the old man, blinking.

"Why," said Alice Hughes. "That's *my* maiden name."

The old man gasped inaudibly, but recovered. "Well, is it? How curious!"

"I wonder if we're related? You—"

"He was my teacher at Central High," said Jonathan Hughes, quickly.

"And still am," said the old man. "And still am."

And they were home.

He could not stop staring. All through dinner, the old man simply sat with his hands empty half the time and stared at the lovely woman across the table from him. Jonathan Hughes fidgeted, talked much too loudly to cover the silences, and ate sparsely. The old man continued to stare as if a miracle was happening every ten seconds. He watched Alice's mouth as if it were giving forth fountains of diamonds. He watched her eyes as if all the hidden wisdoms of the world were there, and now found for the first time. By the look of his face, the old man, stunned, had forgotten why he was there.

"Have I a crumb on my chin?" cried Alice Hughes, suddenly. "Why is everyone *watching* me?"

Whereupon the old man burst into tears that shocked everyone. He could not seem to stop, until at last Alice came around the table to touch his shoulder.

"Forgive me," he said. "It's just that you're so lovely. Please sit down. Forgive."

They finished off the dessert and with a great display of

tossing down his fork and wiping his mouth with his napkin, Jonathan Hughes cried, "That was fabulous. Dear wife, I love you!" He kissed her on the cheek, thought better of it, and rekissed her, on the mouth. "You see?" He glanced at the old man. "I very *much* love my wife."

The old man nodded quietly and said, "Yes, yes, I remember."

"You *remember*?" said Alice, staring.

"A toast!" said Jonathan Hughes, quickly. "To a fine wife, a grand future!"

His wife laughed. She raised her glass.

"Mr. Weldon," she said, after a moment. "You're not drinking?..."

It was strange seeing the old man at the door to the living room.

"Watch this," he said, and closed his eyes. He began to move certainly and surely about the room, eyes shut. "Over here is the pipestand, over here the books. On the fourth shelf down a copy of Eiseley's *The Star Thrower*. One shelf up H. G. Wells's *Time Machine*, most appropriate, and over here the special chair, and me in it."

He sat. He opened his eyes.

Watching from the door, Jonathan Hughes said, "You're not going to cry again, are you?"

"No. No more crying."

There were sounds of washing up from the kitchen. The lovely woman out there hummed under her breath. Both men turned to look out of the room toward that humming.

"Someday," said Jonathan Hughes, "I will hate her? Someday, I will kill her?"

"It doesn't seem possible, does it? I've watched her for an hour and found nothing, no hint, no clue, not the merest period, semicolon or exclamation point of blemish, bump, or hair out of place with her. I've watched you, too, to see if *you* were at fault, *we* were at fault, in all this."

"And?" The young man poured sherry for both of them, and handed over a glass.

"You drink too much is about the sum. Watch it."

Hughes put his drink down without sipping it. "What else?"

"I suppose I should give you a list, make you keep it, look at it every day. Advice from the old crazy to the young fool."

"Whatever you say, I'll remember."

"Will you? For how long? A month, a year, then, like everything else, it'll go. You'll be busy living. You'll be slowly turning into…me. She will slowly be turning into someone worth putting out of the world. Tell her you love her."

"Every day."

"Promise! It's *that* important! Maybe that's where I failed myself, failed us. Every day, without fail!" The old man leaned forward, his face taking fire with his words. "Every day. Every day!"

Alice stood in the doorway, faintly alarmed.

"Anything wrong?"

"No, no." Jonathan Hughes smiled. "We were trying to decide which of us likes you best."

She laughed, shrugged, and went away.

"I think," said Jonathan Hughes, and stopped and closed his eyes, forcing himself to say it, "it's time for you to go."

"Yes, time." But the old man did not move. His voice was very tired, exhausted, sad. "I've been sitting here feeling defeated. I can't find anything wrong. I can't find the flaw. I can't advise you, my God, it's so stupid, I shouldn't have come to upset you, worry you, disturb your life, when I have nothing to offer but vague suggestions, inane cryings of doom. I sat here a moment ago and thought: I'll kill her now, get rid of her now, take the blame now, as an old man, so the young man there, you, can go on into the future and be free of her. Isn't that silly? I wonder if it would work? It's that old time-travel paradox, isn't it? Would I foul up the time flow, the world, the universe, what? Don't worry, no, no, don't look that way. No murder now. It's all been done up ahead, twenty years in your future. The old man having done nothing whatever, having been no help, will now open the door and run away to his madness."

He arose and shut his eyes again.

"Let me see if I can find my way out of my own house, in the dark."

He moved, the young man moved with him to find the closet by the front door and open it and take out the old man's over-coat and slowly shrug him into it.

"You *have* helped," said Jonathan Hughes. "You have told me to tell her I love her."

"Yes, I *did* do that, didn't I?"

They turned to the door.

"Is there hope for us?" the old man asked, suddenly, fiercely.

"Yes. I'll make sure of it," said Jonathan Hughes.

"Good, oh, good. I almost believe!"

The old man put one hand out and blindly opened the front door.

"I won't say goodbye to her. I couldn't stand looking at that lovely face. Tell her the old fool's gone. Where? Up the road to wait for you. You'll arrive someday."

"To become you? Not a chance," said the young man.

"Keep saying that. And—my God—here—" The old man fumbled in his pocket and drew forth a small object wrapped in crumpled newspaper. "You'd better keep this. I can't be trusted, even now. I might do something wild. Here. Here."

He thrust the object into the young man's hands. "Goodbye. Doesn't that mean: God be with you? Yes. Goodbye."

The old man hurried down the walk into the night. A wind shook the trees. A long way off, a train moved in darkness, arriving or departing, no one could tell.

Jonathan Hughes stood in the doorway for a long while, trying to see if there really was someone out there vanishing in the dark.

"Darling," his wife called.

He began to unwrap the small object.

She was in the parlor door behind him now, but her voice sounded as remote as the fading footsteps along the dark street.

"Don't stand there letting the draft in," she said.

He stiffened as he finished unwrapping the object. It lay in his hand, a small revolver.

Far away the train sounded a final cry, which failed in the wind.

"Shut the door," said his wife.

His face was cold. He closed his eyes.

Her voice. Wasn't there just the tiniest touch of petulance there?

He turned slowly, off balance. His shoulder brushed the door. It drifted. Then:

The wind, all by itself, slammed the door with a bang.

The Screaming Woman

My name is Margaret Leary and I'm ten years old and in the fifth grade at Central School. I haven't any brothers or sisters, but I've got a nice father and mother except they don't pay much attention to me. And anyway, we never thought we'd have anything to do with a murdered woman. Or almost, anyway.

When you're just living on a street like we live on, you don't think awful things are going to happen, like shooting or stabbing or burying people under the ground, practically in your back yard. And when it does happen you don't believe it. You just go on buttering your toast or baking a cake.

I got to tell you how it happened. It was a noon in the middle of July. It was hot and Mama said to me, "Margaret, you go to the store and buy some ice cream. It's Saturday, Dad's home for lunch, so we'll have a treat."

I ran out across the empty lot behind our house. It was a big lot, where kids had played baseball, and broken glass and stuff. And on my way back from the store with the ice cream I was just walking along, minding my own business, when all of a sudden it happened.

I heard the Screaming Woman.

I stopped and listened.

It was coming up out of the ground.

A woman was buried under the rocks and dirt and glass, and she was screaming, all wild and horrible, for someone to dig her out.

I just stood there, afraid. She kept screaming, muffled.

Then I started to run. I fell down, got up, and ran some more. I got in the screen door of my house and there was Mama, calm as you please, not knowing what I knew, that there was a real live woman buried out in back of our house, just a hundred yards away, screaming bloody murder.

"Mama," I said.

"Don't stand there with the ice cream," said Mama.

"But, Mama," I said.

"Put it in the icebox," she said.

"Listen, Mama, there's a Screaming Woman in the empty lot."

"And wash your hands," said Mama.

"She was screaming and screaming…"

"Let's see, now, salt and pepper," said Mama, far away.

"Listen to me," I said, loud. "We got to dig her out. She's buried under tons and tons of dirt and if we don't dig her out, she'll choke up and die."

"I'm certain she can wait until after lunch," said Mama.

"Mama, don't you believe me?"

"Of course, dear. Now wash your hands and take this plate of meat in to your father."

"I don't even know who she is or how she got there," I said. "But we got to help her before it's too late."

"Good gosh," said Mama. "Look at this ice cream. What did you do, just stand in the sun and let it melt?"

"Well, the empty lot…"

"Go on, now, scoot."

I went into the dining room.

"Hi, Dad, there's a Screaming Woman in the empty lot."

"I never knew a woman who didn't," said Dad.

"I'm serious," I said.

"You look very grave," said Father.

"We've got to get picks and shovels and excavate, like for an Egyptian mummy," I said.

"I don't feel like an archaeologist, Margaret," said Father. "Now, some nice cool October day, I'll take you up on that."

"But we can't wait that long," I almost screamed. My heart was bursting in me. I was excited and scared and afraid and here was Dad, putting meat on his plate, cutting and chewing and paying me no attention.

"Dad?" I said.

"Mmmm?" he said, chewing.

"Dad, you just gotta come out after lunch and help me," I said. "Dad, Dad, I'll give you all the money in my piggy bank!"

"Well," said Dad. "So it's a business proposition, is it? It must be important for you to offer your perfectly good money. How much money will you pay, by the hour?"

"I got five whole dollars it took me a year to save, and it's all yours."

Dad touched my arm. "I'm touched. I'm really touched. You want me to play with you and you're willing to pay for my time. Honest, Margaret, you make your old Dad feel like a piker. I don't give you enough time. Tell you what, after lunch, I'll come out and listen to your Screaming Woman, free of charge."

"Will you, oh, will you, really?"

"Yes, ma'am, that's what I'll do," said Dad. "But you must promise me one thing?"

"What?"

"If I come out, you must eat all of your lunch first."

"I promise," I said.

"Okay."

Mother came in and sat down and we started to eat.

"Not so fast," said Mama.

I slowed down. Then I started eating fast again.

"You heard your mother," said Dad.

"The Screaming Woman," I said. "We got to hurry."

"I," said Father, "intend sitting here quietly and judiciously giving my attention first to my steak, then to my potatoes, and my salad, of course, and then to my ice cream, and after that to a long drink of iced coffee, if you don't mind. I may be a good hour at it. And another thing, young lady, if you mention her name, this Screaming Whatsis, once more at this table during lunch, I won't go out with you to hear her recital."

"Yes, sir."

"Is that understood?"

"Yes, sir," I said.

Lunch was a million years long. Everybody moved in slow motion, like those films you see at the movies. Mama got up slow and got down slow and forks and knives and spoons moved slow. Even the flies in the room were slow. And Dad's cheek muscles moved slow. It was so slow. I wanted to scream, "Hurry! Oh, please, rush, get up, run around, come on out, run!"

But no, I had to sit, and all the while we sat there slowly, slowly eating our lunch, out there in the empty lot (I could hear her screaming in my mind. *Scream!*) was the Screaming Woman, all alone, while the world ate its lunch and the sun was hot and the lot was empty as the sky.

"There we are," said Dad, finished at last.

"Now will you come out to see the Screaming Woman?" I said.

"First a little more iced coffee," said Dad.

"Speaking of Screaming Women," said Mother, "Charlie Nesbitt and his wife Helen had another fight last night."

"That's nothing new," said Father. "They're always fighting."

"If you ask me, Charlie's no good," said Mother. "Or her, either."

"Oh, I don't know," said Dad. "I think she's pretty nice."

"You're prejudiced. After all, you almost married her."

"You going to bring that up again?" he said. "After all, I was only engaged to her six weeks."

"You showed some sense when you broke it off."

"Oh, you know Helen. Always stagestruck. Wanted to travel in a trunk. I just couldn't see it. That broke it up. She was sweet, though. Sweet and kind."

"What did it get her? A terrible brute of a husband like Charlie."

"Dad," I said.

"I'll give you that. Charlie has got a terrible temper," said Dad. "Remember when Helen had the lead in our high school graduation play? Pretty as a picture. She wrote some songs for it herself. That was the summer she wrote that song for me."

"Ha," said Mother.

"Don't laugh. It was a good song."

"You never told me about that song."

"It was between Helen and me. Let's see, how *did* it go?"

"Dad," I said.

"You'd better take your daughter out in the back lot," said Mother, "before she collapses. You can sing me that wonderful song later."

"Okay, come on, you," said Dad, and I ran him out of the house.

The empty lot was still empty and hot and the glass sparkled green and white and brown all around where the bottles lay. "Now, where's this Screaming Woman?" laughed Dad.

"We forgot the shovels," I cried.

"We'll get them later, after we hear the soloist," said Dad.

I took him over to the spot. "Listen," I said.

We listened.

"I don't hear anything," said Dad, at last.

"Shh," I said. "Wait."

We listened some more. "Hey, there, Screaming Woman!" I cried.

We heard the sun in the sky. We heard the wind in the trees, real quiet. We heard a bus, far away, running along. We heard a car pass.

That was all.

"Margaret," said Father. "I suggest you go lie down and put a damp cloth on your forehead."

"But she was here," I shouted. "I heard her, screaming and screaming and screaming. See, here's where the ground's been dug up." I called frantically at the earth. "Hey there, you down there!"

"Margaret," said Father. "This is the place where Mr. Kelly dug yesterday, a big hole, to bury his trash and garbage in."

"But during the night," I said, "someone else used Mr. Kelly's burying place to bury a woman. And covered it all over again."

"Well, I'm going back in and take a cool shower," said Dad.

"You won't help me dig?"

"Better not stay out here too long," said Dad. "It's hot."

Dad walked off. I heard the back door slam.

I stamped on the ground. "Darn," I said.

The screaming started again.

She screamed and screamed. Maybe she had been tired and was resting and now she began it all over, just for me.

I stood in the empty lot in the hot sun and I felt like crying. I ran back to the house and banged the door.

"Dad, she's screaming again!"

"Sure, sure," said Dad. "Come on." And he led me to my upstairs bedroom. "Here," he said. He made me lie down and put a cold rag on my head. "Just take it easy."

I began to cry. "Oh, Dad, we can't let her die. She's all buried, like that person in that story by Edgar Allan Poe, and think how awful it is to be screaming and no one paying any attention."

"I forbid you to leave the house," said Dad, worried. "You just lie there the rest of the afternoon." He went out and locked the door. I heard him and Mother talking in the front room. After a while I stopped crying. I got up and tiptoed to the window. My room was upstairs. It seemed high.

I took a sheet off the bed and tied it to the bedpost and let it out the window. Then I climbed out the window and shinnied down until I touched the ground. Then I ran to the garage, quiet, and I got a couple of shovels and I ran to the empty lot. It was hotter than ever. And I started to dig, and all the while I dug, the Screaming Woman screamed....

It was hard work. Shoving in the shovel and lifting the rocks and glass. And I knew I'd be doing it all afternoon and maybe I wouldn't finish in time. What could I do? Run tell other people? But they'd be like Mom and Dad, pay no attention. I just kept digging, all by myself.

About ten minutes later, Dippy Smith came along the path through the empty lot. He's my age and goes to my school.

"Hi, Margaret," he said.

"Hi, Dippy," I gasped.

"What you doing?" he asked.

"Digging."

"For what?"

"I got a Screaming Lady in the ground and I'm digging for her," I said.

"I don't hear no screaming," said Dippy.

"You sit down and wait awhile and you'll hear her scream yet. Or better still, help me dig."

"I don't dig unless I hear a scream," he said.

We waited.

"Listen!" I cried. "Did you *hear* it?"

"Hey," said Dippy, with slow appreciation, his eyes gleaming. "That's okay. Do it again."

"Do what again?"

"The scream."

"We got to wait," I said, puzzled.

"Do it again," he insisted, shaking my arm. "Go on." He dug in his pocket for a brown aggie. "Here." He shoved it at me. "I'll give you this marble if you do it again."

A scream came out of the ground.

"Hot dog!" said Dippy. "Teach *me* to do it!" He danced around as if I was a miracle.

"I don't…" I started to say.

"Did you get the *Throw-Your-Voice* book for a dime from that Magic Company in Dallas, Texas?" cried Dippy. "You got one of those tin ventriloquist contraptions in your mouth?"

"Y-yes," I lied, for I wanted him to help. "If you'll help dig, I'll tell you about it later."

"Swell," he said. "Give me a shovel."

We both dug together, and from time to time the woman screamed.

"Boy," said Dippy. "You'd think she was right under foot. You're wonderful, Maggie." Then he said, "What's her name?"

"Who?"

"The Screaming Woman. You must have a name for her."

"Oh, sure." I thought a moment. "Her name's Wilma Schweiger and she's a rich old woman, ninety-six years old, and she was buried by a man named Spike, who counterfeited ten-dollar bills."

"Yes, *sir*," said Dippy.

"And there's hidden treasure buried with her, and I, I'm a grave robber come to dig her out and get it," I gasped, digging excitedly.

Dippy made his eyes Oriental and mysterious. "Can I be a grave robber, too?" He had a better idea. "Let's pretend it's the Princess Ommanatra, an Egyptian queen, covered with diamonds!"

We kept digging and I thought, Oh, we will rescue her, we *will*. If only we keep on!

"Hey, I just got an idea," said Dippy. And he ran off and got a piece of cardboard. He scribbled on it with crayon.

"Keep digging!" I said. "We can't stop!"

"I'm making a sign. See? SLUMBERLAND CEMETERY! We can bury some birds and beetles here, in matchboxes and stuff. I'll go find some butterflies."

"No, Dippy!"

"It's more fun that way. I'll get me a dead cat, too, maybe...."

"Dippy, use your shovel! Please!"

"Aw," said Dippy. "I'm tired. I think I'll go home and take a nap."

"You can't do that."

"Who says so?"

"Dippy, there's something I want to tell you."

"What?"

He gave the shovel a kick.

I whispered in his ear. "There's really a woman buried here."

"Why sure there is," he said. "You said it, Maggie."

"You don't believe me, either."

"Tell me how you throw your voice and I'll keep on digging."

"But I can't tell you, because I'm not doing it," I said. "Look, Dippy. I'll stand way over here and you listen there."

The Screaming Woman screamed again.

"Hey!" said Dippy. "There really *is* a woman here!"

"That's what I tried to say."

"Let's dig!" said Dippy.

We dug for twenty minutes.

"I wonder who she is?"

"I don't know."

"I wonder if it's Mrs. Nelson or Mrs. Turner or Mrs. Bradley. I wonder if she's pretty. Wonder what color her hair is? Wonder if she's thirty or ninety or sixty?"

"Dig!" I said.

The mound grew high.

"Wonder if she'll reward us for digging her up."

"Sure."

"A quarter, do you think?"

"More than that. I bet it's a dollar."

Dippy remembered as he dug, "I read a book once of magic. There was a Hindu with no clothes on who crept down in a grave and slept there sixty days, not eating anything, no malts, no chewing gum or candy, no air, for sixty days." His face fell. "Say, wouldn't it be awful if it was only a radio buried here and us working so hard?"

"A radio's nice, it'd be all ours."

Just then a shadow fell across us.

"Hey, you kids, what you think you're doing?"

We turned. It was Mr. Kelly, the man who owned the empty lot. "Oh, hello, Mr. Kelly," we said.

"Tell you what I want you to do," said Mr. Kelly. "I want you to take those shovels and take that soil and shovel it right back in that hole you been digging. That's what I want you to do."

My heart started beating fast again. I wanted to scream myself.

"But Mr. Kelly, there's a Screaming Woman and…"

"I'm not interested. I don't hear a thing."

"Listen!" I cried.

The scream.

Mr. Kelly listened and shook his head. "Don't hear nothing. Go on now, fill it up and get home with you before I give you my foot!"

We filled the hole all back in again. And all the while we filled it in, Mr. Kelly stood there, arms folded, and the woman screamed, but Mr. Kelly pretended not to hear it.

When we were finished, Mr. Kelly stomped off, saying, "Go on home now. And if I catch you here again…"

I turned to Dippy. "He's the one," I whispered.

"Huh?" said Dippy.

"He *murdered* Mrs. Kelly. He buried her here, after he strangled her, in a box, but she came to. Why, he stood right here and she screamed and he wouldn't pay any attention."

"Hey," said Dippy. "That's right. He stood right here and lied to us."

"There's only one thing to do," I said. "Call the police and have them come arrest Mr. Kelly."

We ran for the corner store telephone.

The police knocked on Mr. Kelly's door five minutes later. Dippy and I were hiding in the bushes, listening.

"Mr. Kelly?" said the police officer.

"Yes, sir, what can I do for you?"

"Is Mrs. Kelly at home?"

"Yes, sir."

"May we see her, sir?"

"Of course. Hey, Anna!"

Mrs. Kelly came to the door and looked out. "Yes, sir?"

"I beg your pardon," apologized the officer. "We had a report that you were buried out in an empty lot, Mrs. Kelly. It sounded like a child made the call, but we had to be certain. Sorry to have troubled you."

"It's those blasted kids," cried Mr. Kelly, angrily. "If I ever catch them, I'll rip them limb from limb!"

"Cheezit!" said Dippy, and we both ran.

"What'll we do now?" I said.

"I got to go home," said Dippy. "Boy, we're really in trouble. We'll get a licking for this."

"But what about the Screaming Woman?"

"To heck with her," said Dippy. "We don't dare go near that empty lot again. Old man Kelly'll be waiting around with his razor strap and lambast heck out'n us. And I just happened to remember, Maggie. Ain't old man Kelly sort of deaf, hard-of-hearing?"

"Oh, my gosh," I said. "No *wonder* he didn't hear the screams."

"So long," said Dippy. "We sure got in trouble over your darn old ventriloquist voice. I'll be seeing you."

I was left all alone in the world, no one to help me, no one to believe me at all. I just wanted to crawl down in that box with the Screaming Woman and die. The police were after me now, for lying to them, only I didn't know it was a lie, and my father was probably looking for me, too, or would be once he found my bed empty. There was only one last thing to do, and I did it.

I went from house to house, all down the street, near the empty lot. And I rang every bell and when the door opened I said: "I beg your pardon, Mrs. Griswold, but is anyone missing from your house?" or "Hello, Mrs. Pikes, you're looking fine today. Glad to see you *home!*" And once I saw that the lady of the house was home I just chatted awhile to be polite, and went on down the street.

The hours were rolling along. It was getting late. I kept thinking, oh, there's only so much air in that box with that woman under the earth, and if I don't hurry, she'll suffocate, and I got to rush! So I rang bells and knocked on doors, and it got later, and I was just about to give up and go home, when I knocked on the last door, which was the door of Mr. Charlie Nesbitt, who lives next to us. I kept knocking and knocking.

Instead of Mrs. Nesbitt, or Helen as my father calls her, coming to the door, why it was Mr. Nesbitt, Charlie, *himself*.

"Oh," he said. "It's you, Margaret."

"Yes," I said. "Good afternoon."

"What can I do for you, kid?" he said.

"Well, I thought I'd like to see your wife, Mrs. Nesbitt," I said.

"Oh," he said.

"May I?"

"Well, she's gone out to the store," he said.

"I'll wait," I said, and slipped in past him.

"Hey," he said.

I sat down in a chair. "My, it's a hot day," I said, trying to be calm, thinking about the empty lot and air going out of the box, and the screams getting weaker and weaker.

"Say, listen, kid," said Charlie, coming over to me, "I don't think you better wait."

"Oh, sure," I said. "Why not?"

"Well, my wife won't be back," he said.

"Oh?"

"Not today, that is. She's gone to the store, like I said, but, but, she's going on from there to visit her mother. Yeah. She's going to visit her mother, in Schenectady. She'll be back, two or three days, maybe a week."

"That's a shame," I said.

"Why?"

"I wanted to tell her something."

"What?"

"I just wanted to tell her there's a woman buried over in the empty lot, screaming under tons and tons of dirt."

Mr. Nesbitt dropped his cigarette.

"You dropped your cigarette, Mr. Nesbitt," I pointed out, with my shoe.

"Oh, did I? Sure. So I did," he mumbled. "Well, I'll tell Helen when she comes home, your story. She'll be glad to hear it."

"Thanks. It's a real woman."

"How do you know it is?"

"I heard her."

"How, how you know it isn't, well, a *mandrake* root?"

"What's that?"

"You know. A mandrake. It's a kind of a plant, kid. They scream. I know, I read it once. How you know it ain't a mandrake?"

"I never thought of that."

"You better start thinking," he said, lighting another cigarette. He tried to be casual. "Say, kid, you, eh, you *say* anything about this to anyone?"

"Sure, I told lots of people."

Mr. Nesbitt burned his hand on his match.

"Anybody doing anything about it?" he asked.

"No," I said. "They won't believe me."

He smiled. "Of course. Naturally. You're nothing but a kid. Why should they listen to you?"

"I'm going back now and dig her out with a spade," I said.

"Wait."

"I got to go," I said.

"Stick around," he insisted.

"Thanks, but no," I said, frantically.

He took my arm. "Know how to play cards, kid? Blackjack?"

"Yes, sir."

He took out a deck of cards from a desk. "We'll have a game."

"I got to go dig."

"Plenty of time for that," he said, quiet. "Anyway, maybe my wife'll be home. Sure. That's it. You wait for her. Wait awhile."

"You think she will be?"

"Sure, kid. Say, about that voice; is it very strong?"

"It gets weaker all the time."

Mr. Nesbitt sighed and smiled. "You and your kid games. Here now, let's play that game of blackjack, it's more fun than Screaming Women."

"I got to go. It's late."

"Stick around, you got nothing to do."

I knew what he was trying to do. He was trying to keep me in his house until the screaming died down and was gone. He was trying to keep me from helping her. "My wife'll be home in ten minutes," he said. "Sure. Ten minutes. You wait. You sit right there."

We played cards. The clock ticked. The sun went down the sky. It was getting late. The screaming got fainter and fainter in my mind. "I got to go," I said.

"Another game," said Mr. Nesbitt. "Wait another hour, kid. My wife'll come yet. Wait."

In another hour he looked at his watch. "Well, kid, I guess you can go now." And I knew what his plan was. He'd sneak down in the middle of the night and dig up his wife, still alive, and take her somewhere else and bury her, good. "So long, kid. So long." He let me go, because he thought that by now the air must all be gone from the box.

The door shut in my face.

I went back near the empty lot and hid in some bushes. What could I do? Tell my folks? But they hadn't believed me. Call the police on Mr. Charlie Nesbitt? But he said his wife was away visiting. Nobody would believe me!

I watched Mr. Kelly's house. He wasn't in sight. I ran over to the place where the screaming had been and just stood there.

The screaming had stopped. It was so quiet I thought I would never hear a scream again. It was all over. I was too late, I thought.

I bent down and put my ear against the ground.

And then I heard it, way down, way deep, and so faint I could hardly hear it.

The woman wasn't screaming any more. She was singing.

Something about, "I loved you fair, I loved you well."

It was sort of a sad song. Very faint. And sort of broken. All of those hours down under the ground in that box must have sort of made her crazy. All she needed was some air and food and she'd be all right. But she just kept singing, not wanting to scream any more, not caring, just singing.

I listened to the song.

And then I turned and walked straight across the lot and up the steps to my house and I opened the front door.

"Father," I said.

"So there you are!" he cried.

"Father," I said.

"You're going to get a licking," he said.

"She's not screaming any more."

"Don't talk about her!"

"She's singing now," I cried.

"You're not telling the truth!"

"Dad," I said. "She's out there and she'll be dead soon if you don't listen to me. She's out there, singing, and this is what she's singing." I hummed the tune. I sang a few of the words. "I loved you fair, I loved you well…"

Dad's face grew pale. He came and took my arm.

"What did you say?" he said.

I sang it again: "I loved you fair, I loved you well."

"Where did you *hear* that song?" he shouted.

"Out in the empty lot, just now."

"But that's *Helen's* song, the one she wrote, years ago, for *me!*" cried Father. "You *can't* know it. *Nobody* knew it, except Helen and me. I never sang it to anyone, not you or anyone."

"Sure," I said.

"Oh, my God!" cried Father, and ran out the door to get a shovel. The last I saw of him he was in the empty lot, digging, and lots of other people with him, digging.

I felt so happy I wanted to cry.

I dialed a number on the phone and when Dippy answered I said, "Hi, Dippy. Everything's fine. Everything's worked out keen. The Screaming Woman isn't screaming any more."

"Swell," said Dippy.

"I'll meet you in the empty lot with a shovel in two minutes," I said.

"Last one there's a monkey! So long!" cried Dippy.

"So long, Dippy!" I said, and ran.

The Trunk Lady

Johnny Menlo kicked his shoes and sat down hard on the bottom of the attic stairs. His teacher, his special private tutor, was *not* coming after all. So he *wouldn't* have someone in the house all to himself.

Downstairs the party was running full blast. The sounds of it came up mockingly—the laughter, the cocktail shakers clinking, the music. Johnny thought he had got away from its sounds, sitting way up here, so lonely. His teacher was supposed to have come today. She hadn't.

Mom and Dad, so busy drinking with people, gave Johnny the kind of look you give your shadow.

Johnny retreated farther up the stairs into the complete musty asylum of the abandoned attic. Even up here the dust and warm afternoon quiet was rustled by the party noises from below.

Johnny glanced around. There were four trunks sitting under veils of webs in the dim corners. A sunbeam fell through a small dirty window, lighted things for Johnny's curious blue eyes.

The trunk in the north corner, for instance. It was always locked, the key hidden somewhere. The hasps were down now, but the brass tongue in the middle was flipped up, unlocked.

Johnny walked to the trunk and pried the hasps open. He pulled the lid up. Suddenly the attic was very cold.

She was inside.

Curled up, her body was, young, pretty. Her slender face was like chalk etched against the blackboard of her hair. Johnny gasped, but not too loudly. He held onto the trunk rim. Only her perfume was still alive. She looked as lonely and abandoned as he felt. He sympathized. Attics are places for things neglected and forgotten.

Death had apparently come through suffocation. Someone had slammed the heavy airtight lid down upon her curled loveliness. Her hand was like a white fragment of it against her filmy pink cocktail dress.

A moment later he found the balled wad of paper on the floor. It was only part of a note, with her writing on it.

—you've got to make it up to me, the way I've been treated. It shouldn't be difficult. I could be Johnny's teacher. That would explain my presence in the house to everyone. ELLIE.

He looked at her quiet beauty. It seemed as if she might have fallen asleep during the cocktail party and had been carried here and the lid slammed down upon her while in slumber!

The attic dimness moved in about Johnny, shaking him, then drawing out, leaving him numbed and saying, "Are you my teacher? Are you the one I was going to have for myself alone? But they—they killed you? Why should anyone kill my teacher?"

Another thought rushed the first away. He, Johnny Menlo, of the society Menlos, had found a body, hadn't he? *Sure.* His eyes widened. Mom and Dad'd *have* to notice him now, more often.

Why, even Grandma would quit playing chess all day with Uncle Flinny, choke on her brandy, stare at him through thick glasses, and cry, "My God, child, your snooping finally came to a profit, did it?"

Sure! Sure! Johnny blinked rapidly, his heart pounding.

Cousin William might even *faint* at the news!

He, Johnny Menlo, had found the body. Pictures in the papers of *himself* instead of Mother beaming out of the society columns!

Hiding the note in his pocket, Johnny took one last long look at the pretty lashes and the pink lips and the dark black hair of the Trunk Lady. He closed the lid on her sleeping.

He'd scream. Yes, at the top of the grand stairs. Scream till the sky fell down, and the party with it! Scream!

His screaming wasn't bad at all.

Down the stairs, across the hall, making a path with his screaming through the startled ranks of people, Johnny reached Mother's glittering cocktail gown and held onto it very tightly.

"Johnny, Johnny, why are you downstairs? What's the matter? I told you—" Mother's girl-face looked down over the glitter. He grabbed another fistful of spangles. He yelled it:

"Mom, there's a body in the attic!"

Like faces in a football stadium, the faces watching them. Mother stiffened, then relaxed. "Let go my dress, darling, you'll get it dirty. Look at your hands, cobwebs and all. Now run up to your room like a good boy." She patted his head.

"But Mom!" he wailed. "There's a body—"

"Good Lord," someone murmured. "Just like his father."

Johnny spun angrily. "You shut up! There is *so* a body!"

Mother didn't see him. She looked at her guests, and all Johnny could see was her lovely swanlike throat, the firm chin with the pulse beating under it, her fingers fixing the chestnut shine of hair swept up from her ears.

"Please forgive Johnny," she was saying. "Children are so imaginative, aren't they?"

Her chin came down. There was no light in her blue eyes. "You'd better go upstairs, Johnny."

"Oh, but, Mom—"

His world was crashing. The spangles slipped from between his fingers. He suddenly hated everyone at the party looking at him.

"You heard what your mother said, General."

That was Dad's resonant voice and it meant the fight was lost. Johnny jerked around, shot one last glare at the people, and ran upstairs, tears coming into his eyes.

He twisted the brass knob of Grandma's door. She sat playing chess with Uncle Flinny before the great glaring window. Sunlight glinted off her glasses. She hardly looked up.

"Pardon me, Granny, but—"

She shifted her cane against her thin knee. "Well?"

"There's a body in the attic and nobody'll believe me—"

"Go away, Johnny!"

"But," he cried, "there's a body!"

"We know it, we know it! Now run get Cousin William a bottle of cognac! Scat! Go!"

Johnny went and got the cognac from the wine pantry, rapped on Cousin William's door, and thought he heard indrawn breath behind the paneling. Then Cousin William whispered quickly.

"Who's there?"

"Cognac."

"Oh, fine, fine!" Cousin William's weak-chinned, rabbity face poked out, his soft hands darting after the offered liquor. "Thank God. Now go away and let me get drunk!"

The door slammed, but before it did Johnny got a brief glimpse of the cluttered, disorderly interior of Cousin William's Designing Room—the mannequins standing stiff around with brilliant silks draped, cut, fixed to them, watercolor sketches of capes, hats, suits, thumbtacked to the plaster walls. Bright heaps of woolens, threaded spools, and all. The door cut it off, locked it in, and Cousin William was nervously attending his cognac behind the shining knob.

Johnny eyed the hall phone, his anger simmering. He thought of Mom and Dad dancing, Uncle Flinny and Grandma playing their eternal chess, Cousin William drinking—and himself a stranger in this great old echoing house. He snatched up the phone.

"Uh—I want—that is—give me the police station."

Another deep voice cut in on the operator's.

"Hang up the phone, Johnny. Hang up and go to bed." Dad's very resonant and cultured voice.

Johnny hung up slowly. So this was his reward for finding a body? He sat and cried with frustration. He felt like the lady in the trunk, the lid slammed in his face by five people! *Slammed!*

He was twisting in bed when Uncle Flinny softly opened the door and poked his curly, soft-haired, big head into the room. His eyes were round, black, gentle, peaceful-looking. He came in with slow, soft movements, sat on the edge of the chair beside the bed like a very quiet little bird. He folded his bird-like fingers.

"Since you're retiring early," he said, "I thought I'd better come tell your bedtime story early too. Yes?"

Johnny felt himself too old for stories. Being raised in such an adult house with few contacts with children, and having an advanced education with such mature talk and mature people around, he felt himself far above bedtime stories. But he resigned himself, sighed, and said, "Okay, Uncle Flinny. Go ahead. Shoot."

Uncle Flinny held onto his neatly pressed black trousers at the knees as if they'd explode and slowly pieced out his tale.

"Well, once there was a young woman who was very beautiful—"

Oh-oh! Johnny'd heard this story a thousand times before. He fidgeted. *A body in the attic and he had to listen to this.*

"And," continued Uncle Flinny, "this beautiful young girl fell in love with and married a young knight. They lived happily for years. Until one day a Dark One kidnapped the beautiful woman and ran away with her." Uncle Flinny looked sad and old.

"And then the husband came home," prompted Johnny.

Uncle Flinny didn't hear him at all. He just kept talking in a funny soft monotone. "The husband chased the Dark One into a Dark Land. But no matter how hard he pleaded, or tried to catch up with the Dark One, he never could. His wife was gone forever. Forever."

Uncle Flinny's breathing was uneven, harsh. His eyes glowed dark, round. His lips trembled. He wasn't himself. He was someone else off a million miles in that Dark Land. He seized his knees tighter and bent over them.

"But the husband searched and searched, vowing that some-day he would find and kill the Dark One, and, wonder of won-ders, he did! He struck the Dark One down, but oh God above, after striking the Dark One he found that somehow the Dark One looked like his beautiful wife! And he found to his horror that he himself was growing—darker and darker...."

The end. Johnny hoped there'd be no more. Uncle Flinny sat sighing in the atmosphere he'd built from the story. He'd forgotten Johnny was a part of the room. His hands were shaking and he was out of breath. He just sat there.

Johnny shivered for no reason he knew. "Thanks. Thanks very much, Uncle Flinny," he said. "Thanks for the swell story."

Uncle Flinny turned blind eyes. "Unh?" He relaxed, recog-nizing Johnny. "Oh, yes. Anytime. Anytime at all."

"You sure get steamed up, Uncle Flinny."

Uncle Flinny quietly opened the door. "Good night, Johnny."

"Oh, Uncle!"

"Yes?"

Johnny stopped himself. "Never mind."

Uncle Flinny shuffled out. The door closed gently.

Johnny bounced furiously on the springs. "The things I've had to do the last few days, to keep this family happy! Listen to Uncle Flinny—wait on Grandma—get out of the way of Mother —obey Father. And keep Cousin William drunk. Guh!"

He was tired of them all. For a change why not some attention for *himself*? He could hear the party continuing downstairs. Slipping from bed, he listened against the door.

In the next hour he heard all varieties of feet upon the stairs, like heartbeats in the house. The crisp, snapping moves of Grandma and her pert cane feeling the layers of altitude. The shuffle of Uncle Flinny. The even long and easy stride of Dad. The glide of Mother. The nervous, uneasy tripping of Cousin William.

And there were voices talking, some arguing, some urging, others hysterical, mixed—Dad calm, Mother criticizing, Grandma stern, Cousin William whimpering, Uncle Flinny quiet. Once or twice the attic door creaked.

No one even came near Johnny's room. The party still existed downstairs, unaware of all this badinage. Night was coming swiftly on with an autumn chill.

Finally it was quiet again. Johnny hurried up the dark, dusty stairs into the attic, heart beating quickly. He'd show *them*!

The trunk was not heavy, strangely enough. One could easily tip it toward the stairs, and the stairs led down to the landing. One more push from the landing and down, down, down into the living room. Yes. They'd have to believe him now!

Johnny tipped the trunk.

People were talking. Music was playing on the radio-phonograph. Mom and Dad mingled with the bright swarm, flames about which social moths beat their sophisticated wings.

It was in the very midst of these things that Johnny's small voice made some sort of declaration from atop the hall staircase. He yelled loudly.

"Mom! Dad!"

Everybody turned and looked, as at a reception.

The woman came down the stairs.

Somebody had to scream. It sounded almost like Cousin William. But everybody watched, falling back, as the woman came down the stairs in her filmy cocktail dress. Well, she didn't exactly *come* down. She *rolled*.

Over and over, arms limp, legs limp, head bobbing, hair flailing in a dark whip, around and down, softly nudging the steps, jointless, boneless, and lifeless. When she reached the bottom Johnny was right after her.

"I told you, Mother! Dad, I found her again! I found her!"

He'd always and forever remember Mother's face in that moment and the way she said his name. "Johnny...!" And the way she struck him across the face.

Someone said, "Call the police!"

Someone else had the phone, ticking it. Dad's face was like a wet gray calm, suddenly old and tired. Johnny fell back from Mother's blow, holding to the banister. He thought She's never hit me before. Never before. Always kind and good, thoughtless at times, maybe, but she never went and hit me before today.

Then it happened. Everybody began laughing. Somebody pointed at the body, their faces got red, and they laughed. Dad laughed, too, with everything but his eyes.

"I'll be damned," someone said. "So that's the body the child found upstairs?"

"A mannequin!" someone declared.

"Of course. A store-window dummy. Easy to see how a child might think it a body." Again, laughter. Lots of it.

"A mannequin." The laughter grew and grew upon itself.

Johnny, trembling, crept and bent and touched the outflung hand, pulled away, touched it again, felt tremblingly the hard cold plastic.

"That's not the body," he said, looking up, bewildered. He shook his head, moving back. "That's not the body at all," he said. "The other body was different. Warmish and soft. It was a real woman!"

"Johnny!"

Dad had stopped smiling. Mother clenched a fist with white knuckles.

Johnny said, "Just the same, it's not the one!" He began to cry. Tears came as on the windshield of a car in a storm, erasing the world in wet portions. "Just the same, she was dead and she wasn't made of plaster!"

The house was full of sounds late that night. People talking in locked rooms. Arguments. Once he thought he heard Cousin William sobbing. Feet climbed stairs, lights clicked on and off. Finally everyone was in bed, and Johnny sat up, throwing back the covers. That clicking was Cousin William double-locking his door. Why?...Because someone or something was walking around in the house?

Johnny started. His doorknob was turning. The door pushed open a few inches. Someone was standing there in the darkness, looking in. A heart is an erratic thing. Like mercury. It scurries all over a person's insides. Johnny's heart was like mercury.

The door remained open. The shadow remained standing in the doorway, staring, looking in. Johnny said nothing. Then, very matter-of-factly, the shadow withdrew, and the door closed.

Rapping the lock home hard, Johnny threw his breath out and lay trembling on the door. Pressure from outside a moment later, from that withdrawn shadow, could not force the bolt. Johnny listened. The shadow went away.

Very weakly Johnny returned to bed, trembling. "Mom! Mom," he said to himself, "are you mad at me for making a scene before all of society? Would *you* kill me, Mom? Was there something about the Trunk Lady and Dad, something you didn't like, and did *you* kill her because of it? Now, when I come around, in the way, what will you do to me? Oh, Mom, it *can't* be you!"

"Dad," he said, the same way, "*you* made me hang up the phone. Are *you* afraid it will get out too? Afraid of your business, your money, your reputation at the club, huh, Dad? Was that you standing in the door, silent and dark and thinking? You've been my favorite in the family. But now, today, you're so quiet and *you* don't even look at me."

Cousin William. He could have changed the bodies, tried to fool Johnny. He could have put one of the mannequins in the trunk instead. Was she Cousin William's girlfriend? Was she causing trouble somehow? Or was Cousin William just afraid for his reputation? Him and his mannequins and his famous, expensive dresses for expensive women. Was it him, twisting the doorknob a moment ago?

Maybe it was Uncle Flinny, with his bedtime stories and his quiet ways. He loved Mother so much—his sister. He'd do anything for her or Dad or Grandma or Cousin William. Would he kill for her or Dad or the others to keep this house whole, intact and untouched?

Grandma. Played her cold game of chess day by day and drank her brandy neat. Her whole life was keeping the house moving together. Her whole life was society and position and taste. What if someone came into the house and tried to do all the ordering instead of her? What would she do to her?

All of them! All of them!

Johnny sank shivering back on the springs. A woman walked into a big mothballed old mansion like this and suddenly everyone was afraid. Just one woman.

On the table beside his bed Johnny groped and found the note he'd discovered in the attic dust. He felt of it, and read it again in his mind:

—you've got to make it up to me, the way I've been treated. It shouldn't be difficult. I could be Johnny's teacher. That would explain my presence in the house to everyone. ELLIE.

Johnny turned over.

"Ellie, my teacher, where are you now?" he asked the darkness. "Lonely and resting in Cousin William's studio with all the other stiffened mannequins? Playing chess with Grandma, only not moving? In the cold, dark basement like the wine casks put away for all the years? Somewhere in this big house tonight. But maybe not tomorrow. Unless I find you before then...."

There was a huge back yard with many acres to it, fruit trees, a flower garden, the swimming pool, the bathhouse, servants' quarters immediately behind the big house. Sunlight caught between a row of sycamore trees and a high green fence that shielded all this from the street. There was an oak tree to dangle from in the afternoon, and a policeman who walked his beat just under that tree on the sidewalk beyond the fence. Johnny climbed up and waited.

The policeman walked below. Johnny rattled leaves.

"Hi, son." The policeman looked up. "Better watch out. You'll fall."

"I don't care," said Johnny. "We got a dead lady in our house and everybody keeps it secret."

The policeman made a smile. "You have, have you?"

Johnny shifted himself. "I found her in a trunk. Somebody killed her. I tried to call the police last night, but Dad wouldn't let me. I tipped the trunk over, and she fell downstairs but she turned out to be a wax doll. It wasn't the lady after all."

"So." The policeman chuckled, enjoying it.

"But the other lady was real," insisted Johnny.

"What other lady?"

"The first one I found. Cousin William's a dress designer. He changed bodies. You should have seen everyone at breakfast this morning. Trying to be happy. Like in the movies. But they can't fool me. They're not happy. Mother looks tired, and she's real touchy. I wonder how long they can go around like this without yelling?"

The policeman scowled. "Honest to God, you sound just like my kid. Him and his Buck Rogers disintegrators and his comic books. Honest to God, it's a crime what they give the younger generation to read. Ruin their minds with it. Killing. Corpses. Ah!"

"But it's true!"

"See you later," said the policeman, and walked on.

Johnny clung there, and the tree trembled in the wind. Then he dropped down across the fence and gave chase. "You got to come look. They'll take her away if you don't—then nobody'll ever find her."

The policeman was patient. "Look, little boy, I can't go no-where without no warrant. How do I know you're not lying?" He was joking now.

"You've just *got* to believe me—that's all."

The policeman stuck out his hand. "Here."

Johnny took it. The policeman walked.

"Where are we going?" asked Johnny.

"To see your mother."

"No!" Johnny squirmed frantically. "That won't help! She'll hate me for it! She'll lie about it!"

The policeman firmly escorted him around front and thumbed the bell. First a maid, and then Mother was at the door, her face pale as milk, her lips a red smear against the white. Her pompadour was a little toppled over. There were blue pouches under her suddenly dull eyes.

"Johnny!"

"Better keep him inside, ma'am." The policeman touched his cap. "He'll get hurt running in the street."

"Thank you, officer."

The officer looked at her, then at Johnny. Johnny started to speak, but he could only sob. Two tears ran down his cheeks as the door closed, shutting the officer outside.

Mother didn't say anything to Johnny. Not a word. She just stood there, lost and white, twisting her fingers. That was all.

Hours later in the day, Johnny wrote it all down upon a nickel tablet of paper. Everything he knew about the Trunk Lady, everything he knew about Cousin William, Mom, Dad, Uncle Flinny, Grandma. Wetting his pencil, Johnny put it out in lines like this:

"The Lady in the Trunk loved Dad. Dad killed her when she came to the house." Johnny pouted over that one. "Either that or Mom killed her." Long years of viewing motion picture murders went through Johnny's mind. "Then, of course, Grandma or Uncle Flinny could have killed her because their authority and security was threatened." Yeah. Johnny scribbled quick. Let's see, now. "And Cousin William? Maybe it was his woman friend, after all." Johnny sort of hoped it was. He wasn't very partial to Cousin W. "Maybe, maybe there was something in Grandma's past? Or Uncle Flinny's?" Now, how about—

"Johnny!"

Grandma's voice. Johnny put away the pad.

Grandma came in the door and guided Johnny out through the hall and into her room, using her cane as a nervous prod. She seated him before the chessboard and nodded at the pale pieces. "Those are yours. Mine are black." She thought it over, eyes closed.

"Mine are always black."

"We can't play," Johnny announced. "Two of your black pieces are missing." He pointed.

She looked. "Uncle Flinny again. He's always taking some of my players. Always and forever. We'll play anyway. I'll use what I have. Move." She jabbed a skinny finger.

"Where's Uncle Flinny?"

"Watering the garden. Move," she ordered.

Her eyes watched his fingers in their path. She leaned forward slowly over the shining pieces. "We're all good people, Johnny. We led a good life these twenty years in this house. You've been in it only part of that twenty. We never asked for no trouble. Don't make us any, Johnny."

He sat there. A fly buzzed against the large window. Far away, below, water ran from a faucet. "I don't want no—trouble," he said.

The chessboard blurred and ran away like colored water. "Dad looked so white and funny at breakfast today. Why should he feel that way over a wax doll, Grandma? And Mom, she looks like she's all twisted up like a spring inside a clock, ready to bust loose. That's no way to act over a doll, is it?"

Grandma deliberated over her bishop, withdrawn into herself like an old hermit crab in a shell of lace. "There was no body. Just your imagination. Forget it. Forget it." She glared at the child as if he were responsible. "Walk light from now on, sonny. Keep quiet and keep out of the way and forget it. Someone's got to tell you these things. Don't know why it's always me. But just forget it!"

They played chess until twilight. Then the house got dark again too quickly, everybody hurried through supper, and it seemed that everybody went to bed early too.

Johnny listened to the hours chiming out one by one. Someone rapped on the door. Johnny said, "Who is it?"

"Uncle Flinny."

"What do you want, Uncle Flinny!"

"Time for your bedtime story, Johnny."

"Oh, well—not tonight, please, Uncle Flinny."

"Yes. Please. This is a very special story. A very extra special bedtime story."

Johnny waited. Then: "I'm tired, Uncle Flinny. Some other time, huh? Not tonight, please."

Uncle Flinny went away and after a while the clock chimed again. It was after ten. More time. After eleven. More time. Almost twelve.

Johnny opened the door.

The house was completely asleep. You could tell by the quiet, untouched gleam on the long hall stairs, clear moonlight pouring through great areas of glass, and no shadow moving.

Johnny closed the door behind him. From off somewhere in a quiet land, Grandma breathed heavily in her great four-postered bed. There was a tinkling noise, very faintly, as if bottles were being cautiously rattled behind Cousin William's door.

Johnny paused at the staircase. All he had to do would be return to bed and forget about it, believe that it was all a mistake, and there would be no trouble. It would be forgotten and things would take up where they'd been a few days ago.

Mother would laugh at her parties. Dad would drive back and forth to the office with his thick briefcase. Grandma would sneak her brandy on the side. Cousin William would insert needles into mannequin flesh, and Uncle Flinny would go on forever telling his feverish bedtime stories that meant nothing.

Yet it was not so easy as that. Things could not go back now. Only ahead. You *can't* forget. Dad, his only friend, was a stranger now, since the—incident. Mother was worse than ever. Her eyes looked like they cried at night. Down under the glitter she had to live too. And Grandma, she'd drink two bottles instead of one bottle of brandy a week. And Cousin William, every time he stuck a pin into a mannequin he'd think of the Trunk Lady, blanch, cringe, and start whimpering over his cognac.

And she—the lovely dark-haired stranger in the musty trunk —had looked so lonely up there where he'd found her. So apart. There was a bond between them. She was a stranger to the house—and was killed for it. Johnny was a stranger in the house now too. He wanted to find her again, because of that. They were almost brother and sister. She needed finding. She needed to be remembered, not to be forgotten.

Johnny went down each step with careful footing. He clung to the banister, sliding his fingers. She would not be in the attic now, nor would she be in any of the upstairs rooms. How could *they* sleep with her so near them?...Downstairs perhaps. Somewhere in the accumulated night of the house. Not in the servants' quarters.

He had just reached the stair bottom when he heard one of the upstairs doors open very slowly and close. After that there was not a sound, but quite calmly, quietly, someone came and stood at the top of the stairs, looking down.

Johnny froze. He leaned against the wall like a shadow. Sweat came out on his face and trickled in the small palms of his hands. He could not see who it was. They just stood there, watching, looking down, silent and waiting.

Things had to go on. You can't lie in bed and forget. Johnny couldn't just forget the stranger, the Trunk Lady, in her lonely attitude of death. The murderer, too, could not forget easily— nor that there was a small boy in the house who was too curious, too incautious.

Johnny breathed very slowly. He waited a moment. Then, when he saw that the person at the top of the stairs was not coming down, he moved quickly down the hall, into the kitchen, and out the back door into the moonlit veldt of the garden.

The swimming pool lay flat and shining square, with a fringe of trees beyond it, stars over it, the bathhouse near it, the low garden rows to left and right. Farther down was the green- house and the garden toolshed. Johnny ran.

The shadows of the toolshed offered temporary haven. Looking back, he detected no movement in the house, no light. The body would most probably be in one of these outlying houses.

His bed would feel nice now. The lock on the door would be nice. Johnny trembled like the water in the pool. Suddenly he saw someone standing in the upstairs hall window. There was just a hint of a standing figure there. Looking down, as it had looked from the top of the stairs....Then—it was gone.

Now, down the gravel drive on the side of the house, foot- steps sounded. Someone was coming from the front of the house, around under the sycamores. Someone moving in syca- more shadows, stealthily and unseen.

Then, very suddenly, breaking into half-light, she was there. She! Not Mother, nor Grandmother. But emerging half into moonlight, half in flecked shadow—was the Trunk Lady.

She looked at Johnny, far across the garden, and said nothing.

Johnny swallowed tightly and blinked. He held onto himself, his thighs, his knees, with clenched fingers. He crouched and squinted and stared in raw disbelief. A night wind set the sycamore leaves to shivering. From a way off an auto horn hooted like a lonely owl.

She was not dead after all. The whole house had tried to fool him. This was some fantastic jest he could not understand. They were all against him. His teacher was *alive*! There was no murder, no death! She was here, for him alone! In his hour of loneliness, she was here!

He darted out into the moonlight. Panting, not yelling, not laughing, he ran toward her across the grass, to the tiles of the swimming pool, across the tiles, around the pool and toward the sycamores.

She stood waiting for him, arms outstretched to take him into their soft embrace, sycamore shadows stirring over her cocktail dress, setting it into dreamy motion.

He said, "Ellie, is that you?"

He reached the rim of stirring shadow and screamed. The universe seemed to explode. The cocktail dress whirled madly, toppling in a drunken insanity. The Trunk Lady bent and there came a hoarse panting sound. She was fainting.

No! She was falling! A shadow hit him across the face, jarring his senses, once, twice, three times. He fell to his knees and before he could rise fingers were over his face, fingers that numbed him, gripping tight his sobbing mouth.

Mother!

The thought slammed him! Mother, dressed in the Trunk Lady's cocktail dress. Decoying him out into her arms, fooling him.

Mother, don't kill me! Don't kill me! he tried to cry. *I'm sorry I tried to bring the police! Mother, you love Father—is that why you killed Ellie? Mother, let me go! Mother, you looked so much like her standing in the sycamore shadows!*

But the hands would not let him go. There was a rushing, a body against him. A series of shocks. The fingers were so strong, so much thicker than they should be. Much thicker! Johnny screamed inwardly, drawing air in an awful slobbering whistle.

The house leaned over him as if to collapse and crush him in its fall. The great old sleeping house with everyone sleeping in it, unaware that this silent struggle was happening by the flat shine of the pool.

Suddenly he realized that it was not Mother, not the Trunk Lady. The fingers were too strong. Who is stronger than Mother, sterner, more quick and hard?

Grandmother, perhaps?

The body was too hard against him. He half broke free and saw the flat of moonlight, the filmy cocktail dress lying alone, sprawled—and a mannequin hand thrown out into light. The mannequin was on the ground, dead, plastic, cold. Someone else was behind Johnny, holding, fighting.

Cousin William!

But there was no smell of cognac. The actions were the actions of a sober man. The breath was clean and clear and quick, almost sobbing.

Father!

Dad he tried to yell. *Don't, don't, please* don't!

Then a voice was talking. Something black and small clattered on the tiles beside the swirling water, and Johnny suddenly knew. The hands were tight, the voice tighter, whispering. "You hurt your mother!"

I didn't mean to, Johnny screamed inwardly.

"If it hadn't been for you," said the voice, whispering, "your mother would never have known about the Dark One dying!"

I didn't mean to find the Trunk Lady, cried Johnny silently, fighting.

"It'll *kill* her, the shock of it. If she dies, I won't want to live. She's all I've had ever since twenty years ago when it all happened!"

The voice husked on: "Ellie came to the party. They tried to fool me, make out she was somebody else. But I guessed. She came upstairs in her cocktail gown and I gave her a glass of brandy with sleeping powder in it, and I put her to gentle sleep in the old old trunk. Nobody would have known if *you* hadn't looked. Ellie would have just disappeared forever. Only Grandma and me would know! But you're Dark, too, you're Dark, just like Ellie!" the voice whispered. "Sometimes, when I look at you, I see *her* face! So, now—"

The Dark One. Johnny's mind spun, ached, and thrust to get free. *Uncle Flinny!*

Uncle Flinny, he thought. Why do you call Ellie the Dark One? Why? Your bedtime stories, Uncle Flinny. For so many years you've told the same story, the same strange story about the Dark One and the beautiful woman, and now the Dark One came to be my teacher, and why did you kill her! What did she do to *you*? Why do you call her the Dark One? What does the bedtime story mean? I don't know.

"Don't kill me, Uncle Flinny. The water's cold and shining tonight. I don't want to be under the cold shine of it."

Johnny grabbed onto the body behind him and fell forward.

The two of them plunged screaming into the pool. There was a great plunging nausea. The fingers released him. There was a fighting in wet darkness, water stabbing his nostrils, bubbles breaking from his lips.

When Johnny broke surface there was a great sound of air rising from below, a dim surging of an old man jerking against the lazy tide. The man never came to the surface again. Just the bubbles came....

Johnny was crying, screaming to himself as he dragged himself from the pool and saw her lying there so lonely and tired—the mannequin in the cocktail dress. His foot knocked something dark and small rolling on the tiles. He picked it up. One of the dark chess pieces Uncle Flinny was always stealing from the chess set in Grandma's room.

Johnny held it tight, not seeing it really, and looked at the pool with the slowing ripples on it where Uncle Flinny slept below. It was crazy, so crazy he couldn't stand it.

He looked at the house through blurred eyes, and he was shaking like a sick dog. Lights were clicking on all over it. Windows in squares of yellow and orange. Father was running downstairs, shouting, and the back door was opening, just as Johnny collapsed, sobbing, upon the cold hard tiles....

Mother sat on one side of the bed, Dad on the other side. Johnny got his crying all out of him and lay back and looked at Dad, then Mom. "Mom?"

She said nothing, but smiled weakly and held onto his hands so tightly.

"Mom, oh, Mom," Johnny said. "I'm so tired, but I can't sleep. Why? Why, Dad?" He looked at Dad again. "Dad, what happened? I don't know."

Dad found it hard to say. He said it anyway. "Uncle Flinny

was married twenty years ago. His wife died when their baby was born. Uncle Flinny loved his wife very much. She was very beautiful and good. Uncle Flinny hated the baby. He'd have nothing to do with it. He thought the baby was a murderer. You can understand how he felt, can't you? You can understand how *I'd* feel if Mother died?"

Johnny nodded weakly, not too sure at all that he understood. "Uncle Flinny put the baby in a girl's home somewhere. He wouldn't tell us where. She grew up, bitter, hating Uncle Flinny because he treated her unfairly. After all, she didn't ask to be born. You see, son?" he said.

"Yeah, Dad."

"Well, just a month ago, Ellie, the baby, grown up now, found out where we lived somehow. She wrote a letter. We offered her a job as your teacher, which was only right and deserving. We thought to keep it secret from your uncle. When Ellie came, and went upstairs during the party, Uncle Flinny guessed who she was."

Dad couldn't speak for a moment. He closed his eyes. "Then—you found her in the attic. We tried to keep it quiet. We tried to make you forget. It was no use. We could never forget, ourselves. It was bound to come out. There was so much at stake, though, all our lives, we tried to work it out quietly. Things like money and reputations and business and what people would say made us do it, son....And—really—they're not worth a damn!"

Johnny turned his head. "I kept poking my nose in—"

"You were our conscience, I guess. A rather active symbol. You kept the house stirred up. Uncle Flinny thought you were hurting your mother. Your mother—his sister—was all he had after his wife's death."

'So he tried to make it look like I was drowned in the pool—"

Mother suddenly bent and held on to Johnny closely. "I'm sorry, Johnny. Sometimes we're blind. I didn't think he'd do that."

"What about the police?"

"The truth. Flinny killed her and committed suicide."

Mother's voice seemed distant and removed and tired. Johnny heard himself talking. "Uncle Flinny used to tell me bedtime stories, Mom. I still don't understand. All about the Dark One and the beautiful wife, and—"

"Someday, when you're older, you'll understand. Poor Ellie. She was always the Dark One."

Things were fading away, away. It was all over, done. "No more bedtime stories, Mom, please. No more, huh?"

Out of the tired darkness, Mom said, "No more, Johnny."

Johnny rolled wearily over into dreams. His left hand opened and the small black object in it fell clattering to the bedroom floor. He was asleep even before the Black Knight ceased rolling.

"I'm Not So Dumb!"

Oh, I'm not so dumb. No, sir. When those men at Spaulding's Corner said there was a dead man hereabouts, you think I ran quick to the Sheriff's office to give in the news?

You got another think coming. I turned around and walked off from them men, looking over my shoulder every second or so to see if they was smiling after me, their eyes shining with a prank, and I went to stare at the body first. It was Mr. Simmons's body in that empty-echoed farmhouse of his where the green weeds grew thick for years and there was a larkspur, bluebird sprouts, and morning-fires fringing the path. I tromped up to the door, knocked, and when nobody said they was home, I squeaked the door open and looked in.

Only then did I get going for the Sheriff.

On the way some kids threw rocks at me and laughed.

I met the Sheriff coming. When I told him he said yes, yes, he knew all about it, get outa the way! and I shied off, letting him and Mr. Crockwell smelling of farm dirt and Mr. Willis smelling of hardware hinges and Jamie MacHugh smelling of soap and scent and Mr. Duffy smelling of bar beer past.

When I got back to the lonely gray house they were inside bending around like a labor crew working a ditch. Can I come in, I wondered, and they grumbled no, no, go away, you would only be underfoot, Peter.

That's the way it is. People always shake me to one side, chortling at me. Those folks who told me about the body, you know what they expected? Expected me to call the Sheriff without stopping to see if they was lying or not. Not me, not anymore. I realized what went on last spring when they sent

me jogging for a skyhook and shore line for the twenty-seventh
time in as many years; and when I sweated all the way down the
shore curve to Wembley's Pier to fetch a pentagonal monkey
wrench which I never found in all my tries from the age of
seventeen on up to now.

So I fooled them this time by checking first and then running for help.

The Sheriff slouched out of the house half an hour later,
shaking his dusty head. "Poor Mr. Simmons, his head is all
rucked in like the skin of a rusted potbelly stove."

"Oh?" I asked.

The Sheriff flickered a mean yellow glance at me, switching
his mustache around on his thin upper lip, balancing it. "You
damn right it is."

"A murder mystery, hunh?" I asked.

"I won't say it's a mystery," said the Sheriff.

"You know who done it?" I asked.

"Not exactly, and shut up," snapped the Sheriff, thumb-rolling
a cigarette; and sucked it into half ash with his first flame. "I'm
thinking."

"Can I help?" I asked.

"You," snorted the Sheriff, looking up at me on top of my
mountain of bones and body, "help? Ha!"

Everybody laughed, holding rib bones like bundles of
breathing sticks and blowing out cheeks and glittering their
sharp shiny eyes. Me help, that was sure something to tickle.

Mr. Crockwell, he was the farmer man, he laughed, and Mr.
Willis, he was the hardware-store man and tough as a rail spike,
he laughed like tapping a sledge on a beam iron, and Mr. Duffy's
Irish bartender laugh made his tongue jig around pink in his
mouth; and Jamie MacHugh, who would run away if you yelled
boo, he laughed too.

"I been reading Sherlock Holmes," I said.

The Sheriff raked me over. "Since when you reading?"

"I can read, never mind," I said.

"Think you can solve mysteries, eh?" cried the Sheriff. "Get the hell away afore I boot the big rump off you!"

"Leave him be, Sheriff," laughed Jamie MacHugh, waving one hand. He clicked his tongue at me. "You're a first-rate sleuth, ain't you, Peter?"

I blinked at him six times.

"Sleuth, detective, Sherlock Holmes, I mean," said Jamie MacHugh.

"Oh," I said.

"Why, why-high," laughed Jamie MacHugh, "I'd bet my money on big Peter here any day, ann-*eee* day! Strong, strapping lad, Sheriff. He could solve this case with one shuffle of his big left shoe, couldn't he, men?"

Mr. Crockwell winked at Mr. Willis and Mr. Willis tonked a laugh out like cleaning your pipe on a flat stone, and everybody shot little sly glances at the Sheriff, nudging one another's ribs and chuckling.

"Sure, I'd bet good money any autumn on Peter there. Here's fifty cents says Peter can solve the case afore the Sheriff!" said Jamie.

"Now, look here!" bellowed the Sheriff, standing stiff.

"Here's seventy cents says the same," drawled Mr. Willis.

And here came round money silver shining, and green money like little wings flapping on their hairy hands.

The Sheriff kicked a boot angrily. "Odd dammit. No feeble-minded giant can solve any murder case with me around!"

Jamie MacHugh tilted back and forth on his heels. "Scared?"

"Hell's gate, no! But you're all riding my goat!"

"We mean it. Here's our money, Sheriff; you meeting it?"

The Sheriff crackled he sure as hell would, and did. Everybody boomed out laughter like on bass drums and with brass trumpets. Somebody slapped me on the back but I didn't feel it. Someone yelled for me to go in there and show him, Peter, show him, but it was all underwater, far away. Blood pounded around on big red boots in my ears, kicking my brain back and forth like a wrinkled football.

The Sheriff looked at me. I looked at him with my heavy hands hanging. He laughed right out.

"God, I'll solve this case before Peter has time to open his mouth for spit!"

The Sheriff wouldn't let me be in the room with the corpse unless I stood on one leg and put both hands out in the air. I had to do it. The others said it was fair. I did it. I must have stood there during most the time we talked, on one leg, hands out to balance, and them snickering when I toppled.

"Well," I said, over the corpse, "he's dead."

"Brilliant!" Jamie MacHugh had a bone of laughter caught in his throat, choking him.

"And he's been head-bashed," I said, "with a heavy thing."

"Colossal! Wonderful!" spluttered Jamie.

"And no woman done it," I said. "Because a woman couldn't have done it so heavy and hard."

Jamie laughed less. "True enough." He glanced at the others, eyebrows up a tremor. "That's true; we didn't think of that."

"That counts out all females," I said.

Mr. Crockwell teased the Sheriff. "You didn't say *that*, Sheriff."

The Sheriff's cigarette hissed sparks in a Fourth of July pin-wheel. "I was going to say it! Damn, anyone can see a woman didn't do it! Peter, you go stand in the corner and do your talking!"

I stood in the corner on one foot.

"And—" I said.

"Shut up," said the Sheriff. "You've had your say, let me have mine." He hitched up his trousers on his rump. Silence. The Sheriff scowled. "Well, like he says, the man's dead, head stove in, and a woman didn't do it and—"

"Ha-ha," said Mr. Crockwell.

The Sheriff shot him a blazing look. Mr. Crockwell covered his mouth with his hand.

"And the body's been dead twenty-four hours," I said, sniffing.

"Any dimwit knows that!" yelled the Sheriff.

"You didn't say that before," said James MacHugh.

"Do I have to say, can't I think a few?"

I looked around the empty room. Mr. Simmons was a strange man, living alone with no furniture in the house and only carpets here and there, and one cot upstairs. Didn't want to spend money on stuff. Saved it.

I said, "There wasn't much fuss or fight; nothing's upset. Must've been killed by someone he trusted."

The Sheriff started to swear but Jamie MacHugh said for him to let me talk, this was damn interesting. The others said so too. I smiled. I closed my eyes, grinning soft, and opened them again and everyone looked at me for the first time in my life as if I was good enough to stand beside them. I stepped from the corner, slowly.

I crouched beside Mr. Simmons, looking. He was blood ripe. The Sheriff quick followed, imitating me, on his knees. I peered close. The Sheriff peered close. I fussed with the rug. Sheriff fussed with the rug. I smoothed Mr. Simmons's right sleeve. Guess who smoothed Mr. Simmons's left sleeve? I made a humming sound like a comb and tissue in my throat. The Sheriff ground his teeth together. Everybody stood high and sweating sour in the summer-heated quiet.

"What was that about him being murdered by a friend?" Mr. Crockwell wanted to know.

"Sure," I said. "Someone he trusted, no commotion."

"That's right," said Mr. Willis, who didn't speak much.

Everybody said it was right, all right.

"Now," I said, "what people didn't like the cold man here?"

The Sheriff's voice was high and stringy with irritation. "Simmons wasn't liked by many. Always fightin' with folks, tetchy-like."

I looked at the men, wondering which one I could detect to be the murderer. My eyes kept snapping in rubber-band moves to Jamie MacHugh. Jamie always was flighty. You lost your match-box and stared at Jamie, he'd whine, guilty, "I didn't take it." If you dropped a nickel and it went away Jamie'd say, "I didn't do it!"

Funny. Something scared him as a kid, all the time he felt guilty, whether or not he was. So I couldn't help but see him now, and go up and down him with my eyes, him so nervous and losing his head over things. Just opposite of Hardware Willis, who would stand rock stiff while lightning bounced around him.

"I heard Jamie say Mr. Simmons should be killed," I said.

Jamie opened his eyes. "I never said that. And if I did, you know how you say things you never mean."

"I heard you say it, anyways."

"Now, now, now," said Jamie three times. "You, you, you are not Sheriff for this city, city. You just shut your trap."

The Sheriff fox-grinned. "What's the matter with you, Jamie? Second ago you was egging Peter on, all het up for his side."

"I don't want anybody accusing me, that's all, you big slob," said Jamie to me. "Go stand on one foot in the corner!"

I didn't blink my eyes. "I heard you say Mr. Simmons should be dead."

"You look sort of nervous, Jamie?" remarked the Sheriff.

"I remember," said Mr. Willis. "You did say that, Jamie. Say, Peter, you got a good memory." He nodded at me smartly. "I bet fingerprints of Jamie are around here," I said.

"Sure," cried Jamie, pale. "Sure, they're here. I was here early yesterday afternoon to try and get back my thirty dollars from that damn scoundrel lying limp on the floor, you elephant!"

"You see," I said. "He was here. His fingerprints all around like ants at a picnic." And I added, "I bet if we looked in his pocket we'd find Mr. Simmons's wallet full of money, I bet we would."

"Nobody looks through my pockets!"

"I'll do it," I said.

"No," said Jamie.

"Sheriff," I said.

The Sheriff looked at me, looked at Jamie. "Jamie," he said.

"Sheriff," said Jamie.

"Who was it picked me to solve this case?" I said. "Jamie did, Sheriff."

The Sheriff's cigarette hung cold on his lip, twitching. "That's right."

"Why'd he want me solving it, Sheriff?" I asked, and answered, "Because he thought I'd only kick up mud in the creek, rile you so you wouldn't get nothing done."

"Well odd damn, imagine that," murmured the others, moving back.

The Sheriff squinted tight.

"Peter, I got to admit, you got something. Jamie was sure hot to bring you up to mess around. He started them goddamn bets. Irritated me with you until I can't see beans from breakfast!"

"Yes," I said.

"Well now, I didn't kill nobody, I didn't sic Peter on you for that purpose, Sheriff, oh, no, I didn't," said Jamie MacHugh, sweat gobbering out his head like water from them fancy park sprinkling systems in the concrete skulls of them pretty naked women statues.

The Sheriff said, "Let Peter search you."

Jamie said no, as I grabbed his wrists with one big hand and held them while I put my other hand in his rear pants pocket and pulled out the dead man's wallet.

"No," whispered Jamie like a ghost.

I let him go. He swung around next thing, gibbering, and slammed out the door, crying, before anybody could stop him.

"Go get him, Peter!" everybody yelled.

"You really want me to?" I asked. "You're not kidding like with the skyhook and shore line?"

"No, no," they cried. "Get him!"

I thundered out the door and ran after Jamie in the hot sun over a green hill, through a little woods. What if Jamie gets away, I thought. No, he can't do that. I'll run fast.

Just near the edge of town I caught up with Jamie.

He never should have tried to fight me.

Crunch.

So now people sit around the Sheriff's office on summer evenings dangling their shoes in a little laced pattern and speaking with smoke blowing from their easy mouths about how the Sheriff let me solve the case. And the Sheriff says he don't care, he's just as pleased that I caught the criminal as if he'd done it himself; but the Sheriff winces when he says this.

Kids on the street don't kick my shins no more or throw rocks at me. They come ask to hold my hands as we walk downtown. They ask me to tell how I did it. Even ladies in pretty blue or green dresses look over back fences and ask. And I shine up the battered silver star the Sheriff had left over from twenty years ago, catch it on my chest where it sparkles, and I tell everybody again how I solved the Simmons case and caught the murderer Jamie MacHugh, who broke his neck trying to get out of my hands.

Nobody ever tells me to run get a skyhook or shore line or a left-handed screwdriver no more. They think my silences are thinking ones. Men nod at me from cars and say hello Peter and they don't laugh so much, they sort of admire me, and just this morning asked if I intended solving any more cases.

I'm very happy. Happier than in all my days. I'm certainly glad now that Mr. Simmons died and I had a chance to catch Jamie MacHugh that way. No telling how much longer these people might have pestered me.

And if you'll promise, cross your heart, hope to die, spit over your left shoulder, not to tell nobody, I'll let you in on a little secret.

I killed Mr. Simmons myself.

You understand why, don't you?

As I said at the beginning—I'm not so dumb.

Killer, Come Back to Me!

CHAPTER ONE
Ricky Wolfe's Woman

If you've never watched an autopsy, then this is what they do. They cut the body down the middle. Not all the way, but far enough for you to see everything from collarbones to kidneys. When the peels of flesh are tethered back with bright surgical clamps, the various organs thus exposed are examined closely before being sliced out with an expert move of the scalpel. They are then set aside for chemical analysis. The brain is removed from its case by the simple expedient of lifting the skull off in a circle from the ears up.

If you're a criminal, you get special attention. You're not much different inside than anybody else, but the doctors keep looking, as if some day they'd actually find a criminal's body that didn't have a heart.

An interesting case turned up at our laboratory this morning. They brought in the cadaver of one John Broghman. He had little blue tattoos dinting his chest and pelvic regions. On second look, you saw they weren't tattoos, but bullet holes.

I'd like to tell John Broghman's story as it came to me, flat and cold and naked on an autopsy table. It's not sugar. It's carbolic and cyanide. It's a heart beating like a tommy-gun, faster, faster and faster until—well....

He had big lungs and good muscles. He had sponge sacs in his rib casings that maybe one day sucked in the air of the world and liked it. From the build of him you could see he was from a small town where those lungs could grow and get started. Then, you can see where his father and mother died; you can see where he had a younger brother who wasn't much help; you can see where they moved in with an aunt and uncle who didn't love them, and you can see where the uncle made Johnny Broghman work—too young and too hard—in a coal shaft. Those spots on Johnny's lungs—that's what tells you all about those years.

Then, you look at Broghman's cold, inert stomach and you see the shaping hand of hunger that had bruised it. Right here. See?

And now, if you'll look closer, deep in this cold, corrugated brain, you'll find the hatred and the wondering and the wanting of Johnny Broghman growing and making a sort of tumor, a fester spot. Inside this brain you'll find....

Broghman stood on the corner of that dusty little town, watching grasshoppers sweeping over the hot blue sky in a curtain.

The bank was across the street. A stolen automobile, its motor still running warm, was parked in front of it. He'd parked it there with his own hands and then strode across the searing hot asphalt to stand here on this corner, sweating, thinking, knowing that there was something ahead of him that he wanted.

He wasn't certain what it was. Maybe it was in the bank. Maybe it had to do with guns, power, danger and—something else.

The gun was heavy in its leather nest under his arm.

Something he wanted for a long time. What? Something he wanted.

A woman walked along with a slow, thoughtful walk. Her eyes went through him, away, and then slid back again to make a man of him, up and down, and her red lips parted as if she knew his mind. Broghman swallowed thickly, trying to look away.

She stood there, eyes narrowing. Then, she revolved slowly, put one foot after the other with a sort of measured rhythm, and went away with her hair like long fire on her neck, and her eyes like amber metal that could catch emotion and keep it there.

Broghman's stomach muscles lay down like crouching animals. He began to walk. Across the streaming street, up the high curb. His big ears pricked, alert. There—the car motor, still muttering inside its casing. Now into the cool cavern of the bank. Cool expanse of marble. Shining cages that kept domesticated animals inside them with cool green money at their pale, domesticated fingertips.

Broghman lifted the dead weight of the gun, fitted into his calloused hand.

From there on, things resolved into slow, sludgy, underwater gestures of people suspended in a slow motion film. Lazily, his face slowly shading white under the regular pallor of his skin, the little teller shifted a slow hand to money stacked in green stratas, extracted it sluggishly, shoved it gradually forward until it sank with agonizing lack of gravity into Broghman's palm. He pocketed the money. It took what seemed like three minutes to do it.

Then things speeded up to triple action. An alarm gong was like a kick of adrenalin setting things into blurred quickness. Echoes of the gong jumped back from marble cliffs, warning.

Broghman ran across smooth stone acres. People shouted. Everything whirled hotly in his eyes when the sun struck him as he entered the daylight.

He didn't know if it was the sun or not, but when he twisted the car door open, he pulled back and gasped.

She waited for him in the car.

That woman with the hair like long fire and the eyes like yellow metal, who'd walked by him a few minutes ago, looking into him and knowing him and walking on. Her hard fingers gripped the steering wheel, so that the knuckles stood out whitely.

Recovering, he swung sideways into the seat, poking the gun. "Get out!"

"No," she said it simply, and meant it.

He pushed the gun further, against her white blouse.

"I said *get out!*"

Her answer was to engage the gears, jump the accelerator, thrusting the car away from the curb, shrieking rubber. She flushed the car to seventy miles an hour before he knew what she was doing. He had glimpses of darting trees, spinning signs, buildings, with her voice biting through it all:

"*I'm* driving! Wherever you want to go, *I'm driving!*"

Sitting there, the color rose in his protruding cheekbones. He glanced back at the vanishing main street. "Move fast, that's all. Take Highway 43."

"Don't be dumb," she snapped it back at him. "That's a graveyard road. We'll go *my* way. I *know* this damned burg inside and out, like a book."

He realized he was shuddering, and had to clasp his knees, bending to ease the sick pain in his belly, as if he'd been shot.

"What's wrong?" she said. "They get you?"

"No." He made himself straight. "I'm all right. I imagine things. Stomach. Like a hot hole in it. *Guh.*"

Then, while the miles spun under them, he kept silent, nursing his pain. Once, glancing up, he saw her sharp profile against running sky-line, green trees, bright gas stations. Her lips were full to stubbornness, and hard like the even teeth backing them up.

The eyes were the startling part, like feral things plucked from a lusting cat animal and caught in her shocking white face. They didn't belong. Not with all that flame on her head falling in loose, whipping fingers of color to her shoulders, tucked behind almost man-like ears.

After about five minutes she said, "We've lost them." She held the speed high, through hot desert. "How much money?"

He counted it. "Seven hundred."

"Chicken feed." He saw her trim ankle muscles tauten, pressing out more mileage. Slowly, he touched the curve of her leg with his blue eyes, coming up along her brown woolen skirt to the small breasts and the open neck of her white blouse where the cords of her throat went stiffly, yet beautifully up.

"Stop the car," he said, quietly.

She ignored him.

"Who in hell are you!" he demanded, hotly, "running me around! This was *my* job!"

"It's *ours*, now." She gave him her brief, metallic glance. "You're no killer. I know. It's not in your face. Your eyes are open too wide for killing."

"Stop the car."

Parked, she looked straight ahead. "I'm cutting myself in," she said to the road. "I been outside a little while, but I'm coming back in."

He twisted her from the wheel.

"You're damn well in."

He kissed her so it hurt them both. The world went away. A siren, if it had whined, would not have been heard, or a gun shooting. Only her cynically stubborn lips existed, moving under his.

She pulled back, eyes angry and yet—puzzled—a moment.

"Don't do that again," she let him know, evenly. She made

the wheels roar again. "I'm the one who does that! Remember from now on, *you!*"

It was his turn to be puzzled. "Okay, okay," he said.

Desert wind came in the windows, searing, burning them.

She parked the car for the night on a little dirt road equipped with stars, a moon, and ranch lights hanging on the foothills.

She slid from the car, shoes rustling in dry thatches of bramble.

He said, "Why'd you climb in my car today?"

She had her answer ready.

"You were headed for the morgue. I put you on a detour. You need training. The way you walk, talk, hold a gun. You looked like a kid waiting for a ticket in front of a dime movie, today."

"Yeah—"

"Let me finish. Remember Ricky Wolfe?"

"God, *yes.*"

"I was with him," she said, "for five years."

The name of Ricky Wolfe was like a hammer striking. Ricky Wolfe, the big-time, all-around gangman. A guy nobody proved nothing on, with a capacity for gin and blood that was legendary.

She stood there and told him about it. "Six weeks ago they killed him. In Iowa. Threw his body in the river. Only way you could tell it was him, was his wallet. They never had a print of his fingers." She breathed deeply. "So I came west again, here to California, covered up awhile working as a waitress—"

"Then I came along."

"Yeah. I saw you and knew that you needed training or you'd be dead too soon. Ricky was different. He was broken in when I got him. But I always wanted to see what I could do with a beginner."

She turned to him. "You're only good as your woman is good.

If she's a heller, a whiner, a baby, you'll be on a dead-slab in no time. She won't let you think clear." She showed him her hard white fingers. "My nails are clipped short for a cat. I won't rip your back. Now—it's up to you. You want to die tomorrow or four years from now?"

"Is it that way?"

"That's the way it is."

He suddenly broke, standing there. He didn't know why but he just had his arms around her, trembling.

"I'm glad you came. I wouldn't want to be alone tonight."

She kissed him, almost clumsily, and he thought he felt her tremble deep inside. Then, she slapped his face with her hands, twice, hard.

"A kiss's for one thing! A slap's for another! You're not a kid! Learn that, if you stick with me! Grow up!"

He stopped shaking.

In his nostrils the warm clean smell of her body, with no dime perfume to spoil its cleanliness, became suddenly apparent.

He waited for her to make the first move.

"I'm not a kid now…" he said.

Their feet rustled in the dry sand.

CHAPTER TWO
L.A. Boss-Man

He was wanted. For the first time in his life people actually were seeking him. The same people who'd shoved him into gutters, starved his parents, ignored him in coal mines, refused him coffee dimes—these same people were horrifiedly aware of him now, and concerned with his welfare, and what he was doing each day. Sure. Sure.

Broghman, in angry, shocked rips, tore the morning paper down and across and down again.

Julie set a steaming coffee mug on the table of the Motel Inn room and ordered, "Drink it. And quit reading papers. They lie like hell."

He felt of his big brown hands and the gun shining on the blue tablecloth. "God's sake, Julie, I'm not a criminal. I'm a human being."

"Sure. Both of us are. Self-preservation you know."

He learned to walk tall, stiffer, with his guts tucked in. She told him how to talk faster, pull a gun by the swiftest, safest method, pressing it close to his body so only a few people would see it. She could have written a book about banks. She wrote on her tongue for him. There were ways of hitting people's nerves with the knife edge of your stiff-hand to knock them out as good as a gun—she showed him. A moustache appeared sandily on his lip. His hair grew sandy on his neck, and grew the way she ordered it to grow.

It was acting, rehearsing for a bigger part.

In his dreams, her voice struck again and again at him:

"No, no, Johnny! Not *that* way, *this* way!"

The day Julie bought the new car and drove into Victorville, Broghman found himself sweltering in the little two-by-four room, rummaging idly through her traveling kit, sorting out handkerchiefs, a lipstick, a packet of photographs.

Shucking them from their envelope, he lined the pictures side by side on the bedspread in the sunlight, it took him a minute to understand what his eyes were looking at.

At first, they had looked like pictures of himself.

This one here, standing by the sedan in a dark suit. There was something about the dark cloth over long, muscled bones. Something suggestive in the posture. And this one. Himself, almost. In hiking breeches, a shabby hat cocked over rebellious hair. And the last one—Julie with her arm around this man who didn't look at all like Johnny Broghman but at the same time did.

It gave him a stunned feeling like having a body in two places at once. "I'll be damned," he said softly.

The door opened a few minutes later, while he was still looking. Julie's hard silhouette stood in a square of sunlight. There was just a flicker of surprise in her cheek muscles, then she shut the door, put one hand on a hip.

"Recognize yourself?"

"That isn't me."

"It's enough like you to make it worth a hundred grand if we work it fast. Worth a million if we stick it a couple years. Those pics were snapped when you were Boss-man of L.A. When you cleared twenty grand a month or you thought things stunk pretty badly."

He just sat there, waiting.

She stepped forward, slowly, her eyes full of funny, intense light. Her voice was like a sing-song prayer:

"Ricky Wolfe's not dead any more. He's back from the grave, in this room, now, sitting there, and he doesn't know it. He's going back. Back to L.A. to be Boss-man again." She stared down into his features, and her eyes were burning amber. "What do you think of that—*Ricky Wolfe?*"

He got it. He got what she meant and it was like a stiff kick in the teeth. He pulled back, yelling it:

"I know what you're thinking. It won't work!"

"Yes, it will. It *has* to!"

"You can't fool people! Stuff like that happens in dreams, in books. Nobody'd believe I was him. I don't look like him! We couldn't get away with it. It doesn't happen!"

"It happens to us, Ricky Wolfe! It happens to us!"

"Like hell it does." He started getting up.

She cracked him across the face, hard, three times. Her lips were shaking, her eyes almost insane.

"It happens to us!"

The new dark suit fitted like grafted skin. One side padded out a little; Ricky'd been built that way. Higher heels added altitude to Broghman. He learned talking with a faint lisp, chewing a cigar; but the thing that he said to Julie was:

"I keep telling you it won't work. I don't look like him. For a moment, yeah, if you look quick, if the light's bad, if you're half-blind. You're crazy. You want to kill us both!"

"Shut up!" she hissed. "Or I'll do the killing now."

He bit his cigar fiercely.

There were lists of facts, names, alibis to digest. Julie fed, crammed them down him. The leaves fell off the calendar like in a high wind. Then Julie, one day, elevated a stein of beer, yellow like her eyes and in a softer voice said:

"Tomorrow's the big day. L.A. here we come." She drank beer. "How's it feel to be Ricky Wolfe?"

His hand shook. He looked at his face mirrored, distorted in the brown hip of the half-emptied bottle. The cigar. The moustache. He wanted to blurt, "It won't work. An old gag like this won't fool people." But there was that look in her eyes, hot as boiling gold, so he shut up.

She was talking again, almost to herself. "I can't say what it was like, that noon at the bank. You standing there. Something about the way you stood, your face, like Ricky made up in a slightly new package. Lord, how it yanked my insides." He thought it was a nice gesture, this next. He clinked his glass against hers. "Let's drink to our new life—together."

She got mad. "No," she snapped. "Let *me* say things like

that. I keep telling you!" Looking at her, trying to understand what ticked, queer, inside her red hair, he sheepishly downed his beer.

It seemed right that she drove the car to L.A. all the way. It was a picture postcard day. She pressed the speed way up and kept it there when it was safe, her hair streaming like a scarlet banner....They swerved corners to Spring Street and Third, parked the car, and walked—two dark suits reflected in shop windows—toward the bookie joint. He couldn't figure it out. It was crazy—but he was actually enjoying it.

Broghman knew the place from Julie's pungent description. A huge magazine shop smelling of ancient pulp magazines and old books in musty pyramids; dimly lighted; slouched figures moving around in the dimness, phones jangling far back in the twenty aisles and hundreds of tables.

Back in that dusty place, where naked light bulbs hung dying in the high ceiling, the biggest horse racket in L.A. tucked away its profits and shilled its suckers.

The door to hell. Broghman felt his heart pounding. What if he forgot facts, figures, words, names—

Julie shoved him on. It took a moment for his eyes to adjust to the dark after sun. People's faces blurred in the gloom, and he was moving, his hard heels rapping like knuckles, following the sullen redhead with the pendulum walk.

A lot of seated men jerked up, a lot of reading men stopped reading, a lot of talking men caught their tongues in their teeth, a lot of smoking men choked on their cigarettes. It was like flinging a boulder into a stagnant pond, watching ripples skim out and rush back:

"Ricky! For God's sake, fellas, it's him!"

"Ricky!"

"I'm seein' things!"

A sound of bodies stirring, shadows moving, and then one single voice saying:

"That's not Ricky Wolfe." And again, "That's not Ricky."

It was a flat statement.

Broghman felt his gun in his palm slip like a frightened animal. His breath hissed in his nostrils. In the silence that followed, he stopped dead still and there was only the sound of Julie's high heels tacking along the wooden floor and slowly, with a kind of frozen dread, coming to a halt, too.

Broghman turned. Out of the shadow a guy slipped who was too well-dressed for his own good. With a long white horse-face and red-rimmed, tired eyes and sweat on his cheeks. A sort of balding guy, whose features set off a trigger in Broghman's mind. Merritt. Julie'd given a description. Merritt, from the old days. One of Ricky's sidekicks, a jealous kind of gunsel. Merritt. The name clicked.

There was something in Julie's expression. Almost fear. It looked strange on her. Out of place. Lost. Lost and crying in the dark. Her hand crawled along her dark purse, vaguely.

Broghman knew it was no use. It was no use all along.

"That's right," somebody else agreed. "It ain't Ricky at all." The voice sounded awed, funny, disappointed in its surprise.

Merritt said, "What you trying to pull, wise guy? You and the redhead?"

Broghman's jaw stiffened.

"No," he admitted evenly. "No, I'm not Ricky."

He heard Julie's gasp. He continued:

"I'm not Ricky Wolfe. Not at all. I don't have to be him. I'm me. I'm myself! You, you Merritt, you don't count for beans!"

The darkness began to swim. Everybody was sort of held by Broghman's voice, waiting.

"You can't get away with an old trick like that," was Merritt's quick reply. "What are you—kids to try something like this?"

Broghman pulled his gun, and while the darkness got darker, and there was only Merritt in front of him, and the others waiting, he swore, tightened up and fired three shots.

Merritt folded over the bullets, taking them into him with curious, pushing, helpful fingers. He fell flat down on his head, choking.

"Ricky!" it was Julie's voice. He had a flash of the metal jaws of her purse flipping wide, her gloved hand burrowing like a white squirrel inside, extracting a little blue gun.

"I'm in!" said Broghman. There was a sort of power to the way he mouthed it. He sort of grew upward. He seemed to fit his suit better. Everybody else still stood, looking at his face, like they were seeing the devil and couldn't run away.

Broghman took in every face. Names, data, facts, figures that Julie'd given him. Here. One face, a fat red one with beer smelling from its lips. "Kelly!" he snicked it out, with a jerk of his gun. "You know what to do. Get moving with this body!"

"Sure, Boss!" Kelly moved his big stomach and big shoulders and fat, long arms.

Broghman glanced around. "You, Rhodes, help him. Get your car around in the alley, on the double."

Rhodes hesitated.

"Well?" asked Broghman.

"Sure," said Rhodes, hastily. "Sure, Boss."

Other shadows were becoming men now, taking the cue from the others. Someone grabbed Merritt's feet, someone else his arms; and there was a shuffling of running feet back through the dark little office, more orders, more swearing.

You keep people running so they don't have time to think.

No time to get mad, thought Broghman. Keep them excited, keep their eyes fixed on something else, *then you fool them*.

. It didn't take more than a minute for the body to vanish through the back door into the alley. A car roared outside. A small crowd gathered in the front door of the shop.

"Clear them away!" Broghman flipped his gun through the air. "Catch, Sammy," he told one of them. Sammy scuttled through the back office with the gun. To the others Broghman gave a brief going over. "Any of you want to pull out, pull now. Any of you don't like me, say so. I'm *in*."

Kelly emerged from back, wheezing, mopping sweat off his huge pink face. "Everything's okay, Ricky." He caught himself. "I mean—" He groped for a name.

Broghman gave him one. "If it makes you feel better—call me Ricky, too."

Kelly felt better. He grinned. "Okay—Ricky. We always did get along, didn't we?" He stopped and thought about that. "Didn't we—almost—I guess—" He stood there.

There'd be a cop in a moment. Broghman shook his head, and he and Julie and Kelly went into the back office with two others. Before closing the door, he poked a finger at the young guy named Knight. "For the cops it was all a mistake. Nothing happened. You don't know anything."

He slammed the door hard. His hands began to shake so he hid them in his pockets.

Julie was just watching him, all this while, holding onto her purse, examining his face. "It happened," she said. "It happened when you shot Merritt."

"What?" he asked.

She didn't have to answer. A cracked mirror hanging on the dirty wall told him. He saw his eyes there, and shivered.

Out of the past he heard Julie's voice saying, "You're no

killer. It's not in your face. Your eyes are open too wide for killing."

In the mirror, now, they were narrowed to hard slits.

Maybe there was more than one way to be like Ricky Wolfe. Maybe you didn't have to *look* like him. But you could act like him. The guts inside made the difference. And—the eyes.

He broke away from looking at himself. "Let's move. Brentwood. That's where my house is, the one with the swimming pool, huh, Julie?"

"Sure," she said, softly. "Sure it is."

"Come on, then. You too, Kelly. And you boys. Lots of work for us."

"Sure, Boss."

They meant a lot, those two words: "Sure, Boss."

They all went out together.

CHAPTER THREE

Guns Are Old-Fashioned

It was a big impressive house in Brentwood; you could fall in its swimming pool if you didn't watch out; the bathrooms had glass doors. It glittered.

Walking around the huge garden surrounding the place, Broghman figured how it had all worked, how Merritt had been an unpopular sort of guy, how Ricky's spot had been vacant, discounting Merritt, for weeks now following Ricky's death. Things hadn't jelled yet.

So a lot of guys had wanted Ricky back. When people want things bad enough, they get them. Even if they have to make believe. So Broghman filled the part. He was near enough to the original, so they made him into a kind of duplicate of the old boss. Something strictly from a psychological text. Something for mind doctors to kick around. Mob instinct, leader instinct, desire to put upon a pedestal.... What the hell. He was IN, now. That counted. No matter how a psychiatrist explained it—the wishful thinking, the acceptance of a new shape from the old mold, he was *in!*

But, seeing the house and the garden, now after all the excitement died down, he realized that it meant nothing to him. Not a thing. What in hell did he want then? What? Even, there was something about Julie....

There had to be a party.

So Los Angeles could meet a guy named Broghman.

He bought a corsage for Julie for the party. He gave it to her in a cellophane box and watched her face change at sight of it. She twisted the box apart and tore the flower into pieces and dropped it on the floor:

"That's not what I want. I keep telling you. Don't give me anything like that."

She walked off.

He picked up the mashed flower, smelled it. It smelled all right. He shook his head.

The house was full of mist from cigarettes, coming and going in great nicotine fog-banks. Bottles rattled shapely glass hips one against another, champagne tumbled into glasses, everybody talked too much. It was Friday night, Merritt had been killed and taken away Wednesday. Broghman stood in the middle of the noise. This was the circus Julie ringmastered for him, so all the big lions could look at their new tamer, sit up, give a jealous greeting, shake hands maybe. Things were smooth. Julie saw to it that people who were small-time stayed on the outer fringe, while the big Joes got through. There were plenty of them—

"So they call you Ricky, too?"

This was an old man with white hair. Name of Vanning. Some sort of contact with one of the biggest lawyers. Soft pink face, long and intelligent looking, slightly wrinkled, constantly smoking imported cigars. "Like to see you after the party, Ricky," he said, softly.

"What about?"

Vanning chuckled a little. "We're surprised at your showing up, Ricky. We're respectable business men, yes we are. It's like having a ghost coming among us. But I must admit you were clever. Used a psychological trick. Very good."

"Keep talking."

"In spite of the fact that you showed some originality in the way you took Ricky Wolfe's place, you're still one of the old school gangsters. The kind of person who used to rob a bank with a gun—"

"What's wrong with that!"

"Unscientific. We're—businessmen. We do our work with hints, words, a little pressure here and there. Quiet transactions. We use psychology, too, but use it all the time." The old man brushed back his soft white hair. "Now, listen to me, young man. From now on, criminality works behind a desk. It's been tending that way a long time, but now it's here to stay. Science prevents you from being out in the open any more. People won't stand for it."

"So what do we talk about after the party?"

"About you quieting down, my boy. You attract attention. You're old-fashioned, make too much noise."

"So I gotta change!"

"We can give you an office downtown—"

"I'm not made that way!"

The old man kept smiling, his eyes twinkling. "On occasion, if we are forced to, we can revert to old-fashioned gangsterism, too, let me tell you. We can kill you, legally, any time, and take credit for having done the public a service. See how clever we are?"

Broghman considered Vanning a moment, his heart pounding, his eyes narrowed down to hard slits.

Vanning looked at Broghman's eyes. "Hill Street and Sixth. The Leighton Building, after midnight."

"I'll think about it."

When Vanning walked away, Julie's face said "No," to Broghman, with an exclamation point after it. But liquor and self-power both were fogging his brain and he could hardly see her.

The rest of the party wasn't even a decent memory. It was blotted out by a kind of excitement, the same excitement that had followed him ever since he met Julie. It was like a big drum being pounded in his brain, louder and louder and louder.

The door slammed on the last of the departing guests. Julie held onto the doorknob, feeling it. All of the steel had poured out of her as if through a secret release. She was hardly a healthy cat animal any more. She trembled.

They padded upstairs together, through the suddenly quiet house, no words passing between them. They closed the door to her room and the first words that she said were:

"You're not going down tonight to see Vanning. He knows he can't handle you. He's afraid of you. So he'll kill you!"

He kissed her on her full, obstinate lips. She smelled fresh after the nicotine and liquor. He kissed her on the neck, the ears, the cheeks, and again on the lips, and she responded. It was a long kiss.

Her fingers bit into his arms.

"Oh, Ricky, Ricky," she gasped.

He let her go.

He fell back as if she had struck his face.

She put up her hand, as if to catch those words, but she was too late. She couldn't bring them back.

He just looked at her as if she were invisible and said: "What did you say?"

"I didn't mean it."

"You said *Ricky!* You said it!"

Weakly, then, dazed, he repeated her words and then said, "You love him. You love a dead man. I should have guessed. You made me try to look like him, you risked your life on it. You made me look, walk, talk like him, so *he* could hold you again, so *he* could kiss you again, hurt you again!"

"Please…Johnny!"

His eyes were wide open again. "You don't love me. You tried to dig up Ricky out of the grave. I should have guessed when the gang acted the way it did at the magazine shop. They wanted Ricky back, too. They took a substitute for want of the real article. And all the other little things—"

He started groping for the door like a blind man. "You didn't want me to kiss you. *You* kissed *me*. That's the way it was with Ricky. You did things *for* him. When *I* did things, you resented it, you slapped me. It was off-key, off-character. It wasn't Ricky, it wasn't him at all. The flower I gave you, you didn't want. Ricky never gave flowers. And if I said nice things, you were angry—"

Julie got in front of the door, her breath hissing. "You can't go out! Vanning'll kill you."

"You afraid I'll get killed? Afraid *Ricky* will die again?"

He beat it at her, like fists, while his unfeeling hand sought the gun in its leather vest under his arm. "Afraid Ricky'll die again! Couldn't stand that, could you? Couldn't stand having him killed again!"

"No." She said the word so simply, so softly. "I couldn't stand it. I'm sorry, Johnny, but that's how it is."

She shook her head, as though trying to fight out of a dream. "Don't you see, Johnny? We're both the same. I'm not Julie. You don't want me. You want—your mother. Somebody you can cling to. Somebody to take care of you. The mother you never had, Johnny. And I—I want Ricky. We met in front of a bank, Johnny, you and I, and we both wanted something and we tried to get it and it fell apart in our faces." She gripped him, spoke convulsively, "Oh, Ricky, hold onto me tight—"

Ricky! The name was like an iron poked into his brain, stirring all the self-doubts and longings that wracked him. He didn't say anything, but what he was thinking through the liquor fog was, "I'm Johnny Broghman! I'm myself! Damn them—all of them, I don't need a woman to lean on. Not my mother, not Julie…not anybody. I'm Johnny Broghman—the strongest thing in the world."

He tried to push her away and she only clung tighter. Like a leech she was, feeding on his strength, trying to make him into somebody who wasn't Johnny Broghman. As if Johnny Broghman wasn't good enough.…

What his hands couldn't do, his gun did for him.

He didn't will it precisely. But there it was. His eyes were closed almost down, the Ricky way. His gun shot twice and knocked her back. He could feel her hands pull away from him, clinging to the last. She fell, sprawled, and lay unmoving on the floor.

He leaned against the door, swallowing, wiping at his eyes which were blurred. Then he went downstairs, the gun still in his hand. With every step he could feel himself growing stronger. Now he was free. He didn't need a woman to lean on, and now he had proved it.

He had killed twice and now he would kill again. The old

man with the pink face, Vanning. The one who called himself a businessman, and who thought he could make a desk punk out of Johnny Broghman. Vanning, who thought he could boss Johnny Broghman the way he had bossed Ricky Wolfe. Johnny Broghman was a better man than Ricky Wolfe had ever been. Julie had found that out.

Broghman opened the front door....He got it before he had walked halfway down the drive to his car. Vanning's men, in the black car parked in the night shade of bulking trees, reached for him with tommy-guns. The line of bullets hit him and he folded over them like a man folds over an invisible wall.

The guns kept spitting long after Johnny Broghman slumped down like a little kid on the lawn to take his evening sleep....

So that's Johnny Broghman's story, take it or leave it, with or without the benefit of the scalpel. It's all here on the slab.

Now, I'll take the heart of Johnny Broghman's and place it back inside the body where it never had a chance to love, but was only a guy in a cell. I'll put all of Johnny back inside himself where it belongs, all the agony and hatred and sullen burning flame of Johnny, back in upon himself in the cold cavern of the bullet-torn body, and I'll perform suture upon it with a needle and thread. Drop one, purl one, sewing Humpty-Dumpty back up again so they can bury him. I'll go on to other bodies, but I won't be able to write stories about them like Johnny's story. I won't be able to scalpel those brains apart, to know how the heart pulsed or the stomach turned in agony.

Johnny Broghman was my brother.

Hand me the suture, nurse.

Next!

Dead Men Rise Up Never

When Sherry began to scream I gripped the steering wheel and started sweating. I smelled her sweet and warm in the backseat between the stale smell of Willie and the sharp smell of Mark, and my nostrils took Hamphill into account too. Hamphill smelled soap-clean up in the front seat with me, and he tried to talk to her, calm her. He held her hand.

"Sherry, this is for your own good. Please listen to me, Sherry. We only got you away from your house in time. Finlay's men, the ones who threatened you, would have kidnapped you today. I swear it. In God's name. Sherry, we're only protecting you."

She didn't believe Hamphill. I saw her dark shining eyes caught, held like crazy, wild things, in the rearview mirror. The car's speed was up to sixty-five. Listen to him, Sherry, I thought, damn you, he loves you, so give him a chance!

"No! I don't believe you," was what she said. "You're gangsters too! I know you!"

She tried to fling herself out of the car. Maybe she didn't know how fast we were traveling. The ground ran past in a windy blur. She struggled. Mark held on to her. There was a shouting, a sudden scream, and silence....

Sherry relaxed too suddenly in the backseat. Willie must have blinked at her dully, not understanding.

"Stop the car." Hamphill groped at my elbow.

"But, boss..." I said.

"You heard me, Hank, stop it."

The car sound died away and all you could hear was the ocean moaning along the skirt of the cliff. We were on top of it.

Hamphill stared over into the rear seat and Willie's dull voice said, "She's gone to sleep, boss. Guess maybe she's tired."

I didn't turn around. I looked at the gray clouds in the sky and the seagulls looping and crying—at Hamphill's long lean face next to me, bleached to a beaten, shocked white, like a carved wooden mask left to bake and crumble on the sands.

The ocean came in once, twice, three times. Each time Hamphill breathed through his tiny, constricted nostrils. Then, holding her wrists, searching for a pulse he couldn't find, he shut his eyes—tight.

I stared ahead. "There's the cliff house, boss, just ahead. We better get inside it, in case Finlay and his men are following us. I bet they're damn mad at us for this trick...." I trailed off.

Hamphill didn't know I was alive. He resembled something as old suddenly as that ancient wind-shaped, paint-flaked mansion standing on the rim of the stony cliffs.

Loving Sherry had made him young awhile. Now the salt sea wind was at him, rimming his hair above the ears, peeling away his new youth; the tide pounded his guts and sucked away his thinking.

I started the car and drove the last half mile to the cliff house very slowly. I climbed out of the car and slammed the door to waken the boss from his nightmare.

We walked into the house, the four of us carrying her. The front steps groaned when our feet touched them.

Upstairs in a west room with a view we laid Sherry on an old overstuffed sofa. A fine dust puffed from upholstery pores, hovering over her in a powdery sunlit veil. Death had quieted her features and she was beautiful as polished ivory, her hair like the color of waxed chestnuts.

Very slowly Hamphill sank beside her and told her what he thought of her, soft, like a kid talking to a fairy goddess. He didn't sound like Hamphill, the beer baron; or Hamphill, the numbers man; or Hamphill, the racing boss. The wind whined behind his voice, because Sherry was dead and the day was over....

A car passed on the highway and I shivered. Any minute now, maybe, if we hadn't ditched them, some of Finlay's boys might show up—

The room felt crowded. There were only two people who needed to be in it. I pushed Willie and nodded at Mark. We went out and I closed the door and we stood with our hands deep in our pockets, in the hall, thinking many thoughts.

"You didn't have to scare her," I said.

"Me?" asked Mark, jerking a match on the wall and putting the flame unevenly against his cigarette. "She started yelling like a steam whistle."

"You scared her with your talk," I said. "After all, it wasn't a regular kidnapping. We were shielding her from Finlay. You know how soft the boss was on her—special."

"I knew," said Mark, "that we'd collect money on her, then frame Finlay for the deal, have him jailed, leaving us in the clear."

"You got the general idea," I said gently, "only let me bring out the details. The whole thing depended on Sherry's cooperation, once she learned our intentions were for her own good. There wasn't much time to explain today, when we heard Finlay was coming after her, so we grabbed her and ran. The blueprint was for us to hide her, then trap Finlay, let Sherry get a look at him and tell the police it was Finlay kidnapped her. Then they'd salt Finlay away and the whole business would be over."

Mark flicked ashes on the rug. "Only trouble is, Sherry's dead now. Nobody'll believe we didn't kidnap her ourselves. Ain't that swell!" One of Mark's little pointed, shiny black shoes kicked the wall. "Well, I don't want nothing else to do with her. She's dead. I hate dead people. Let's load her in a canvas tied with weights and put her out in the bay somewhere deep, then get out of here, get our money and—"

The door opened. Hamphill came out of it, pale.

"Willie, go watch over her while I talk to the boys," he said slowly, not thinking of the words. Willie beamed proudly and lumbered in. The three of us went into another room.

Mark has a mouth the shape of his own foot. "When we gonna get the money and scram, boss?" He shut the door and leaned on it.

"Money?" The boss held the word up like something strange found on the beach, turning it over. "Money." He focused dazedly on Mark. "I didn't want any *money*. I wasn't in this for the *money*—"

Mark shifted his delicate weight. "But you said—"

"I said. *I* said." Hamphill thought back, putting his thin fingers to his brow to force the thinking. "In order to make you play along, Mark, I said about money, didn't I? It was a lie, Mark, all a lie. Yes. All a lie. I only wanted Sherry. No money. Just her. I was going to pay you out of my own pocket. Right, Hank?" He stared strangely at me. "Right, Hank?"

"Right," I said.

"Well, of all the—" Angry color rose in Mark's cheeks. "This whole damn setup's nothing but nursemaiding a coupla lovebirds!"

"No money!" shouted Hamphill, straightening up. "No money! I was only kicking down the Christmas tree to get the star on top. And you—you always said it was wrong for me to love her, said it wouldn't work. But I planned everything. A week here. A trip to Mexico City later, after she got to know me, after fixing Finlay so he wouldn't bother her again! And you, Mark, you sniffing your damn nose at me, goddamn you!"

Mark grinned. "You should've said about it, boss, how you never intended getting money from kidnapping her, to make me understand. Why, sure, there was no use lying to me. Why, no, boss; no, of course not."

"Careful," I muttered.

"I'm sure sorry," said Mark, lidding his small green eyes. "Sure am. And, by the way, boss, how long we going to be here? I'm just curious, of course."

"I promised Sherry a week's vacation. We stay here that long."

One week. My brows went up. I said nothing.

"One week here, without trying to get the money, sitting, waiting for the cops to find us? Oh, that's swell, boss. I'm right in there with you, I sure am, I'm with you," said Mark. He turned, twisted the doorknob hard one way, stepped out, slammed it.

I put my right hand against Hamphill's heaving chest to stop his move. "No boss," I whispered. "No. He ain't living. He never lived. Why bother killing him? He's dead, I tell you. He was born dead."

The boss would have spoken except that we both heard a voice talking across the hall behind the other door. We opened the door, crossed the hall, and opened the other door slowly, looking in.

Willie sat on the couch-end like a large gray stone idol, his round face half blank, half animated, like a rock with lights playing over it. "You just rest there, Miss Bourne," he said to Sherry earnestly. "You look tired. You just rest. Mr. Hamphill thinks a lot of you. He told me so. He planned this whole setup for weeks, ever since he met you that night in Frisco. He didn't sleep, thinking about you—"

Two days passed. How many seagulls cried and looped over us, I don't remember. Mark counted them with his green eyes, and for every seagull, he threw away a cigarette butt burnt hungrily down to a nub. And when Mark ran out of smokes he counted waves, shells.

I sat playing blackjack. I'd put the cards down slow and pick them up and put them down slow again and shuffle them and cut them and lay them down. Maybe now and then I whistled. I've been around long enough so waiting makes no difference. When you been in the game as long as I have you don't find any difference in anything. Dying is as good as living; waiting is as good as rushing.

Hamphill was either up in *her* room, talking like a man in a confessional, soft and low, gentle and odd, or he was walking the beach, climbing the cliff stones. He'd tell Willie to squat on a rock. Willie'd perch there in the foggy sun with salt rime on his pink ears for five hours, waiting until the boss came back and said to jump down.

I played blackjack.

Mark kicked the table with his foot. "Talk, talk, talk, that's all he does upstairs at night, on and on, dammit! How long do we stick here? How long are we waiting?"

I laid down some cards. "Let the boss take his vacation any way he pleases," I said.

Mark watched me walk out on the porch. He shut the door after me, and though I couldn't be sure, I thought I heard the phone inside being ticked and spun by his fingers....

Late that evening the fog crept in thicker, and I stood upstairs in a north room with Hamphill, waiting.

He looked down out of the window. "Remember the first time we saw her? The way she held herself, the way she took her hair in her hand, the way she laughed? I knew then it would take all the education and smartness and niceness in me to ever get her. Was I a fool, Hank?"

"A fool can't answer that," I said.

He nodded at the sea breaking over rocks, toward a point where fog bands crossed a jut of land that fingered out to sea. "Look beyond that curve, Hank? There's an old California mission out there."

"Under water?"

"About twenty feet under. On a clear day when the sun cuts down, the water's a blue diamond with the mission held inside it."

"Still there, intact?"

"Most of it. They say some of the first padres built it, but the land settled slowly and the little cathedral sank. On clear days you can see it lying there in the water, very quiet. Maybe it's just a ruin, but you imagine you see the whole thing; the stained glass windows, the bronze tower bell, the eucalyptus trees in the wind—"

"Seaweed and the tide, huh?"

"Same thing. Same effect. I wanted Sherry to see it. I wanted to walk along the cliff bottoms, over those big rocks with her, and bake in the sun. Bake all the old poison out of me and all the doubt out of her. The wind does that to you. I thought maybe I could show Sherry the little cathedral and maybe in a day or so she'd breathe easy and sit on a rock with me to see if we could hear the bell in the church tower ringing."

"That's from the bell-buoy at the point," I said.

"No," he said, "that's farther over. This bell rings from in the water, but you have to listen close when the wind dies."

"I hear a siren!" I cried suddenly, whirling. "The police!" Hamphill took my shoulder. "No, that's only the wind in the holes of the cliff. I've been here before. I know. You get used to it."

I felt my heart pounding. "Boss, what do we do now?"

I shut up. I looked down at the white concrete road shimmering in the night and the fog. I saw the car sweeping down the highway, cutting through the fog with scythes of light.

"Boss," I said. "Take a look out this window."

"You look for me."

"A car. It's Finlay's sedan, I'd know it anywhere!"

Hamphill didn't move. "Finlay. I'm glad he's come. He's the one that caused all this. He's the one I want to see. Finlay." He nodded. "I want to talk to him. Go let him in, quietly."

The car ground to a stop below; its doors burst open. Men piled out, crossed the drive swiftly, crossed the porch; one ran around back. I saw guns with fog wet on them. I saw white faces with fog on them.

The downstairs bell rang.

I went down the stairs alone, empty-handed, clenched my teeth together, and opened the door. "Come on in," I said.

Finlay thrust his bodyguard in ahead of himself. The guard had his gun ready and was pop-eyed to see me just standing there. "Where's Hamphill?" Finlay demanded. A second gunsel stayed just outside the door.

"He'll be down in a minute."

"It's a good thing you didn't try any rough stuff."

"Oh, hell," I said.

"Where's Sherry?"

"Upstairs."

"I want her down here."

"Particular, aren't you?"

"Shall I hit him?" Finlay's bodyguard asked him.

Finlay looked up the dark stairs at the light in the opening door above. "Never mind."

Hamphill came down very quietly, one step at a time, pausing on each one with pain, as if his body were old, tired, and it was no longer fun to live and walk around. He got about halfway down when he saw Finlay. "What do you want?" he said.

"It's about Sherry," said Finlay.

I tightened up. The boss said, far away, "What about Sherry?"

"I want her back."

Hamphill said, "No."

"Maybe you didn't hear me right. I said I wanted her back, now!"

"No," said Hamphill.

"I don't want no trouble," said Finlay. His eyes moved from my empty hands to Hamphill's empty hands, puzzled at our strange actions.

"You can't have her," said Hamphill slowly. "Nobody can have her. She's gone."

"How'd you find us?" I asked.

"None of your damn business," said Finlay, glaring. To Hamphill: "You're lying!" To me: "Ain't he lying?"

"Talk quiet," I said. "Talk quiet in a house with someone dead in it."

"Dead?"

"Sherry's dead. Upstairs. Keep your voice down. You're too late. You better go back to town. It's all over."

Finlay lowered his gun. "I'm not going anywhere until I see her with my own eyes."

Hamphill said, "No."

"Like hell." Finlay looked at Hamphill's face and saw how much it looked like bone with the skin peeled away, white and hard. "Okay, so she's dead," he said, finally believing. He swallowed. He looked over his shoulder. "So we can still collect money on her, can't we?"

"No," said the boss.

"Nobody knows she's dead except us. We can still get the money. We'll just borrow a bit of her coat, a buckle, a button, a clip of her hair—You can keep the body, Hampy, old boy, with our compliments," Finlay assured him. "We'll just need a few things like her rings or compact to mail to her father for the dough."

A vein in Hamphill's hard-boned brow began to pulse. He leaned forward, stiffening, his eyes shining.

Finlay went on, "You can have the body, we'll leave you here with it, so you guys can take the rap."

"Sounds familiar," I said, remembering our plan to do the same for Finlay. That's life.

"Step aside, Hampy," said Finlay, walking big.

Hamphill fooled everyone the quiet way he stepped aside, turned as if to lead Finlay upstairs, took two steps up, then whirled. Finlay shouted as Hamphill pumped two shots into his big chest.

I shot the gun from one gunsel's hand. The second gunsel, outside, cursed, banged the door open, and sprang inward, his revolver aimed. The second gunsel shot Hamphill in the left arm just as Hamphill clutched Finlay, and they fell downward, collapsing together.

I got the second gunsel easily with one shot. The first one stood holding his awful red hand. Footsteps came in the back door. Willie came lumbering downstairs, bleating. "Boss, you all right?"

"Upstairs!" I said, helping the boss to his feet from Finlay's quiet body. "Willie, take him up!"

The third bodyguard rushed in, maybe expecting to see us all laid out stiff. I made a mess of his hand too.

Willie helped the boss upstairs and came down with some rope he'd found. There were no more footsteps outside. I pulled the door wide, letting the mist in, cooling my face. It smelled so good I just lay against the wall, smelling and liking it. The car was parked, its lights dark, but there was no movement. We'd taken care of everybody.

"Okay, Willie," I said. "Let's tie 'em up."

°

Hamphill lay like a long gray stick on the couch in the west room, nursing his wound. I closed the door.

"We got a setup, if we want to use it," I said.

He swabbed the wound with a white handkerchief.

I looked at him steadily. "This is the way it'll look to the cops: Finlay and his boys fight over money and shoot each other four ways from Christmas. The police find them here, anytime we want to call and tell them."

Hamphill's eyes fluttered weakly, his voice was small. "Later," he gasped. "Later, Hank. Not now."

"We've got to talk about it now," I said. "It's important."

"I don't want to leave Sherry."

"Look, boss, you're hit bad. You don't feel well."

"Later, Hank," he sighed.

"Yeah," I said feeling cold, but understanding. "Later. Okay."

Downstairs, Mark looked white as new snow. His hands shook as he sucked deeply on a cigarette he'd found on Finlay's body.

"Where were you when the shooting started?" I asked.

"Down at the boathouse on the beach, walking around. I ran up as quick as I could."

"You must be getting old," I said. "What sort of deal did you make on the phone with Finlay?"

Mark jerked, blew out smoke, drew his shaking hand across his unshaven cheek, and looked at his cigarette, then straight at me.

"The fog got me. The waiting got me. My guts got like *that*." He showed a tightened fist to me. "The boss upstairs, talking to her—like water dripping and dripping on my head. So I figured it out neat. You listening?"

"Talk."

"I called Finlay, told him I was double-crossing you guys, that I wanted a cut, that they could have Sherry. I knew Finlay'd come down and we'd get him and his gang and let them take the rap."

"You knew that, did you?"

"You calling me a liar!"

"You were sure quiet about it. We mighta got shot. It mighta worked both ways. We won, you stick with us. If Finlay'd won, you'd be with him, huh? Maybe."

"Hell, no! It was a chance, that's all. Either the cops found us here with Sherry and we got the gas chamber, or we had it out with Finlay. I couldn't tell you or the boss because if he knew he'd have shot me. I got nervous waiting. I wanted a fall guy. Finlay was it. I just didn't think he'd get here when he did; that's why I was down on the beach when things popped. I hoped that Finlay would swipe Sherry, even, and then we'd *have* to get out!"

"Okay," I said, nodding. "But there's still one thing gimmixed up. The boss won't move. After all your trouble fixing a frame, he won't move. So what'll you do now, junior?"

Mark swore. "How long'll we stay here? God, next week, next *month*?"

I pushed him away. "It smells in here. Go open the window."

I was dead tired. I checked the ropes on the three men to be sure they were tied tight, then I stretched out on the couch. Mark went upstairs. I could hear the boss up there, too, talking to somebody now, grunting with pain.

I slept deep, dreaming I walked under green water into that little church off the point, where fish swam with me in a congregation, and the underwater bronze bell rang, and a large squid draped itself like a soiled altar cloth across the pulpit...

I woke about four in the morning to the ticking of my watch. I had a feeling something was wrong. It was so wrong that I didn't have time to do anything about it. Someone hit me over the head. I fell, face forward, on the floor. That was all for a while.

I had a terrific headache when I came to. I blinked around in the dark, found my hands tied. It took five minutes to work out of the rope. I switched on a light.

Two of Finlay's men were gone!

I cursed myself out of the ropes tying my feet and raced upstairs.

Hamphill lay exhausted, in deep sleep. He didn't stir, even when I called his name. I shut the door softly and went to Sherry's room.

The couch where Sherry Bourne had lain was empty. Sherry was gone....

The ocean came and dropped itself on the sand and slid out with a foaming sigh as my feet crunched the sand down.

Squinting out, I saw the rowboat—a gray rowboat, barely visible in the moonlight just breaking through the fog.

A large man stood in the boat, with long thick arms and a big head. Willie.

Mark stood on the beach where the waves didn't quite touch his small dark shoes. He turned as I walked up. I looked at Willie in the boat. Mark looked as if he hadn't expected me to show up.

"Where's Willie going?" I said.

Mark looked out at Willie too. "He's got a load."

"A load of what?"

"Canvas with chains around it and bricks inside."

"What's he doing with that at four in the morning?"

"Dumping it. It's Finlay."

"Finlay!"

"I couldn't sleep downstairs with him there. And if you didn't like my plan, I wanted to get him out of the way. One corpse less, if the cops came." He looked at my head. "Somebody hit you?"

"About half an hour ago, and tied me up. While you were down here fussing around, two of the Finlay boys got free and whacked me." I smiled a little, too, to be friendly. "Then they took Sherry and drove off, just a few minutes ago. What do you think of that story?"

"They stole Sherry!" Mark's eyes widened, his jaw dropped.

"You're a damn good actor," I said.

"What do you mean?"

"I mean, why didn't they shoot me and the boss? We shot Finlay, didn't we? So why'd they hit me over the head when a shot in the guts would be better? It doesn't click. It's too damn convenient, you being down here, twice now, when everything begins to pop. Too damn neat you being down here with Finlay's body, giving them a chance to lam."

"I don't get what you're squawking at," snapped Mark. "If you ask me, you should be glad Sherry's gone. Now we won't have to stay here nursemaiding Hamphill!"

"You're just a little *too* glad," I said.

Willie was way out in the night now, looking back, waving at us.

Mark and I watched as Willie lifted the canvas thing and dropped it over the boat side. It made a big splash with ripples.

"Oh, God," I said. I took Mark quietly by his lapels, holding him close so I breathed in his face. "Know what I think?" I breathed. I gripped him. "I think you wanted to get out of here, bad. So you hit me on the head, tied me up, then you took Finlay's men, toted them out to their car, pushed them inside, drove the car down the road, parked it off behind some shrubs, lights out, left them, and came back. A good setup. You tell the boss they slipped their ropes, swiped Sherry and escaped." I looked at Willie in the boat. "All while you were dropping a body in the ocean—only, not Finlay's body!"

"Yes, it is!" He struggled, but I held him.

"You can't prove anything. I don't know anything about Sherry!"

"You should've shot me, Mark, it would have been more convincing." I released him. "You got the cards stacked. I can't prove that was Sherry inside the canvas with the chains and weights. Getting rid of Sherry was the most important thing in your life, wasn't it? No evidence. Gone for good. And that meant we could move on. We'd *have* to move on. The boss'd chase after the escaped Finlay gang to get Sherry back, only it'd be a wild goose chase, because Sherry isn't anywhere but out there, about forty feet under, where that little cathedral is!"

Willie turned the boat around and started rowing clumsily back with slow strokes. I started a cigarette and let the wind whip away the smoke.

"Funny you thought of putting her out there. There's not a better place. If the boss knew, I think he'd like her being there with the bronze bell in the tower and all. It's just your motive for putting her there that spoils it, Mark. You made something dirty out of something that could've been—well—beautiful."

"You aren't going to tell Hamphill!"

"I don't know. In a way I guess it might be best for us to move on. I don't know."

Willie beached his rowboat, grinning.

I said, "Hi, Willie."

"Hello, Hank. That takes care of Mr. Finlay, don't it?"

"It sure does, Willie. It sure does."

"He wasn't very heavy," said Willie, puzzled.

There was a crunching of feet on the sandy concrete stairway coming down the cliff. I heard Hamphill coming down, sobbing with pain and moaning something that sounded like "Sherry's gone. Sherry's gone!" He burst toward us from the base of the steps. "Sherry's gone!"

"Gone?" said Mark, playing it. "Gone!" said Willie.

I said nothing.

"Finlay's car's gone too. Hank, get our car, we've got to go after them. They can't take Sherry—" He saw the rowboat. "What's that for?"

Mark laughed. "I got Willie to give me a hand with Finlay."

"Yeah," said Willie. "Plunk—overboard. He wasn't heavy at all. Light as a feather."

Mark's cheek twitched. "You're just bragging, Willie. Oh, Hank, you better go get the car ready."

Maybe I showed something in my eyes. Hamphill glanced first at me, then at Mark, then at Willie, then at the boat.

"Where—where were you, Hank? Did you help load Finlay and drop him?"

"No. I was asleep. Somebody hit me on the head."

Hamphill shambled forward in the sand.

"What's wrong?" cried Mark.

"Hold still!" commanded Hamphill. He plunged his hand into one of Mark's coat pockets, then the other. He drew something out into the moonlight.

Sherry's bracelet and ring.

Hamphill's face was like nothing I'd ever seen before in my life. He stared blindly at the boat and his voice was far away as he said, "So Finlay was light as a feather, was he, Willie?"

"Yes, sir," said Willie.

Hamphill said slowly, "What were you going to do, Mark, use the bracelet and ring on your own time, to get the money?" He jerked a hand at Willie. "Willie, grab him!"

Willie grabbed. Mark yelled. Willie coiled him in like a boa constrictor enfolding a boar.

Hamphill said, "Walk out into the water with him, Willie."

"Yes, boss."

"And come back alone."

"Yes, boss."

"Boss, cut it out. Cut it, boss!" Mark screamed, thrashing wildly.

Willie began walking. The first shell of water poured over his big feet. A second skin of water slid in, foaming soft. Mark shouted and a wave thundered, roared around the shout, folding it as Willie folded Mark. Willie stopped.

"Keep going," said Hamphill.

Willie went in to his knees, then up, inch by inch, over his big stomach, to his chest. Mark's yelling was farther away now because the night wind covered it over.

Hamphill stood watching like a frozen god. A wave broke over Willie into custard foam, leveled out, as Willie plunged ahead with Mark and vanished. Six waves came in, broke.

Then a huge water wall rushed in, casting Willie, alone, at our feet. He stood up, shaking water off his thick arms. "Yes, boss."

"Go up to the car and wait there, Willie," said Hamphill. Willie lumbered off.

Hamphill looked out at the point, listening. "Now what in hell are you up to?" I said.

"None of your damn business."

He began walking toward the water. I put out my hands. He pulled away from me and there was a gun in one hand. "Get going. Go on up to the car with Willie. I got a date for a high mass," he said. "And I don't want to be late. Now, Hank."

He walked out into the cold water, straight ahead. I stood watching him as long as I could see his tall striding figure. Then one big wave came and spread everything into a salt solitude....

I climbed back up to the car, opened the door, and slid in beside Willie.

"Where's the boss?" asked Willie.

"I'll tell you all about it in the morning," I said. I sat there and Willie dripped water.

"Listen," I said and held my breath.

We heard the waves go in and out, in and out, like mighty organ music. "Hear 'em, Willie? That's Sherry taking the soprano and the boss on the baritone. They're in the choir loft, Willie, sending way up high after that gloria. That is real singing, Willie—listen to it while you can. You'll never hear anything like it again."

"I don't hear nothing," said Willie.

"You poor guy," I said, started the car, and drove away....

Where Everything Ends

In the old days a circus had dumped its ancient red wagons and yellow-painted cages into the canal. It looked as if a long parade had rolled and rumbled off the rim to pile up and rust brown under the grey motionless waters. There were about ten cages, wheels turned up, the paint of old years flaking like leaves from a calendar.

Steve Michaels stood on the edge of it, looking down and seeing it through a red mist.

Thirty years ago this was called Venice by the Sea, California. Like Italy. Gondolas had skimmed brightly, with green lanterns in the night, up and down, people singing, everything clean and new. That was all gone. Now it was a dump for empty cages.

Steve didn't know it was five in the afternoon. He didn't seem to notice the winter sun hung on a misty grey sky. The silence held onto him and wouldn't let him breathe.

All of a sudden Lisa was beside him. She made the winter air warm and sweet. Her voice was low,

"Steve, you can't stand here forever."

His grey eyes didn't look up.

"I can try."

"Come home to the L.A. office, Steve. You can come out again tomorrow."

"Yeah. After the funeral," Steve said, "I can come down and look at Charlie's bloodstains on the sidewalk. If it rains I can watch the rain wash them away." He stared at the concrete beneath his feet with its funny color. "I wish it could rain in my head and do the same."

Lisa waited. "All right," she sighed. "What do we do?"

His shoulders came up. He threw away a dead cigarette he'd forgotten to use.

"Walk. Come on, Lisa. We're looking for a murderer who lives in a house on the canal."

They walked south.

The territory was familiar. Steve explained. "The houses start here, thick, and peter out four miles down the coast. You find oil wells there, pumping, and the canal waters get dirty black with it. It—smells like old blood."

The cold light made Steve's face whiter, the skin of it boned tight on his cheeks, his eyes lonelier and colorless, and his hair blacker in contrast.

"While you were in El Monte yesterday, Lisa, someone phoned the office. An old man named Gerbelow who works an oil well on the Venice flatlands, said he was being blackmailed. Blackmailer's alias is Markham. Funny things were happening."

"What things?"

"Accidents at night, to oil equipment. Someone slipping around in the dark doing it. Charlie figured whoever was responsible lived nearby the canal system, I guess. So many nights, funny hours. I stuck in the office. Charlie interviewed Gerbelow, first, then strolled along the whole canal system, looking for some clue to the setup—"

Lisa's hand tightened on his arm. "The papers said it was accidental. Charlie Brandon walked off the pavement in the dark, struck his head and drowned in six feet of water..."

Steve's jaw muscles tightened. "I let the cops think it was accidental, too. Didn't want them plowing around. This is *my* case, mine and Charlie's." He looked at all the mouse-colored houses, each a grey replica of its brother. One-story flats with mist to tuck them in at twilight, and a salt wind blowing fury at morning. "Charlie must've figured some theory, walking around. I wish I knew what it was."

"Have you seen old man Gerbelow yet?"

"I phoned him and told him we'd be down. He said he'd only seen Markham once, a couple months ago when Markham first started his game. Gerbelow's got bad eyes. The only thing he said was that Markham had a young voice; young and cocky."

Steve walked faster.

"Is that where we're going, Steve? To Gerbelow's?"

"Yeah. It's a four-mile walk. We can look for *things* on the way down."

Lisa shivered and half turned as they walked. It was almost completely dark now.

"Funny how you think someone's following you—and it's only the wind."

Four miles down, the canal begins to veer toward the sea. The beat of the ocean comes in a kind of salt anger upon piers, rocks and sand flats. There, the oil wells knit land and sea together with pumping black fingers. You hear them groaning, creaking over their work. You can't see what they're doing in the dark, but you hear them complaining all the while.

A wind raked away the fog-clouds for a moment, like pale leaves on a big dark lawn, to let stars come through like funny far away flowers coming in bud. Steve whistled through his teeth.

Lisa went with him toward this one particular oil well that was set back from the canal about a hundred yards among a dozen others that climbed up and up and didn't want to stop. An oil well looks like the kind of thing the Guy uses to take down stars every night and shine them with a rag; a regular ladder up.

There was a light shining in a small shack. The teeter-totter of the oil pump moved up and down, up and down with a sighing, creaking, blowing; like a nervous finger.

"Hey, Pop!"

No answer. Steve heard Lisa whimper and a moment later she held onto him and said, "There he is, Steve. Up there, with his head under the power-shaft."

It was no place for a head. Steve gagged as he climbed the ladder up and stood atop the machinery shed where old man Gerbelow lay like a man sleeping, his head stuck under a shaft that went up and down, up and down. Steve's eyes followed it, up, down, up, down, until they blurred it out, wet, sick. He couldn't see. He could only kneel and a moment later say,

"Did it rain today, Lisa?"

"No."

"That's funny. The top of the shed's wet, and it's not blood. The fog's only been in a short while, no time for condensation there. Funny," he said, turning away. He came down into the raw wind and shadows, looking at the canal. Nothing moved anywhere for a moment. Then there was a shadow. Steve saw it running, far off, maybe a hundred yards away.

Steve had his gun out before he'd run four steps, but by that time the shadow was gone, and when Steve reached the canal there was nothing, only the sound of Lisa running on high heels after him. He looked upward at the towers with their platforms and ladders and webs of metal. Good hiding place, those, scuttle up in the shadows and lie watching and waiting over people below. So many towers. Too many. So many platforms and ladders and places to hide. Steve sighed. "Let's go back to Gerbelow's. There's been another accident. An old man tinkered with his machinery and got his head under the wrong dingus."

It was just about then they heard the scream.

o

They ran back.

They found a little man thin as steel wire quivering on Gerbelow's shack wall, pouring vomit over a fence in a kind of hot, acrid protest to the species of death that lay up there on the roof. In between awful sucks of breath the little man sobbed, "God Almighty, he's dead! If he'd kept his mouth shut, he'd be alive. You see, see him up there, you!" And he made sick again. "I was just—coming by to pay a visit, and—and—"

The little man wiped his mouth with a hairy, fumbling wrist and got Steve and Lisa in a kind of frightened focus. "You. YOU killed him! You—Markham!"

Steve held his badge in his hand like a pebble. The little man eyed it, swore softly, shook like the skin of a horse's flank. "Police. Detectives. Ah. They come a couple nights, get tired waiting, go away. Soons they go—huh—Markham slips out of hiding. He watches. He knows, by damn, by damn. Police always too early or too late. Damn." He bent over, coughing.

Steve quietly asked the man where he lived. The man shook an unsteady hand at the next well. "My name's Black. Oh, God, my stomach, my heart, my eyes. I don't want no trouble, don't make me none!"

"You knew what was happening to Gerbelow?"

Black knew, and kept his voice low about it. "He paid money to Markham so Markham would let him alone. Lots of people paid rather than have their machinery smashed. Machinery's rare, hard to get, hard to repair; the war and all. Oh, God, look at his head up there!" He retched again.

Steve lit a cigarette and gave it to Black to calm him. Black sucked it hungrily, eyes glinting at Lisa, then Steve. He couldn't keep quiet. "Now, look, I—I never seen this—blackmailer."

"No?"

"No. Nobody ever saw him. He telephoned. I wasn't bothered, myself. He didn't ask much money from the others. Just a little. Everybody paid, it was such a small amount of their total profit, and kept their machines whole."

Black went on and on. He told about an oiler named Big Irish Kelly who burned up, screaming, in his shack one night three months before. Markham had set the fire, not intending to murder. But Kelly was caught inside, anyhow, and that was the first blood on Markham's hands. An accident, but good as murder.

Steve interrupted the nervous flow of Black's tongue with: "Time's moving. Look, now, Black, show us around the fields. We're new here."

Black put his small back to the fence and trembled. "Not on your life. Look what it got Gerbelow! This Markham comes night after night. No noise. No sound. Only the fog." He whispered it. "Coming like the fog he would, soft, and going like a wave pulling back into the sea, leaving nothing. People set traps. Did they work? Hell, no. Markham knows everybody's mind. We found ropes on the towers. Figured maybe he swings like an ape around up in the girders in the wind. Surrounded a tower once, but everybody was scared to climb up, scared of being booted off and down. The police came, but they didn't find anything but some sacks shaped like a body, stuffed and propped up in the girders. Markham was gone, like one of them Hindu rope climbers into air."

"Did he ever bring a car with him?"

No car. Lisa suggested a canal boat.

Black was getting calmer now, and snorted smoke. "Hell, no. He never ran away from us, not far anyway before'd vanish. He didn't drive; no car in miles, and no boats. And if he'd swum we'd seen him, sure!"

Steve threw away his cigarette and casually asked,

"By the way, how is your oil well pumping these days, Black?"

That rocked him. Black closed his eyes, waited, opened them again, sullen and dark and replied, "If you want to know—my well's bone dry…"

Steve watched Lisa thoughtfully. In the dim light she looked beautiful; she smelled new, freshly young against the old smell of the sea, the primordial odor of oil.

Black's voice was sullen, like his eyes. Steve watched him, now, and said, "Your well's dry. So you're jealous of your neighbors and their riches. You live close by. You know the lay of the land. You could be the blackmailer, and come and go like the fog, eh? Couldn't you?"

"Gerbelow and the other people could tell you the blackmailer's voice is young. That don't fit me!"

It didn't. And anyway, Steve figured, it would be pretty dumb to kill someone right next door. And the fact that Charlie'd searched miles down the canal pretty well eliminated Black, anyway.

Steve put away his gun. "You'll have to escort us, whether you like the idea or not, Black. I can't have you running around behind me. There's a lot I want to see and hear. You lead the way."

Black led, grumbling. They walked toward the sea. On the way, Steve considered a few things. Gerbelow and Charlie'd both been killed when they were warm on the trail. Markham seemed like the patient kind of guy who'd wait a few months for it to blow over, and come back later. Meanwhile, though, he'd keep his eye peeled on Lisa and Black and himself. Might even be around right now, listening, hiding. If we get too warm, he'll try and conk us, too. One killing leads to another. You go on, day after day, trying to cover up…

❖

Steve began talking it out to Lisa as they walked down toward
the sea, led by Black. "We found Charlie lying in the water near
a bunch of abandoned circus wagons at the far end of the canal.
So the murderer doesn't live there, Lisa. He wouldn't kill a
man in front of his own house."

Lisa looked at all the black shacks and the fog rolling between
them. "Here then, Steve?"

Steve exhaled slowly. "Maybe here. It would be someone
who's lived here all his life, knows the whole territory and the
people. Maybe it was someone I played with when I was a kid,
living down on Windward Avenue. That would be something.
Yeah."

They reached the ocean to watch the breakers crash and
shake the sand underfoot. A foghorn blew melancholy notes
way out toward Catalina Island.

"You think the murderer came this way, Steve?"

"No. Breakers are too damn big, and the Coast Guard is too
damn vigilant these days. No." He lit another cigarette. "The
more I think about it, Lisa, the more I think the murderer
doesn't live here among his victims, or at the end of the canal
where we found Charlie. No, a happy medium would be better.
Somewhere between here and where we found Charlie. That
might be it."

The first iron wrench flew through the dark like a metal bird.

Black grunted and fell down and never got up again.

Lisa screamed and twisted about. Steve knocked her down
himself. The second iron wrench smashed off his right side, on
the lower rib casing, glancing it. By the impact of it, Steve wondered how much was left of Black's skull if that first wrench hit
him square.

Steve fell with it, letting it rock him back. He let go of his muscles and lay watching a shadow run off by itself. Steve's first two shots from his gun richocheted off iron; the third went into air, the shadow with it, behind wooden girders, Steve up and after it, quick. He left Lisa behind, and in the middle of his running he heard her footsteps ticking after. He cut off down a gravel path to the north, instead of going straight ahead, in case the murderer was waiting with another wrench in the shadows.

He reached the canal, breathing hard. A moment later Lisa grabbed him and sobbed on his lapel. It seemed that Black was dead, too. It seemed that Steve had been the object of that thrown wrench, but Black had gotten in the way. Lisa sobbed about it.

He held onto her, keeping his eyes on everything at once. The oil towers looked like they wanted to fall down on you, leaning way over, dark and high, with fog playing their timbers like a harp.

"Oh, Steve, Steve—"

"Hold onto yourself, sweets. Our little playboy's let himself in for too much playing. He should have been satisfied killing Gerbelow. But he stuck around to see what *we* thought, too. I guess he didn't like the way I talked back there."

They stood there together, like a couple kids, a couple kids in Gigantica. A thousand towers marching through the fog over them, grunting and puffing and steaming. Steve breathed easier, but the pain on his right side was knotting up like a snail in a hot shell.

Lisa said, "This's been an awful night, Steve. We're not any better off than we were. Let's get out of here, let's go home."

He felt tired, himself, sucked out, hot, cold, old, worn. But he swore under his breath and stepped away from her, scowling.

"Charlie's funeral is tomorrow. I can't go look him in the face without doing something about it, now."

There was a long silence. Lisa's voice was funny when she said, "What sort of person was Charlie when he was a kid?"

"Charlie?" He thought about it, uneasy and talking just to hear himself in the dark. "The old days? We ran around at the beach, played on the piers, fooled around the canal. Charlie's mother used to whip him for playing near the canal. I remember, one time—" The *canal*...

Steve shut up and walked. Lisa followed without a word, looking aside at his suddenly hard white face. He practically ran down three hundred yards of canal looking for something. When he found it he stopped and stood over it.

A trail of water across cement, dripped and spread and soaking into it.

"There was water on top of Gerbelow's shed, Lisa, by his body. There's water, here, too, where Markham came out of the canal."

"Are you sure, Steve?"

"Yeah. For the first time, I think I am."

"But nobody ever saw anybody swimming in the canal, Steve."

"There are ways and ways of doing things. I got a screwy, half-baked idea. All that crap about climbing towers like an ape-man was so much hash. Markham threw that in to confuse everybody. He didn't want people thinking about the canal too much. He wanted them to suspect one another. But he was an outsider, and this is where he came in."

Steve peeled off his coat in a cold dream. He unlaced his shoes, slowly, quietly, and then said, "You know what Markham looks like? Once you've found a main clue in a setup like this, the other pieces fall in place." He shucked his socks. "Markham's young. Maybe twenty-five, maybe thirty. Not much older. Young and healthy. He's got a chest development that would do for a horse."

"How do you know that?"

"The murderer felt safe in murdering three people. Why? Because he had a good means of escape and didn't live near where any of the bodies were found. But we KNOW where Charlie was looking, *along the canal*. Mathematically then, if the killer doesn't live at either end of the canal where the murders took place, he *must* live in the middle. And his method of travel gives us a general description of his age and health. Markham was always very careful to emerge from the canal a helluva distance beyond the place where he intended causing trouble. That's why nobody ever found his water trail, they didn't look far enough down and away from where the disturbance started on certain nights."

He nodded at the canal.

"The canal told me. Another thing—he's got a healthy tan. He lives on the canal. Sure." Steve folded all his clothes, including his pants, in a little pile on the cold cement beside the canal waters.

"I don't get it, Steve."

"Markham spends a lot of time on the beach every day. Lives a life of leisure, never does much. Black said he didn't ask for much money from his victims. A little bit from each one. Six or seven people kicking out with thirty bucks a month, or maybe fifty. Our blackmailer has plenty of leisure, plenty of time. That's a pretty good description of him. If I went to a row of houses and asked for a guy answering that description I should be able to find him, eventually, yes? Right. An athlete with a good chest expansion, a healthy tan, idle, young."

Steve was down to the skin and a pair of shorts now. He

didn't even see Lisa there in front of him. He just rose and stood by the waters, looking down. "The water's cold tonight. Probably wasn't bad in the summer, but I bet it's cold tonight." He leaned forward. "Nobody ever saw Markham come or go. Like the fog, they said, drifting. Or a wave from the sea. Silent and easy." He looked up at Lisa with the face of a lost child. "Have the police come to the end of the canal in about an hour, Lisa. I'll see you there."

She started to argue.

Steve said, "Nobody ever saw a car come by, or saw a boat on the canal, or saw anybody swimming across the canal. I'll show you how Markham was so mysterious, Lisa. Goodnight, sweets. See you in an hour."

"Steve!"

He was gone. Slipping like something white and of the fog, cleaving the water without a sound, so only a ripple came in to mark his vanishing, he went. Dark waters closed. The whole canal lay cold.

Lisa watched for five minutes, but she never saw Steve come up for air again, no matter how hard she stared.

The fog wrapped her up. The oil wells churned. The ocean pounded the shore. The foghorn sounded off in another world. Lisa, cold and shivering, gathered up the clothes and went to phone the police.

Steve was far away from Lisa, going north, when he came to the surface. He felt air break about nostrils, drew it in with a deep move of his lungs, and sank. The first cold shock of water wore off. Pain had gone from his side.

Pulling with great strokes of his arms, back, he skimmed through bottom darkness. Slime touched his fingers when they brushed the bottom. The water itself was clean here. It got sluggish, tepid with oil down further toward the sea. He could see about twenty feet ahead before intense black closed down. The lighting system on the Venice canal is lousy. One feeble lamp throwing diffused light from a base ten feet back from the canal; one feeble lamp every hundred yards. At night, with light like that, you'd never see anyone swimming five feet under.

When he rose again, with just a soft easy gesture of his body, he heard the oil wells throbbing like black hearts in the cliffs of silence on either side. Going down, he felt the extreme quiet of this mode of travel. No one to see you walking or running along sidewalks or dodging in shadows. Just the cold canal under stars, under fog, under wind. No ruffle on the water from swimming the surface. You kept deep and yanked cold wet power back, kicking away, holding breath, releasing it only in small bubble dribbles, gliding on.

With good lungs, a healthy young body, young and healthier than Steve's, you could swim a long cold way without having air. You rose quiet, gaped, sank, and shot on your dim way like a shark in familiar sounds.

Like a shark. Steve grinned against the passing water's pressure. You get like a fish after months of practice. Less and less air, longer down, easier strokes. No wonder the police never saw anything.

You can follow a guy for miles if he's walking on the sidewalk, and he won't know you're following. You pace him, get ahead of him, idle back, sink, and wait.

Steve came up again, slow and quiet as a fin breaking water.

"Charlie," he thought, "you walked here last night. You knew what you were looking for. Gerbelow told you his suspicions. You went on from there. It's fantastic, but it's true. You figured out how Markham worked, too. You figured him for a deep water shark."

Steve shoved under again, thinking, pushing. The cold wasn't half bad, now. But it'd been a long time since he'd swam late at night this way.

There was a hole gaping in the canal wall. Part of an old storm drain. Steve investigated. It all fell into place in his mind. Swim up the drain, under the ground a few feet to where the water recedes, crouch with your head out of water, bumping the tile walls of the tube, and you could hide all night if you had to, out of sight like a crocodile in a burrow of a river bank. There were storm drains emptying into the canal all along the way. Convenient burrows to rest in when one is tired of swimming. Rest in one for ten minutes, then swim on. Just enough air between top of tube and water for breathing. No wonder Markham fooled everyone!

Steve went on.

"Remember, Charlie, you and me and the canal when we were kids?" Steve gritted his teeth. "We three, you and me, and the canal. Funny how life begins and ends in the same place, sometimes. Yeah.

"So he followed you, Charlie. Like I'm after him. How far, Charlie? I'll tell you. Figure how far a man can swim underwater, with little rests maybe, until he's tired. One mile, two miles down the canal. No further. Just far enough away so the cops won't find you. Far enough away from your crimes.

"You figured it, Charlie, walking, smoking your cigars. You didn't know Markham was swimming that night, watching, waiting. Right in front of his house, he dragged you under! Hit you with a pipe, then, so you wouldn't be found there, towed you down to the end of the canal, where everything ends; including the circus and the cages and the old splintered wheels, and he laid you there. Then he swam home, slow, climbed out, went in and dried off, and maybe ate a late supper. Damn!"

Something lay shining in the water at the base of the canal.

Tin cans. A dozen of them, filled with cement, lined up in a neat row. Nothing wrong with tin cans. But they indicated the halfway mark, perhaps. They were put there, maybe, to help a swimmer orient himself without having to lift his head high above water and expose himself to view. Just a row of cans, nobody would notice but a shark.

It must have been fun for awhile, scaring people in the fog, making easy money. Playing like a kid, running around in the salt shadows, vanishing and leaving shivers behind you. Fun making your money that way, lying on the beach by day, getting exercise by night. Fun until the murdering began. You never plan for that. You *never* do.

Tiredness got a start in his arm muscles first. The blow struck by the thrown wrench was really hot, now, a heat almost glowing in the water, cringing with every stroke.

Getting tired. Steve thought quickly. How much further? As far as I can go and be dead tired, and then about one block, two blocks farther, counting in the added strength of an athlete like Markham. That should make it.

The shark came silent, swift and neat.

Shining only faintly, bubbles trailing from it, it shot from dimness, the strength of it becoming hands, legs, a man's face and body!

Steve shouted under water! The anger only shot up in frothed foam!

Markham!

When you take someone into your arms it is to love or to kill. There was no love here. Only the shock of bodies throwing cushions of water, fingers coming up like spiders on Steve's face, trying to poke into his eyes. Instinctively, he balled himself and kicked into that shimmering face, using it as a something to push on at the same time.

Markham came back. This time Steve was ready and used the canal side for traction, striking ahead to meet him. They exploded upward into the fog world, yelling for air, and then down. Muscles and training are not good things to meet. The underwater world was no place for a guy who hadn't been down in it for years.

Markham swarmed over Steve as they sank in a fury of split water. When it came to holding breath Markham had lungs for it, big and long-trained. Just by holding onto Steve and sinking and staying on the bottom, he could win out. Steve would eventually breathe water.

Markham tried that.

Steve relaxed on purpose, just wriggling one arm, one hand. He saved his air, his legs locked against Markham's. Funny. A guy named Markham. Fighting him underwater. Never seen his face before, can't even see it now, thought Steve, and here I am fighting with a name and a lot of muscles and bubbles! They plummeted and struck the canal floor, like they were caught in the falling drapery of a stage's scenery, long yards of green and black velvet tangled around them in the midst of a thunderstorm. Lightning blew Steve's brain apart, he saw fires and comets behind closed eyes. *Air!* In another second his lungs would—

Steve got his right hand on Markham's nose, thrust sharply upward. Markham's mouth broke open, an open trap, air gurgling out sharp, quick, awful. He broke away from Steve as a crab would, scuttling.

Steve knew what happened next. Markham would rise up for air, come down again quick and hold Steve before Steve could get any air at all. Next time there'd be no failure. Only lungs getting cold and dead and soggy.

Steve did it first. He came up, swearing. You can't swear underwater, only in your mind. The swearing is caught in you, just as you are caught in the cold web of water. Steve swore to the night, the insane pulse of oil pumps, the ocean colliding in mighty blows upon some far beach. Then he fell down upon the upcoming Markham, and Markham was wriggling like bait in a can!

Steve held his precious cache of air in raw lungs. His ears were shaking like hunks of tin hung in a high wind, beaten by great timbers of wood.

This is for you, Charlie! He made a slow beat against the slime with Markham's jerking head. *For you, Charlie!* And for Big Irish and the burning shack and old man Gerbelow and the man-shark that swam in calm waters and left no print but a trail of water where he came and went, that evaporated by morning and was gone!

Two beats, three beats.

"Give up your air, you bastard! Give up your air!"

Four beats. Markham laxed. Steve held on in a tight fury. Held until the head got drowsy and all the air regurgitated. With an intake, a rushing, Markham breathed of the good cold canal water where children played in the old days, of the good cold canal water where Charlie and Steve and a little boy who grew up to be a shark played in the warm sun, where all three fell into it and, now, only one would come up alive!

Steve held on until the intake was complete.

A drowsy nightmare. He came up to the outer world, glad for lungs, glad for the miracle of air. He simply clung limp to the side of the canal for fifteen minutes and sucked in and breathed out, in and out, enjoying it.

Then, treading water very slowly, he went down and found what had to be found, and taking *it* by the hand, swam slowly toward the end of the canal. It seemed a million miles away, so he took it easy, stopping every now and then, and going on again, like two kids going home hand in hand, one leading the other through the cold waters.

The end of the canal. Steve thought of that, thought of Charlie walking, thought of the circus wagons; and then the ironic idea came of itself. With his last strength, he'd do it.

The end of the canal. He reached it. He went under.

When he came up, a moment later, alone, he heard noises. A siren coming in from the suburbs, car motors slowing down, brakes, doors opening. Steve climbed from the water. He heard car doors slam, feet running.

The water ran off him in cold drippings. He shivered with it. His throat was raw, cold agony, and the world suddenly became six flashlights blazing over his wet body.

Lisa was there, crying, suddenly. A siren was just dying. She grabbed hold of him.

"Steve, Steve, you're all right."

"Sure, sure, Lisa sweets. You'll get yourself wet."

"Oh, Steve…"

He let her shake against him, so warm, so sweet, and over her shoulder he closed his eyes, felt the water running from his dark hair, running, running. He thought, it's raining in my brain. This'll help wash away part of Charlie's blood. Yeah. Wash away.

His teeth chattering, holding onto Lisa like she was a warm buoy in a sea of fog, he forced the words out of himself:

"Call the wagon. Get the hooks. There's a new kind of animal down in one of those cages. I think I got him tamed. Yeah—"

The lights turned down, burning the cold water through in slashes. Bars. Rusted Bars. And a white animal drifting sluggish behind the bars. Behind the bars. Behind the bars.

Steve laughed crazy and held Lisa close.

"Don't go away."

Corpse Carnival

It was unthinkable! Raoul recoiled from it, but was forced to face its reality because convulsions were surging sympathetically through his nervous system. Over him the tall circus banners in red, blue, and yellow fluttered somber and high in the night wind; the fat woman, the skeleton man, the armless, legless horrors, staring down at him with the same fierce hatred and violence they expressed in real life. Raoul heard Roger tugging at the knife in his chest.

"Roger, don't die! Hold on, Roger!" Raoul screamed.

They lay side by side on the warm grass, a sprinkle of odorous sawdust under them. Through the wide flaps of the main tent, which flipped like the leathery wings of some prehistoric monster, Raoul could see the empty apparatus at the tent top where Deirdre, like a lovely bird, soared each night. Her name flashed in his mind. He didn't want to die. He only wanted Deirdre.

"Roger, can you hear me, Roger?"

Roger managed to nod, his face clenched into a shapeless ball by pain. Raoul looked at that face: the thin, sharp lines; the pallor; the arrogant handsomeness; the dark, deep-set eyes; the cynical lip; the high forehead; the long black hair—and seeing Roger was like gazing into a mirror at one's own death.

"Who did it?" Raoul struggled, got his frantically working lips to Roger's ear. "One of the other freaks? The Cyclops? Lal?"

"I—I—" sobbed Roger. "Didn't see. Dark. Dark. Something white, quick. Dark." He sucked in a rattling breath.

"Don't die, Roger!"

"Selfish!" hissed Roger. "Selfish!"

"How can I be any other way; you know how I feel! Selfish! How would any man feel with half his body, soul, and life cast off, a leg amputated, an arm yanked away! Selfish, Roger. Oh, God!"

The calliope ceased, the steam of it went on hissing, and Tiny Mathews, who had been practicing, came running through the summer grass, around the side of the tent.

"Roger, Raoul, what happened!"

"Get the doctor, quick, get the doctor!" gibbered Raoul. "Roger's hurt badly. He's been stabbed!"

The midget darted off, mouselike, shrilling. It seemed like an hour before he returned with the doctor, who bent down and ripped Roger's sequined blue shirt from his thin, wet chest.

Raoul shut his eyes tight. "Doctor! Is he dead?"

"Almost," said the doctor. "Nothing I can do."

"There is," whispered Raoul, reaching out, seizing the doctor's coat, clenching it as if to crush away his fear. "Use your scalpel!"

"No," replied the doctor. "There are no antiseptic conditions."

"Yes, yes, I beg of you, cut us apart! Cut us apart before it's too late! I've got to be free! I want to live! Please!"

The calliope steamed and hissed and chugged; the brutal roustabouts looked down. Tears squeezed from under Raoul's lids. "Please, there's no need of both of us dying!"

The doctor reached for his black bag. The roustabouts did not turn away as he ripped cloth and bared the thin spines of Raoul and Roger. A hypodermic load of sedative was injected efficiently.

Then the doctor set to work at the thin epidermal skin structure that had joined Raoul to Roger, one to the other, ever since the day of their birth twenty-seven years before.

Lying there Roger said nothing, but Raoul screamed.

o

Fever flooded him to the brim for days. Drenching the bed with sweat, crying out, he looked over his shoulder to talk with Roger but—*Roger wasn't there! Roger would never be there again!*

Roger *had* been there for twenty-seven years. They'd walked together, fallen together, liked and disliked together, one the echo of the other, one the mirror, slightly distorted by the other's perverse individuality. Back to back they had fought the surrounding world. Now Raoul felt himself a turtle unshelled, a snail irretrievably dehoused from its armor. He had no wall to back against for protection. The world circled behind him now, came rushing in to strike his back!

"Deirdre!"

He cried her name in his fever, and at last saw her leaning over his bed, her dark hair drawn tight to a gleaming knot behind her ears. In memory, too, he saw her whirling one hundred times over on her hempen rope at the top of the tent in her tight costume. "I love you, Raoul. Roger's dead. The circus is going on to Seattle. When you're well, you can catch up with us. I love you, Raoul."

"Deirdre, don't you go away too!"

Weeks passed. Often he lay until dawn with the memory of Roger next to him in the old bondage. "Roger?" Silence. Long silence.

Then he would look behind himself and weep. A vacuum lived there now. He must learn never to look back. How many months he hung on the raw edge of life, he had no accounting of. Pain, fear, horror, pressured him and he was reborn again in silence, alone, one instead of two, and life had to start all over.

He tried to recall the murderer's face or figure, but could not. Twisting, he thought of the days before the murder—Roger's insults to the other freaks, his adamant refusal to get along with anyone, even his own twin. Raoul winced. The freaks hated Roger, even if Raoul gave them no irritation. They'd demanded that the circus get rid of the twins for once and all!

Well, the twins were gone now. One into the earth. The other into a bed. And Raoul lay planning, thinking of the day when he might return to the show, hunting the murderer, to live his life, to see Father Dan, the circus owner, to kiss Deirdre again, to see the freaks and search their faces to see which one had done this to him. He would let no one know that he had not seen the killer's face in the deep shadows that night. He would let the killer simmer in his juices, wondering if Raoul knew more than he had said!

It was a hot summer twilight. Animal odors sprang up all around him in infinite acrid varieties. Raoul walked across the tanbark uneasily, seeing the first evening star, unused to this freedom, always peering behind himself to make certain Roger wasn't lagging.

For the first time in his life Raoul realized he was being ignored! The sight of him and Roger had gathered crowds anywhere, anytime. And now the people looked only at the lurid canvases, and Raoul noticed, with a turn of his heart, that the canvas painting of himself and Roger had been taken down. There was an empty space, as if a tooth had been extracted from the midway. Raoul resented this sudden neglect, but at the same time he glowed with a new sensation of individuality.

He could run! He wouldn't have to tell Roger: "Turn here!" or "Watch it, I'm falling!" And he wouldn't have to put up with Roger's bitter comments: "Clumsy! No, no, not *that* direction. I want to go this way. Come on!"

A red face poked out of a tent. "What the hell?" cried the man. "I'll be damned! Raoul!" He plunged forward. "Raoul, you've come back! Didn't recognize you because—" He glanced behind Raoul. "That is, well, dammit, welcome home!"

"Hello, Father Dan!"

Sitting in Father Dan's tent they clinked glasses. Father Dan was a small, violently red-haired Irishman and he shouted a lot. "God, boy, it's good to see you. Sorry the show had to push on, leave you behind that way. Lord! Deirdre's been a sick cow over you, waiting. Now, now, don't fidget, you'll see her soon enough. Drink up that brandy." Father Dan smacked his lips.

Raoul drank his down, burning. "I never thought I'd come back. Legend says that if one Siamese twin dies, so does the other. I guess Doc Christy did a good job with his surgery. Did the police bother you much, Father Dan?"

"A coupla days. Didn't find a thing. They get after you?"

"I talked a whole day with them before coming west. They let me go. I didn't like talking to them anyway. This business is between Roger and me and the killer." Raoul leaned back. "And now—"

Father Dan swallowed thickly. "And now—" he muttered.

"I know what you're thinking," said Raoul.

"Me?" guffawed Father Dan too heartily, smacking Raoul's knee. "You know I never think!"

"The fact is, you know it, I know it, Papa Dan, that I'm no longer a Siamese twin," said Raoul. His hand trembled. "I'm just Raoul Charles DeCaines, unemployed, no abilities other than gin rummy, playing a poor saxophone, and telling a very few feeble quips. I can raise tents for you, Papa Dan, or sell tickets, or shovel manure, or I might leap from the highest trapeze some night without a net; you could charge five bucks a seat. You'd have to break in a new man for *that* act every night."

"Shut up!" cried Father Dan, his pink face getting pinker. "Damn you, feeling sorry for yourself! Tell you what you'll get from me, Raoul DeCaines—hard work! Damn right you'll heave elephant manure and camel dung, but—maybe later when you're strong, you can work the trapezes with the Condiellas."

"The Condiellas!" Raoul stared, not believing.

"Maybe, I said. Just maybe!" retorted F.D., snorting. "And I hope you break your scrawny neck, damn you! Here, drink up, boy, drink up!"

The canvas flap rattled, opened, a man with staring blind eyes set in a dark Hindu face felt his way inside. "Father Dan?"

"I'm here," said Father Dan. "Come in, Lal."

Lal hesitated, his thin nostrils drawing small. "Someone else here?" His body stiffened. "Ah." Blind eyes shone wetly. "They are back. I smell the double sweat of them."

"It's just me," said Raoul, feeling cold, his heart pumping. "No," insisted Lal gently. "I smell the two of you." Lal groped forward in his own darkness, his delicate limbs moving in his old silks, the knife he used in his act gleaming at his waist.

"Let's forget the past, Lal."

"After Roger's insults?" cried Lal softly. "Ah, no. After the two of you stole the show from us, treated us like filth, so we went on strike against you? Forget?"

Lal's blind eyes narrowed to slits. "Raoul, you had better go away. If you remain you will not be happy. I will tell the police about the split canvas, and then you will not be happy."

"The split canvas?"

"The sideshow canvas painting of you and Roger in yellow and red and pink which hung on the runway with the printed words SIAMESE TWINS! on it. One night four weeks ago I heard a ripping sound in the dark. I ran forward and stumbled over the canvas. I showed it to the others. They told me it was the painting of you and Roger, ripped down the middle, separating you. If I tell the police of that, you will not be happy. I have kept the split canvas in my tent—"

"What has that to do with me?" demanded Raoul angrily.

"Only you can answer that," replied Lal quietly. "Perhaps I'm blackmailing you. If you go away, I will not tell who it was who ripped the canvas in half that night. If you stay I may be forced to explain to the police why you yourself sometimes wished Roger dead and gone from you."

"Get out!" roared Father Dan. "Get out of here! It's time for the show!"

The tent flaps rustled; Lal was gone.

The riot began just as they were finishing off the bottle, starting with the lions roaring and jolting their cages until the bars rattled like loose iron teeth. Elephants trumpeted, camels humped skyward in clouds of dust, the electric light system blacked out, attendants ran shouting, horses burst from their roped stalls and rattled around the menagerie, spreading tumult; the lions roared louder, splitting the night down the seams; Father Dan, cursing, smashed his bottle to the ground and flung himself outside, swearing, swinging his arms, catching attendants, roaring directions into their startled ears. Someone screamed, but the scream was lost in the incredible dinning, the confusion, the chaotic hoofing of animals. A swell and tide of terror sounded from the throats of the crowd waiting by the boxes to buy tickets; people scattered, children squealed!

Raoul grabbed a tent pole and hung on as a cluster of horses thundered past him.

A moment later the lights came on again; the attendants gathered the horses together in five minutes. The damage was estimated as minor by a sweating, pink-faced, foul-tongued Papa Dan, and everything quieted down. Everybody was okay, except Lal, the Hindu. Lal was dead.

"Come see what the elephants did to him, Father Dan," someone said.

The elephants had walked on Lal as if he were a small dark

carpet of woven grasses; his sharp face was crushed far down into the sawdust, very silent and crimson wet.

Raoul got sick to his stomach and had to turn away, gritting his teeth. In the confusion, he suddenly found himself standing outside the geeks' tent, the place where he and Roger had lived ten years of their odd nightmarish life. He hesitated, then poked through the flaps and walked in.

The tent smelled the same, full of memories. The canvas sagged like a melancholy gray belly from the blue poles. Beneath the stomaching canvas, in a rectangle, the flake-painted platforms, bearing their freak burdens of fat, thin, armless, legless, eyeless misery, stood ancient and stark under the naked electric light bulbs. The bulbs buzzed in the air, large fat Mazda beetles, shedding light on all the numbed, sullen faces of the queer humans.

The freaks focused their vague uneasy eyes on Raoul, then their eyes darted swiftly behind him, seeking Roger, not finding him. Raoul felt the scar, the empty livid stitchings on his back take fire. Out of memory Roger came. Roger's remembered voice called the freaks by the acrid names Roger had thought up for them: "Hi, Blimp!" for the Fat Lady. "Hello, Popeye!" This for the Cyclops Man. "And you, Encyclopaedia Britannica!" That could only mean the Tattooed Man. "And you, Venus de Milo!" Raoul nodded at the armless blond woman. Even six feet of earth could not muffle Roger's insolent voice. "Shorty!" There sat the legless man on his crimson velvet pillow. "Hi, Shorty!" Raoul clapped his hand over his mouth. Had he said it *aloud*? Or was it just Roger's cynical voice in his brain?

Tattoo, with many heads painted on his body, seemed like a vast crowd milling forward. "Raoul!" he shouted happily. He flexed muscles proudly, making the tattoos cavort like a three-ring act. He held his shaved head high because the Eiffel Tower, indelible on his spine, must never sag. On each shoulder blade hung puffy blue clouds. Pushing shoulder blades together, laughing, he'd shout, "See! Storm clouds over the Eiffel! Ha!"

But the sly eyes of the other freaks were like so many sharp needles weaving a fabric of hate around him.

Raoul shook his head. "I can't understand you people! You hated both of us once for a reason; we outshone, outbilled, out-salaried you. But now—how can you still hate *me*?"

Tattoo made the eye around his navel almost wink. "I'll tell you," he said. "They hated you when you were more abnormal than they were." He chuckled. "Now they hate you even more because you're released from freakdom." Tattoo shrugged. "Me, I'm not jealous. I'm no freak." He shot a casual glance at them. "They never liked being what they are. They didn't plan their act; their glands did. Me, my mind did all this to me, these pink chest gunboats, my abdominal island ladies, my flower fingers! It's different—mine's ego. Theirs was a lousy accident of nature. Congratulations, Raoul, on escaping."

A sigh rose from the dozen platforms, angry, high, as if for the first time the freaks realized that Raoul would be the only one of their number ever to be free of the taint of geekdom and staring people.

"We'll strike!" complained the Cyclops. "You and Roger always caused trouble. Now Lal's dead. We'll strike and make Father Dan throw you out!"

Raoul heard his own voice burst out. "I came back because one of you killed Roger! Besides that, the circus was and is my life, and Deirdre is here. None of you can stop me from staying and finding my brother's murderer in my own time, in my own way."

"We were all in bed that night," whined Fat Lady.

"Yes, yes, we were, we were," they all said in unison.

"It's too late," said Skyscraper. "You'll never find anything!"

The armless lady kicked her legs, mocking. "I didn't kill him. I can't hold a knife except by lying on my back, using my feet!"

"I'm half blind!" said Cyclops.

"I'm too fat to move!" whined Fat Lady.

"Stop it, stop it!" Raoul couldn't stand it. Raging, he bolted from the tent, ran through darkness some ten feet. Then suddenly he saw her, standing in the shadows, waiting for him.

"Deirdre!"

She was the white thing of the upper spaces, a creature winging a canvas void each night, whirling propeller-wise one hundred times around to the enumeration of the strident ringmaster: "—eighty-eight!" A whirl. "Eighty-nine!" A curling. "Ninety!" Her strong right arm bedded with hard muscles, the fingers bony, grasping the hemp loop; the wrists, the elbow, the biceps drawing her torso, her tiny bird-wing feet on up, over, and down; on up, over, and down; with a boom of the brass kettle as she finished each roll.

Now, against the stars, her strong curved right arm raised to a guy wire, she poised forward, looking at Raoul in the half-light, her fingers clenching, relaxing, clenching.

"They've been at you, haven't they?" she asked, whispering, looking past him, inward to those tawdry platforms and their warped cargo, her eyes blazing. "Well, I've got power too. I'm a big act. I've got pull with Papa Dan. I'll have my say, darling."

At the word "darling" she relaxed. Her tight hand fell. She stood, hands down, eyes half-closed, waiting for Raoul to come and put his arms about her. "What a homecoming we've given you," she sighed. "I'm so sorry, Raoul." She was warmly alive against him. "Oh, darling, these eight weeks have been ten years."

Warm, close, good, his arms bound her closer. And for the first time in all his life, Roger was not muttering at Raoul's back: "Oh, for God's sake, get it over with!"

They stood in the runway at nine o'clock. The fanfare. Deirdre kissed his cheek. "Be back in a few minutes." The ringmaster called her name. "Raoul, you must get up, away from the freaks. Tomorrow you rehearse with the Condiellas."

"Won't the freaks detest me for leaving them on the ground? They killed Roger; now, if I outshine them again, they'll get me!"

"To hell with the freaks, to hell with everything but you and me," she declared, her iron fingers working, testing a practice hemp floured with resin. She heard her entrance music. Her eyes clouded. "Darling, did you ever see a Tibetan monk's prayer wheel? Each time the wheel revolves it's one prayer to heaven—*oom mani padme hum.*" Raoul gazed at the high rope where she'd swing in a moment. "Every night, Raoul, every time I go around one revolution, it'll mean I love you, I love you, I love you, like that—over and over."

The music towered. "One other thing," she added quickly. "Promise you'll forget the past. Lal's dead, he committed suicide. Father Dan's told the police another story that doesn't implicate you, so let's forget the whole sorry mess. As far as the police know Lal was blind and in the confusion of the lights going off, when the animals got free, he was killed."

"Lal didn't commit suicide, Deirdre. And it wasn't an accident." Raoul could hardly say it, look at her. "When I returned, the real killer got panicky and wanted a cover-up. Lal suspected the killer, too, so there was a double motive. Lal was pushed under those elephants to make me think my search was over and done. It's not. It's just beginning. Lal wasn't the kind to commit suicide."

"But he hated Roger."

"So did *all* the geeks. And then there's the matter of Roger's picture and mine torn in two pieces."

Deirdre stood there. They called her name. "Raoul, if you're right, then they'll kill you. If the killer was trying to throw you off-trail, and you go on and on—" She had to run then, off into the music, the applause, the noise. She swung up, up, high, higher.

A large-petaled flower floated on the darkness and came to rest on Raoul's shoulder. "Oh, it's you, Tattoo."

The Eiffel Tower was sagging. Twin flowers were twitching at Tattoo's sides as in a high storm. "The geeks," he muttered sullenly. "They've gone on hands and knees to Father Dan!"

"What!"

"Yeah. The armless lady is gesturin' around with her damn big feet, yellin'. The legless man waves his arms, the midget walks the table top, the tall man thumps the canvas ceiling! Oh, God, they're wild mad. Fat Lady'll bust like a rotten melon, I swear! Thin Man'll fall like a broken xylophone!

"They say you killed Lal and they're going to tell the police. The police just got done talking with Father Dan and he convinced them Lal's death was pure accident. Now, the geeks say either Father Dan kicks you out or they go on strike and tell the cops to boot. So Father Dan says for you to hop on over to his tent, *tout de suite*. Good luck, kid."

Father Dan sloshed his whiskey into a glass and glared at it, then at Raoul. "It's not what you did or didn't do that counts, it's what the geeks *believe*. They're boiling. They say you killed Lal because he knew the truth about you and your brother—"

"The truth!" cried Raoul. "What *is* the truth?"

Father Dan couldn't face him, he had to look away. "That you were fed up, sick of being tied to Roger like a horse to a tree, that you—that you killed your brother to be free—that's what they say!" Father Dan sprang to his feet and paced the sawdust. "I'm not believing it—yet."

"But," cried Raoul. "*But*, maybe it would've been worth risking, isn't that what you mean?"

"Look here, Raoul, it stands to reason, if one of the geeks killed Roger, why in hell are you alive? Why didn't he kill you? Would he chance having you catch up with him? Not on your busted tintype. Hell. None of the geeks killed Roger."

"Maybe he got scared. Maybe he wanted me to live and suffer. That would be real irony, don't you see?" pleaded Raoul, bewildered.

Father Dan closed his eyes. "I see that I've got my head way out *here*." He shoved out his hand. "And this business of the torn painting of you and Roger that Lal found. It points to the fact that someone wanted Roger dead and you alive, so maybe you paid one of the other geeks to do the job, maybe you didn't have the nerve yourself—" Father Dan paced swiftly. "And after the job was done, your murderer friend tore the picture triumphantly in two pieces!" Father Dan stopped for breath, looked at Raoul's numbed, beaten face. "All right," he shouted, "maybe I'm drunk. Maybe I'm crazy. So maybe you *didn't* kill him. You'll still have to pull out. I can't take a chance on you, Raoul, much as I like you. I can't lose my whole sideshow over you."

Raoul rose unsteadily. The tent tilted around him. His ears hammered crazily. He heard his own strange voice saying, "Give me two more days, Father Dan. That's all I ask. When I find the killer, things will quiet down, I promise. If I don't find him. I'll go away, I promise that too."

Father Dan stared morosely at his boot tip in the sawdust. Then he roused himself uneasily. "Two days, then. But that's all. Two days, and no more. You're a hard man to down, aren't you, number two twin?"

✿

They rode on horseback down past the slumbering town, tethered up by a creek, and talked earnestly and kissed quietly. He
told her about Father Dan, the split canvas, Lal, and the danger
to his job. She held his face in her hands, looking up.

"Darling, let's go away. I don't want you hurt."

"Only two more days. If I find the murderer, we can stay."

"But there are other circuses, other places." Her gray eyes
were tormented. "I'd give up my job to keep us safe." She
seized his shoulders. "Is Roger that important to you?" Before
he knew what she intended, she had whirled him in the dark,
locked her elbows in his, and pressured her slender back to his
scarred spine. Whispering softly, she said, "I have you now, for
the first time, alone, don't go away from me." She released him
slowly, and he turned and held her again. She said, so softly,
"Don't go away from me, Raoul, I don't want anything to inter-
fere again...."

Instantly time flew backward. In Raoul's mind he heard
Deirdre on another day, asking Roger why he and Raoul had
never submitted themselves to the surgeon's scalpel. And Roger's
cynic's face rose like driftwood from the tide pool of Raoul's
memory, laughing curtly at Deirdre and retorting, "No, my dear
Deirdre, no. It takes two to agree to an operation. I refuse."

Raoul kissed Deirdre, trying to forget Roger's bitter com-
ment. He recalled his first kiss from Deirdre and Roger's abrupt
voice: "Kiss her this way, Raoul! Here, let *me* show you! May I
cut in? No, no, Raoul, you're unromantic! That's better. Mind if
I fan myself?" Another chortle. "It's a bit warm."

"Shut up, shut up, shut up!" screamed Raoul. He shook violently, jolting himself back into the present—into Deirdre's
arms—

He woke in the morning with an uncontrollable desire to

run, get Deirdre, pack, catch a train, and get out now, get away
from things forever. He paced his hotel room. To go away, he
thought, to leave and never know any more about the half
of himself that was buried in a cemetery hundreds of miles
away— But he *had* to know.

Noon bugle. The carnies, geeks, finkers, and palefaces, the
shills and the shanties, lined the timber tables as Raoul picked
vaguely at his plated meat. There was a way to find the murderer. A sure way.

"Tonight I'm turning the murderer over to the police," said
Raoul, murmuring.

Tattoo almost dropped his fork. "You mean it?"

"Pass the white top tent," someone interrupted. Cake was
handed past Raoul's grim face as he said:

"I've been waiting—biding my time since I got back—
watching the killer. I saw his face the night he got Roger. I
didn't tell the police that. I didn't tell anybody that. I been
waiting—just waiting—for the right time and place to even up
the score. I didn't want the police doing my work for me. I
wanted to fix him in my own way."

"It wasn't Lal, then?"

"No."

"You let Lal be killed?"

"I didn't think he would be. He should have kept quiet. I'm
sorry about Lal. But the score'll be evened tonight. I'll turn the
killer's body over to the police personally. And it'll be in self-
defense. They won't hold me. I'll tell you that, painted man."

"What if he gets you first?"

"I'm half dead now. I'm ready." Raoul leaned forward
earnestly, holding Tattoo's blue wrist. "You won't tell anyone
about this, of course?"

"Who? Me? Ha, ha, not *me*, Raoul."

✿

The choice news passed from Tattoo to Blimp to Skeleton to Armless to Cyclops to Shorty and on around. Raoul could almost see it go. And he knew that now the matter would be settled; either he'd get the killer or the killer'd get him. Simple. Corner a rat and have it out. But what if nothing happened?

He frequented all the dark places when the sun set. He strolled under tall crimson wagons where buckets might drop off and crush his head. None dropped. He idled behind cat cages where a sprung door could release fangs on his scarred spine. No cats leaped. He sprawled under an ornate blue wagon wheel waiting for it to revolve, killing him. The wheel did not revolve, nor did elephants trample him, nor tent poles collapse across him, nor guns shoot him. Only the rhythmed music of the band blared out into the starry sky, and he grew more unhappy and solemn in his death-walking.

He began walking faster, whistling loudly against the thoughts in his mind. Roger had been killed for a purpose. Raoul was *purposely* left alive.

A wave of applause echoed from the big top. A lion snarled. Raoul put his hands to his head and closed his eyes. The geeks were innocent. He knew that now. If Lal or Tattoo or Fat Lady or Armless or Legless was guilty, they'd have killed both Roger and Raoul. There was only one solution. It was clear as a blast of a new trumpet.

He began walking toward the runway entrance, shuffling his feet. There'd be no fight, no blood spilled, no accusations or angers.

"I will live for a long time," he said to himself, wearily. "But what will there be to live for, after tonight?"

What good to stick with the show now, what good if the

freaks did settle down to accepting him? What good to know the killer's name. No good—no damned good at all. In his frantic search for one thing he'd lost another. He was alive. His heart pounded hot and heavy in him, sweat poured from his armpits, down his back, on his brow, in his hands. Alive. And the very fact of his aliveness, his living, his heart pulsing, his feet moving, was proof of the killer's identity. It is not often, he thought grimly, that a killer is found through a live man being alive, usually it is through a dead man's being dead. I wish I were dead. I wish I were dead.

This was the last performance in the circus in his life. He found himself shuffling down the runway, heard the whirling din of music, the applause, the laughter as clowns tumbled and wrestled in the red rings.

Deirdre stood in the runway, looking like a miracle of stars and whiteness, pure and clean and birdlike. She turned as he came up, her face pale, small blue petals under each eye from sleepless nights; but beautiful. She watched the way Raoul walked with his head down.

The music held them. He raised his head and didn't look at her.

"Raoul," she said, "what's wrong?"

He said, "I've found the killer."

A cymbal crashed. Deirdre looked at him for a long time. "Who is it?"

He didn't answer, but talked to himself, low, like a prayer, staring straight out at the rings and the people: "You get caught. No matter what you do, you're helpless. With Roger I was unhappy: without him I'm worse. When I had Roger I wanted you; now, with Roger gone, I can never have you. If I'd given up the hunt, I'd never have been happy. Now that the hunt is over, I'm even more miserable with what I've found."

"You're—you're going to turn the killer in, then?" she asked, finally, after a long time.

He just stood there, saying nothing, not able to think or see or talk. He felt the music rise, high. He heard, far off, the announcer giving Deirdre's name, he felt her hard fingers hold him for a moment, tightly, and her warm lips kiss him hard.

"Goodbye, darling."

Running lightly, the sequins all flashing and flittering like huge reflecting wings, Deirdre went over the tanbark, into the storm of applause, her face upward, staring at her ropes and her heaven, the music beating down on her like rain. The rope pulled her up, up, and up. The music cut. The trap drum pattered smoothly, monotonously. She began her loops.

A man walked out of the shadows when Raoul motioned to him, smoking a cigar, chewing it thoughtfully. He stopped beside Raoul and they were wordless for a time, staring upward.

There was Deirdre, caught high in the tent by a white beam of steady light. Grasping the slender rope strand, her legs swung up over her curved body in a great circle, over, up and down.

The ringmaster bawled out the revolutions one by one: "One—two—three—four—!"

Over and over went Deirdre, like a white moth spinning a cocoon. *Remember, Raoul, when I go around; the monk's prayer wheel.* Raoul's face fell apart. *Oom mani padme hum. I love, I love you, I love you.*

"She's pretty, ain't she?" said the detective at Raoul's side.

"Yes, and she's the one you want," said Raoul slowly, not believing the words he had to speak. "I'm alive tonight. That proves it. She killed Roger and ripped our canvas painting in half. She killed Lal." He passed a trembling hand over his eyes. "She'll be down in about five minutes, you can arrest her then."

They both stared upward together, as if they didn't quite believe she was there.

"Forty-one, forty-two, forty-three, forty-four, forty-five," counted the detective. "Hey, what're you crying about? Forty-six, forty-seven, forty-..."

And So Died Riabouchinska

The cellar was cold cement and the dead man was cold stone and the air was filled with an invisible fall of rain, while the people gathered to look at the body as if it had been washed in on an empty shore at morning. The gravity of the earth was drawn to a focus here in this single basement room—a gravity so immense that it pulled their faces down, bent their mouths at the corners and drained their cheeks. Their hands hung weighted and their feet were planted so they could not move without seeming to walk underwater.

A voice was calling, but nobody listened.

The voice called again and only after a long time did the people turn and look, momentarily, into the air. They were at the seashore in November and this was a gull crying over their heads in the gray color of dawn. It was a sad crying, like the birds going south for the steel winter to come. It was an ocean sounding the shore so far away that it was only a whisper of sand and wind in a seashell.

The people in the basement room shifted their gaze to a table and a golden box resting there, no more than twenty-four inches long, inscribed with the name RIABOUCHINSKA. Under the lid of this small coffin the voice at last settled with finality, and the people stared at the box, and the dead man lay on the floor, not hearing the soft cry.

"Let me out, let me out, oh, please, please, someone let me out."

And finally Mr. Fabian, the ventriloquist, bent and whispered to the golden box, "No, Ria, this is serious business.

Later. Be quiet, now, that's a good girl." He shut his eyes and tried to laugh.

From under the polished lid her calm voice said, "Please don't laugh. You should be much kinder now after what's happened."

Detective Lieutenant Krovitch touched Fabian's arm. "If you don't mind, we'll save your dummy act for later. Right now there's all *this* to clean up." He glanced at the woman, who had now taken a folding chair. "Mrs. Fabian." He nodded to the young man sitting next to her. "Mr. Douglas, you're Mr. Fabian's press agent and manager?"

The young man said he was. Krovitch looked at the face of the man on the floor. "Fabian, Mrs. Fabian, Mr. Douglas—all of you say you don't know this man who was murdered here last night, never heard the name Ockham before. Yet Ockham earlier told the stage manager he knew Fabian and had to see him about something vitally important."

The voice in the box began again quietly.

Krovitch shouted. "*Damn* it, Fabian!"

Under the lid, the voice laughed. It was like a muffled bell ringing.

"Pay no attention to her, Lieutenant," said Fabian.

"Her? Or *you*, damn it! What is this? Get together, you two!"

"We'll never be together," said the quiet voice, "never again after tonight."

Krovitch put out his hand. "Give me the key, Fabian."

In the silence there was the rattle of the key in the small lock, the squeal of the miniature hinges as the lid was opened and laid back against the table top.

"Thank you," said Riabouchinska.

Krovitch stood motionless, just looking down and seeing Riabouchinska in her box and not quite believing what he saw.

The face was white and it was cut from marble or from the whitest wood he had ever seen. It might have been cut from snow. And the neck that held the head which was as dainty as a porcelain cup with the sun shining through the thinness of it, the neck was also white. And the hands could have been ivory and they were thin small things with tiny fingernails and whorls on the pads of the fingers, little delicate spirals and lines.

She was all white stone, with light pouring through the stone and light coming out of the dark eyes with blue tones beneath like fresh mulberries. He was reminded of milk glass and of cream poured into a crystal tumbler. The brows were arched and black and thin and the cheeks were hollowed and there was a faint pink vein in each temple and a faint blue vein barely visible above the slender bridge of the nose, between the shining dark eyes.

Her lips were half parted and it looked as if they might be slightly damp, and the nostrils were arched and modeled perfectly, as were the ears. The hair was black and it was parted in the middle and drawn back of the ears and it was real—he could see every single strand of hair. Her gown was as black as her hair and draped in such a fashion as to show her shoulders, which were carved wood as white as a stone that has lain a long time in the sun. She was very beautiful. Krovitch felt his throat move and then he stopped and did not say anything.

Fabian took Riabouchinska from her box. "My lovely lady," he said. "Carved from the rarest imported woods. She's appeared in Paris, Rome, Istanbul. Everyone in the world loves her and thinks she's really human, some sort of incredibly delicate midget creature. They won't accept that she was once part of many forests growing far away from cities and idiotic people."

Fabian's wife, Alyce, watched her husband, not taking her eyes from his mouth. Her eyes did not blink once in all the time he was telling of the doll he held in his arms. He in turn seemed aware of no one but the doll; the cellar and its people were lost in a mist that settled everywhere.

But finally the small figure stirred and quivered. "Please, don't talk about me! You know Alyce doesn't like it."

"Alyce never has liked it."

"Shh, don't!" cried Riabouchinska. "Not here, not now." And then, swiftly, she turned to Krovitch and her tiny lips moved. "How did it all happen? Mr. Ockham, I mean, Mr. Ockham."

Fabian said, "You'd better go to sleep now, Ria."

"But I don't want to," she replied. "I've as much right to listen and talk, I'm as much a part of this murder as Alyce or—or Mr. Douglas even!"

The press agent threw down his cigarette. "Don't drag me into this, you—" And he looked at the doll as if it had suddenly become six feet tall and were breathing there before him.

"It's just that I want the truth to be told." Riabouchinska turned her head to see all of the room. "And if I'm locked in my coffin there'll be no truth, for John's a consummate liar and I must watch after him, isn't that right, John?"

"Yes," he said, his eyes shut, "I suppose it is."

"John loves me best of all the women in the world and I love him and try to understand his wrong way of thinking."

Krovitch hit the table with his fist. "God damn, oh, God *damn* it, Fabian! If you think you can—"

"I'm helpless," said Fabian.

"But she's—"

"I know, I know what you want to say," said Fabian quietly, looking at the detective. "She's in my throat, is that it? No, no. She's not in my throat. She's somewhere else. I don't know. Here, or here." He touched his chest, his head.

"She's quick to hide. Sometimes there's nothing I can do.

Sometimes she is only herself, nothing of me at all. Sometimes she tells me what to do and I must do it. She stands guard, she reprimands me, is honest where I am dishonest, good when I am wicked as all the sins that ever were. She lives a life apart. She's raised a wall in my head and lives there, ignoring me if I try to make her say improper things, cooperating if I suggest the right words and pantomime." Fabian sighed. "So if you intend going on I'm afraid Ria must be present. Locking her up will do no good, no good at all."

Lieutenant Krovitch sat silently for the better part of a minute, then made his decision. "All right. Let her stay. It just may be, by God, that before the night's over I'll be tired enough to ask even a ventriloquist's dummy questions."

Krovitch unwrapped a fresh cigar, lit it and puffed smoke. "So you don't recognize the dead man, Mr. Douglas?"

"He looks vaguely familiar. Could be an actor."

Krovitch swore. "Let's all stop lying, what do you say? Look at Ockham's shoes, his clothing. It's obvious he needed money and came here tonight to beg, borrow or steal some. Let me ask you this, Douglas. Are you in love with Mrs. Fabian?"

"Now, wait just a moment!" cried Alyce Fabian.

Krovitch motioned her down. "You sit there, side by side, the two of you. I'm not exactly blind. When a press agent sits where the husband should be sitting, consoling the wife, well! The way you look at the marionette's coffin, Mrs. Fabian, holding your breath when she appears. You make fists when she talks. Hell, you're obvious."

"If you think for one moment I'm jealous of a stick of wood!"

"Aren't you?"

"No, no, I'm not!"

Fabian moved. "You needn't tell him anything, Alyce."

"Let her!"

They all jerked their heads and stared at the small figurine, whose mouth was now slowly shutting. Even Fabian looked at the marionette as if it had struck him a blow.

After a long while Alyce Fabian began to speak.

"I married John seven years ago because he said he loved me and because I loved him and I loved Riabouchinska. At first, anyway. But then I began to see that he really lived all of his life and paid most of his attentions to her and I was a shadow waiting in the wings every night.

"He spent fifty thousand dollars a year on her wardrobe—a hundred thousand dollars for a dollhouse with gold and silver and platinum furniture. He tucked her in a small satin bed each night and talked to her. I thought it was all an elaborate joke at first and I was wonderfully amused. But when it finally came to me that I was indeed merely an assistant in his act I began to feel a vague sort of hatred and distrust—not for the marionette, because after all it wasn't her doing, but I felt a terrible growing dislike and hatred for John, because it *was* his fault. He, after all, was the control, and all of his cleverness and natural sadism came out through his relationship with the wooden doll.

"And when I finally became very jealous, how silly of me! It was the greatest tribute I could have paid him and the way he had gone about perfecting the art of throwing his voice. It was all so idiotic, it was all so strange. And yet I knew that something had hold of John, just as people who drink have a hungry animal somewhere in them, starving to death.

"So I moved back and forth from anger to pity, from jealousy to understanding. There were long periods when I didn't hate him at all, and I never hated the thing that Ria was in him, for she was the best half, the good part, the honest and the lovely part of him. She was everything that he never let himself try to be."

Alyce Fabian stopped talking and the basement room was silent.

"Tell about Mr. Douglas," said a voice, whispering.

Mrs. Fabian did not look up at the marionette. With an effort she finished it out. "When the years passed and there was so little love and understanding from John, I guess it was natural I turned to—Mr. Douglas."

Krovitch nodded. "Everything begins to fall into place. Mr. Ockham was a very poor man, down on his luck, and he came to this theater tonight because he knew something about you and Mr. Douglas. Perhaps he threatened to speak to Mr. Fabian if you didn't buy him off. That would give you the best of reasons to get rid of him."

"That's even sillier than all the rest," said Alyce Fabian tiredly. "I didn't kill him."

"Mr. Douglas might have and not told you."

"Why kill a man?" said Douglas. "John knew all about us."

"I did indeed," said John Fabian, and laughed.

He stopped laughing and his hand twitched, hidden in the snowflake interior of the tiny doll, and her mouth opened and shut, opened and shut. He was trying to make her carry the laughter on after he had stopped, but there was no sound, save the little empty whisper of her lips moving and gasping, while Fabian stared down at the little face and perspiration came out, shining, upon his cheeks.

The next afternoon Lieutenant Krovitch moved through the theater darkness backstage, found the iron stairs and climbed with great thought, taking as much time as he deemed necessary on each step, up to the second-level dressing rooms. He rapped on one of the thin-paneled doors.

"Come in," said Fabian's voice from what seemed a great distance.

Krovitch entered and closed the door and stood looking at the man who was slumped before his dressing mirror. "I have something I'd like to show you," Krovitch said. His face showing no emotion whatever, he opened a manila folder and pulled out a glossy photograph, which he placed on the dressing table.

John Fabian raised his eyebrows, glanced quickly up at Krovitch and then settled slowly back in his chair. He put his fingers to the bridge of his nose and massaged his face carefully, as if he had a headache. Krovitch turned the picture over and began to read from the typewritten data on the back. "Name, Miss Ilyana Riamonova. One hundred pounds. Blue eyes. Black hair. Oval face. Born 1914, New York City. Disappeared 1934. Believed a victim of amnesia. Of Russo–Slav parentage. Etcetera. Etcetera."

Fabian's lip twitched.

Krovitch laid the photograph down, shaking his head thoughtfully. "It was pretty silly of me to go through police files for a picture of a marionette. You should have heard the laughter at headquarters. *God.* Still, here she is—Riabouchinska. *Not* papier-mâché, *not* wood, *not* a puppet, but a woman who once lived and moved around and—disappeared." He looked steadily at Fabian. "Suppose you take it from there?"

Fabian half smiled. "There's nothing to it at all. I saw this woman's picture a long time ago, liked her looks and copied my marionette after her."

"Nothing to it at all." Krovitch took a deep breath and exhaled, wiping his face with a huge handkerchief. "Fabian, this very morning I shuffled through a stack of *Billboard* magazines that high. In the year 1934 I found an interesting article concerning an act which played on a second-rate circuit, known as Fabian and Sweet William. Sweet William was a little boy dummy. There was a girl assistant—Ilyana Riamonova. No picture of her in the article, but I at least had a name, the name of a real person, to go on. It was simple to check police files then and dig up this picture. The resemblance, needless to say, between the live woman on one hand and the puppet on the other is nothing short of incredible. Suppose you go back and tell your story over again, Fabian."

"She was my assistant, that's all. I simply used her as a model."

"You're making me sweat," said the detective. "Do you think I'm a fool? Do you think I don't know love when I see it? I've watched you handle the marionette, I've seen you talk to it, I've seen how you make it react to you. You're in love with the puppet naturally, because you loved the original woman very, very much. I've lived too long not to sense that. Hell, Fabian, stop fencing around."

Fabian lifted his pale slender hands, turned them over, examined them and let them fall.

"All right. In 1934 I was billed as Fabian and Sweet William. Sweet William was a small bulb-nosed boy dummy I carved a long time ago. I was in Los Angeles when this girl appeared at the stage door one night. She'd followed my work for years. She was desperate for a job and she hoped to be my assistant...."

He remembered her in the half light of the alley behind the theater and how startled he was at her freshness and eagerness to work with and for him and the way the cool rain touched softly down through the narrow alleyway and caught in small spangles through her hair, melting in dark warmness, and the rain beaded upon her white porcelain hand holding her coat together at her neck.

He saw her lips' motion in the dark and her voice, separated off on another sound track, it seemed, speaking to him in the autumn wind, and he remembered that without his saying yes or no or perhaps she was suddenly on the stage with him, in the great pouring bright light, and in two months he, who had always prided himself on his cynicism and disbelief, had stepped off the rim of the world after her, plunging down a bottomless place of no limit and no light anywhere.

Arguments followed, and more than arguments—things said and done that lacked all sense and sanity and fairness. She had edged away from him at last, causing his rages and remarkable hysterias. Once he burned her entire wardrobe in a fit of jealousy. She had taken this quietly. But then one night he handed her a week's notice, accused her of monstrous disloyalty, shouted at her, seized her, slapped her again and again across the face, bullied her about and thrust her out the door, slamming it!

She disappeared that night.

When he found the next day that she was really gone and there was nowhere to find her, it was like standing in the center of a titanic explosion. All the world was smashed flat and all the echoes of the explosion came back to reverberate at midnight, at four in the morning, at dawn, and he was up early, stunned with the sound of coffee simmering and the sound of matches being struck and cigarettes lit and himself trying to shave and looking at mirrors that were sickening in their distortion.

He clipped out all the advertisements that he took in the papers and pasted them in neat rows in a scrapbook—all the ads describing her and telling about her and asking for her back. He even put a private detective on the case. People talked. The police dropped by to question him. There was more talk.

But she was gone like a piece of white incredibly fragile tissue paper, blown over the sky and down. A record of her was sent to the largest cities, and that was the end of it for the police. But not for Fabian. She might be dead or just running away, but wherever she was he knew that somehow and in some way he would have her back.

One night he came home, bringing his own darkness with him, and collapsed upon a chair, and before he knew it he found himself speaking to Sweet William in the totally black room.

"William, it's all over and done. I can't keep it up!"

And William cried, "Coward! Coward!" from the air above his head, out of the emptiness. "You can get her back if you want!"

Sweet William squeaked and clappered at him in the night. "Yes, you can! *Think!*" he insisted. "Think of a way. You can do it. Put me aside, lock me up. Start all over."

"Start all over?"

"Yes," whispered Sweet William, and darkness moved within darkness. "Yes. Buy wood. Buy fine new wood. Buy hard-grained wood. Buy beautiful fresh new wood. And carve. Carve slowly and carve carefully. Whittle away. Cut delicately. Make the little nostrils so. And cut her thin black eyebrows round and high, so, and make her cheeks in small hollows. Carve, carve…"

"No! It's foolish. I could never do it!"

"Yes, you could. Yes you could, could, could, could…"

The voice faded, a ripple of water in an underground stream. The stream rose up and swallowed him. His head fell forward. Sweet William sighed. And then the two of them lay like stones buried under a waterfall.

The next morning, John Fabian bought the hardest, finest-grained piece of wood that he could find and brought it home and laid it on the table, but could not touch it. He sat for hours staring at it. It was impossible to think that out of this cold chunk of material he expected his hands and his memory to re-create something warm and pliable and familiar. There was no way even faintly to approximate that quality of rain and summer and the first powderings of snow upon a clear pane of glass in the middle of a December night. No way, no way at all to catch the snowflake without having it melt swiftly in your clumsy fingers.

And yet Sweet William spoke out, sighing and whispering, after midnight, "You can do it. Oh, yes, yes, you can do it!"

And so he began. It took him an entire month to carve her hands into things as natural and beautiful as shells lying in the sun. Another month and the skeleton, like a fossil imprint he was searching out, stamped and hidden in the wood, was revealed, all febrile and so infinitely delicate as to suggest the veins in the white flesh of an apple.

And all the while Sweet William lay mantled in dust in his box that was fast becoming a very real coffin. Sweet William croaking and wheezing some feeble sarcasm, some sour criticism, some hint, some help, but dying all the time, fading, soon to be untouched, soon to be like a sheath molted in summer and left behind to blow in the wind.

As the weeks passed and Fabian molded and scraped and polished the new wood, Sweet William lay longer and longer in stricken silence, and one day as Fabian held the puppet in his hand Sweet William seemed to look at him a moment with puzzled eyes and then there was a death rattle in his throat.

And Sweet William was gone.

Now as he worked, a fluttering, a faint motion of speech began far back in his throat, echoing and re-echoing, speaking silently like a breeze among dry leaves. And then for the first time he held the doll in a certain way in his hands and memory moved down his arms and into his fingers and from his fingers into the hollowed wood and the tiny hands flickered and the body became suddenly soft and pliable and her eyes opened and looked up at him.

And the small mouth opened the merest fraction of an inch

and she was ready to speak and he knew all of the things that she must say to him, he knew the first and the second and the third things he would have her say. There was a whisper, a whisper, a whisper.

The tiny head turned this way gently, that way gently. The mouth half opened again and began to speak. And as it spoke he bent his head and he could feel the warm breath—of *course* it was there!—coming from her mouth, and when he listened very carefully, holding her to his head, his eyes shut, wasn't *it* there, too, softly, *gently*—the beating of her heart?

Krovitch sat in a chair for a full minute after Fabian stopped talking. Finally he said, "I *see*. And your wife?"

"Alyce? She was my second assistant, of course. She worked very hard and, God help her, she loved me. It's hard now to know why I ever married her. It was unfair of me."

"What about the dead man—Ockham?"

"I never saw him before you showed me his body in the theater basement yesterday."

"Fabian," said the detective.

"It's the truth!"

"Fabian."

"The truth, the truth, damn it, I swear it's the truth!"

"The truth." There was a whisper like the sea coming in on the gray shore at early morning. The water was ebbing in a fine lace on the sand. The sky was cold and empty. There were no people on the shore. The sun was gone. And the whisper said again, "The truth."

Fabian sat up straight and took hold of his knees with his thin hands. His face was rigid. Krovitch found himself making the same motion he had made the day before—looking at the gray ceiling as if it were a November sky and a lonely bird going over and away, gray within the cold grayness.

"The truth." Fading. "The truth."

Krovitch lifted himself and moved as carefully as he could to the far side of the dressing room where the golden box lay open and inside the box the thing that whispered and talked and could laugh sometimes and could sometimes sing. He carried the golden box over and set it down in front of Fabian and waited for him to put his living hand within the gloved delicate hollowness, waited for the fine small mouth to quiver and the eyes to focus. He did not have to wait long.

"The first letter came a month ago."

"No."

"The first letter came a month ago."

"No, *no!*"

"The letter said, 'Riabouchinska, born 1914, died 1934. Born again in 1935.' Mr. Ockham was a juggler. He'd been on the same bill with John and Sweet William years before. He remembered that once there had been a woman, before there was a puppet."

"No, that's not true!"

"Yes," said the voice.

Snow was falling in silences and even deeper silences through the dressing room. Fabian's mouth trembled. He stared at the blank walls as if seeking some new door by which to escape. He half rose from his chair. "Please…"

"Ockham threatened to tell about us to everyone in the world."

Krovitch saw the doll quiver, saw the fluttering of the lips, saw Fabian's eyes widen and fix and his throat convulse and tighten as if to stop the whispering.

"I—I was in the room when Mr. Ockham came. I lay in my box and I listened and heard, and I *know.*" The voice blurred, then recovered and went on. "Mr. Ockham threatened to tear me up, burn me into ashes if John didn't pay him a thousand dollars.

"Then suddenly there was a falling sound. A cry. Mr. Ockham's head must have struck the floor. I heard John cry out and I heard him swearing, I heard him sobbing. I heard a gasping and a choking sound."

"You heard nothing! You're deaf, you're blind! You're wood!" cried Fabian.

"But I *hear*!" she said, and stopped as if someone had put a hand to her mouth.

Fabian had leaped to his feet now and stood with the doll in his hand. The mouth clapped twice, three times, then finally made words. "The choking sound stopped. I heard John drag Mr. Ockham down the stairs under the theater to the old dressing rooms that haven't been used in years. Down, down, down, I heard them going away and away—down..."

Krovitch stepped back as if he were watching a motion picture that had suddenly grown monstrously tall. The figures terrified and frightened him, they were immense, they towered! They threatened to inundate him with size. Someone had turned up the sound so that it screamed.

He saw Fabian's teeth, a grimace, a whisper, a clenching. He saw the man's eyes squeeze shut.

Now the soft voice was so high and faint it trembled toward nothingness.

"I'm not made to live this way. This way. There's nothing for us now. Everyone will know, everyone will. Even when you killed him and I lay asleep last night, I dreamed. I knew, I realized. We both knew, we both realized that these would be our last days, our last hours. Because while I've lived with your weakness and I've lived with your lies, I can't live with something that kills and hurts in killing. There's no way to go on from here. How *can* I live alongside such knowledge?..."

Fabian held her into the sunlight which shone dimly through

the small dressing-room window. She looked at him and there was nothing in her eyes. His hand shook and in shaking made the marionette tremble, too. Her mouth closed and opened, closed and opened, closed and opened, again and again and again. Silence.

Fabian moved his fingers unbelievingly to his own mouth.

A film slid across his eyes. He looked like a man lost in the street, trying to remember the number of a certain house, trying to find a certain window with a certain light. He swayed about, staring at the walls, at Krovitch, at the doll, at his free hand, turning the fingers over, touching his throat, opening his mouth. He listened.

Miles away in a cave, a single wave came in from the sea and whispered down in foam. A gull moved soundlessly, not beating its wings—a shadow.

"She's gone. She's gone. I can't find her. She's run off. I can't find her. I can't find her. I try, I try, but she's run away off far. Will you help me? Will you help me find her? Will you help me find her? Will you please help me find her?"

Riabouchinska slipped bonelessly from his limp hand, folded over and glided noiselessly down to lie upon the cold floor, her eyes closed, her mouth shut.

Fabian did not look at her as Krovitch led him out the door.

Yesterday I Lived!

Years went by and after all the years of raining and cold and fog going and coming through Hollywood Cemetery over a stone with the name Diana Coyle on it, Cleve Morris walked into the studio projection room out of the storm and looked up at the screen.

She was there. The long, lazy body of hers, the shining red hair and bright complementary green eyes.

And Cleve thought, *Is it cold out there, Diana? Is it cold out there tonight? Is the rain to you yet? Have the years pierced the bronze walls of your resting place and are you still—beautiful?*

He watched her glide across the screen, heard her laughter, and his wet eyes shimmered her into bright quivering color streaks.

It's so warm in here tonight, Diana. You're here, all the warmth of you, and yet it's only so much illusion. They buried you three years ago, and now the autograph hunters are crazy over some new actress here at the studio.

He choked on that. No reason for this feeling, but everyone felt that way about her. Everyone loved her, hated her for being so lovely. But maybe *you* loved her more than the others.

Who in hell are you? She hardly ever saw you. Cleve Morris, a desk sergeant spending two hours a day at the front desk buzzing people through locked doors and six hours strolling around dim soundstages, checking things. She hardly knew you. It was always, "Hello, Diana," and "Hi, Sarge!" and "Good night, Diana," when her long evening gown rustled from the stages, and over her smooth shoulder one eye winking. "Night, Sarge; be a good boy!"

174   RAY BRADBURY

Three years ago. Cleve slid down in his projection room
loge. The watch on his wrist ticked eight o'clock. The studio
was dead, lights fading one by one. Tomorrow, action lots of it.
But now, tonight, he was alone in this room, looking over the
old films of Diana Coyle. In the projection booth behind him,
checking the compact spools of film, Jamie Winters, the studio's
A-1 cameraman, did the honors of projection.

So here you are, the two of you, late at night. The film
flickers, marring her lovely face. It flickers again, and you're
irritated. It flickers twice more, a long time, then smooths out.
Bad print. Cleve sinks lower in his seat, thinking back three
years ago, along about this same hour of night, just about the
same day of the month...three years ago...same hour...rain in
the dark sky...three years ago....

Cleve was at his desk that night. People strode through doors,
rain-spangled, never seeing him. He felt like a mummy in a
museum where the attendants had long ago tired of noticing
him. Just a fixture to buzz doors open for them.

"Good evening, Mr. Guilding."

R. J. Guilding thought it over and vetoed the suggestion with
a jerk of one gray-gloved hand. His white head jerked too. "Is
it?" he wanted to know. You get that way being a producer.

Buzz. Door open. *Slam*.

"Good evening, Diana!"

"What?" She walked from the rainy night with it shining in
little clear gems on her white oval face. He'd like to have kissed
them away. She looked lost and alone. "Oh, hello, Cleve. Working
late. The darn picture's almost finished. Gosh, I'm tired."

Buzz. Door open. *Slam*.

He looked after her and kept her perfume as long as he
could.

"Ah, flatfoot," somebody said. Leaning over the desk, smiling ironically, was a pretty man named Robert Denim. "Open the door for me, country boy. They never should've put you on this job. You're glamor-struck. Poor kid."

Cleve looked at him strangely. "She doesn't belong to you anymore, does she?"

Denim's face was suddenly not pretty. He didn't say anything for a moment, but by the look in his eyes Cleve's doubts were removed. Denim grabbed the door and jerked it viciously.

Cleve purposely left the buzzer untouched. Denim swore and turned around, one gloved hand balled into a fist. Cleve buzzed the buzzer, smiling. It was the kind of smile that drained Denim's hesitation, made him decide to pull the knob again and stride off down away into the halls, into the studio.

A few minutes later Jamie Winters entered, shaking off rain, but holding onto a man-sized peeve. "That Diana Coyle woman; I tell you, Cleve. She stays up late at night and expects me to photograph her like a twelve-year-old kid! What a job I got! Fooey."

Behind Jamie Winters came Georgie Kroll, and Tally Durham hanging onto him so that Diana couldn't get him. But it was too late. By Georgie's face he was already got; and by Tally's she knew it but couldn't believe it.

Slam.

Cleve checked his name chart, found that everybody who was working tonight was already in. He relaxed. This was a dark hive, and Diana was the queen bee with all the other bees humming around her. The studio worked late tonight, just for her, all the lights, sound, color, activity. Cleve smoked a cigarette quietly, leaning back, smiling over his thoughts. *Diana, let's just you and me buy a little home in San Fernando where the flood washes you out every year, and the wild flowers spring up when the flood is gone. Nice paddling in a canoe with you, Diana, even in a flood. We got flowers, hay, sunlight, and peace in the valley, Diana.*

The only sound to Cleve was the rain beating at the windows, an occasional flare of thunder, and his watch ticking like a termite boring a hole in the structure of silence.

Tictictictictic...

The scream pulled him out of his chair and half across the reception room, echoed through the building. A script girl burst into view, shambling with dead kind of feet, babbling. Cleve grabbed her and held her still.

"She's dead! She's dead!"

The watch went *tic*, *tic*, *tic* all over again.

Lightning blew up around the place, and a cold wind hit Cleve's neck. His stomach turned over and he was afraid to ask the simple question he would eventually have to ask. Instead he stalled the inevitable, locking the bronze front doors and making secure any windows that were open. When he turned, the script girl was leaning against his desk, a tremble in her like something shattered in a finely integrated machine, shaking it to pieces.

"On stage twelve. Just now," she gasped. "Diana Coyle."

Cleve ran through the dim alleys of the studio, the sound of his running lonely in the big empty spaces. Ahead of him brilliant lights poured from opened stage doors; people stood framed in the vast square, shocked, not moving.

He ran onto the set and stopped, his heart pounding, to look down.

She was the most beautiful person who ever died.

Her silver evening gown was a small lake around her. Her fingernails were five scarlet beetles dead and shining on either side of her slumped body.

All the hot lights looked down, trying to keep her warm when she was fast cooling. My blood too, thought Cleve. Keep me warm, lights!

The shock of it held everybody as in a still photo.

Denim, fumbling with a cigarette, spoke first.

"We were in the middle of a scene. She just fell down and that was all."

Tally Durham, about the size of a salt shaker, wandered blindly about the stage telling everybody, "We thought she fainted, that's all! I got the smelling salts!"

Denim sucked, deeply nervous, on his smoke. "The smelling salts didn't work…"

For the first time in his life Cleve touched Diana Coyle.

But it was too late now. What good to touch cold clay that didn't laugh back at you using green eyes and curved lips?

He touched her and said, "She's been poisoned."

The word "poison" spread out through the dim sound stage behind the glaring lights. Echoes came back with it.

Georgie Kroll stuttered. "She—she got a drink—from the soft drinks—box—a couple minutes ago. Maybe—"

Cleve found the soft drinks dispenser blindly. He smelled one bottle and tucked it aside carefully, using a handkerchief, into a lunchbox that was studio property. "Nobody touch that."

The floor was rubbery to walk on. "Anybody see anybody else touch that bottle before Diana drank out of it?"

Way up in the glaring electrical heaven, a guy looked down like a short-circuited god and called, "Hey, Cleve, just before the last scene we had light trouble. Somebody conked a main switch. The lights were doused for about a minute and a half. Plenty time for someone to fix that bottle!"

"Thanks." Cleve turned to Jamie Winters, the cameraman. "You got film in your camera? Got a picture of—her—dying?"

"I guess so. Sure!"

"How soon can you have it developed?"

"Two, three hours. Got to call Juke Davis and have him come to the studio, though."

"Phone him, then. Take two watchmen with you to guard that film. Beat it!"

Far away the sirens were singing and Hollywood was going to sleep. Somebody onstage suddenly realized Diana was dead and started sobbing.

I wish I could do that, thought Cleve. *I wish I could cry. What am I supposed to do now, act tough, be a Sherlock? Question everyone, when my heart isn't working?* Cleve heard his voice going on alone.

"We'll be working late tonight, everybody. We'll be working until we get this scene right. And if we don't get it right, I guess we don't go home. Before the homicide squad gets here, every-one to their places. We'll do the scene over. Places, everybody."

They did the scene over.

The homicide squad arrived. There was one detective named Foley and another named Sadlowe. One was small, the other big. One talked a lot, and the other listened. Foley did the talking and it gave Cleve a sick headache.

R. J. Guilding, the director and producer of the film, slumped in his canvas chair, wiping his face and trying to tell Foley that he wanted this whole mess kept out of the papers and quiet.

Foley told him to shut up. Foley glared at Cleve as if he were also a suspect. "What've you found out, son?"

"There was film in the camera. Film of Diana—Miss Coyle's death."

Foley's eyebrows went like that. "Well, hell, let's see it!"

They walked over into the film laboratory to get the film. Cleve was frankly afraid of the place. Always had been. It was

a huge dark mortuary building with dead-end passages and
labyrinths of black walls to cut the light. You stumbled through
pitch dark, touching the walls, careening, turning, cursing,
twisting around cutouts; walked south, east, west, south again
and suddenly found yourself in a green-freckled space as big as
the universe. Nothing to see but green welts and splashes of
light, dim snakes of film climbing, winding over spools from
floor to high ceiling and back down. The one brilliant light was
a printing light that shot from a projector and printed negative
to positive as they slid by in parallel slots. The positive then
coiled over and down into a long series of developing baths.
The place was a whining morgue. Juke Davis moved around in
it with ghoul-like movements.

"There's no soundtrack. I'll develop it and splice it in later,"
said Davis. "Here you are, Mr. Foley. Here's your film."

They took the film and retreated back through the labyrinth.

In the projection room Cleve and the detectives Foley and
Sadlowe, with Jamie Winters operating the projector in the booth,
watched the death scene printed on the screen for them. Stage
twelve had been slammed shut, and other officers were back
there, talking, grilling everyone in alphabetical order.

On the screen Diana laughed. Robert Denim laughed back.
It was very silent. They opened mouths but no sounds came
out. People danced behind them. Diana and Robert Denim
danced now, gracefully, quietly, leisurely. When they stopped
dancing they talked seriously with—Tally Durham and Georgie
Kroll.

Foley spoke. "You say that this fellow Kroll loved Diana too?"

Cleve nodded. "Who didn't?"

Foley said, "Yeah. Who didn't. Well—" He stared with suspi-
cion at the screen. "How about this Tally Durham woman. Was
she jealous?"

Was there any woman in Hollywood who didn't hate Diana

because she was perfect? Cleve spoke of Tally's love for Georgie Kroll.

"It never fails," replied Foley with a shake of his head.

Cleve said, "Tally may have killed Diana. Who knows. Georgie'd have a motive too. Diana treated him like a rag doll. He wanted her and couldn't have her. That happened to a lot of men in Diana's life. If she ever loved anybody, it was Robert Denim, and that didn't last. Denim is a little too—tough, I guess that's how you'd put it."

Foley snorted. "Good going. We got three suspects in one scene. Any one of them could have dosed that pop bottle with nicotine. The lights were out for a minute and a half. In that time any guy who ever bought Black Leaf Forty nicotine sulfate at the corner garden store could have tossed twenty drops of it in her drink and gone back playing innocent when the lights bloomed again. Nuts."

Sadlowe spoke for the first time that evening. "There ought to be some way to splice out the innocents from this film." A brilliant observation.

Cleve caught his breath. *She* was dying.

She died like she had done everything in her life. You had to admire the way she did it, with the grace, fire, and control of a fine cat-animal. In the middle of the scene she forgot her lines. Her fingers crawled slowly to her throat and she turned. Her face changed. She looked straight out at you from the screen as if she knew this was her biggest and, to a cynic, her best scene.

Then she fell, like a silken canopy from which the supports had been instantly withdrawn.

Denim crouched over her, mouthing the word, "Diana!"

And Tally Durham screamed a silent scream as the film shivered and fluttered into blackness, numbers, amber colors, and then nothing but glaring light.

Oh, God, press a button somewhere! Run the reel backward and bring her back to life! Press a button as you see in those comic newsreels; in which smashed trains are reintegrated, fallen emperors are enthroned, the sun rises in the west and—Diana Coyle rises from the dead!

From the booth Jamie Winters's voice said, "That's it. That's all of it. You want to see it again?"

Foley said, "Yeah. Show it to us half a dozen times."

"Excuse me," gasped Cleve.

"Where you going?"

He went out into the rain. It beat cold on him. Behind him, inside, Diana was dying again and again and again, like a trained puppet. Cleve clenched his jaw and looked straight up at the sky and let the night cry on him, all over him, soaking him through and through; in perfect harmony, the night and he and the crying dark....

The storm lasted until morning both inside and outside the studio. Foley yelled at everybody. Everybody answered back calmly that they weren't guilty; yes, they had hated Diana, but at the same time loved her, yes, they were jealous of her, but she was a good girl too.

Foley evolved a colossal idea, invited all suspects to the projection room and scared hell out of everyone, proving nothing, by showing them Diana's last scene. R. J. Guilding broke down and sobbed, Georgie squeaked, and Tally screamed. Cleve got sick to his stomach, and the night went on and on.

Georgie said yes, yes, he'd loved Diana; Tally said yes, yes, she'd hated her; Guilding reaffirmed the fact that Diana had stalled production, causing trouble; and Robert Denim admitted to an attempted reconciliation between himself and his former wife. Jamie Winters told how Diana had stayed up late nights, ruining her face for proper photography. And R. J. Guilding snapped, "Diana told me you were photographing her poorly, on purpose!"

Jamie Winters was calm. "That's not true. She was trying to shove the blame for her complexion off on someone else, me."

Foley said, "You were in love with her too?"

Winters replied, "Why do you think I became her photographer?"

So when dawn came Diana was still as dead as the night before. Big stage doors thundered aside and the suspects wearily shambled out to climb into their cars and start home.

Cleve watched them through aching eyes. Silently he walked around the studio, checking everything when it didn't need checking. He smelled the sweet green odor of the cemetery over the wall.

Funny Hollywood. It builds a studio next door to a graveyard. Right over that wall there. Sometimes it seemed everyone in movietown tried to scale that wall. Some poured themselves over in a whiskey tide, some smoked themselves over; all of them looked forward to an office in Hollywood Cemetery—with no phones. Well, Diana didn't have to climb that wall.

Someone had pushed her over....

Cleve held on to the steering wheel, tight, hard, wanting to break it, telling the world to get out of the way, dammit! He was beginning to get mad!

They buried her on a bright California day with a stiff wind blowing and too many red and yellow and blue flowers and the wrong kind of tears.

That was the first day Cleve ever drank enough to get drunk. He would always remember that day.

The studio phoned three days later.

"Say, Morris, what's eating you? Where you been?"

"In my apartment," said Cleve dully.

He kept the radio off, he didn't walk the streets like he used to at night, dreaming. He neglected the newspapers; they had big pictures of her in them. The radio talked about her, so he almost wrecked the thing. When the week was over she was safely in the earth, and the newspapers had tapered off the black ink wreaths, were telling her life story on page two the following Wednesday; page four Thursday; page five Friday; page ten Saturday; and by the following Monday they wrote the concluding chapter and slipped it in among the stock-market reports on page twenty-nine.

You're slipping, Diana! Slipping! You used to make page one!
Cleve went back to work.

By Friday there was nothing left but that new stone in Hollywood Cemetery. Papers rotted in the flooded gutters, washing away the ink of her name; the radio blatted war, and Cleve worked with his eyes looking funny and changed.

He buzzed doors all day, and people went in and out. He watched Tally dance in every morning, smaller and chipper, and happy now that Diana was gone, holding on to Georgie, who was all hers now, except his mind and soul. He watched Robert Denim walk in, and they never spoke to each other. He waved hello to Jamie Winters and was courteous to R. J. Guilding.

But he watched them all, like a dialogue director waiting for one muffed line or missed cue.

And finally the papers announced casually that her death had been attributed to suicide, and it was a closed chapter.

A couple of weeks later Cleve was still sticking to his apartment, reading and thinking, when the phone rang.

"Cleve? This is Jamie Winters. Look, cop-man, come out of it. You're wanted at a party, now, tonight. I got some film clips from Gable's last picture."

There was argument. In the end Cleve gave in and went to the party. They sat in Jamie Winters's parlor facing a small-size screen. Winters showed them scenes from pictures that never reached the theater. Garbo tripping over a light cord and falling on her platform. Spencer Tracy blowing his lines and swearing. William Powell sticking his tongue out at the camera when he forgot his next cue. Cleve laughed for the first time in a million years.

Jamie Winters had an endless collection of film clips of famous stars blowing up and saying censorable things.

And when Diana Coyle showed up, it was like a kick in the stomach. Like being shot with two barrels of a shotgun! Cleve jerked and gasped, and shut his eyes, clenching the chair.

Then, suddenly, he was very cool. He had an idea. Looking at the screen, it came to him, like cold rain on his cheeks. "Jamie!" he said.

In the sprocketing darkness, Jamie replied, "Yes?"

"I've got to see you in the kitchen, Jamie."

"Why?"

"Never mind why. Let the camera run itself and come on."

In the kitchen Cleve held on to Jamie. "It's about those films you're showing us. The mistakes. The censored clips. Have you any clips from Diana's last picture? Spoiled scenes, blow-ups, I mean?"

"Yeah. At the studio. I collect them. It's a hobby. That stuff usually goes in the trash can. I keep them for laughs."

Cleve sucked in his breath. "Can you get that film for me; all of it; bring it here tomorrow night and go over it with me?"

"Sure, if you want me to. I don't see—"

"Never mind, Jamie. Just do like I say, huh? Bring me all the cutouts, the scenes that were bad. I want to see who spoiled the scenes, who caused the most trouble, and why! Will you do it, Jamie?"

"Sure. Sure I will, Cleve. Take it easy. Here, sit down. Have a drink."

Cleve didn't eat much the next day. The hours went too slowly. At night he ate a little supper and swallowed four aspirins. Then he drove in a mechanical nightmare to Jamie Winters's house.

Jamie was waiting with drinks and film in the camera.

"Thanks, Jamie." Cleve sat down and drank nervously. "All right. Shall we see them?"

"Action!" said Jamie.

Light on the screen. "Take one, scene seven. *The Gilded Virgin*: Diana Coyle, Robert Denim."

Clack!

The scene faded in. There was a terrace by an ocean scene in moonlight. Diana was talking.

"It's a lovely night. So lovely I can't believe in it."

Robert Denim, holding her hands in his, looked at her and said, "I think I can make you believe in it. I'll—damn it!"

"Cut!" cried Guilding's voice offscreen.

The film ran on. Denim's face was ugly, getting dark and lined.

"There you go, hogging the camera again!"

"Me?" Diana wasn't beautiful anymore. Not *this* way. She shook the gilt off her wings in an angry powder. "Me, you two-bit thespian, you loud-mouthed, dirty—"

Flick. Dark. End of film.

Cleve sat there, staring. After a while he said, "They didn't get along, did they?" And then, to himself, almost, "I'm glad."

"Here's another one," said Winters. The camera ticked rapidly. Another scene. A party scene. Laughter and music; and cutting across it, dark, snapping, bitter and accusative:

"—damn you!"

"—if you fed me the wrong cue on purpose! Of all the cheap, common little—"

Diana and Robert Denim, at it again!

Another scene, and another, and another. Six, seven, eight!

Here was one of Denim saying, "Honest to God, someone ought to shut you up for good, lady!"

"Who?" cried Diana, eyes flashing like little green stones. "You? You snivel-nosed ham!"

And Denim, glaring back, saying quietly, "Yes. Maybe me. Why not? It's an idea."

There were some bristling hot scenes with Tally Durham too. And one in which Diana browbeat little Georgie Kroll until he was nervous and sweating out an apology. All on film; all good evidence. But the ratio was seven of Denim's blow-ups to one of Tally's or Georgie's. On and on and on and on!

"Stop it, stop it!" Cleve got up from his chair. His figure cut the light, threw a shadow on the screen, swaying.

"Thanks for the trouble, Jamie. I'm tired too. Can—can I have these film clips of Denim?"

"Sure."

"I'm going downtown to police headquarters tonight and turn in Robert Denim for the murder of Diana Coyle. Thanks again, Jamie. You been a great help. Night."

Five, ten, fifteen, twenty hours. Count 'em by twos, by fours, by sixes. Rush the hours by. Argue with the cops and go home and flop in bed.

Toddle off to your gas chamber, Robert Denim: that's a good little killer!

And then in the middle of deep slumber, your phone rang.

"Hullo."

And a voice said over the phone in the night, "Cleve?"

"Yeah?"

And the voice said, "This is Juke Davis at the film laboratory. Come quick, Cleve. I been hurt, I been hurt, oh, I been hurt...."

A body fell at the other end of the line.

Silence.

✿

He found Juke lying in a chemical bath. Red chemical from his own body where a knife had dug out his dreams and his living and his talking forever and spread it around in a scarlet lake.

A phone receiver hung dangling on one greenish wall. It was dark in the laboratory. Someone had shuffled in through the dim tunnels, come out of the dark, and now, standing there, Cleve heard nothing but the film moving forever on its trellises, like some vine going up through the midnight room trying to find the sun. Numbly, Cleve knelt beside Juke. The man lay half propped against the film machinery where the printing light shot out and imprinted negative to positive. He had crawled there, across the room.

In one clenched fist, Cleve found a frame of film; the faces of Tally, Georgie, Diana, and Robert Denim on it. Juke had found out something, something about this film, something about a killer; and his reward had come swiftly to him through the studio dark.

Cleve used the phone.

"This is Cleve Morris. Is Robert Denim still being held at Central Jail?"

"He's in his cell, and he won't talk. I tell you, Morris, you gave us a bum steer with them film clips...."

"Thanks." Cleve hung up. He looked at Juke lying there by the machinery. "Well, who was it. Juke? It wasn't Denim. That leaves Georgie and Tally? Well?"

Juke said nothing and the machinery sang a low sad song.

One year went by. Another year followed. And then a third.

Robert Denim contracted out to another studio. Tally married Georgie, Guilding died at a New Year's party of over-drinking and a bad heart, time went on, everybody forgot. Well, almost everybody....

Diana, child, is it cold out there tonight—?

Cleve rose in his seat. Three years ago. He blinked his eyes. Same kind of night as this, cold and raining.

The screen flickered.

Cleve paid little attention. It kept on flickering strangely. Cleve stiffened. His heart beat with the sprocketing noise of the machine. He bent forward.

"Jamie, will you run that last one hundred feet over again?"

"Sure thing, Cleve."

Flickers on film. Imperfections. Long blotches, short blobs. Cleve spelled it out. W...I...N...

Cleve opened the door of the projection room so softly Jamie Winters didn't hear him. Winters was glaring out at the film on the screen, and there was a strange, happy look on his face. The look of a saint seeing a new miracle.

"Enjoying yourself, Jamie boy?"

Jamie Winters shook himself and turned and smiled uneasily.

Cleve locked the door. He gave a little soft lecture: "It's been a long time. I haven't slept well many nights. Three years, Jamie. And tonight you had nothing to do so you ran off some film so you could gloat over it. Gloat over Diana and think how clever you were. Maybe it was fun to see me suffer too; you knew how much I liked her. Have you come here often in the past three years to gloat over her, Jamie?" he asked softly.

Winters laughed good-naturedly.

Cleve said, "She didn't love you, did she? You were her photographer. So to even things up, you began photographing her badly. It fits in. Her last two films were poor. She looked tired. It wasn't her fault; you did things with your camera. So Diana threatened to tell on you. You would've been blackballed at every studio. You couldn't have her love, and she threatened your career, so what did you do, Jamie Winters? You killed her."

"This is a poor idea of a joke," said Winters, hardening.

Cleve went on, "Diana looked at the camera when she died. She looked at you. We never thought of that. In a theater you always feel as if she were looking at the audience, not the man behind the camera. She died. You took a picture of her dying. Then, later, you invited me to a party, fed me the bait, with those film clips showing Denim in a suspicious light. I fell for it. You destroyed all the other film that put Denim in a good position. Juke Davis found out what you were doing. He worked with film all the time, he knew you were juggling clips. You wanted to frame Denim because there had to be a fall guy and you'd be clear. Juke questioned you, you stabbed him. You stole and destroyed the few extra clips Juke had discovered. Juke couldn't talk over the phone, but he shoved his hand in the printing light of the developing machine and printed your name W-I-N-T-E-R-S in black splotches as the film moved. He happened to be printing the negative of Diana's last film that night! And you began running it off to me ten minutes ago, thinking it was only a damaged film!"

Jamie Winters moved quickly, like a cat. He ripped open the projector and tore the film out in one vicious animal movement.

Cleve hit him. He pulled way back and blasted loose.

The case was really over now. But he wasn't happy or glad or anything but blind red angry, flooded with hot fury.

All he could think of now while he hit the face of Winters again and again and again, holding him tight with one hand, beating him over and over with the other, all he could think of was—

A stone in the yard of the cemetery just over the wall from the studio; a stone sweating blue rain over her bronzed name. All he could say in a hoarse, choked whisper was:

"Is it cold out there tonight, Diana; is it cold, little girl?"

And Cleve hit him again and again and again!

The Town Where No One Got Off

Crossing the continental United States by night, by day, on the train, you flash past town after wilderness town where nobody ever gets off. Or rather, no person who doesn't *belong*, no person who hasn't roots in these country graveyards ever bothers to visit their lonely stations or attend their lonely views.

I spoke of this to a fellow passenger, another salesman like myself, on the Chicago–Los Angeles train as we crossed Iowa.

"True," he said. "People get off in Chicago; everyone gets off there. People get off in New York, get off in Boston, get off in L.A. People who don't live there go there to see and come back to tell. But what tourist ever just got off at Fox Hill, Nebraska, to *look* at it? You? Me? No! I don't know anyone, got no business there, it's no health resort, so why bother?"

"Wouldn't it be a fascinating change," I said, "some year to plan a really different vacation? Pick some village lost on the plains where you don't know a soul and go there for the hell of it?"

"You'd be bored stiff."

"I'm not bored thinking of it!" I peered out the window. "What's the next town coming up on this line?"

"Rampart Junction."

I smiled. "Sounds good. I might get off there."

"You're a liar and a fool. What you want? Adventure? Romance? Go ahead. Jump off the train. Ten seconds later you'll call yourself an idiot, grab a taxi, and race us to the next town."

"Maybe."

I watched telephone poles flick by, flick by, flick by. Far ahead I could see the first faint outlines of a town.

"But I don't think so," I heard myself say.

The salesman across from me looked faintly surprised.

For slowly, very slowly, I was rising to stand. I reached for my hat. I saw my hand fumble for my one suitcase. I was surprised myself.

"Hold on!" said the salesman. "What're you doing?"

The train rounded a curve suddenly. I swayed. Far ahead I saw one church spire, a deep forest, a field of summer wheat.

"It looks like I'm getting off the train," I said.

"Sit down," he said.

"No," I said. "There's something about that town up ahead. I've got to go see. I've got the time. I don't have to be in L.A., really, until next Monday. If I don't get off the train now, I'll always wonder what I missed, what I let slip by when I had the chance to see it."

"We were just talking. There's nothing there."

"You're wrong," I said. "There is."

I put my hat on my head and lifted the suitcase in my hand.

"By God," said the salesman, "I think you're really going to do it."

My heart beat quickly. My face was flushed.

The train whistled. The train rushed down the track. The town was near!

"Wish me luck," I said.

"Luck!" he cried.

I ran for the porter, yelling.

There was an ancient flake-painted chair tilted back against the station-platform wall. In this chair, completely relaxed so he sank into his clothes, was a man of some seventy years whose timbers looked as if he'd been nailed there since the station was built. The sun had burned his face dark and tracked his cheek with lizard folds and stitches that held his eyes in a perpetual squint. His hair smoked ash-white in the summer wind. His blue shirt, open at the neck to show white clock springs, was bleached like the staring late afternoon sky. His shoes were blistered as if he had held them, uncaring, in the mouth of a stove, motionless, forever. His shadow under him was stenciled a permanent black.

As I stepped down, the old man's eyes flicked every door on the train and stopped, surprised, at me.

I thought he might wave.

But there was only a sudden coloring of his secret eyes; a chemical change that was recognition. Yet he had not twitched so much as his mouth, an eyelid, a finger. An invisible bulk had shifted inside him.

The moving train gave me an excuse to follow it with my eyes. There was no one else on the platform. No autos waited by the cobwebbed, nailed-shut office. I alone had departed the iron thunder to set foot on the choppy waves of platform lumber.

The train whistled over the hill.

Fool! I thought. My fellow passenger had been right. I would panic at the boredom I already sensed in this place. All right, I thought, fool, yes, but run, no!

I walked my suitcase down the platform, not looking at the old man. As I passed, I felt his thin bulk shift again, this time so I could hear it. His feet were coming down to touch and tap the mushy boards.

I kept walking.

"Afternoon," a voice said faintly.

I knew he did not look at me but only at that great cloudless spread of shimmering sky.

"Afternoon," I said.

I started up the dirt road toward the town. One hundred yards away, I glanced back.

The old man, still seated there, stared at the sun, as if posing a question.

I hurried on.

I moved through the dreaming late afternoon town, utterly anonymous and alone, a trout going upstream, not touching the banks of a clear-running river of life that drifted all about me.

My suspicions were confirmed: it was a town where nothing happened, where occurred only the following events:

At four o'clock sharp, the Honneger Hardware door slammed as a dog came out to dust himself in the road. Four-thirty, a straw sucked emptily at the bottom of a soda glass, making a sound like a great cataract in the drugstore silence. Five o'clock, boys and pebbles plunged in the town river. Five-fifteen, ants paraded in the slanting light under some elm trees.

And yet—I turned in a slow circle—somewhere in this town there must be something worth seeing. I knew it was there. I knew I had to keep walking and looking. I knew I would find it.

I walked. I looked.

All through the afternoon there was only one constant and unchanging factor: the old man in the bleached blue pants and shirt was never far away. When I sat in the drugstore he was out front spitting tobacco that rolled itself into tumblebugs in the dust. When I stood by the river he was crouched downstream making a great thing of washing his hands.

Along about seven-thirty in the evening, I was walking for the seventh or eighth time through the quiet streets when I heard footsteps beside me.

I looked over, and the old man was pacing me, looking straight ahead, a piece of dried grass in his stained teeth.

"It's been a long time," he said quietly.

We walked along in the twilight.

"A long time," he said, "waitin' on that station platform."

"You?" I said.

"Me." He nodded in the tree shadows.

"Were you waiting for someone at the station?"

"Yes," he said. "You."

"Me?" The surprise must have shown in my voice. "But why…? You never saw me before in your life."

"Did I say I did? I just said I was waitin'."

We were on the edge of town now. He had turned and I had turned with him along the darkening riverbank toward the trestle where the night trains ran over going east, going west, but stopping rare few times.

"You want to know anything about me?" I asked suddenly. "You the sheriff?"

"No, not the sheriff. And no, I don't want to know nothin' about you." He put his hands in his pockets. The sun was set now. The air was suddenly cool. "I'm just surprised you're here at last, is all."

"Surprised?"

"Surprised," he said, "and…pleased."

I stopped abruptly and looked straight at him.

"How long have you been sitting on that station platform?"

"Twenty years, give or take a few."

I knew he was telling the truth; his voice was as easy and quiet as the river.

"Waiting for me?" I said.

"Or someone like you," he said.

We walked on in the growing dark.

"How you like our town?"

"Nice, quiet," I said.

"Nice, quiet." He nodded. "Like the people?"

"People look nice and quiet."

"They are," he said. "Nice, quiet."

I was ready to turn back but the old man kept talking and in order to listen and be polite I had to walk with him in the vaster darkness, the tides of field and meadow beyond town.

"Yes," said the old man, "the day I retired, twenty years ago, I sat down on that station platform and there I been, sittin', doin' nothin', waitin' for somethin' to happen, I didn't know what, I didn't know, I couldn't say. But when it finally happened, I'd know it, I'd look at it and say, Yes, sir, that's what I was waitin' for. Train wreck? No. Old woman friend come back to town after fifty years? No. No. It's hard to say. Someone. Somethin'. And it seems to have somethin' to do with you. I wish I could say—"

"Why don't you try?" I said.

The stars were coming out. We walked on.

"Well," he said slowly, "you know much about your own insides?"

"You mean my stomach or you mean psychologically?"

"That's the word. I mean your head, your brain, you know much about *that*?"

The grass whispered under my feet. "A little."

"You hate many people in your time?"

"Some."

"We all do. It's normal enough to hate, ain't it, and not only hate but, while we don't talk about it, don't we sometimes want to hit people who hurt us, even *kill* them?"

"Hardly a week passes we don't get that feeling," I said, "and put it away."

"We put away all our lives," he said. "The town says thus and so, Mom and Dad say this and that, the law says such and such. So you put away one killin' and another and two more after that. By the time you're my age, you got lots of that kind of stuff between your ears. And unless you went to war, nothin' ever happened to get rid of it."

"Some men trapshoot or hunt ducks," I said. "Some men box or wrestle."

"And some don't. I'm talkin' about them that don't. Me. All my life I've been saltin' down those bodies, puttin' 'em away on ice in my head. Sometimes you get mad at a town and the people in it for makin' you put things aside like that. You like the old cave men who just gave a hell of a yell and whanged someone on the head with a club."

"Which all leads up to…?"

"Which all leads up to: Everybody'd like to do one killin' in his life, to sort of work off that big load of stuff, all those killin's in his mind he never did have the guts to do. And once in a while a man has a chance. Someone runs in front of his car and he forgets the brakes and keeps goin'. Nobody can prove nothin' with that sort of thing. The man don't even tell himself he did it. He just didn't get his foot on the brake in time. But you know and I know what really happened, don't we?"

"Yes," I said.

The town was far away now. We moved over a small stream on a wooden bridge, just near the railway embankment.

"Now," said the old man, looking at the water, "the only kind of killin' worth doin' is the one where nobody can guess who did it or why they did it or who they did it to, right? Well, I got this idea maybe twenty years ago. I don't think about it every day or every week. Sometimes months go by, but the idea's this: Only one train stops here each day, sometimes not even that. Now, if you wanted to kill someone you'd have to wait, wouldn't you, for years and years, until a complete and actual stranger came to your town, a stranger who got off the train for no reason, a man nobody knows and who don't know nobody in the town. Then, and only then, I thought, sittin' there on the station chair, you could just go up and when nobody's around, kill him and throw him in the river. He'd be found miles downstream. Maybe he'd never be found. Nobody would ever think to come to Rampart Junction to find him. He wasn't goin' there. He was on his way someplace else. There, that's my whole idea. And I'd know that man the minute he got off the train. Know him, just as clear…"

I had stopped walking. It was dark. The moon would not be up for an hour.

"Would you?" I said.

"Yes," he said. I saw the motion of his head looking at the stars. "Well, I've talked enough." He sidled close and touched my elbow. His hand was feverish, as if he had held it to a stove before touching me. His other hand, his right hand, was hidden, tight and bunched, in his pocket. "I've talked enough."

Something screamed.

I jerked my head.

Above, a fast-flying night express razored along the unseen tracks, flourished light on hill, forest, farm, town dwellings, field, ditch, meadow, plowed earth and water, then, raving high, cut off away, shrieking, gone. The rails trembled for a little while after that. Then, silence.

The old man and I stood looking at each other in the dark. His left hand was still holding my elbow. His other hand was still hidden.

"May I say something?" I said at last.

The old man nodded.

"About myself," I said. I had to stop. I could hardly breathe. I forced myself to go on. "It's funny. I've often thought the same way as you. Sure, just today, going cross-country, I thought, How perfect, how perfect, how really perfect it could be. Business has been bad for me, lately. Wife sick. Good friend died last week. War in the world. Full of boils, myself. It would do me a world of good—"

"What?" the old man said, his hand on my arm.

"To get off this train in a small town," I said, "where nobody knows me, with this gun under my arm, and find someone and kill them and bury them and go back down to the station and get on and go home and nobody the wiser and nobody ever to know who did it, ever. Perfect, I thought, a perfect crime. And I got off the train."

We stood there in the dark for another minute, staring at each other. Perhaps we were listening to each other's hearts beating very fast, very fast indeed.

The world turned under me. I clenched my fists. I wanted to fall. I wanted to scream like the train.

For suddenly I saw that all the things I had just said were not lies put forth to save my life.

All the things I had just said to this man were true.

And now I knew why I had stepped from the train and walked up through this town. I knew what I had been looking for.

I heard the old man breathing hard and fast. His hand was tight on my arm as if he might fall. His teeth were clenched. He leaned toward me as I leaned toward him. There was a terrible silent moment of immense strain as before an explosion.

He forced himself to speak at last. It was the voice of a man crushed by a monstrous burden.

"How do I know you got a gun under your arm?"

"You don't know." My voice was blurred. "You can't be sure."

He waited. I thought he was going to faint.

"That's how it is?" he said.

"That's how it is," I said.

He shut his eyes tight. He shut his mouth tight.

After another five seconds, very slowly, heavily, he managed to take his hand away from my own immensely heavy arm. He looked down at his right hand then, and took it, empty, out of his pocket.

Slowly, with great weight, we turned away from each other and started walking blind, completely blind, in the dark.

◦

The midnight passenger-to-be-picked-up flare sputtered on the tracks. Only when the train was pulling out of the station did I lean from the open Pullman door and look back.

The old man was seated there with his chair tilted against the station wall, with his faded blue pants and shirt and his sun-baked face and his sun-bleached eyes. He did not glance at me as the train slid past. He was gazing east along the empty rails where tomorrow or the next day or the day after the day after that, a train, some train, any train, might fly by here, might slow, might stop. His face was fixed, his eyes were blindly frozen, toward the east. He looked a hundred years old.

The train wailed.

Suddenly old myself, I leaned out, squinting.

Now the darkness that had brought us together stood between. The old man, the station, the town, the forest, were lost in the night.

For an hour I stood in the roaring blast staring back at all that darkness.

The Whole Town's Sleeping

It was a warm summer night in the middle of Illinois country. The little town was deep far away from everything, kept to itself by a river and a forest and a ravine. In the town the sidewalks were still scorched. The stores were closing and the streets were turning dark. There were two moons: a clock moon with four faces in four night directions above the solemn black courthouse, and the real moon that was slowly rising in vanilla whiteness from the dark east.

In the downtown drugstore, fans whispered in the high ceiling air. In the rococo shade of porches, invisible people sat. On the purple bricks of the summer twilight streets, children ran. Screen doors whined their springs and banged. The heat was breathing from the dry lawns and trees.

On her solitary porch, Lavinia Nebbs, aged 37, very straight and slim, sat with a tinkling lemonade in her white fingers, tapping it to her lips, waiting.

"Here I am, Lavinia."

Lavinia turned. There was Francine, at the bottom porch step, in the smell of zinnias and hibiscus. Francine was all in snow white and she didn't look 35.

Ms. Lavinia Nebbs rose and locked her front door, leaving her lemonade glass standing half empty on the porch rail. "It's a fine night for the movie."

"Where you going, ladies?" cried Grandma Hanlon from her shadowy porch across the street.

They called back through the soft ocean of darkness: "To the Elite Theater to see Harold Lloyd in *Welcome, Danger!*"

"Won't catch *me* out on no night like this," wailed Grandma Hanlon. "Not with The Lonely One strangling women. Lock myself in with my *gun!*"

Grandma's door slammed and locked.

The two maiden ladies drifted on. Lavinia felt the warm breath of the summer night shimmering off the oven-baked sidewalk. It was like walking on a hard crust of freshly warmed bread. The heat pulsed under your dress and along your legs with a stealthy sense of invasion.

"Lavinia, you don't believe all that gossip about The Lonely One, do you?"

"Those women like to see their tongues dance."

"Just the same, Hattie McDollis was killed a month ago. And Roberta Ferry the month before. And now Eliza Ramsell has disappeared..."

"Hattie McDollis walked off with a traveling man, I bet."

"But the others—strangled—four of them, their tongues sticking out their mouths, they say."

They stood on the edge of the ravine that cut the town in two. Behind them were the lighted houses and faint radio music; ahead was deepness, moistness, fireflies, and dark.

"Maybe we shouldn't go to the movie," said Francine. "The Lonely One might follow and kill us. I don't like that ravine. Look how black, smell it, and *listen.*"

The ravine was a dynamo that never stopped running, night or day: there was a great moving hum among the secret mists and washed shales, and the odors of a rank greenhouse. Always the black dynamo was humming, with green electric sparkles where fireflies hovered.

"And it won't be *me*," said Francine, "coming back through this terrible dark ravine tonight, late. It'll be you, Lavinia, you down the steps and over that rickety bridge and maybe the

Lonely One standing behind a tree. I'd never have gone over to church this afternoon if I had to walk through here all alone, even in daylight."

"Bosh," said Lavinia Nebbs.

"It'll be you alone on the path, listening to your shoes, not me. And shadows. You *all alone* on the way back home. Lavinia, don't you get lonely living by yourself in that house?"

"Old maids love to live alone," said Lavinia. She pointed to a hot shadowy path. "Let's walk the short cut."

"I'm afraid."

"It's early. The Lonely One won't be out till late." Lavinia, as cool as mint ice cream, took the other woman's arm and led her down the dark winding path into cricket-warmth and frog-sound, and mosquito-delicate silence.

"Let's run," gasped Francine.

"No."

If Lavinia hadn't turned her head just then, she wouldn't have seen it. But she did turn her head, and it was there. And then Francine looked over and she saw it too, and they stood there on the path, not believing what they saw.

In the singing deep night, back among a clump of bushes—half hidden, but laid out as if she had put herself down there to enjoy the soft stars—lay Eliza Ramsell.

Francine screamed.

The woman lay as if she were floating there, her face moon-freckled, her eyes like white marble, her tongue clamped in her lips.

Lavinia felt the ravine turning like a gigantic black merry-go-round underfoot. Francine was gasping and choking, and a long while later Lavinia heard herself say, "We'd better get the police."

❖

"Hold me, Lavinia, please hold me, I'm cold. Oh, I've never been so cold since winter."

Lavinia held Francine and the policemen were all around in the ravine grass. Flashlights darted about, voices mingled, and the night grew toward 8:30.

"It's like December. I need a sweater," said Francine, eyes shut, against Lavinia's shoulder.

The policeman said, "I guess you can go now, ladies. You might drop by the station tomorrow for a little more questioning."

Lavinia and Francine walked away from the police and the delicate sheet-covered thing on the ravine grass.

Lavinia felt her heart going loudly within her and she was cold, too, with a February cold. There were bits of sudden snow all over her flesh and the moon washed her brittle fingers whiter, and she remembered doing all the talking while Francine just sobbed.

A police voice called, "You want an escort, ladies?"

"No, we'll make it," said Lavinia, and they walked on. I can't remember anything now, she thought. I can't remember how she looked lying there, or anything. I don't believe it happened. Already I'm forgetting. I'm making myself forget.

"I've never *seen* a dead person before," said Francine.

Lavinia looked at her wrist watch, which seemed impossibly far away. "It's only 8:30. We'll pick up Helen and get on to the show."

"The show!"

"It's what we *need*."

"Lavinia, you don't *mean* it!"

"We've got to forget this. It's not good to remember."

"But Eliza's back there now and—"

"We need to laugh. We'll go on to the show as if nothing happened."

"But Eliza was once your friend, *my* friend—"

"We can't help her; we can only help ourselves forget. I insist. I won't go home and brood over it. I won't *think* of it. I'll fill my mind with everything else *but*."

They started up the side of the ravine on a stony path in the dark. They heard voices and stopped.

Below, near the creek waters, a voice was murmuring, "I am The Lonely One. I am The Lonely One. I *kill* people."

"And I'm Eliza Ramsell. Look. And I'm dead. See my tongue out my mouth, see!"

Francine shrieked. "You, there! Children, you nasty children! Get home, get out of the ravine, you hear me? Get home, get home, get home!"

The children fled from their game. The night swallowed their laughter away up the distant hills into the warm darkness.

Francine sobbed and walked on.

"I thought you ladies'd never come!" Helen Greer tapped her foot atop her porch steps. "You're only an hour late, that's all."

"We—" started Francine.

Lavinia clutched her arm. "There was a commotion. Someone found Eliza Ramsell dead in the ravine."

Helen gasped. "Who found her?"

"We don't know."

The three maiden ladies stood in the summer night looking at one another. "I've got a notion to lock myself in my house," said Helen at last.

But finally she went to fetch a sweater, and while she was gone Francine whispered frantically, "Why didn't you *tell* her?"

"Why upset her? Time enough tomorrow," replied Lavinia.

The three women moved along the street under the black trees through a town that was slamming and locking doors, pulling down windows and shades and turning on blazing lights. They saw eyes peering out at them from curtained windows.

How strange, thought Lavinia Nebbs, the ice-cream night, the Popsicles dropped in puddles of lime and chocolate where they fell when the children were scooped indoors. Baseballs and bats lie upon the unfootprinted lawns. A half-drawn, white chalk hopscotch line is there on the steamed sidewalk.

"We're crazy out on a night like this," said Helen.

"Lonely One can't kill three ladies," said Lavinia. "There's safety in numbers. Besides, it's too soon. The murders never come less than a month apart."

A shadow fell across their faces. A figure loomed. As if someone had struck an organ a terrible blow, the three women shrieked.

"*Got* you!" The man jumped from behind a tree. Rearing into the moonlight, he laughed. Leaning on the tree, he laughed again.

"Hey, I'm the—The Lonely One!"

"Tom Dillon!"

"Tom!"

"Tom," said Lavinia. "If you ever do a childish thing like that again, may you be riddled with bullets by mistake!"

Francine began to cry.

Tom Dillon stopped smiling. "Hey, I'm sorry."

"Haven't you heard about Eliza Ramsell?" snapped Lavinia. "She's dead, and you scaring women. You should be ashamed. Don't speak to us again."

"Aw—"

He moved to follow them.

"Stay right there, Mr. Lonely One, and scare yourself," said Lavinia. "Go see Eliza Ramsell's face and see if it's funny!" She pushed the other two on along the street of trees and stars, Francine holding a handkerchief to her face.

"Francine," pleaded Helen, "it was only a joke. Why's she crying so hard?"

"I guess we better tell you, Helen. *We* found Eliza. And it wasn't pretty. And we're trying to forget. We're going to the show to help and let's not talk about it. Enough's enough. Get your ticket money ready, we're almost downtown!"

The drug store was a small pool of sluggish air which the great wooden fans stirred in tides of arnica and tonic and soda-smell out into the brick streets.

"A nickel's worth of green mint chews," said Lavinia to the druggist. His face was set and pale, like all the faces they had seen on the half-empty streets. "For eating in the show," she explained, as the druggist dropped the mints into a sack with a silver shovel.

"Sure look pretty tonight," said the druggist. "You looked cool this noon, Miss Lavinia, when you was in here for chocolates. So cool and nice that someone asked after you."

"Oh?"

"You're getting popular. Man sitting at the counter—" he rustled a few more mints in the sack— "watched you walk out and he said to me, 'Say, who's *that*?' Man in a dark suit, thin pale face. 'Why, that's Lavinia Nebbs, prettiest maiden lady in town,' *I* said. 'Beautiful,' *he* said. 'Where's she live?' " Here the druggist paused and looked away.

"You *didn't*?" wailed Francine. "You didn't give him her address, I hope? You *didn't*!"

"Sorry, guess I didn't think. I said, 'Oh, over on Park Street, you know, near the ravine.' Casual remark. But now, tonight, them finding the body, I heard a minute ago, I suddenly thought, what've I *done*!" He handed over the package, much too full.

"You fool!" cried Francine, and tears were in her eyes.

"I'm sorry. 'Course, maybe it was nothing."

"Nothing, nothing!" said Francine.

Lavinia stood with the three people looking at her, staring at her. She didn't know what or how to feel. She felt nothing—except perhaps the slightest prickle of excitement in her throat. She held out her money automatically.

"No charge on those peppermints." The druggist turned down his eyes and shuffled some papers.

"Well, I know what we're going to do right *now*!" Helen stalked out of the drug shop. "We're going right straight home. I'm not going to be part of any hunting party for you, Lavinia. That man was asking for you. You're *next*! You want to be dead in that ravine?"

"It was just a man," said Lavinia slowly, eyes on the streets.

"So's Tom Dillon a man, but maybe he's The Lonely One."

"We're all overwrought," said Lavinia reasonably. "I won't miss the movie now. If I'm the next victim, let me *be* the next victim. A lady has all too little excitement in her life, especially an old maid, a lady thirty-seven like me, so don't you mind if I enjoy it. And I'm being sensible. Stands to reason he won't be out tonight, so soon after a murder. A month from now, yes, when the police've relaxed and when he *feels* like another murder. You've got to *feel* like murdering people, you know. At least that kind of murderer does. And he's just resting up now. And anyway I'm not going home to stew in my own juices."

"But Eliza's face, there in the ravine!"

"After the first look I never looked again. I didn't *drink* it in, if that's what you mean. I can see a thing and tell myself I never saw it, that's how strong *I* am. And the whole argument's silly anyhow, because I'm not beautiful."

"Oh, but you are, Lavinia. You're the loveliest maiden lady

in town, now that Eliza's—" Francine stopped. "If you'd only relaxed, you'd been married years ago—"

"Stop sniveling, Francine. Here's the box office. You and Helen go on home. I'll sit alone and go home alone."

"Lavinia, you're crazy. We can't leave you here—"

They argued for five minutes. Helen started to walk away but came back when she saw Lavinia thump down her money for a solitary movie ticket. Helen and Francine followed her silently into the theater.

The first show was over. In the dim auditorium, as they sat in the odor of ancient brass polish, the manager appeared before the worn red velvet curtains for an announcement:

"The police have asked for an early closing tonight. So everyone can be home at a decent hour. So we are cutting our short subjects and putting on our feature film again now. The show will be over at 11. Everyone's advised to go straight home and not linger on the streets. Our police force is pretty small and will be spread around pretty thin."

"That means us, Lavinia! *Us!*" Lavinia felt the hands tugging at her elbows on either side.

Harold Lloyd in Welcome, Danger! said the screen in the dark.

"Lavinia," Helen whispered.

"What?"

"As we came in, a man in a dark suit, across the street, crossed over. He just came in. He just sat in the row behind us."

"Oh, Helen."

"He's right behind us *now*."

Lavinia looked at the screen.

Helen turned slowly and glanced back. "I'm calling the manager!" she cried and leaped up. "Stop the film! Lights!"

"Helen, come back!" said Lavinia, her eyes shut.

o

When they set down their empty soda glasses, each of the ladies had a chocolate mustache on her upper lip. They removed them with their tongues, laughing.

"You see how *silly* it was?" said Lavinia. "All that riot for nothing. How embarrassing!"

The drug store clock said 11:25. They had come out of the theater and the laughter and the enjoyment feeling new. And now they were laughing at Helen, and Helen was laughing at herself.

Lavinia said, "When you ran up that aisle crying, 'Lights!' I thought I'd die!"

"That poor man!"

"The theater manager's brother from Racine!"

"I apologized," said Helen.

"You *see* what panic can do?"

The great fans still whirled and whirled in the warm night air, stirring and restirring the smells of vanilla, raspberry, peppermint and disinfectant in the drug store.

"We shouldn't have stopped for these sodas. The police said—"

"Oh, bosh the police," laughed Lavinia. "I'm not afraid of anything. The Lonely One is a million miles away now. He won't be back for weeks, and the police'll get him then, just wait. Wasn't the film *funny*?"

The streets were clean and empty. Not a car or a truck or a person was in sight. The bright lights were still lit in the small store windows where the hot wax dummies stood. Their blank blue eyes watched as the ladies walked past them, down the night street.

"Do you suppose if we screamed they'd do anything?"

"Who?"

"The dummies, the window people."

"Oh, Francine."

"Well…"

There were a hundred people in the windows, stiff and silent, and three people on the street, the echoes following like gunshots when they tapped their heels on the baked pavement.

A red neon sign flickered dimly, buzzing like a dying insect. They walked past it.

Baked and white, the long avenue lay ahead. Blowing and tall in a wind that touched only their leafy summits, the trees stood on either side of the three small women.

"First, we'll walk you home, Francine."

"No, I'll walk *you* home."

"Don't be silly. You live the nearest. If you walked me home you'd have to come back across the ravine all by yourself. And if so much as a leaf fell on you, you'd drop dead."

Francine said, "I can stay the night at your house. You're the *pretty* one!"

"No."

So they drifted like three prim clothes-forms over a moonlit sea of lawn and concrete and trees. To Lavinia, watching the black trees flit by, listening to the voices of her friends, the night seemed to quicken. They seemed to be running while walking slowly. Everything seemed fast, and the color of hot snow.

"Let's sing," said Lavinia.

They sang sweetly and quietly, arm in arm, not looking back. They felt the hot sidewalk cooling underfoot, moving, moving.

"Listen," said Lavinia.

They listened to the summer night, to the crickets and the far-off tone of the courthouse clock making it fifteen minutes to 12.

"Listen."

A porch swing creaked in the dark. And there was Mr. Terle,

silent, alone on his porch as they passed, having a last cigar.
They could see the pink cigar fire idling to and fro.

Now the lights were going, going, gone. The little house
lights and big house lights, the yellow lights and green hurri-
cane lights, the candles and oil lamps and porch lights, and
everything felt locked up in brass and iron and steel. Everything, thought Lavinia, is boxed and wrapped and shaded. She
imagined the people in their moonlit beds, and their breathing
in the summer night, safe and together. And here we are, she
thought, listening to our solitary footsteps on the baked summer-
evening sidewalk. And above us the lonely street lights shining
down, making a million wild shadows.

"Here's your house, Francine. Good night."

"Lavinia, Helen, stay here tonight. It's late, almost midnight
now. Mrs. Murdock has an extra room. You can sleep in the
parlor. I'll make hot chocolate. It'd be ever such fun!" Francine
was holding them both close to her.

"No, thanks," said Lavinia.

And Francine began to cry.

"Oh, not *again*, Francine," said Lavinia.

"I don't want you dead," sobbed Francine, the tears running
straight down her cheeks. "You're so fine and nice, I want you
alive. Please, oh, please!"

"Francine, I didn't realize how much this has affected you.
But I promise you I'll phone when I get home, right away."

"Oh, *will* you?"

"And tell you I'm safe, yes. And tomorrow we'll have a picnic
lunch at Electric Park, all right? With ham sandwiches I'll make
myself. How's that? You'll see; I'm going to live forever!"

"You'll phone?"

"I promised, didn't I?"

"Good night, good night!" Francine was gone behind her
door, locked tight in an instant.

"Now," said Lavinia to Helen, "I'll walk *you* home."

The courthouse clock struck the hour.

The sounds went across a town that was empty, emptier than it had ever been before. Over empty streets and empty lots and empty lawns the sound went.

"Ten, eleven, *twelve*," counted Lavinia, with Helen on her arm.

"Don't you feel *funny*?" asked Helen.

"How do you mean?"

"When you think of us being out here on the sidewalk, under the trees, and all those people safe behind locked doors lying in their beds. We're practically the only walking people out in the open in a thousand miles, I bet." The sound of the deep warm dark ravine came near.

In a minute they stood before Helen's house, looking at each other for a long time. The wind blew the odor of cut grass and wet lilacs between them. The moon was high in a sky that was beginning to cloud over. "I don't suppose it's any use asking you to stay, Lavinia?"

"I'll be going on."

"Sometimes…"

"Sometimes what?"

"Sometimes I think people *want* to die. You've certainly acted odd all evening."

"I'm just not afraid," said Lavinia. "And I'm curious, I suppose. And I'm using my head. Logically, The Lonely One can't be around. The police and all."

"*Our* police? *Our* little old force? They're home in bed too, the covers up over their ears."

"Let's just say I'm enjoying myself, precariously but safely. If there were any *real* chance of anything happening to me, I'd stay here with you, you can be sure of that."

"Maybe your subconscious doesn't want you to live anymore."

"You and Francine, honestly!"

"I feel so guilty. I'll be drinking hot cocoa just as you reach the ravine bottom and walk on the bridge in the dark."

"Drink a cup for me. Good night."

Lavinia Nebbs walked down the midnight street, down the late summer night silence. She saw the houses with their dark windows and far away she heard a dog barking. In five minutes, she thought, I'll be safe home. In five minutes I'll be phoning silly little Francine. I'll—

She heard the man's voice singing far away among the trees.

She walked a little faster.

Coming down the street toward her in the dimming moonlight was a man. He was walking casually.

I can run knock on one of these doors, thought Lavinia. If necessary.

The man was singing, *Shine On, Harvest Moon*, and he carried a long club in his hand. "Well, look who's here! What a time of night for you to be out, Miss Nebbs!"

"Officer Kennedy!"

And that's who it was, of course—Officer Kennedy on his beat.

"I'd better see you home."

"Never mind, I'll make it."

"But you live across the ravine."

Yes, she thought, but I won't walk the ravine with *any* man. How do I know *who* The Lonely One is? "No, thanks," she said.

"I'll wait right here then," he said. "If you need help, give a yell. I'll come running."

She went on, leaving him under a light, humming to himself, alone.

Here I am, she thought.

The ravine.

She stood on the top of the 113 steps down the steep, brambled bank that led across the creaking bridge and up through the black hills to Park Street. And only one lantern to see by. Three minutes from now, she thought, I'll be putting my key in my house door. Nothing can happen in just 180 seconds.

She started down the dark green steps into the deep ravine night.

"One, two, three, four, five, six, seven, eight, nine steps," she whispered.

She felt she was running but she was not running.

"Fifteen, sixteen, seventeen, eighteen, nineteen steps," she counted aloud.

The ravine was deep, black and black, black. And the world was gone, the world of safe people in bed. The locked doors, the town, the drug store, the theater, the lights, everything was gone. Only the ravine existed and lived, black and huge about her.

"Nothing's happened, has it? No one around, *is* there? Twenty-four, twenty-five steps. Remember that old ghost story you told each other when you were children?"

She listened to her feet on the steps.

"The story about the dark man coming in your house and you upstairs in bed. And now he's at the *first* step coming up to your room. Now he's at the *second* step. Now he's at the third and the fourth and the *fifth* step! Oh, how you laughed and screamed at that story! And now the horrid dark man is at the twelfth step, opening your door, and now he's standing by your bed. I *got you*!"

She screamed. It was like nothing she'd ever heard, that scream. She had never screamed that loud in her life. She stopped, she froze, she clung to the wooden banister. Her heart exploded in her. The sound of its terrified beating filled the universe.

"There, there!" she screamed to herself. "At the bottom of

the steps. A man, under the light! No, now he's gone! He was *waiting* there!"

She listened.

Silence. The bridge was empty.

Nothing, she thought, holding her heart. Nothing. Fool. That story I told myself. How silly. What shall I do?

Her heartbeats faded.

Shall I call the officer, did he hear my scream? Or was it only loud to *me*? Was it really just a small scream after all?

She listened. Nothing. Nothing.

I'll go back to Helen's and sleep there tonight. But even while she thought this she moved down again. No, it's nearer home now. Thirty-eight, thirty-nine steps, careful, don't fall. Oh, I *am* a fool. Forty steps. Forty-one. Almost halfway now. She froze again.

"Wait," she told herself. She took a step.

There was an echo.

She took another step. Another echo—just a fraction of a moment later.

"Someone's following me," she whispered to the ravine, to the black crickets and dark-green frogs and the black stream. "Someone's on the steps behind me. I don't dare turn around."

Another step, another echo.

Every time I take a step, *they* take one.

A step and an echo.

Weakly she asked of the ravine, "Officer Kennedy, is that *you*?"

The crickets were suddenly still. The crickets were listening. The night was listening to *her*. For a moment all the far summer-night meadows and close summer-night trees were suspending motion. Leaf, shrub, star, and meadowgrass had ceased their particular tremors and were listening to Lavinia Nebbs's heart.

And perhaps a thousand miles away, across locomotive-lonely country, in an empty way-station, a lonely night traveler reading a dim newspaper under a naked light-bulb might raise his head, listen, and think, What's that?—and decide, Only a woodchuck, surely, beating a hollow log. But it was Lavinia Nebbs, it was the heart of Lavinia Nebbs.

Faster. Faster. She went down the steps.

Run!

She heard music. In a mad way, in a silly way, she heard the huge surge of music that pounded at her, and she realized as she ran—as she ran in panic and terror—that some part of her mind was dramatizing, borrowing from the turbulent score of some private film. The music was rushing and plunging her faster, faster, plummeting and scurrying, down, and down into the pit of the ravine!

"Only a little way," she prayed. "One hundred ten, eleven, twelve, thirteen steps! The bottom! Now, run! Across the bridge!"

She spoke to her legs, her arms, her body, her terror; she advised all parts of herself in this white and terrible instant. Over the roaring creek waters, on the swaying, almost-alive bridge planks she ran, followed by the wild footsteps behind, with the music following too, the music shrieking and babbling.

He's following. Don't turn, don't look—if you see him, you'll not be able to move! You'll be frightened, you'll freeze! Just run, run, *run!*

She ran across the bridge.

Oh, God! God, please, please let me get up the hill! Now up, up the path, now between the hills. Oh, God, it's dark, and everything so far away! If I screamed now it wouldn't help; I can't scream anyway! Here's the top of the path, here's the street. Thank God I wore my low-heeled shoes, I can run, I can run! Oh, God, please let me be safe. If I get home safe I'll never go out alone, I was a fool, let me admit it, a fool! I didn't know what terror was! I wouldn't let myself think, but if you let me get home from this I'll never go out without Helen or Francine again! Here's the street. Across the street now!

She crossed the street and rushed up the sidewalk.

Oh, God, the porch! My house!

In the middle of her running, she saw the half-filled lemonade glass where she had left it hours before, in the good easy lazy time, left it on the railing. She wished she was back in that time now, drinking from it, the night still young and not begun.

"Oh, please, please, give me time to get inside and lock the door and I'll be safe!"

She heard her clumsy feet on the porch, felt her hands scrabbling and ripping at the lock with the key. She heard her heart. She heard her inner voice screaming.

The key fit.

"Unlock the door, quick, quick!"

The door opened.

"Now, inside. *Slam* it!"

She slammed the door.

"Now lock it, bar it, lock it!" she cried. "Lock it *tight*!"

The door was locked and barred and bolted.

The music stopped. She listened to her heart again and the sound of it diminishing into silence.

Home.

Oh, safe at home! Safe, safe and safe at home! She slumped against the door. Safe, safe. Listen. Not a sound. Safe, safe, oh, thank God, safe at home. I'll never go out at night again. Safe, oh, safe, safe, home, so good, so safe. Safe inside, the door locked. Wait. Look out the window.

She looked. She gazed out the window for a full half-minute.

"Why, there's no one there at all! Nobody! There was no one

following me at all. Nobody running after me." She caught her breath and almost laughed at herself. "It stands to reason. If a man *had* been following me, he'd have *caught* me. I'm not a fast runner. There's no one on the porch or in the yard. How silly of me! I wasn't running from anything except *me*. That ravine was safer than safe. Just the same, though, it's nice to be home. Home's the really good warm safe place, the *only* place to be.

She put her hand out to the light switch and stopped.

"What?" she asked. "What, *what*?"

Behind her, in the black living room, someone cleared his throat....

At Midnight, In the Month of June

He had been waiting a long, long time in the summer night, as the darkness pressed warmer to the earth and the stars turned slowly over the sky. He sat in total darkness, his hands lying easily on the arms of the Morris chair. He heard the town clock strike nine and ten and eleven, and then at last twelve. The breeze from an open back window flowed through the midnight house in an unlit stream that touched him like a dark rock where he sat silently watching the front door—silently watching.

At midnight, in the month of June....

The cool night poem by Mr. Edgar Allan Poe slid over his mind like the waters of a shadowed creek.

The lady sleeps! Oh, may her sleep,
Which is enduring, so be deep!

He moved down the black shapeless halls of the house, stepped out of the back window, feeling the town locked away in bed, in dream, in night. He saw the shining snake of garden hose coiled resiliently in the grass. He turned on the water. Standing alone, watering the flower bed, he imagined himself a conductor leading an orchestra that only night-strolling dogs might hear, passing on their way to nowhere with strange white smiles. Very carefully he planted both feet and his tall weight into the mud beneath the window, making deep, well-outlined prints. He stepped inside again and walked, leaving mud, down the absolutely unseen hall, his hands seeing for him.

Through the front porch window he made out the faint out-
line of a lemonade glass, half full, sitting on the porch rail
where *she* had left it. He trembled quietly.

Now, he could feel her coming home. He could feel her
moving across town, far away, in the summer night. He shut his
eyes and put his mind out to find her, and felt her moving along
in the dark; he knew just where she stepped down from a curb
and crossed a street, and up on a curb and tack-tacking, tack-
tacking along under the June elms and the last of the lilacs,
with a friend. Walking the empty desert of night, he *was* she.
He felt a purse in his hands. He felt long hair prickle his neck,
and his mouth turn greasy with lipstick. Sitting still, he was
walking, walking, walking on home after midnight.

"Good night!"

He heard but did not hear the voices, and she was coming
nearer, and now she was only a mile away and now only a matter
of a thousand yards, and now she was sinking, like a beautiful
white lantern on an invisible wire, down into the cricket and
frog and water-sounding ravine. And he knew the texture of the
wooden ravine stairs as if, a boy, he was rushing down them,
feeling the rough grain and the dust and the leftover heat of
the day....

He put his hands out on the air, open. The thumbs of his
hands touched, and then the fingers, so that his hands made a
circle, enclosing emptiness, there before him. Then, very slowly,
he squeezed his hands tighter and tighter together, his mouth
open, his eyes shut.

He stopped squeezing and put his hands, trembling, back on
the arms of the chair. He kept his eyes shut.

Long ago, he had climbed, one night, to the top of the courthouse tower fire escape, and looked out at the silver town, at
the town of the moon, and the town of summer. And he had

seen all the dark houses with two things in them, people and sleep, the two elements joined in bed and all their tiredness and terror breathed upon the still air, siphoned back quietly, and breathed out again, until that element was purified, the problems and hatreds and horrors of the previous day exorcised long before morning and done away with forever.

He had been enchanted with the hour, and the town, and he had felt very powerful, like the magic man with the marionettes who strung destinies across a stage on spider threads. On the very top of the courthouse tower he could see the least flicker of leaf turning in the moonlight five miles away; the last light, like a pink pumpkin eye, wink out. The town did not escape his eye—it could do nothing without his knowing its every tremble and gesture.

And so it was tonight. He felt himself a tower with the clock in it pounding slow and announcing hours in a great bronze tone, and gazing upon a town where a woman, hurried or slowed by fitful gusts and breezes now of terror and now of self-confidence, took the chalk-white midnight sidewalks home, fording solid avenues of tar and stone, drifting among fresh-cut lawns, and now running, running down the steps, through the ravine, up the hill, up the hill!

He heard her footsteps before he really heard them. He heard her gasping before there was a gasping. He fixed his gaze to the lemonade glass outside, on the banister. Then the real sound, the real running, the gasping, echoed wildly outside. He sat up. The footsteps raced across the street, the sidewalk, in a panic. There was a babble, a clumsy stumble up the porch steps, a key ratcheting the door, a voice yelling in a whisper, praying to itself. "Oh, God, dear God!" Whisper! Whisper! And the woman crashing in the door, slamming it, bolting it, talking, whispering, talking to herself in the dark room.

He felt, rather than saw, her hand move toward the light switch.

He cleared his throat.

She stood against the door in the dark. If moonlight could have struck in upon her, she would have shimmered like a small pool of water on a windy night. He felt the fine sapphire jewels come out upon her face, and her face all glittering with brine.

"Lavinia," he whispered.

Her arms were raised across the door like a crucifix. He heard her mouth open and her lungs push a warmness upon the air. She was a beautiful dim white moth; with the sharp needle point of terror he had her pinned against the wooden door. He could walk all around the specimen, if he wished, and look at her, look at her.

"Lavinia," he whispered.

He heard her heart beating. She did not move.

"It's me," he whispered.

"Who?" she said, so faint it was a small pulse-beat in her throat.

"I won't tell you," he whispered. He stood perfectly straight in the center of the room. God, but he felt *tall*! Tall and dark and very beautiful to himself, and the way his hands were out before him was as if he might play a piano at any moment, a lovely melody, a waltzing tune. The hands were wet, they felt as if he had dipped them into a bed of mint and cool menthol.

"If I told you who I am, you might not be afraid," he whispered. "I want you to be afraid. Are you afraid?"

She said nothing. She breathed out and in, out and in, a small bellows which, pumped steadily, blew upon her fear and kept it going, kept it alight.

"Why did you go to the show tonight?" he whispered. "*Why* did you go to the show?"

No answer.

He took a step forward, heard her breath take itself, like a sword hissing in its sheath.

"Why did you come back through the ravine, alone?" he whispered. "You *did* come back alone, didn't you? Did you think you'd meet me in the middle of the bridge? Why did you go to the show tonight? Why did you come back through the ravine, alone?"

"I—" she gasped.

"You," he whispered.

"No—" she cried, in a whisper.

"Lavinia," he said. He took another step.

"Please," she said.

"Open the door. Get out. And run," he whispered.

She did not move.

"Lavinia, open the door."

She began to whimper in her throat.

"Run," he said.

In moving he felt something touch his knee. He pushed, something tilted in space and fell over, a table, a basket, and a half-dozen unseen balls of yarn tumbled like cats in the dark, rolling softly. In the one moonlit space on the floor beneath the window, like a metal sign pointing, lay the sewing shears. They were winter ice in his hand. He held them out to her suddenly, through the still air.

"Here," he whispered.

He touched them to her hand. She snatched her hand back.

"Here," he urged.

"Take this," he said, after a pause.

He opened her fingers that were already dead and cold to the touch, and stiff and strange to manage, and he pressed the scissors into them. "Now," he said.

He looked out at the moonlit sky for a long moment, and

when he glanced back it was some time before he could see her in the dark.

"I waited," he said. "But that's the way it's always been. I waited for the others, too. But they all came looking for me, finally. It was that easy. Five lovely ladies in the last two years. I waited for them in the ravine, in the country, by the lake, everywhere I waited, and they came out to find me, and found me. It was always nice, the next day, reading the newspapers. And you went looking tonight, I know, or you wouldn't have come back alone through the ravine. Did you scare yourself there, and run? Did you think I was down there waiting for you? You should have *heard* yourself running up the walk! Through the door! And *locking* it! You thought you were safe inside, home at last, safe, safe, safe, didn't you?"

She held the scissors in one dead hand, and she began to cry. He saw the merest gleam, like water upon the wall of a dim cave. He heard the sounds she made.

"No," he whispered. "You have the scissors. Don't cry."

She cried. She did not move at all. She stood there, shivering, her head back against the door, beginning to slide down the length of the door toward the floor.

"Don't cry," he whispered.

"I don't like to hear you cry," he said. "I can't stand to hear that."

He held his hands out, and moved them through the air until one of them touched her cheek. He felt the wetness of that cheek, he felt her warm breath touch his palm like a summer moth. Then he said only one more thing:

"Lavinia," he said, gently. "Lavinia."

How clearly he remembered the old nights in the old times, in the times when he was a boy and them all running, and running, and hiding and hiding, and playing hide-and-seek. In the first spring nights and in the warm summer nights and in the late summer evenings and in those first sharp autumn nights when doors were shutting early and porches were empty except for blowing leaves. The game of hide-and-seek went on as long as there was sun to see by, or the rising snow-crusted moon. Their feet upon the green lawns were like the scattered throwing of soft peaches and crab apples, and the counting of the Seeker with his arms cradling his buried head, chanting to the night: five, ten, fifteen, twenty, twenty-five, thirty, thirty-five, forty, forty-five, fifty....And the sound of thrown apples fading, the children all safely closeted in tree or bush shade, under the latticed porches with the clever dogs minding not to wag their tails and give their secret away. And the counting done: eighty-five, ninety, ninety-five, a hundred!

Ready or not, here I come!

And the Seeker running out through the town wilderness to find the Hiders, and the Hiders keeping their secret laughter in their mouths, like precious June strawberries, with the help of clasped hands. And the Seeker seeking after the smallest heartbeat in the high elm tree or the glint of a dog's eye in a bush, or a small water sound of laughter that could not help but burst out as the Seeker ran right on by and did not see the shadow within the shadow....

He moved into the bathroom of the quiet house, thinking all this, enjoying the clear rush, the tumultuous gushing of memories like a waterfalling of the mind over a steep precipice, falling and falling toward the bottom of his head.

God, how secret and tall they had felt, hidden away God, how the shadows mothered and kept them, sheathed in their own triumph. Glowing with perspiration, how they crouched like idols and thought they might hide *forever*! While the silly Seeker went pelting by on his way to failure and inevitable frustration.

Sometimes the Seeker stopped right *at* your tree and peered up at you crouched there in your visible warm wings, in your great colorless windowpane bat wings, and said, "I *see* you there!" But you said nothing. "You're *up* there all right." But you said nothing. "Come on *down!*" But not a word, only a victorious Cheshire smile. And doubt coming over the Seeker below. "It is *you*, isn't it?" The backing off and away. "Aw, I *know* you're up there!" No answer. Only the tree sitting in the night and shaking quietly, leaf upon leaf. And the Seeker, afraid of the dark within darkness, loping away to seek easier game, something to be named and certain of. "All right for *you!*"

He washed his hands in the bathroom, and thought, Why am I washing my hands? And then the grains of time sucked back up the flue of the hourglass again and it was another year....

He remembered that sometimes when he played hide-and-seek they did not find him at all; he would not let them find him. He said not a word, he stayed so long in the apple tree that he was a white-fleshed apple; he lingered so long in the chestnut tree that he had the hardness and the brown brightness of the autumn nut. And God, how powerful to be undiscovered, how immense it made you, until your arms were branching, growing out in all directions, pulled by the stars and the tidal moon until your secretness enclosed the town and mothered it with your compassion and tolerance. You could do anything in the shadows, anything. If you chose to do it, you could do it. How powerful to sit above the sidewalk and see people pass under, never aware you were there and watching, and might put out an arm to brush their noses with the five-legged spider of your hand and brush their thinking minds with terror.

He finished washing his hands and wiped them on a towel.

But there was always an end to the game. When the Seeker had found all the other Hiders and these Hiders in turn were

Seekers and they were all spreading out, calling your name, looking for you, how much more powerful and important *that* made you.

"Hey, hey! Where *are* you! Come in, the game's over!"

But you not moving or coming in. Even when they all collected under your tree and saw, or thought they saw you there at the very top, and called up at you. "Oh, come down! Stop fooling! Hey! We see you. We know you're there!"

Not answering even then—not until the final, the fatal thing happened. Far off, a block away, a silver whistle screaming, and the voice of your mother calling your name, and the whistle again. "Nine o'clock!" her voice wailed. "Nine o'clock! Home!"

But you waited until all the children were gone. Then, very carefully unfolding yourself and your warmth and secretness, and keeping out of the lantern light at corners, you ran home alone, alone in darkness and shadow, hardly breathing, keeping the sound of your heart quiet and in yourself, so if people heard anything at all they might think it was only the wind blowing a dry leaf by in the night. And your mother standing there, with the screen door wide....

He finished wiping his hands on the towel. He stood a moment thinking of how it had been the last two years here in town. The old game going on, by himself, playing it alone, the children gone, grown into settled middle age, but now, as before, himself the final and last and only Hider, and the whole town seeking and seeing nothing and going on home to lock their doors.

But tonight, out of a time long past, and on many nights now, he had heard that old sound, the sound of the silver whistle, blowing and blowing. It was certainly not a night bird singing, for he knew each sound so well. But the whistle kept calling and calling and a voice said, *Home* and *Nine o'clock*, even though it was now long after midnight. He listened. There was the silver whistle. Even though his mother had died many years ago, after having put his father in an early grave with her temper and her tongue. "Do this, do that, do this, do that, do this, do that, do this, do that...." A phonograph record, broken, playing the same cracked turn again, again, again, her voice, her cadence, around, around, around, around, repeat, repeat, repeat.

And the clear silver whistle blowing and the game of hide-and-seek over. No more of walking in the town and standing behind trees and bushes and smiling a smile that burned through the thickest foliage. An automatic thing was happening. His feet were walking and his hands were doing and he knew everything that must be done now.

His hands did not belong to him.

He tore a button off his coat and let it drop into the deep dark well of the room. It never seemed to hit bottom. It floated down. He waited.

It seemed never to stop rolling. Finally, it stopped.

His hands did not belong to him.

He took his pipe and flung that into the depths of the room. Without waiting for it to strike emptiness, he walked quietly back through the kitchen and peered outside the open, blowing, white-curtained window at the footprints he had made there. He was the Seeker, seeking now, instead of the Hider hiding. He was the quiet searcher finding and sifting and putting away clues, and those footprints were now as alien to him as something from a prehistoric age. They had been made a million years ago by some other man on some other business; they were no part of him at all. He marveled at their precision and deepness and form in the moonlight. He put his hand down almost to touch them, like a great and beautiful archaeological discovery! Then he was gone, back through the rooms, ripping a piece of material from his pants cuff and blowing it off his open palm like a moth.

His hands were not his hands anymore, or his body his body.

He opened the front door and went out and sat for a moment on the porch rail. He picked up the lemonade glass and drank what was left, made warm by an evening's waiting, and pressed his fingers tight to the glass, tight, tight, very tight. Then he put the glass down on the railing.

The silver whistle!

Yes, he thought. Coming, coming.

The silver whistle!

Yes, he thought. Nine o'clock. Home, home. Nine o'clock. Studies and milk and graham crackers and white cool bed, home, home; nine o'clock and the silver whistle.

He was off the porch in an instant, running softly, lightly, with hardly a breath or a heartbeat, as one barefooted runs, as one all leaf and green June grass and night can run, all shadow, forever running, away from the silent house and across the street, and down into the ravine....

He pushed the door wide and stepped into the Owl Diner, this long railroad car that, removed from its track, had been put to a solitary and unmoving destiny in the center of town. The place was empty. At the far end of the counter, the counterman glanced up as the door shut and the customer walked along the line of empty swivel seats. The counterman took the toothpick from his mouth.

"Tom Dillon, you old so-and-so! What *you* doing up this time of night, Tom?"

Tom Dillon ordered without the menu. While the food was being prepared, he dropped a nickel in the wall phone, got his number, and spoke quietly for a time. He hung up, came back, and sat, listening. Sixty seconds later, both he and the counterman heard the police siren wail by at fifty miles an hour. "Well—hell!" said the counterman. "Go get 'em boys!"

He set out a tall glass of milk and a plate of six fresh graham crackers.

Tom Dillon sat there for a long while, looking secretly down at his ripped pants cuff and muddied shoes. The light in the diner was raw and bright, and he felt as if he were on a stage. He held the tall cool glass of milk in his hand, sipping it, eyes shut, chewing the good texture of the graham crackers, feeling it all through his mouth, coating his tongue.

"Would or would you not," he asked, quietly, "call this a hearty meal?"

"I'd call that very hearty indeed," said the counterman, smiling.

Tom Dillon chewed another graham cracker with great concentration, feeling all of it in his mouth. It's just a matter of time, he thought, waiting.

"More milk?"

"Yes," said Tom.

And he watched with steady interest, with the purest and most alert concentration in all of his life, as the white carton tilted and gleamed, and the snowy milk poured out, cool and quiet, like the sound of a running spring at night, and filled the glass up all the way, to the very brim, to the very brim, and over....

The Smiling People

It was the sensation of silence that was the most notable aspect of the house. As Mr. Greppin came through the front door the oiled silence of it opening and swinging closed behind him was like an opening and shutting dream, a thing accomplished on rubber pads, bathed in lubricant, slow and unmaterialistic. The double carpet in the hall, which he himself had so recently laid, gave off no sound from his movements. And when the wind shook the house late of nights there was not a rattle of eave or tremor of loose sash. He had himself checked the storm windows. The screen doors were securely hooked with bright new, firm hooks, and the furnace did not knock but sent a silent whisper of warm wind up the throats of the heating system that sighed ever so quietly, moving the cuffs of his trousers as he stood, now, warming himself from the bitter afternoon.

Weighing the silence with the remarkable instruments of pitch and balance in his small ears, he nodded with satisfaction that the silence was so unified and finished. Because there *had* been nights when rats had walked between wall-layers and it had taken baited traps and poisoned food before the walls were mute. Even the grandfather clock had been stilled, its brass pendulum hung frozen and gleaming in its long cedar, glass-fronted coffin.

They were waiting for him in the dining room.

He listened. They made no sound. Good. Excellent, in fact. They had learned, then, to be silent. You had to teach people, but it was worthwhile—there was not a rattle of knife or fork from the dining table. He worked off his thick gray gloves, hung up his cold armor of overcoat and stood there with an expression of urgency yet indecisiveness…thinking of what had to be done.

Mr. Greppin proceeded with familiar certainty and economy of motion into the dining room, where the four individuals seated at the waiting table did not move or speak a word. The only sound was the merest allowable pad of his shoes on the deep carpet.

His eyes, as usual, instinctively, fastened upon the lady heading the table. Passing, he waved a finger near her cheek. She did not blink.

Aunt Rose sat firmly at the head of the table and if a mote of dust floated lightly down out of the ceiling spaces, did her eye trace its orbit? Did the eye revolve in its shellacked socket, with glassy cold precision? And if the dust mote happened upon the shell of her wet eye did the eye batten? Did the muscles clinch, the lashes close?

No.

Aunt Rose's hand lay on the table like cutlery, rare and fine and old; tarnished. Her bosom was hidden in a salad of fluffy linen.

Beneath the table her stick legs in high-buttoned shoes went up into a pipe of dress. You felt that the legs terminated at the skirt line and from there on she was a department store dummy, all wax and nothingness responding, probably, with much the same chill waxen movements, with as much enthusiasm and response as a mannequin.

So here was Aunt Rose, staring straight at Greppin—he choked out a laugh and clapped hands derisively shut—there were the first hints of a dust mustache gathering across her upper lip!

"Good evening, Aunt Rose," he said, bowing. "Good evening, Uncle Dimity," he said, graciously. "No, not a word," he held up his hand. "Not a word from any of you." He bowed again. "Ah, good evening, cousin Lila, and you, cousin Sam."

Lila sat upon his left, her hair like golden shavings from a tube of lathed brass. Sam, opposite her, told all directions with *his* hair.

They were both young, he fourteen, she sixteen. Uncle Dimity, their father (but "father" was a nasty word!) sat next to Lila, placed in this secondary niche long, long ago because Aunt Rose said the window draft might get his neck if he sat at the head of the table. Ah, Aunt Rose!

Mr. Greppin drew the chair under his tight-clothed little rump and put a casual elbow to the linen.

"I've something to say," he said. "It's very important. This has gone on for weeks now. It can't go any further. I'm in love. Oh, but I've told you that long ago. On the day I made you all smile, remember?"

The eyes of the four seated people did not blink, the hands did not move.

Greppin became introspective. The day he had made them smile. Two weeks ago it was. He had come home, walked in, looked at them and said, "I'm to be married!"

They had all whirled with expressions as if someone had just smashed the window.

"You're WHAT?" cried Aunt Rose.

"To Alice Jane Ballard!" he had said, stiffening somewhat.

"Congratulations," said Uncle Dimity. "I guess," he added, looking at his wife. He cleared his throat. "But isn't it a little early, son?" He looked at his wife again. "Yes. Yes, I think it's a little early. I wouldn't advise it yet, not just yet, no."

"The house is in a terrible way," said Aunt Rose. "We won't have it fixed for a year yet."

"That's what you said last year and the year before," said Mr. Greppin. "And anyway," he said bluntly, "this is my house."

Aunt Rose's jaw had clamped at that. "After all these years for us to be bodily thrown out, why I—"

"You won't be thrown out, don't be idiotic," said Greppin, furiously.

"Now, Rose—" said Uncle Dimity in a pale tone.

Aunt Rose dropped her hands. "After all I've done—"

In that instant Greppin had known they would have to go, all of them. First he would make them silent, then he would make them smile, then, later, he would move them out like luggage. He couldn't bring Alice Jane into a house full of grims such as these, where Aunt Rose followed you wherever you went even when she wasn't following you, and the children performed indignities upon you at a glance from their maternal parent, and the father, no better than a third child, carefully rearranged his advice to you on being a bachelor. Greppin stared at them. It was their fault that his loving and living was all wrong. If he did something about them—then his warm bright dreams of soft bodies glowing with an anxious perspiration of love might become tangible and near. Then he would have the house all to himself and—and Alice Jane. Yes, Alice Jane.

They would have to go. Quickly. If he told them to go, as he had often done, twenty years might pass as Aunt Rose gathered sunbleached sachets and Edison phonographs. Long before then Alice Jane herself would be moved and gone.

Greppin looked at them as he picked up the carving knife.

Greppin's head snapped with tiredness.

He flicked his eyes open. Eh? Oh, he had been drowsing, thinking.

All *that* had occurred two weeks ago. Two weeks ago this

very night that conversation about marriage, moving, Alice Jane, had come about. Two weeks ago it had been. Two weeks ago he had made them smile.

Now, recovering from his reverie, he smiled around at the silent and motionless figures. They smiled back in peculiarly pleasing fashion.

"I hate you, old woman," he said to Aunt Rose, directly. "Two weeks ago I wouldn't have dared say that. Tonight, ah, well—" he lazed his voice, turning. "Uncle Dimity, let me give you a little advice, old man—"

He talked small talk, picked up a spoon, pretended to eat peaches from an empty dish. He had already eaten downtown in a tray cafeteria; pork, potatoes, apple pie, string beans, beets, potato salad. But now he made dessert-eating motions because he enjoyed this little act. He made as if he were chewing.

"So—tonight you are finally, once and for all, moving out. I've waited two weeks, thinking it all over. In a way I guess I've kept you here this long because I wanted to keep an eye on you. Once you're gone, I can't be sure—" And here his eyes gleamed with fear. "You might come prowling around, making noises at night, and I couldn't stand that. I can't ever have noises in this house, not even when Alice moves in...."

The double carpet was thick and soundless underfoot, re-assuring.

"Alice wants to move in day after tomorrow. We're getting married."

Aunt Rose winked evilly, doubtfully at him.

"Ah!" he cried, leaping up, then, staring, he sank down, mouth convulsing. He released the tension in him, laughing. "Oh, I see. It was a fly." He watched the fly crawl with slow precision on the ivory cheek of Aunt Rose and dart away. Why did it have to pick that instant to make her eye appear to blink, to doubt. "Do you doubt I ever will marry, Aunt Rose? Do you think me incapable of marriage, of love and love's duties? Do you think me immature, unable to cope with a woman and her ways of living? Do you think me a child, only daydreaming? Well!" He calmed himself with an effort, shaking his head. "Man, man," he argued to himself. "It was only a fly, and does a fly make doubt of love, or did you make it into a fly and a wink? Damn it!" He pointed at the four of them.

"I'm going to fix the furnace hotter. In an hour I'll be moving you out of the house once and for all. You comprehend? Good. I see you do."

Outside, it was beginning to rain, a cold drizzling downpour that drenched the house. A look of irritation came to Greppin's face. The sound of the rain was the one thing he couldn't stop, couldn't be helped. No way to buy new hinges or lubricants or hooks for that. You might tent the house-top with lengths of cloth to soften the sound, mightn't you? That's going a bit far. No. No way of preventing the rain sounds.

He wanted silence now, where he had never wanted it before in his life so much. Each sound was a fear. So each sound had to be muffled, gotten to and eliminated.

The drum of rain was like the knuckles of an impatient man on a surface. He lapsed again into remembering.

He remembered the rest of it. The rest of that hour on that day two weeks ago when he had made them smile....

He had taken up the carving knife and prepared to cut the bird upon the table. As usual the family had been gathered, all wearing their solemn, puritanical masks. If the children smiled the smiles were stepped on like nasty bugs by Aunt Rose.

Aunt Rose criticized the angle of Greppin's elbows as he cut the bird. The knife, she made him understand also, was not sharp enough. Oh, yes, the sharpness of the knife. At this point in his memory he stopped, rolled-tilted his eyes, and laughed. Dutifully, then, he had crisped the knife on the sharpening rod and again set upon the fowl.

He had severed away much of it in some minutes before he slowly looked up at their solemn, critical faces, like puddings with agate eyes, and after staring at them a moment, as if discovered with a naked woman instead of a naked-limbed partridge, he lifted the knife and cried hoarsely, "Why in God's name can't you, any of you, ever smile? I'll *make* you smile!"

He raised the knife a number of times like a magician's wand.

And, in a short interval—behold! they were *all* of them smiling!

He broke that memory in half, crumpled it, balled it, tossed it down. Rising briskly, he went to the hall, down the hall to the kitchen, and from there down the dim stairs into the cellar where he opened the furnace door and built the fire steadily and expertly into wonderful flame.

Walking upstairs again he looked about him. He would have cleaners come and clean the empty house, redecorators slide down the dull drapes and hoist new shimmery banners up. New thick Oriental rugs purchased for the floors would subtly insure the silence he desired and would need at least for the next month, if not for the entire year.

He put his hands to his face. What if Alice Jane made noise moving about the house? Some noise, some how, some place!

And then he laughed. It was quite a joke. That problem was already solved. Yes, it was solved. He need fear no noise from Alice Jane. It was all absurdly simple. He would have all the pleasure of Alice Jane and none of the dream-destroying distractions and discomforts.

There was one other addition needed to the quality of silence.

Upon the tops of the doors that the wind sucked shut with a bang at frequent intervals he would install air-compression brakes, those kind they have on library doors that hiss gently as their levers seal.

He passed through the dining room. The figures had not moved from their tableau. Their hands remained affixed in familiar positions, and their indifference to him was not impoliteness.

He climbed the hall stairs to change his clothing, preparatory to the task of moving the family. Taking the links from his fine cuffs, he swung his head to one side. Music. At first he paid it no mind. Then, slowly, his face swinging to the ceiling, the color drained out of his cheeks.

At the very apex of the house the music began, note by note, one note following another, and it terrified him.

Each note came like a plucking of one single harp thread. In the complete silence the small sound of it was made larger until it grew all out of proportion to itself, gone mad with all this soundlessness to stretch about in.

The door opened in an explosion from his hands, the next thing his feet were trying the stairs to the third level of the house, the banister twisted in a long polished snake under his tightening, relaxing, reaching-up, pulling hands! The steps went under to be replaced by longer, higher, darker steps. He had started the game at the bottom with a slow stumbling, now he was running with full impetus and if a wall had suddenly confronted him he would not have stopped for it until he saw blood on it and fingernail scratches where he tried to pass through.

He felt like a mouse running in a great clear space of a bell. And high in the bell sphere the one harp thread hummed. It drew him on, caught him up with an umbilical of sound, gave his fear sustenance and life, mothered him. Fears passed between mother and groping child. He sought to shear the connection with his hands, could not. He felt as if someone had given a heave on the cord, wriggling.

Another clear threaded tone. And another.

"No, keep quiet," he shouted. "There can't be noise in my house. Not since two weeks ago. I said there would be no more noise. So it can't be—it's impossible! Keep quiet!"

He burst upward into the attic.

Relief can be hysteria.

Teardrops fell from a vent in the roof and struck, shattering upon a tall neck of Swedish cut-glass flowerware with resonant tone.

He shattered the vase with one swift move of his triumphant foot!

Picking out and putting on an old shirt and old pair of pants in his room, he chuckled. The music was gone, the vent plugged, the silence again insured. There are silences and silences. Each with its own identity. There were summer night silences, which weren't silences at all, but layer on layer of insect chorals and the sound of electric arc lamps swaying in lonely small orbits on lonely country roads, casting out feeble rings of illumination upon which the night fed—summer night silence which, to be a silence, demanded an indolence and a neglect and an indifference upon the part of the listener. Not a silence at all! And there was a winter silence, but it was an incoffined silence, ready to burst out at the first touch of spring, things had a compression, a not-for-long feel, the silence made a sound unto itself, the freezing was so complete it made chimes of everything or detonations of a single breath or word you spoke at midnight in the diamond air. No, it was not a silence worthy of the name. A silence between two lovers, when there need be no words. Color came in his cheeks, he shut his eyes. It was a most pleasant silence, a perfect silence with Alice Jane. He had seen to that. *Everything* was perfect.

Whispering.

He hoped the neighbors hadn't heard him shrieking like a fool.

A faint whispering.

Now, about silences. The best silence was one conceived in every aspect by an individual, himself, so that there could be no bursting of crystal bonds, or electric-insect hummings, the human mind could cope with each sound, each emergency, until such a complete silence was achieved that one could hear one's cells adjust in one's hand.

A whispering.

He shook his head. There was no whispering. There could be none in *his* house. Sweat began to seep down his body, he began to shake in small, imperceptible shakings, his jaw loosened, his eyes were turned free in their sockets.

Whispering. Low rumors of talk.

"I tell you I'm getting married," he said, weakly, loosely.

"You're lying," said the whispers.

His head fell forward on its neck as if hung, chin on chest.

"Her name is Alice Jane Ballard—" he mouthed it between soft, wet lips and the words were formless. One of his eyes began to jitter its lid up and down as if blinking out a message to some unseen guest. "You can't stop me from loving her, I love her—"

Whispering.

He took a blind step forward.

The cuff of his pants leg quivered as he reached the floor grille of the ventilator. A hot rise of air followed his cuffs. Whispering.

The furnace.

*

He was on his way downstairs when someone knocked on the front door. He leaned against it. "Who is it?"

"Mr. Greppin?"

Greppin drew in his breath. "Yes?"

"Will you let us in, please?"

"Well, who is it?"

"The police," said the man outside.

"What do you want, I'm just sitting down to supper!"

"Just want a talk with you. The neighbors phoned. Said they hadn't seen your aunt and uncle for two weeks. Heard a noise awhile ago—"

"I assure you everything is all right." He forced a laugh.

"Well, then," continued the voice outside, "we can talk it over in friendly style if you'll only open the door."

"I'm sorry," insisted Greppin. "I'm tired and hungry, come back tomorrow. I'll talk to you then, if you want me to."

"I'll have to insist, Mr. Greppin."

They began to beat against the door.

Greppin turned automatically, stiffly, walked down the hall past the old clock, into the dining room, without a word. He seated himself without looking at any one in particular and then he began to talk, slowly at first, then more rapidly.

"Some pests at the door. You'll talk to them, won't you, Aunt Rose? You'll tell them to go away, won't you, we're eating dinner? Everyone else go on eating and look pleasant and they'll go away, if they do come in. Aunt Rose you *will* talk to them, won't you? And now that things are happening I have something to tell you." A few hot tears fell for no reason. He looked at them as they soaked and spread in the white linen, vanishing. "I don't know anyone named Alice Jane Ballard. I never knew anyone named Alice Jane Ballard. It was all—all—I don't know.

I said I loved her and wanted to marry her to get around somehow to make you smile. Yes, I said it because I planned to make
you smile, that was the only reason. I'm never going to have a
woman, I always knew for years I never would have. Will you
please pass the potatoes, Aunt Rose?"

The front door splintered and fell. A heavy softened rushing
filled the hall. Men broke into the dining room.

A hesitation.

The police inspector hastily removed his hat.

"Oh, I beg your pardon," he apologized. "I didn't mean to
intrude upon your supper, I—"

The sudden halting of the police was such that their movement shook the room. The movement catapulted the bodies of
Aunt Rose and Uncle Dimity straight away to the carpet, where
they lay, their throats severed in a half moon from ear to ear—
which caused them, like the children seated at the table, to
have what was the horrid illusion of a smile under their chins,
ragged smiles that welcomed in the late arrivals and told them
everything with a simple grimace....

The Fruit at the Bottom of the Bowl

William Acton rose to his feet. The clock on the mantel ticked midnight.

He looked at his fingers and he looked at the large room around him and he looked at the man lying on the floor. William Acton, whose fingers had stroked typewriter keys and made love and fried ham and eggs for early breakfasts, had now accomplished a murder with those same ten whorled fingers.

He had never thought of himself as a sculptor and yet, in this moment, looking down between his hands at the body upon the polished hardwood floor, he realized that by some sculptural clenching and remodeling and twisting of human clay he had taken hold of this man named Donald Huxley and changed his physiognomy, the very frame of his body.

With a twist of his fingers he had wiped away the exacting glitter of Huxley's eyes; replaced it with a blind dullness of eye cold in socket. The lips, always pink and sensuous, were gaped to show the equine teeth, the yellow incisors, the nicotined canines, the gold-inlaid molars. The nose, pink also, was now mottled, pale, discolored, as were the ears. Huxley's hands, upon the floor, were open, pleading for the first time in their lives, instead of demanding.

Yes, it was an artistic conception. On the whole, the change had done Huxley a share of good. Death made him a handsomer man to deal with. You could talk to him now and he'd have to listen.

William Acton looked at his own fingers.

It was done. He could not change it back. Had anyone heard?

He listened. Outside, the normal late sounds of street traffic continued. There was no banging of the house door, no shoulder wrecking the portal into kindling, no voices demanding entrance. The murder, the sculpturing of clay from warmth to coldness was done, and nobody knew.

Now what? The clock ticked midnight. His every impulse exploded him in a hysteria toward the door. Rush, get away, run, never come back, board a train, hail a taxi, get, go, run, walk, saunter, but get the blazes out of here!

His hands hovered before his eyes, floating, turning.

He twisted them in slow deliberation; they felt airy and feather-light. Why was he staring at them this way? he inquired of himself. Was there something in them of immense interest that he should pause now, after a successful throttling, and examine them whorl by whorl?

They were ordinary hands. Not thick, not thin, not long, not short, not hairy, not naked, not manicured and yet not dirty, not soft and yet not callused, not wrinkled and yet not smooth; not murdering hands at all—and yet not innocent. He seemed to find them miracles to look upon.

It was not the hands as hands he was interested in, nor the fingers as fingers. In the numb timelessness after an accomplished violence he found interest only in the *tips* of his fingers.

The clock ticked upon the mantel.

He knelt by Huxley's body, took a handkerchief from Huxley's pocket, and began methodically to swab Huxley's throat with it. He brushed and massaged the throat and wiped the face and the back of the neck with fierce energy. Then he stood up.

He looked at the throat. He looked at the polished floor. He bent slowly and gave the floor a few dabs with the handkerchief, then he scowled and swabbed the floor; first, near the head of the corpse; secondly, near the arms. Then he polished the floor all around the body. He polished the floor one yard from the body on all sides. Then he polished the floor two yards from the body on all sides. The he polished the floor three yards from the body in all directions. Then he—

He stopped.

There was a moment when he saw the entire house, the mirrored halls, the carved doors, the splendid furniture; and, as clearly as if it were being repeated word for word, he heard Huxley talking and himself just the way they had talked only an hour ago.

Finger on Huxley's doorbell. Huxley's door opening.

"Oh!" Huxley shocked. "It's you, Acton."

"Where's my wife, Huxley?"

"Do you think I'd tell you, really? Don't stand out there, you idiot. If you want to talk business, come in. Through that door. There. Into the library."

Acton had *touched* the library door.

"Drink?"

"I need one. I can't believe Lily is gone, that she—"

"There's a bottle of burgundy, Acton. Mind fetching it from that cabinet?"

Yes, fetch it. *Handle* it. Touch it. He did.

"Some interesting first editions there, Acton. Feel this binding. *Feel* of it."

"I didn't come to see books, I—"

He had *touched* the books and the library table and *touched* the burgundy bottle and burgundy glasses.

Now, squatting on the floor beside Huxley's cold body with the polishing handkerchief in his fingers, motionless, he stared at the house, the walls, the furniture about him, his eyes widening, his mouth dropping, stunned by what he realized and what he saw. He shut his eyes, dropped his head, crushed the handkerchief between his hands, wadding it, biting his lips with his teeth, pulling in on himself.

The fingerprints were everywhere, *everywhere*!

"Mind getting the burgundy, Acton, eh? The burgundy bottle, eh? With your fingers, eh? I'm terribly tired. You understand?"

A pair of gloves.

Before he did one more thing, before he polished another area, he must have a pair of gloves, or he might unintentionally, after cleaning a surface, redistribute his identity.

He put his hands in his pockets. He walked through the house to the hall umbrella stand, the hatrack. Huxley's overcoat. He pulled out the overcoat pockets.

No gloves.

His hands in his pockets again, he walked upstairs, moving with a controlled swiftness, allowing himself nothing frantic, nothing wild. He had made the initial error of not wearing gloves (but, after all, he hadn't *planned* a murder, and his subconscious, which may have known of the crime before its commitment, had not even hinted he might need gloves before the night was finished), so now he had to sweat for his sin of omission. Somewhere in the house there must be at least one pair of gloves. He would have to hurry; there was every chance that someone might visit Huxley, even at this hour. Rich friends drinking themselves in and out the door, laughing, shouting, coming and going without so much as hello–goodbye. He would have until six in the morning, at the outside, when Huxley's friends were to pick Huxley up for the trip to the airport and Mexico City....

Acton hurried about upstairs opening drawers, using the handkerchief as blotter. He untidied seventy or eighty drawers in six rooms, left them with their tongues, so to speak, hanging out, ran on to new ones. He felt naked, unable to do anything until he found gloves. He might scour the entire house with the handkerchief, buffing every possible surface where fingerprints might lie, then accidentally bump a wall here or there, thus sealing his own fate with one microscopic, whorling symbol! It would be putting his stamp of approval on the murder, that's what it would be! Like those waxen seals in the old days when they rattled papyrus, flourished ink, dusted all with sand to dry the ink, and pressed their signet rings in hot crimson tallow at the bottom. So it would be if he left one, mind you, one fingerprint upon the scene! His approval of the murder did not extend as far as affixing said seal.

More drawers! Be quiet, be curious, be careful, he told himself.

At the bottom of the eighty-fifth drawer he found gloves.

"Oh, my Lord, my Lord!" He slumped against the bureau, sighing. He tried the gloves on, held them up, proudly flexed them, buttoned them. They were soft, gray, thick, impregnable. He could do all sorts of tricks with hands now and leave no trace. He thumbed his nose in the bedroom mirror, sucking his teeth.

"NO!" cried Huxley.

What a wicked plan it had been.

Huxley had fallen to the floor, *purposely*! Oh, what a wickedly clever man! Down onto the hardwood floor had dropped Huxley, with Acton after him. They had rolled and tussled and clawed at the floor, printing and printing it with their frantic fingertips! Huxley had slipped away a few feet, Acton crawling after to lay hands on his neck and squeeze until the life came out like paste from a tube!

Gloved, William Acton returned to the room and knelt down upon the floor and laboriously began the task of swabbing every wildly infested inch of it. Inch by inch, inch by inch, he polished and polished until he could almost see his intent, sweating face in it. Then he came to a table and polished the leg of it, on up its solid body and along the knobs and over the top. He came to a bowl of wax fruit, burnished the filigree silver, plucked out the wax fruit and wiped them clean, leaving the fruit at the bottom unpolished.

"I'm *sure* I didn't touch *them*," he said.

After rubbing the table he came to a picture frame hung over it.

"I'm certain I didn't touch *that*," he said.

He stood looking at it.

He glanced at all the doors in the room. Which doors had he used tonight? He couldn't remember. Polish all of them, then. He started on the doorknobs, shined them all up, and then he curried the doors from head to foot, taking no chances. Then he went to all the furniture in the room and wiped the chair arms.

"That chair you're sitting in, Acton, is an old Louis XIV piece. *Feel* that material," said Huxley.

"I didn't come to talk furniture, Huxley! I came about Lily."

"Oh, come off it, you're not that serious about her. She doesn't love you, you know. She's told me she'll go with me to Mexico City tomorrow."

"You and your money and your damned furniture!"

"It's nice furniture, Acton; be a good guest and feel of it."

Fingerprints can be found on fabric.

"Huxley!" William Acton stared at the body. "Did you guess I was going to kill you? Did your subconscious suspect, just as my subconscious suspected? And did your subconscious tell you to make me run about the house handling, touching, *fondling* books, dishes, doors, chairs? Were you *that* clever and *that* mean?"

He washed the chairs dryly with the clenched handkerchief. Then he remembered the body—he hadn't dry-washed it. He went to it and turned it now this way, now that, and burnished every surface of it. He even shined the shoes, charging nothing.

While shining the shoes his face took on a little tremor of worry, and after a moment he got up and walked over to that table.

He took out and polished the wax fruit at the bottom of the bowl.

"Better," he whispered, and went back to the body.

But as he crouched over the body his eyelids twitched and his jaw moved from side to side and he debated, then he got up and walked once more to the table.

He polished the picture frame.

While polishing the picture frame he discovered—

The wall.

"That," he said, "is *silly*."

"Oh!" cried Huxley, fending him off. He gave Acton a shove as they struggled. Acton fell, got up, *touching* the wall, and ran toward Huxley again. He strangled Huxley. Huxley died.

Acton turned steadfastly from the wall, with equilibrium and decision. The harsh words and the action faded in his mind; he hid them away. He glanced at the four walls.

"Ridiculous!" he said.

From the corners of his eyes he saw something on one wall.

"I refuse to pay attention," he said to distract himself. "The next room, now! I'll be methodical. Let's see—altogether we were in the hall, the library, *this* room, and the dining room and the kitchen."

There was a spot on the wall behind him.

Well, *wasn't* there?

He turned angrily. "All right, all right, just to be *sure*," and he went over and couldn't find any spot. Oh, a *little* one, yes, right—there. He dabbed it. It wasn't a fingerprint anyhow. He finished with it, and his gloved hand leaned against the wall and he looked at the wall and the way it went over to his right and over to his left and how it went down to his feet and up over his head and he said softly, "No." He looked up and down and over and across and he said quietly, "That would be too much." How many square feet? "I don't give a good damn," he said. But unknown to his eyes, his gloved fingers moved in a little rubbing rhythm on the wall.

He peered at his hand and the wallpaper. He looked over his shoulder at the other room. "I must go in there and polish the essentials," he told himself, but his hand remained, as if to hold the wall, or himself, up. His face hardened.

Without a word he began to scrub the wall, up and down, back and forth, up and down, as high as he could stretch and as low as he could bend.

"Ridiculous, oh my Lord, ridiculous!"

But you must be certain, his thought said to him.

"Yes, one *must* be certain," he replied.

He got one wall finished, and then...

He came to another wall.

"What time is it?"

He looked at the mantel clock. An hour gone. It was five after one.

The doorbell rang.

Acton froze, staring at the door, the clock, the door, the clock.

Someone rapped loudly.

A long moment passed. Acton did not breathe. Without new air in his body he began to fail away, to sway; his head roared a silence of cold waves thundering onto heavy rocks.

"Hey, in there!" cried a drunken voice. "I know you're in

there, Huxley! Open up, dammit! This is Billy-boy, drunk as an owl, Huxley, old pal, drunker than two owls."

"Go away," whispered Acton soundlessly, crushed.

"Huxley, you're in there, I hear you breathing!" cried the drunken voice.

"Yes, I'm in here," whispered Acton, feeling long and sprawled and clumsy on the floor, clumsy and cold and silent. "Yes."

"Hell!" said the voice, fading away into mist. The footsteps shuffled off. "Hell…"

Acton stood a long time feeling the red heart beat inside his shut eyes, within his head. When at last he opened his eyes he looked at the new fresh wall straight ahead of him and finally got courage to speak. "Silly," he said. "This wall's flawless. I won't touch it. Got to hurry. Got to hurry. Time, time. Only a few hours before those damn-fool friends blunder in!" He turned away.

From the corners of his eyes he saw the little webs. When his back was turned the little spiders came out of the woodwork and delicately spun their fragile little half-invisible webs. Not upon the wall at his left, which was already washed fresh, but upon the three walls as yet untouched. Each time he stared directly at them the spiders dropped back into the woodwork, only to spindle out as he retreated. "Those walls are all right," he insisted in a half shout. "I won't *touch* them!"

He went to a writing desk at which Huxley had been seated earlier. He opened a drawer and took out what he was looking for. A little magnifying glass Huxley sometimes used for reading. He took the magnifier and approached the wall uneasily.

Fingerprints.

"But those aren't mine!" He laughed unsteadily. "I *didn't* put them there! I'm sure I didn't! A servant, a butler, or a maid perhaps!"

The wall was full of them.

"Look at this one here," he said. "Long and tapered, a woman's, I'd bet money on it."

"Would you?"

"I would!"

"Are you certain?"

"Yes!"

"Positive?"

"Well—yes."

"Absolutely?"

"Yes, damn it, yes!"

"Wipe it out, anyway, why don't you?"

"There, by God!"

"Out damned spot, eh, Acton?"

"And this one, over here," scoffed Acton. "That's the print of a fat man."

"Are you sure?"

"Don't start that again!" he snapped, and rubbed it out. He pulled off a glove and held his hand up, trembling, in the glary light.

"Look at it, you idiot! See how the whorls go? See?"

"That proves nothing!"

"Oh, all right!" Raging, he swept the wall up and down, back and forth, with gloved hands, sweating, grunting, swearing, bending, rising, and getting redder of face.

He took off his coat, put it on a chair.

"Two o'clock," he said, finishing the wall, glaring at the clock.

He walked over to the bowl and took out the wax fruit and polished the ones at the bottom and put them back, and polished the picture frame.

He gazed up at the chandelier.

His fingers twitched at his sides.

His mouth slipped open and the tongue moved along his lips and he looked at the chandelier and looked away and looked back at the chandelier and looked at Huxley's body and then at the crystal chandelier with its long pearls of rainbow glass.

He got a chair and brought it over under the chandelier and put one foot up on it and took it down and threw the chair, violently, laughing, into a corner. Then he ran out of the room, leaving one wall as yet unwashed.

In the dining room he came to a table.

"I want to show you my Gregorian cutlery, Acton," Huxley had said. Oh, that casual, that *hypnotic* voice!

"I haven't time," Acton said. "I've got to see Lily—".

"Nonsense, look at this silver, this exquisite craftsmanship."

Acton paused over the table where the boxes of cutlery were laid out, hearing once more Huxley's voice, remembering all the touchings and gesturings.

Now Acton wiped the forks and spoons and took down all the plaques and special ceramic dishes from the wall itself....

"Here's a lovely bit of ceramics by Gertrude and Otto Natzler, Acton. Are you familiar with their work?"

"It *is* lovely."

"Pick it up. Turn it over. See the fine thinness of the bowl, hand-thrown on a turntable, thin as eggshell, incredible. And the amazing volcanic glaze. Handle it, go ahead. I don't mind."

HANDLE IT. GO AHEAD. PICK IT UP!

Acton sobbed unevenly. He hurled the pottery against the wall. It shattered and spread, flaking wildly, upon the floor.

An instant later he was on his knees. Every piece, every shard of it, must be found. Fool, fool, fool! he cried to himself, shaking his head and shutting and opening his eyes and bending under the table. Find every piece, idiot, not one fragment of it must be left behind. Fool, fool! He gathered them. Are they all here? He looked at them on the table before him. He looked under the table again and under the chairs and the service bureaus, and found one more piece by match light and started to polish each little fragment as if it were a precious stone. He laid them all out neatly upon the shining polished table.

"A lovely bit of ceramics, Acton. Go ahead—*handle* it."

He took out the linen and wiped it and wiped the chairs and tables and doorknobs and windowpanes and ledges and drapes and wiped the floor and found the kitchen, panting, breathing violently, and took off his vest and adjusted his gloves and wiped the glittering chromium…."I want to show you my house, Acton," said Huxley. "Come along…." And he wiped all the utensils and the silver faucets and the mixing bowls, for now he had forgotten what he had touched and what he had not. Huxley and he had lingered here, in the kitchen, Huxley prideful of its array, covering his nervousness at the presence of a potential killer, perhaps wanting to be near the knives if they were needed. They had idled, touched this, that, something else—there was no remembering what or how much or how many—and he finished the kitchen and came through the hall into the room where Huxley lay.

He cried out.

He had forgotten to wash the fourth wall of the room! And while he was gone the little spiders had popped from the fourth, unwashed wall and swarmed over the already clean walls, dirtying them again! On the ceilings, from the chandelier, in the corners, on the floor, a million little whorled webs hung billowing at his scream! Tiny, tiny little webs, no bigger than, ironically, your—finger!

As he watched, the webs were woven over the picture frame, the fruit bowl, the body, the floor. Prints wielded the paper knife, pulled out drawers, touched the tabletop, touched, touched, touched everything everywhere.

He polished the floor wildly, wildly. He rolled the body over and cried on it while he washed it, and got up and walked over and polished the fruit at the bottom of the bowl. Then he put a chair under the chandelier and got up and polished each little hanging fire of it, shaking it like a crystal tambourine until it tilted bellwise in the air. Then he leaped off the chair and gripped the doorknobs and got up on other chairs and swabbed the walls higher and higher and ran to the kitchen and got a broom and wiped the webs down from the ceiling and polished the bottom fruit of the bowl and washed the body and door-knobs and silverware and found the hall banister and followed the banister upstairs.

Three o'clock! Everywhere, with a fierce, mechanical inten-sity, clocks ticked! There were twelve rooms downstairs and eight above. He figured the yards and yards of space and time needed. One hundred chairs, six sofas, twenty-seven tables, six radios. And under and on top and behind. He yanked fur-niture out away from walls and, sobbing, wiped them clean of years-old dust, and staggered and followed the banister up, up the stairs, handling, erasing, rubbing, polishing, because if he left one little print it would reproduce and make a million more!—and the job would have to be done all over again and now it was four o'clock!—and his arms ached and his eyes were swollen and staring and he moved sluggishly about, on strange legs, his head down, his arms moving, swabbing and rubbing, bedroom by bedroom, closet by closet....

They found him at six-thirty that morning.

In the attic.

The entire house was polished to a brilliance. Vases shone like glass stars. Chairs were burnished. Bronzes, brasses, and cop-pers were all aglint. Floors sparkled. Banisters gleamed.

Everything glittered. Everything shone, everything was bright! They found him in the attic, polishing the old trunks and the old frames and the old chairs and the old carriages and toys and music boxes and vases and cutlery and rocking horses and dusty Civil War coins. He was half through the attic when the police officer walked up behind him with a gun.

"Done!"

On the way out of the house Acton polished the front door-knob with his handkerchief and slammed it in triumph!

The Small Assassin

Just when the idea occurred to her that she was being murdered she could not tell. There had been little subtle signs, little suspicions for the past month; things as deep as sea tides in her, like looking at a perfectly calm stretch of tropic water, wanting to bathe in it and finding, just as the tide takes your body, that monsters dwell just under the surface, things unseen, bloated, many-armed, sharp-finned, malignant and inescapable.

A room floated around her in an effluvium of hysteria. Sharp instruments hovered and there were voices, and people in sterile white masks.

My name, she thought, what is it?

Alice Leiber. It came to her. David Leiber's wife. But it gave her no comfort. She was alone with these silent, whispering white people and there was great pain and nausea and death-fear in her.

I am being murdered before their eyes. These doctors, these nurses don't realize what hidden thing has happened to me. David doesn't know. Nobody knows except me and—the killer, the little murderer, the small assassin.

I am dying and I can't tell them now. They'd laugh and call me one in delirium. They'll see the murderer and hold him and never think him responsible for my death. But here I am, in front of God and man, dying, no one to believe my story, everyone to doubt me, comfort me with lies, bury me in ignorance, mourn me and salvage my destroyer.

Where is David? she wondered. In the waiting room, smoking

one cigarette after another, listening to the long tickings of the very slow clock?

Sweat exploded from all of her body at once, and with it an agonized cry. Now. Now! Try and kill me, she screamed. Try, try, but I won't die! I won't!

There was a hollowness. A vacuum. Suddenly the pain fell away. Exhaustion, and dusk came around. It was over. Oh, God! She plummeted down and struck a black nothingness which gave way to nothingness and nothingness and another and still another....

Footsteps. Gentle, approaching footsteps.

Far away, a voice said, "She's asleep. Don't disturb her."

An odor of tweeds, a pipe, a certain shaving lotion. David was standing over her. And beyond him the immaculate smell of Dr. Jeffers.

She did not open her eyes. "I'm awake," she said, quietly. It was a surprise, a relief to be able to speak, to not be dead.

"Alice," someone said, and it was David beyond her closed eyes, holding her tired hands.

Would you like to meet the murderer, David? she thought. I hear your voice asking to see him, so there's nothing but for me to point him out to you.

David stood over her. She opened her eyes. The room came into focus. Moving a weak hand, she pulled aside a coverlet.

The murderer looked up at David Leiber with a small, red-faced, blue-eyed calm. Its eyes were deep and sparkling.

"Why!" cried David Leiber, smiling. "He's a *fine* baby!"

Dr. Jeffers was waiting for David Leiber the day he came to take his wife and new child home. He motioned Leiber to a chair in his office, gave him a cigar, lit one for himself, sat on the edge of his desk, puffing solemnly for a long moment. Then he cleared his throat, looked David Leiber straight on and said, "Your wife doesn't like her child, Dave."

"What!"

"It's been a hard thing for her. She'll need a lot of love this next year. I didn't say much at the time, but she was hysterical in the delivery room. The strange things she said—I won't repeat them. All I'll say is that she feels alien to the child. Now, this may simply be a thing we can clear up with one or two questions." He sucked on his cigar another moment, then said, "Is this child a 'wanted' child, Dave?"

"Why do you ask?"

"It's vital."

"Yes. Yes, it is a 'wanted' child. We planned it together. Alice was so happy, a year ago, when—"

"Mmmm—that makes it more difficult. Because if the child was unplanned, it would be a simple case of a woman hating the idea of motherhood. That doesn't fit Alice." Dr. Jeffers took his cigar from his lips, rubbed his hand across his jaw. "It must be something else, then. Perhaps something buried in her childhood that's coming out now. Or it might be the simple temporary doubt and distrust of any mother who's gone through the unusual pain and near-death that Alice has. If so, then a little time should heal that. I thought I'd tell you, though, Dave. It'll help you be easy and tolerant with her if she says anything about—well—about wishing the child had been born dead. And if things don't go well, the three of you drop in on me. I'm always glad to see old friends, eh? Here, take another cigar along for—ah—for the baby."

It was a bright spring afternoon. Their car hummed along wide, tree-lined boulevards. Blue sky, flowers, a warm wind. David talked a lot, lit his cigar, talked some more. Alice answered directly, softly, relaxing a bit more as the trip progressed. But she held the baby not tightly or warmly or motherly enough to satisfy the queer ache in Dave's mind. She seemed to be merely carrying a porcelain figurine.

"Well," he said, at last, smiling. "What'll we name him?"

Alice Leiber watched green trees slide by. "Let's not decide yet. I'd rather wait until we get an exceptional name for him. Don't blow smoke in his face." Her sentences ran together with no change of tone. The last statement held no motherly reproof, no interest, no irritation. She just mouthed it and it was said.

The husband, disquieted, dropped the cigar from the window. "Sorry," he said.

The baby rested in the crook of his mother's arm, shadows of sun and tree changing his face. His blue eyes opened like fresh blue spring flowers. Moist noises came from the tiny, pink, elastic mouth.

Alice gave her baby a quick glance. Her husband felt her shiver against him.

"Cold?" he asked.

"A chill. Better raise the window, David."

It was more than a chill. He rolled the window slowly up.

Suppertime.

Dave had brought the child from the nursery, propped him at a tiny, bewildered angle, supported by many pillows, in a newly purchased high chair.

Alice watched her knife and fork move. "He's not high-chair size," she said.

"Fun having him here, anyway," said Dave, feeling fine. "Everything's fun. At the office, too. Orders up to my nose. If I don't watch myself I'll make another fifteen thousand this year. Hey, look at Junior, will you? Drooling all down his chin!" He reached over to wipe the baby's mouth with his napkin. From the corner of his eye he realized that Alice wasn't even watching. He finished the job.

"I guess it wasn't very interesting," he said, back again at his food. "But one would think a mother'd take some interest in her own child!"

Alice jerked her chin up. "Don't speak that way! Not in front of him! Later, if you must."

"Later?" he cried. "In front of, in back of, what's the difference?" He quieted suddenly, swallowed, was sorry. "All right. Okay. I know how it is."

After dinner she let him carry the baby upstairs. She didn't tell him to; she *let* him.

Coming down, he found her standing by the radio, listening to music she didn't hear. Her eyes were closed, her whole attitude one of wondering, self-questioning. She started when he appeared.

Suddenly, she was at him, against him, soft, quick; the same. Her lips found him, kept him. He was stunned. Now that the baby was gone, upstairs, out of the room, she began to breathe again, live again. She was free. She was whispering, rapidly, endlessly.

"Thank you, thank you, darling. For being yourself, always. Dependable, so very dependable!"

He had to laugh. "My father told me, 'Son, provide for your family!' "

Wearily, she rested her dark, shining hair against his neck. "You've overdone it. Sometimes I wish we were just the way we were when we were first married. No responsibilities, nothing but ourselves. No—no babies."

She crushed his hand in hers, a supernatural whiteness in her face.

"Oh, Dave, once it was just you and me. We protected each

other, and now we protect the baby, but get no protection from it. Do you understand? Lying in the hospital I had time to think a lot of things. The world is evil—"

"Is it?"

"Yes. It is. But laws protect us from it. And when there aren't laws, then love does the protecting. You're protected from my hurting you, by my love. You're vulnerable to me, of all people, but love shields you. I feel no fear of you, because love cushions all your irritations, unnatural instincts, hatreds and immaturities. But—what about the baby? It's too young to know love, or a law of love, or anything, until we teach it. And in the meantime be vulnerable to it."

"Vulnerable to a baby?" He held her away and laughed gently.

"Does a baby know the difference between right and wrong?" she asked.

"No. But it'll learn."

"But a baby is so new, so amoral, so conscience-free." She stopped. Her arms dropped from him and she turned swiftly. "That noise? What was it?"

Leiber looked around the room. "I didn't hear—"

She stared at the library door. "In there," she said, slowly. Leiber crossed the room, opened the door and switched the library lights on and off. "Not a thing." He came back to her. "You're worn out. To bed with you—right now."

Turning out the lights together, they walked slowly up the soundless hall stairs, not speaking. At the top she apologized. "My wild talk, darling. Forgive me. I'm exhausted."

He understood, and said so.

She paused, undecided, by the nursery door. Then she fingered the brass knob sharply, walked in. He watched her approach the crib much too carefully, look down, and stiffen as if she'd been struck in the face. "David!"

Leiber stepped forward, reached the crib.

The baby's face was bright red and very moist; his small pink mouth opened and shut, opened and shut; his eyes were a fiery blue. His hands leapt about on the air.

"Oh," said Dave, "he's just been crying."

"Has he?" Alice Leiber seized the crib-railing to balance herself. "I didn't hear him."

"The door was closed."

"Is that why he breathes so hard, why his face is red?"

"Sure. Poor little guy. Crying all alone in the dark. He can sleep in our room tonight, just in case he cries."

"You'll spoil him," his wife said.

Leiber felt her eyes follow as he rolled the crib into their bedroom. He undressed silently, sat on the edge of the bed. Suddenly he lifted his head, swore under his breath, snapped his fingers. "Damn it! Forgot to tell you. I must fly to Chicago Friday."

"Oh, David." Her voice was lost in the room.

"I've put this trip off for two months, and now it's so critical I just *have* to go."

"I'm afraid to be alone."

"We'll have the new cook by Friday. She'll be here all the time. I'll only be gone a few days."

"I'm afraid. I don't know of what. You wouldn't believe me if I told you. I guess I'm crazy."

He was in bed now. She darkened the room; he heard her walk around the bed, throw back the cover, slide in. He smelled the warm woman-smell of her next to him. He said, "If you want me to wait a few days, perhaps I could—"

"No," she said, unconvinced. "You go. I know it's important. It's just that I keep thinking about what I told you. Laws and love and protection. Love protects you from me. But, the baby—" She took a breath. "What protects you from him, David?"

Before he could answer, before he could tell her how silly it was, speaking so of infants, she switched on the bed light, abruptly.

"Look," she said, pointing.

The baby lay wide awake in its crib, staring straight at him, with deep, sharp blue eyes.

The lights went out again. She trembled against him.

"It's not nice being afraid of the thing you birthed." Her whisper lowered, became harsh, fierce, swift. "He tried to kill me! He lies there, listens to us talking, waiting for you to go away so he can try to kill me again! I swear it!" Sobs broke from her.

"Please," he kept saying, soothing her. "Stop it, stop it. Please."

She cried in the dark for a long time. Very late she relaxed, shakingly, against him. Her breathing came soft, warm, regular, her body twitched its worn reflexes and she slept.

He drowsed.

And just before his eyes lidded wearily down, sinking him into deeper and yet deeper tides, he heard a strange little sound of awareness and awakeness in the room.

The sound of small, moist, pinkly elastic lips.

The baby.

And then—sleep.

In the morning, the sun blazed. Alice smiled.

David Leiber dangled his watch over the crib. "See, baby? Something bright. Something pretty. Sure. Sure. Something bright. Something pretty."

Alice smiled. She told him to go ahead, fly to Chicago, she'd be very brave, no need to worry. She'd take care of baby. Oh, yes, she'd take care of him, all right.

The airplane went east. There was a lot of sky, a lot of sun and clouds and Chicago running over the horizon. Dave was dropped into the rush of ordering, planning, banqueting, telephoning, arguing in conference. But he wrote letters each day and sent telegrams to Alice and the baby.

On the evening of his sixth day away from home he received the long-distance phone call. Los Angeles.

"Alice?"

"No, Dave. This is Jeffers speaking."

"Doctor!"

"Hold on to yourself, son. Alice is sick. You'd better get the next plane home. It's pneumonia. I'll do everything I can, boy. If only it wasn't so soon after the baby. She needs strength."

Leiber dropped the phone into its cradle. He got up, with no feet under him, and no hands and no body. The hotel room blurred and fell apart.

"Alice," he said, blindly, starting for the door.

The propellers spun about, whirled, fluttered, stopped; time and space were put behind. Under his hand, David felt the doorknob turn; under his feet the floor assumed reality, around him flowed the walls of a bedroom, and in the late-afternoon sunlight Dr. Jeffers stood, turning from a window, as Alice lay waiting in her bed, something carved from a fall of winter snow. Then Dr. Jeffers was talking, talking continuously, gently, the sound rising and falling through the lamplight, a soft flutter, a white murmur of voice.

"Your wife's too good a mother, Dave. She worried more about the baby than herself...."

Somewhere in the paleness of Alice's face, there was a sudden constriction which smoothed itself out before it was realized. Then, slowly, half-smiling, she began to talk and she talked as a mother should about this, that, and the other thing, the telling detail, the minute-by-minute and hour-by-hour report of a mother concerned with a dollhouse world and the miniature life of that world. But she could not stop; the spring was wound tight, and her voice rushed on to anger, fear and the faintest touch of revulsion, which did not change Dr. Jeffers' expression, but caused Dave's heart to match the rhythm of this talk that quickened and could not stop:

"The baby wouldn't sleep. I thought he was sick. He just lay, staring, in his crib, and late at night he'd cry. So loud, he'd cry, and he'd cry all night and all night. I couldn't quiet him, and I couldn't rest."

Dr. Jeffers' head nodded slowly, slowly. "Tired herself right into pneumonia. But she's full of sulfa now and on the safe side of the whole damn thing."

Dave felt ill. "The baby, what about the baby?"

"Fit as a fiddle; cock of the walk!"

"Thanks, Doctor."

The doctor walked off away and down the stairs, opened the front door faintly, and was gone.

"David!"

He turned to her frightened whisper.

"It was the baby again." She clutched his hand. "I try to lie to myself and say that I'm a fool, but the baby knew I was weak from the hospital, so he cried all night every night, and when he wasn't crying he'd be much too quiet. I knew if I switched on the light he'd be there, staring up at me."

David felt his body close in on itself like a fist. He remembered seeing the baby, feeling the baby, awake in the dark, awake very late at night when babies should be asleep. Awake and lying there, silent as thought, not crying, but watching from its crib. He thrust the thought aside. It was insane.

Alice went on. "I was going to kill the baby. Yes, I was. When you'd been gone only a day on your trip I went to his room and put my hands about his neck; and I stood there, for a long time, thinking, afraid. Then I put the covers up over his face and turned him over on his face and pressed him down and left him that way and ran out of the room."

He tried to stop her.

"No, let me finish," she said, hoarsely, looking at the wall. "When I left his room I thought, It's simple. Babies smother every day. No one'll ever know. But when I came back to see him dead, David, he was alive! Yes, alive, turned over on his back, alive and smiling and breathing. And I couldn't touch him again after that. I left him there and I didn't come back, not to feed him or look at him or do anything. Perhaps the cook tended to him. I don't know. All I know is that his crying kept me awake, and I thought all through the night, and walked around the rooms and now I'm sick." She was almost finished now. "The baby lies there and thinks of ways to kill me. Simple ways. Because he knows I know so much about him. I have no love for him; there is no protection between us; there never will be."

She was through. She collapsed inward on herself and finally slept. David Leiber stood for a long time over her, not able to move. His blood was frozen in his body, not a cell stirred anywhere, anywhere at all.

The next morning there was only one thing to do. He did it. He walked into Dr. Jeffers' office and told him the whole thing, and listened to Jeffers' tolerant replies:

"Let's take this thing slowly, son. It's quite natural for mothers

to hate their children, sometimes. We have a label for it—
ambivalence. The ability to hate, while loving. Lovers hate each
other, frequently. Children detest their mothers—"

Leiber interrupted. "I never hated my mother."

"You won't admit it, naturally. People don't enjoy admitting
hatred for their loved ones."

"So Alice hates her baby."

"Better say she has an obsession. She's gone a step further
than plain, ordinary ambivalence. A Caesarean operation brought
the child into the world and almost took Alice out of it. She
blames the child for her near-death and her pneumonia. She's
projecting her troubles, blaming them on the handiest object
she can use as a source of blame. We *all* do it. We stumble into a
chair and curse the furniture, not our own clumsiness. We miss a
golf-stroke and damn the turf or our club, or the make of ball. If
our business fails we blame the gods, the weather, our luck. All I
can tell you is what I told you before. Love her. Finest medicine
in the world. Find little ways of showing your affection, give her
security. Find ways of showing her how harmless and innocent
the child is. Make her feel that the baby was worth the risk. After
a while, she'll settle down, forget about death, and begin to love
the child. If she doesn't come around in the next month or so,
ask me. I'll recommend a good psychiatrist. Go on along now,
and take that look off your face."

When summer came, things seemed to settle, become easier.
Dave worked, immersed himself in office detail, but found
much time for his wife. She, in turn, took long walks, gained
strength, played an occasional light game of badminton. She
rarely burst out any more. She seemed to have rid herself of
her fears.

Except on one certain midnight when a sudden summer

wind swept around the house, warm and swift, shaking the trees like so many shining tambourines. Alice wakened, trembling, and slid over into her husband's arms, and let him console her, and ask her what was wrong.

She said, "Something's here in the room, watching us."

He switched on the light. "Dreaming again," he said. "You're better, though. Haven't been troubled for a long time."

She sighed as he clicked off the light again, and suddenly she slept. He held her, considering what a sweet, weird creature she was, for about half an hour.

He heard the bedroom door sway open a few inches.

There was nobody at the door. No reason for it to come open. The wind had died.

He waited. It seemed like an hour he lay silently, in the dark.

Then, far away, wailing like some small meteor dying in the vast inky gulf of space, the baby began to cry in his nursery.

It was a small, lonely sound in the middle of the stars and the dark and the breathing of this woman in his arms and the wind beginning to sweep through the trees again.

Leiber counted to one hundred, slowly. The crying continued.

Carefully disengaging Alice's arm he slipped from bed, put on his slippers, robe, and moved quietly from the room.

He'd go downstairs, he thought, fix some warm milk, bring it up, and—

The blackness dropped out from under him. His foot slipped and plunged. Slipped on something soft. Plunged into nothingness.

He thrust his hands out, caught frantically at the railing. His body stopped falling. He held. He cursed.

The "something soft" that caused his feet to slip rustled and thumped down a few steps. His head rang. His heart hammered at the base of his throat, thick and shot with pain.

Why do careless people leave things strewn about a house? He groped carefully with his fingers for the object that had almost spilled him headlong down the stairs.

His hand froze, startled. His breath went in. His heart held one or two beats.

The thing he held in his hand was a toy. A large cumbersome, patchwork doll he had bought as a joke, for—

For the baby.

Alice drove him to work the next day.

She slowed the car halfway downtown, pulled to the curb and stopped it. Then she turned on the seat and looked at her husband.

"I want to go away on a vacation. I don't know if you can make it now, darling, but if not, please let me go alone. We can get someone to take care of the baby, I'm sure. But I just have to get away. I thought I was growing out of this—this *feeling.* But I haven't. I can't stand being in the room with him. He looks up at me as if he hates me, too. I can't put my finger on it; all I know is I want to get away before something happens."

He got out on his side of the car, came around, motioned to her to move over, got in. "The only thing you're going to do is see a good psychiatrist. And if he suggests a vacation, well, okay. But this can't go on; my stomach's in knots all the time." He started the car. "I'll drive the rest of the way."

Her head was down; she was trying to keep back tears. She looked up when they reached his office building. "All right. Make the appointment. I'll go talk to anyone you want, David."

He kissed her. "Now, you're talking sense, lady. Think you can drive home okay?"

"Of course, silly."

"See you at supper, then. Drive carefully."

"Don't I always? 'Bye."

He stood on the curb, watching her drive off, the wind taking hold of her long, dark, shining hair. Upstairs, a minute later, he phoned Jeffers and arranged an appointment with a reliable neuro-psychiatrist.

The day's work went uneasily. Things fogged over; and in the fog he kept seeing Alice lost and calling his name. So much of her fear had come over to him. She actually had him convinced that the child was in some ways not quite natural.

He dictated long, uninspired letters. He checked some shipments downstairs. Assistants had to be questioned, and kept going. At the end of the day he was exhausted, his head throbbed, and he was very glad to go home.

On the way down in the elevator he wondered, What if I told Alice about the toy—that patchwork doll—I slipped on on the stairs last night? Lord, wouldn't *that* back her off? No, I won't ever tell her. Accidents are, after all, accidents.

Daylight lingered in the sky as he drove home in a taxi. In front of the house he paid the driver and walked slowly up the cement walk, enjoying the light that was still in the sky and the trees. The white colonial front of the house looked unnaturally silent and uninhabited, and then, quietly, he remembered this was Thursday, and the hired help they were able to obtain from time to time were all gone for the day.

He took a deep breath of air. A bird sang behind the house. Traffic moved on the boulevard a block away. He twisted the key in the door. The knob turned under his fingers, oiled, silent.

The door opened. He stepped in, put his hat on the chair with his briefcase, started to shrug out of his coat, when he looked up.

Late sunlight streamed down the stairwell from the window near the top of the hall. Where the sunlight touched it took on the bright color of the patchwork doll sprawled at the bottom of the stairs.

But he paid no attention to the toy.

He could only look, and not move, and look again at Alice.

Alice lay in a broken, grotesque, pallid gesturing and angling of her thin body, at the bottom of the stairs, like a crumpled doll that doesn't want to play any more, ever.

Alice was dead.

The house remained quiet, except for the sound of his heart.

She was dead.

He held her head in his hands, he felt her fingers. He held her body. But she wouldn't live. She wouldn't even try to live. He said her name, out loud, many times, and he tried, once again, by holding her to him, to give her back some of the warmth she had lost, but that didn't help.

He stood up. He must have made a phone call. He didn't remember. He found himself, suddenly, upstairs. He opened the nursery door and walked inside and stared blankly at the crib. His stomach was sick. He couldn't see very well.

The baby's eyes were closed, but his face was red, moist with perspiration, as if he'd been crying long and hard.

"She's dead," said Leiber to the baby. "She's dead."

Then he started laughing low and soft and continuously for a long time until Dr. Jeffers walked in out of the night and slapped him again and again across the face.

"Snap out of it! Pull yourself together!"

"She fell down the stairs, Doctor. She tripped on a patch-work doll and fell. I almost slipped on it the other night, myself. And now—"

The doctor shook him.

"Doc, Doc, Doc," said Dave, hazily. "Funny thing. Funny. I—I finally thought of a name for the baby."

The doctor said nothing.

Leiber put his head back in his trembling hands and spoke the words. "I'm going to have him christened, next Sunday. Know what name I'm giving him? I'm going to call him Lucifer."

It was eleven at night. A lot of strange people had come and gone through the house, taking the essential flame with them— Alice. David Leiber sat across from the doctor in the library.

"Alice wasn't crazy," he said, slowly. "She had good reason to fear the baby."

Jeffers exhaled. "Don't follow after her! She blamed the child for her sickness, now you blame it for her death. She stumbled on a toy, remember that. You can't blame the child."

"You mean Lucifer?"

"Stop calling him that!"

Leiber shook his head. "Alice heard things at night, moving in the halls. You want to know what made those noises, Doctor? They were made by the baby. Four months old, moving in the dark, listening to us talk. Listening to every word!" He held to the sides of the chair. "And if I turned the lights on, a baby is so small. It can hide behind furniture, a door, against a wall— below eye-level."

"I want you to stop this!" said Jeffers.

"Let me say what I think or I'll go crazy. When I went to Chicago, who was it kept Alice awake, tiring her into pneumonia? The baby! And when Alice didn't die, then he tried killing me. It was simple; leave a toy on the stairs, cry in the night until your father goes downstairs to fetch your milk, and stumbles. A crude trick, but effective. It didn't get me. But it killed Alice dead." David Leiber stopped long enough to light a cigarette. "I should have caught on. I'd turn on the lights in the middle of the night, many nights, and the baby'd be lying there, eyes wide. Most babies sleep all the time. Not this one. He stayed awake, thinking."

"Babies don't think."

"He stayed awake doing whatever he *could* do with his brain, then. What in hell do we know about a baby's mind? He had every reason to hate Alice; she suspected him for what he was —certainly not a normal child. Something—different. What do you know of babies, Doctor? The general run, yes. You know, of course, how babies kill their mothers at birth. Why? Could it be resentment at being forced into a lousy world like this one?"

Leiber leaned toward the doctor, tiredly. "It all ties up. Suppose that a few babies out of all the millions born are instantaneously able to move, see, hear, think, like many animals and insects can. Insects are born self-sufficient. In a few weeks most mammals and birds adjust. But children take years to speak and learn to stumble around on their weak legs.

"But suppose one child in a billion is—strange? Born perfectly aware, able to think, instinctively. Wouldn't it be a perfect setup, a perfect blind for anything the baby might want to do? He could pretend to be ordinary, weak, crying, ignorant. With just a *little* expenditure of energy he could crawl about a darkened house, listening. And how easy to place obstacles at the top of stairs. How easy to cry all night and tire a mother into pneumonia. How easy, right at birth, to be so close to the mother that *a few deft maneuvers might cause peritonitis!*"

"For God's sake!" Jeffers was on his feet. "That's a repulsive thing to say!"

"It's a repulsive thing I'm speaking of. How many mothers have died at the birth of their children? How many have suckled strange little improbabilities who cause death one way or another? Strange, red little creatures with brains that work in a bloody darkness we can't even guess at. Elemental little brains, warm with racial memory, hatred, and raw cruelty, with no more thought than self-preservation. And self-preservation in this case consisted of eliminating a mother who realized what a horror she had birthed. I ask you, Doctor, what is there in the world more selfish than a baby? Nothing!"

Jeffers scowled and shook his head, helplessly.

Leiber dropped his cigarette down. "I'm not claiming any great strength for the child. Just enough to crawl around a little, a few months ahead of schedule. Just enough to listen all the time. Just enough to cry late at night. That's enough, more than enough."

Jeffers tried ridicule. "Call it murder, then. But murder must be motivated. What motive had the child?"

Leiber was ready with the answer. "What is more at peace, more dreamfully content, at ease, at rest, fed, comforted, unbothered, than an unborn child? Nothing. It floats in a sleepy, timeless wonder of nourishment and silence. Then, suddenly, it is asked to give up its berth, is forced to vacate, rushed out into a noisy, uncaring, selfish world where it is asked to shift for itself, to hunt, to feed from the hunting, to seek after a vanishing love that once was its unquestionable right, to meet confusion instead of inner silence and conservative slumber! And the child resents it! Resents the cold air, the huge spaces, the sudden departure from familiar things. And in the tiny filament of brain the only thing the child knows is selfishness and hatred because the spell has been rudely shattered. Who is responsible for this disenchantment, this rude breaking of the spell? The mother. So here the new child has someone to hate with all its unreasoning mind. The mother has cast it out, rejected it. And the father is no better, kill him, too! He's responsible in *his* way!"

Jeffers interrupted. "If what you say is true, then every woman in the world would have to look on her baby as something to dread, something to wonder about."

"And why not? Hasn't the child a perfect alibi? A thousand years of accepted medical belief protects him. By all natural accounts he is helpless, not responsible. The child is born hating. And things grow worse, instead of better. At first the baby gets a certain amount of attention and mothering. But then as time passes, things change. When very new, a baby has the power to make parents do silly things when it cries or sneezes, jump when it makes a noise. As the years pass, the baby feels even that small power slip rapidly, forever away, never to return. Why shouldn't it grasp all the power it can have? Why shouldn't it jockey for position while it has all the advantages? In later years it would be too late to express its hatred. *Now* would be the time to strike."

Leiber's voice was very soft, very low.

"My little boy baby, lying in his crib nights, his face moist and red and out of breath. From crying? No. From climbing slowly out of his crib, from crawling long distances through darkened hallways. My little boy baby. I want to kill him."

The doctor handed him a water glass and some pills. "You're not killing anyone. You're going to sleep for twenty-four hours. Sleep'll change your mind. Take this."

Leiber drank down the pills and let himself be led upstairs to his bedroom, crying, and felt himself being put to bed. The doctor waited until he was moving deep into sleep, then left the house.

Leiber, alone, drifted down, down.

He heard a noise. "What's—what's *that*?" he demanded, feebly.

Something moved in the hall.

David Leiber slept.

○

Very early the next morning, Dr. Jeffers drove up to the house. It was a good morning, and he was here to drive Leiber to the country for a rest. Leiber would still be asleep upstairs. Jeffers had given him enough sedative to knock him out for at least fifteen hours.

He rang the doorbell. No answer. The servants were probably not up. Jeffers tried the front door, found it open, stepped in. He put his medical kit on the nearest chair.

Something white moved out of sight at the top of the stairs. Just a suggestion of a movement. Jeffers hardly noticed it.

The smell of gas was in the house.

Jeffers ran upstairs, crashed into Leiber's bedroom.

Leiber lay motionless on the bed, and the room billowed with gas, which hissed from a released jet at the base of the wall near the door. Jeffers twisted it off, then forced up all the windows and ran back to Leiber's body.

The body was cold. It had been dead quite a few hours.

Coughing violently, the doctor hurried from the room, eyes watering. Leiber hadn't turned on the gas himself. He *couldn't* have. Those sedatives had knocked him out, he wouldn't have wakened until noon. It wasn't suicide. Or was there the faintest possibility?

Jeffers stood in the hall for five minutes. Then he walked to the door of the nursery. It was shut. He opened it. He walked inside and to the crib.

The crib was empty.

He stood swaying by the crib for half a minute, then he said something to nobody in particular.

"The nursery door blew shut. You couldn't get back into your crib where it was safe. You didn't plan on the door blowing shut. A little thing like a slammed door can ruin the best of plans. I'll find you somewhere in the house, hiding, pretending to be something you are not." The doctor looked dazed. He put his hand to his head and smiled palely. "Now I'm talking like Alice and David talked. But, I can't take any chances. I'm not sure of anything, but I can't take chances."

He walked downstairs, opened his medical bag on the chair, took something out of it and held it in his hands.

Something rustled down the hall. Something very small and very quiet. Jeffers turned rapidly.

I had to operate to bring you into this world, he thought. Now I guess I can operate to take you out of it....

He took half a dozen slow, sure steps forward into the hall. He raised his hand into the sunlight.

"See, baby! Something bright—something pretty!"

A scalpel.

Marionettes, Inc.

They walked slowly down the street at about ten in the evening, talking calmly. They were both about thirty-five, both eminently sober.

"But why so early?" said Smith.

"Because," said Braling.

"Your first night out in years and you go home at ten o'clock."

"Nerves, I suppose."

"What I wonder *is* how you ever managed it. I've been trying to get you out for ten years for a quiet drink. And now, on the one night, you insist on turning in early."

"Mustn't crowd my luck," said Braling.

"What did you do, put sleeping powder in your wife's coffee?"

"No, that would be unethical. You'll see soon enough."

They turned a corner. "Honestly, Braling, I hate to say this, but you *have* been patient with her. You may not admit it to me, but marriage has been awful for you, hasn't it?"

"I wouldn't say that."

"It's got around, anyway, here and there, how she got you to marry her. That time back in 1979 when you were going to Rio—"

"Dear Rio. I never *did* see it after all my plans."

"And how she tore her clothes and rumpled her hair and threatened to call the police unless you married her."

"She always was nervous, Smith, understand."

"It was more than unfair. You didn't love her. You told her as much, didn't you?"

"I recall that I was quite firm on the subject."

"But you married her anyhow."

"I had my business to think of, as well as my mother and father. A thing like that would have killed them."

"And it's been ten years."

"Yes," said Braling, his gray eyes steady. "But I think perhaps it might change now. I think what I've waited for has come about. Look here."

He drew forth a long blue ticket.

"Why, it's a ticket for Rio on the Thursday rocket!"

"Yes, I'm finally going to make it."

"But how wonderful! You *do* deserve it! But won't *she* object? Cause trouble?"

Braling smiled nervously. "She won't know I'm gone. I'll be back in a month and no one the wiser, except you."

Smith sighed. "I wish I were going with you."

"Poor Smith, *your* marriage hasn't exactly been roses, has it?"

"Not exactly, married to a woman who overdoes it. I mean, after all, when you've been married ten years, you don't expect a woman to sit on your lap for two hours every evening, call you at work twelve times a day and talk baby talk. And it seems to me that in the last month she's gotten worse. I wonder if perhaps she isn't a little simple-minded?"

"Ah, Smith, always the conservative. Well, here's my house. Now, would you like to know my secret? How I made it out this evening?"

"Will you really tell?"

"Look up, there!" said Braling.

They both stared up through the dark air.

In the window above them, on the second floor, a shade was raised. A man about thirty-five years old, with a touch of gray at either temple, sad gray eyes, and a small thin mustache looked down at them.

"Why, that's *you*!" cried Smith.

"Sh-h-h, not so loud!" Braling waved upward. The man in the window gestured significantly and vanished.

"I must be insane," said Smith.

"Hold on a moment."

They waited.

The street door of the apartment opened and the tall spare gentleman with the mustache and the grieved eyes came out to meet them.

"Hello, Braling," he said.

"Hello, Braling," said Braling.

They were identical.

Smith stared. "Is this your twin brother? I never knew—"

"No, no," said Braling quietly. "Bend close. Put your ear to Braling Two's chest."

Smith hesitated and then leaned forward to place his head against the uncomplaining ribs.

Tick-tick-tick-tick-tick-tick-tick-tick.

"Oh no! It *can't* be!"

"It is."

"Let me listen again."

Tick-tick-tick-tick-tick-tick-tick-tick.

Smith staggered back and fluttered his eyelids, appalled. He reached out and touched the warm hands and the cheeks of the thing.

"Where'd you get him?"

"Isn't he excellently fashioned?"

"Incredible. Where?"

"Give the man your card, Braling Two."

Braling Two did a magic trick and produced a white card:

MARIONETTES, INC.
Duplicate self or friends; new humanoid plastic 1990 models, guaranteed against all physical wear. From $7,600 to our $15,000 deluxe model.

"No," said Smith.

"Yes," said Braling.

"Naturally," said Braling Two.

"How long has this gone on?"

"I've had him for a month. I keep him in the cellar in a toolbox. My wife never goes downstairs, and I have the only lock and key to that box. Tonight I said I wished to take a walk to buy a cigar. I went down cellar and took Braling Two out of his box and sent him back up to sit with my wife while I came on out to see you, Smith."

"Wonderful! He even *smells* like you: Bond Street and Melachrinos!"

"It may be splitting hairs, but I think it highly ethical. After all, what my wife wants most of all is *me*. This marionette *is* me to the hairiest detail. I've been home all evening. I shall be home with her for the next month. In the meantime another gentleman will be in Rio after ten years of waiting. When I return from Rio, Braling Two here will go back in his box."

Smith thought that over a minute or two. "Will he walk around without sustenance for a month?" he finally asked.

"For six months if necessary. And he's built to do everything—eat, sleep, perspire—everything, natural as natural is. You'll take good care of my wife, won't you, Braling Two?"

"Your wife is rather nice," said Braling Two. "I've grown rather fond of her."

Smith was beginning to tremble. "How long has Marionettes, Inc., been in business?"

"Secretly, for two years."

"Could I—I mean, is there a possibility—" Smith took his friend's elbow earnestly. "Can you tell me where I can get one, a robot, a marionette, for myself? You *will* give me the address, won't you?"

"Here you are."

Smith took the card and turned it round and round. "Thank you," he said. "You don't know what this means. Just a little respite. A night or so, once a month even. My wife loves me so much she can't bear to have me gone an hour. I love her dearly, you know, but remember the old poem: 'Love will fly if held too lightly, love will die if held too tightly.' I just want her to relax her grip a little bit."

"You're lucky, at least, that your wife loves you. Hate's my problem. Not so easy."

"Oh, Nettie loves me madly. It will be my task to make her love me comfortably."

"Good luck to you, Smith. Do drop around while I'm in Rio. It will seem strange, if you suddenly stop calling by, to my wife. You're to treat Braling Two, here, just like me."

"Right! Goodbye. And thank you."

Smith went smiling down the street. Braling and Braling Two turned and walked into the apartment hall.

On the crosstown bus Smith whistled softly, turning the white card in his fingers:

Clients must be pledged to secrecy, for while an act is pending in Congress to legalize Marionettes, Inc., it is still a felony, if caught, to use one.

"Well," said Smith.

Clients must have a mold made of their body and a color index check of their eyes, lips, hair, skin, etc. Clients must expect to wait for two months until their model is finished.

Not so long, thought Smith. Two months from now my ribs will have a chance to mend from the crushing they've taken. Two months from now my hand will heal from being so constantly held. Two months from now my bruised underlip will begin to reshape itself. I don't mean to sound *ungrateful*.... He flipped the card over.

> *Marionettes, Inc., is two years old and has a fine record of satisfied customers behind it. Our motto is "No Strings Attached." Address: 43 South Wesley Drive.*

The bus pulled to his stop; he alighted, and while humming up the stairs he thought, Nettie and I have fifteen thousand in our joint bank account. I'll just slip eight thousand out as a business venture, you might say. The marionette will probably pay back my money, with interest, in many ways. Nettie needn't know. He unlocked the door and in a minute was in the bedroom. There lay Nettie, pale, huge, and piously asleep.

"Dear Nettie." He was almost overwhelmed with remorse at her innocent face there in the semidarkness. "If you were awake you would smother me with kisses and coo in my ear. Really, you make me feel like a criminal. You have been such a good, loving wife. Sometimes it is impossible for me to believe you married me instead of that Bud Chapman you once liked. It seems that in the last month you have loved me more wildly than *ever* before."

Tears came to his eyes. Suddenly he wished to kiss her, confess his love, tear up the card, forget the whole business. But as he moved to do this, his hand ached and his ribs cracked and groaned. He stopped, with a pained look in his eyes, and turned away. He moved out into the hall and through the dark rooms. Humming, he opened the kidney desk in the library and filched the bankbook. "Just take eight thousand dollars is all," he said. "No more than that." He stopped. "Wait a minute."

He rechecked the bankbook frantically. "Hold on here!" he cried. "Ten thousand dollars is missing!" He leaped up. "There's only five thousand left! What's she done? What's Nettie done with it? More hats, more clothes, more perfume! Or, wait— I know! She bought that little house on the Hudson she's been talking about for months, without so much as a by your leave!"

He stormed into the bedroom, righteous and indignant. What did she mean, taking their money like this? He bent over her. "Nettie!" he shouted. "Nettie, wake up!"

She did not stir. "What've you done with my money!" he bellowed.

She stirred fitfully. The light from the street flushed over her beautiful cheeks.

There was something about her. His heart throbbed violently. His tongue dried. He shivered. His knees suddenly turned to water. He collapsed. "Nettie, Nettie!" he cried. "What've you done with my money!"

And then, the horrid thought. And then the terror and the loneliness engulfed him. And then the fever and disillusionment. For, without desiring to do so, he bent forward and yet forward again until his fevered ear was resting firmly and irrevocably upon her round pink bosom. "Nettie!" he cried.

Tick-tick-tick-tick-tick-tick-tick-tick-tick-tick-tick.

As Smith walked away down the avenue in the night, Braling and Braling Two turned in at the door to the apartment. "I'm glad he'll be happy too," said Braling.

"Yes," said Braling Two abstractedly.

"Well, it's the cellar box for you, B-Two." Braling guided the other creature's elbow down the stairs to the cellar.

"That's what I want to talk to you about," said Braling Two, as they reached the concrete floor and walked across it. "The cellar. I don't like it. I don't like that toolbox."

"I'll try and fix up something more comfortable."

"Marionettes are made to move, not lie still. How would you like to lie in a box most of the time?"

"Well—"

"You wouldn't like it at all. I keep running. There's no way to shut me off. I'm perfectly alive and I have feelings."

"It'll only be a few days now. I'll be off to Rio and you won't have to stay in the box. You can live upstairs."

Braling Two gestured irritably. "And when you come back from having a good time, back in the box I go."

Braling said, "They didn't tell me at the marionette shop that I'd get a difficult specimen."

"There's a lot they don't know about us," said Braling Two. "We're pretty new. And we're sensitive. I hate the idea of you going off and laughing and lying in the sun in Rio while we're stuck here in the cold."

"But I've wanted that trip all my life," said Braling quietly.

He squinted his eyes and could see the sea and the mountains and the yellow sand. The sound of the waves was good to his inward mind. The sun was fine on his bared shoulders. The wine was most excellent.

"*I'll* never get to go to Rio," said the other man. "Have you thought of that?"

"No, I—"

"And another thing. Your wife."

"What about her?" asked Braling, beginning to edge toward the door.

"I've grown quite fond of her."

"I'm glad you're enjoying your employment." Braling licked his lips nervously.

"I'm afraid you don't understand. I think—I'm in love with her."

Braling took another step and froze. "You're *what*?"

"And I've been thinking," said Braling Two, "how nice it is in

Rio and how I'll never get there, and I've thought about your wife and—I think we could be very happy."

"Th-that's nice." Braling strolled as casually as he could to the cellar door. "You won't mind waiting a moment, will you? I have to make a phone call."

"To whom?" Braling Two frowned.

"No one important."

"To Marionettes, Incorporated? To tell them to come get me?"

"No, no—nothing like that!" He tried to rush out the door.

A metal-firm grip seized his wrists. "Don't run!"

"Take your hands off!"

"No."

"Did my wife put you up to this?"

"No."

"Did she guess? Did she talk to you? Does she know? Is *that* it?" He screamed. A hand clapped over his mouth.

"You'll never know, will you?" Braling Two smiled delicately. "You'll never know."

Braling struggled. "She *must* have guessed; she *must* have affected you!"

Braling Two said, "I'm going to put you in the box, lock it, and lose the key. Then I'll buy another Rio ticket for your wife."

"Now, now, wait a minute. Hold on. Don't be rash. Let's talk this over!"

"Goodbye, Braling."

Braling stiffened. "What do you mean, 'goodbye'?"

Ten minutes later Mrs. Braling awoke. She put her hand to her cheek. Someone had just kissed it. She shivered and looked up. "Why—you haven't done that in years," she murmured.

"We'll see what we can do about that," someone said.

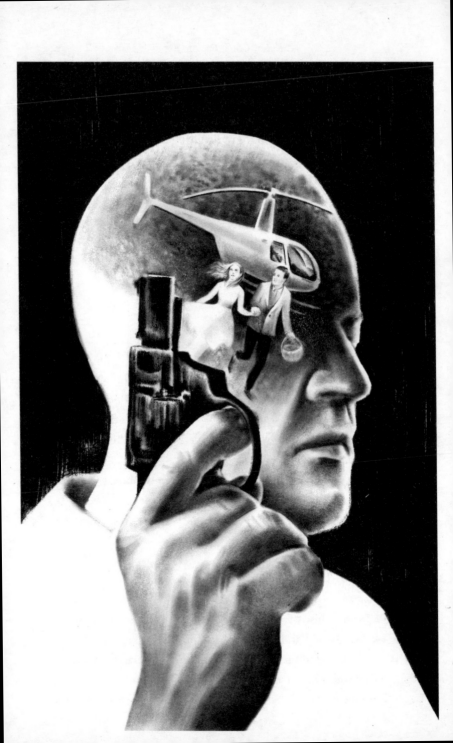

Punishment Without Crime

"You wish to kill your wife?" said the dark man at the desk.

"Yes. No...not exactly. I mean..."

"Name?"

"Hers or mine?"

"Yours."

"George Hill."

"Address?"

"Eleven South Saint James, Glenview."

The man wrote this down, emotionlessly. "Your wife's name?"

"Katherine."

"Age?"

"Thirty-one."

Then came a swift series of questions. Color of hair, eyes, skin, favorite perfume, texture and size index. "Have you a dimensional photo of her? A tape recording of her voice? Ah, I see you do. Good. Now—"

An hour later, George Hill was perspiring.

"That's all." The dark man arose and scowled. "You still want to go through with it."

"Yes."

"Sign here."

He signed.

"You know this is illegal?"

"Yes."

"And that we're in no way responsible for what happens to you as a result of your request?"

"For God's sake!" cried George. "You've kept me long enough. Let's get on!"

The man smiled faintly. "It'll take nine hours to prepare the marionette of your wife. Sleep awhile, it'll help your nerves. The third mirror room on your left is unoccupied."

George moved in a slow numbness to the mirror room. He lay on the blue velvet cot, his body pressure causing the mirrors in the ceiling to whirl. A soft voice sang, "Sleep...sleep... sleep..."

George murmured, "Katherine, I didn't want to come here. You forced me into it. You made me do it. God, I wish I weren't here. I wish I could go back. I don't want to kill you."

The mirrors glittered as they rotated softly.

He slept.

He dreamed he was forty-one again, he and Katie running on a green hill somewhere with a picnic lunch, their helicopter beside them. The wind blew Katie's hair in golden strands and she was laughing. They kissed and held hands, not eating. They read poems; it seemed they were always reading poems.

Other scenes. Quick changes of color, in flight. He and Katie flying over Greece and Italy and Switzerland, in that clear, long autumn of 1997! Flying and never stopping!

And then—nightmare. Katie and Leonard Phelps. George cried out in his sleep. How had it happened? Where had Phelps sprung from? Why had he interfered? Why couldn't life be simple and good? Was it the difference in age? George touching fifty, and Katie so young, so very young. Why, why?

The scene was unforgettably vivid. Leonard Phelps and Katherine in a green park beyond the city. George himself appearing on a path only in time to see the kissing of their mouths.

The rage. The struggle. The attempt to kill Leonard Phelps.

More days, more nightmares.

George Hill awoke, weeping.

✿

"Mr. Hill, we're ready for you now."

Hill arose clumsily. He saw himself in the high and now-silent mirrors, and he looked every one of his years. It had been a wretched error. Better men than he had taken young wives only to have them dissolve away in their hands like sugar crystals under water. He eyed himself, monstrously. A little too much stomach. A little too much chin. Somewhat too much pepper in the hair and not enough in the limbs...

The dark man led him to a room.

George Hill gasped. "This is *Katie's* room!"

"We try to have everything perfect."

"It *is*, to the last detail!"

George Hill drew forth a signed check for ten thousand dollars. The man departed with it.

The room was silent and warm.

George sat and felt for the gun in his pocket. A lot of money. But rich men can afford the luxury of cathartic murder. The violent unviolence. The death without death. The murder without murdering. He felt better. He was suddenly calm. He watched the door. This was a thing he had anticipated for six months and now it was to be ended. In a moment the beautiful robot, the stringless marionette, would appear, and...

"Hello, George."

"Katie!"

He whirled.

"Katie." He let his breath out.

She stood in the doorway behind him. She was dressed in a feather-soft green gown. On her feet were woven gold-twine sandals. Her hair was bright about her throat and her eyes were blue and clear.

He did not speak for a long while. "You're beautiful," he said at last, shocked.

"How else could I be?"

His voice was slow and unreal. "Let me look at you."

He put out his vague hands like a sleepwalker. His heart pounded sluggishly. He moved forward as if walking under a deep pressure of water. He walked around and around her, touching her.

"Haven't you seen enough of me in all these years?"

"Never enough," he said, and his eyes were filled with tears.

"What did you want to talk to me about?"

"Give me time, please, a little time." He sat down weakly and put his trembling hands to his chest. He blinked. "It's incredible. Another nightmare. How did they *make* you?"

"We're not allowed to talk of that; it spoils the illusion."

"It's magic!"

"Science."

Her touch was warm. Her fingernails were perfect as seashells. There was no seam, no flaw. He looked upon her. He remembered again the words they had read so often in the good days. *Behold, thou art fair, my love; behold, thou art fair; thou hast doves' eyes within thy locks....Thy lips are like a thread of scarlet, and thy speech is comely....Thy two breasts are like two young roes that are twins, which feed among the lilies... there is no spot in thee.*

"George?"

"What?" His eyes were cold glass.

He wanted to kiss her lips.

Honey and milk are under thy tongue.

And the smell of thy garments is like the smell of Lebanon.

"George."

A vast humming. The room began to whirl.

"Yes, yes, a moment, a moment." He shook his humming head.

How beautiful are thy feet with shoes, O prince's daughter!

the joints of thy thighs are like jewels, the work of the hands of
a cunning workman....

"How did they do it?" he cried. In so short a time. Nine hours, while he slept. Had they melted gold, fixed delicate watch springs, diamonds, glitter, confetti, rich rubies, liquid silver, copper thread? Had metal insects spun her hair? Had they poured yellow fire in molds and set it to freeze?

"No," she said. "If you talk that way, I'll go."

"Don't!"

"Come to business, then," she said, coldly. "You want to talk to me about Leonard."

"Give me time, I'll get to it."

"Now," she insisted.

He knew no anger. It had washed out of him at her appearance. He felt childishly dirty.

"Why did you come to see me?" She was not smiling.

"Please."

"I insist. Wasn't it about Leonard? You know I love him, don't you?"

"Stop it!" He put his hands to his ears.

She kept at him. "You know, I spend all of my time with him now. Where you and I used to go, now Leonard and I stay. Remember the picnic green on Mount Verde? We were there last week. We flew to Athens a month ago, with a case of champagne."

He licked his lips. "You're not guilty, you're *not*." He rose and held her wrists. "You're fresh, you're not her. She's guilty, not you. You're different!"

"On the contrary," said the woman. "I *am* her. I can act only as she acts. No part of me is alien to her. For all intents and purposes we are one."

"But you did not do what she has done!"

"I did all those things. I kissed him."

"You can't have, you're just born!"

"Out of her past and from your mind."

"Look," he pleaded, shaking her to gain her attention. "Isn't there some way, can't I—pay more money? Take you away with me? We'll go to Paris or Stockholm or any place you like!"

She laughed. "The marionettes only rent. They never sell."

"But I've money!"

"It was tried, long ago. It leads to insanity. It's not possible. Even this much is illegal, you *know* that. We exist only through governmental sufferance."

"All I want is to live with you, Katie."

"That can never be, because I am Katie, every bit of me is her. We do not want competition. Marionettes can't leave the premises; dissection might reveal our secrets. Enough of this. I warned you, we mustn't speak of these things. You'll spoil the illusion. You'll feel frustrated when you leave. You paid your money, now do what you came to do."

"I don't want to kill you."

"One part of you does. You're walling it in, you're trying not to let it out."

He took the gun from his pocket. "I'm an old fool. I should never have come. You're so beautiful."

"I'm going to see Leonard tonight."

"Don't talk."

"We're flying to Paris in the morning."

"You heard what I said!"

"And then to Stockholm." She laughed sweetly and caressed his chin. "My little fat man."

Something began to stir in him. His face grew pale. He knew what was happening. The hidden anger and revulsion and hatred in him were sending out faint pulses of thought. And the delicate telepathic web in her wondrous head was receiving the death impulse. The marionette. The invisible strings. He himself manipulating her body.

"Plump, odd little man, who once was so fair."

"Don't," he said.

"Old while I am only thirty-one, ah, George, you were blind, working years to give me time to fall in love again. Don't you think Leonard is lovely?"

He raised the gun blindly.

"Katie."

"His head is as the most fine gold—" she whispered.

"Katie, don't!" he screamed.

"His locks are bushy, and black as a raven....His hands are as gold rings set with the beryl—"

How could she speak those words! It was in *his* mind, how could *she* mouth it!

"Katie, don't make me do this!"

"His cheeks are as a bed of spices," she murmured, eyes closed, moving about the room softly. *"His belly is as bright ivory overlaid with sapphires. His legs are as pillars of marble—"*

"Katie!" he shrieked.

"His mouth is most sweet—"

One shot.

"—this is my beloved—"

Another shot.

She fell.

"Katie, Katie, Katie!"

Four more times he pumped bullets into her body.

She lay shuddering. Her senseless mouth clicked wide and some insanely warped mechanism had caused her to repeat again and again, *"Beloved, beloved, beloved, beloved, beloved…"*

George Hill fainted.

He awakened to a cool cloth on his brow.

"It's all over," said the dark man.

"Over?" George Hill whispered.

The dark man nodded.

George Hill looked weakly down at his hands. They had been covered with blood. When he fainted he had dropped to the floor. The last thing he remembered was the feeling of the real blood pouring upon his hands in a freshet.

His hands were now clean-washed.

"I've got to leave," said George Hill.

"If you feel capable."

"I'm all right." He got up. "I'll go to Paris now, start over. I'm not to try to phone Katie or anything, am I."

"Katie is dead."

"Yes. I killed her, didn't I? God, the blood, it was *real*!"

"We are proud of that touch."

He went down in the elevator to the street. It was raining, and he wanted to walk for hours. The anger and destruction were purged away. The memory was so terrible that he would never wish to kill again. Even if the real Katie were to appear before him now, he would only thank God, and fall senselessly to his knees. She was dead now. He had had his way. He had broken the law and no one would know.

The rain fell cool on his face. He must leave immediately, while the purge was in effect. After all, what was the use of such purges if one took up the old threads? The marionettes' function was primarily to prevent actual crime. If you wanted to kill, hit, or torture someone, you took it out on one of those unstringed automatons. It wouldn't do to return to the apartment now. Katie might be there. He wanted only to think of her as dead, a thing attended to in deserving fashion.

He stopped at the curb and watched the traffic flash by. He took deep breaths of the good air and began to relax.

"Mr. Hill?" said a voice at his elbow.

"Yes?"

A manacle was snapped to Hill's wrist. "You're under arrest."

"But—"

"Come along. Smith, take the other men upstairs, make the arrests!"

"You can't do this to me," said George Hill.

"For murder, yes, we can."

Thunder sounded in the sky.

It was eight-fifteen at night. It had been raining for ten days. It rained now on the prison walls. He put his hands out to feel the drops gather in pools on his trembling palms.

A door clanged and he did not move but stood with his hands in the rain. His lawyer looked up at him on his chair and said, "It's all over. You'll be executed tonight."

George Hill listened to the rain.

"She wasn't real. I didn't kill her."

"It's the law, anyhow. You remember. The others are sentenced, too. The president of Marionettes, Incorporated, will die at midnight. His three assistants will die at one. You'll go about one-thirty."

"Thanks," said George. "You did all you could. I guess it was murder, no matter how you look at it, image or not. The idea was there, the plot and the plan were there. It lacked only the real Katie herself."

"It's a matter of timing, too," said the lawyer. "Ten years ago you wouldn't have got the death penalty. Ten years from now you wouldn't, either. But they had to have an object case, a whipping boy. The use of marionettes has grown so in the last year it's fantastic. The public must be scared out of it, and scared badly. God knows where it would all wind up if it went on. There's the spiritual side of it, too, where does life begin or end? Are the robots alive or dead? More than one church has been split up the seams on the question. If they aren't alive, they're the next thing to it; they react, they even think. You know the 'live robot' law that was passed two months ago; you come under that. Just bad timing, is all, bad timing."

"The government's right. I see that now," said George Hill.

"I'm glad you understand the attitude of the law."

"Yes. After all, they can't let murder be legal. Even if it's done with machines and telepathy and wax. They'd be hypocrites to let me get away with my crime. For it *was* a crime. I've felt guilty about it ever since. I've felt the need of punishment. Isn't that odd? That's how society gets to you. It makes you feel guilty even when you see no reason to be...."

"I have to go now. Is there anything you want?"

"Nothing, thanks."

"Goodbye then, Mr. Hill."

The door shut.

George Hill stood up on the chair, his hands twisting together, wet, outside the window bars. A red light burned in the wall suddenly. A voice came over the audio: "Mr. Hill, your wife is here to see you."

He gripped the bars.

She's dead, he thought.

"Mr. Hill?" asked the voice.

"She's dead. I killed her."

"Your wife is waiting in the anteroom, will you see her?"

"I saw her fall, I shot her, I saw her fall dead!"

"Mr. Hill, do you hear me?"

"Yes!" he shouted, pounding at the wall with his fists. "I hear you. I hear you! She's dead, she's dead, can't she let me be! I killed her, I won't see her, she's dead!"

A pause. "Very well, Mr. Hill," murmured the voice.

The red light winked off.

Lightning flashed through the sky and lit his face. He pressed his hot cheeks to the cold bars and waited, while the rain fell. After a long time, a door opened somewhere onto the street and he saw two caped figures emerge from the prison office below. They paused under an arc light and glanced up.

It was Katie. And beside her, Leonard Phelps.

"Katie!"

Her face turned away. The man took her arm. They hurried across the avenue in the black rain and got into a low car.

"Katie!" He wrenched at the bars. He screamed and beat and pulled at the concrete ledge. "She's alive! Guard! Guard! I saw her! She's not dead, I didn't kill her, now you can let me out! I didn't murder anyone, it's all a joke, a mistake, I saw her, I saw her! Katie, come back, tell them, Katie, say you're alive! Katie!"

The guards came running.

"You can't kill me! I didn't do anything! Katie's alive, I saw her!"

"We saw her, too, sir."

"But let me free, then! Let me free!" It was insane. He choked and almost fell.

"We've been through all that, sir, at the trial."

"It's not fair!" He leaped up and clawed at the window, bellowing.

The car drove away, Katie and Leonard inside it. Drove away to Paris and Athens and Venice and London next spring and Stockholm next summer and Vienna in the fall.

"Katie, come back, you can't *do* this to me!"

The red taillights of the car dwindled in the cold rain. Behind him, the guards moved forward to take hold of him while he screamed.

Some Live Like Lazarus

You won't believe it when I tell you I waited more than sixty years for a murder, hoped as only a woman can hope that it might happen, and didn't move a finger to stop it when it finally drew near. Anna Marie, I thought, you can't stand guard forever. Murder, when ten thousand days have passed, is more than a surprise, it is a miracle.

"Hold on! Don't let me fall!"

Mrs. Harrison's voice.

Did I ever, in half a century, hear it whisper? Was it always screaming, shrieking, demanding, threatening?

Yes, always.

"Come along, Mother. There you are, Mother."

Her son Roger's voice.

Did I ever in all the years hear it rise above a murmur, protest, or, even faintly birdlike, argue?

No. Always the loving monotone.

This morning, no different than any other of their first mornings, they arrived in their great black hearse for their annual Green Bay summer. There he was, thrusting his hand in to hoist the window dummy after him, an ancient sachet of bones and talcum dust that was named, surely for some terrible practical joke, Mother.

"Easy does it, Mother."

"You're bruising my arm!"

"Sorry, Mother."

I watched from a window of the lake pavilion as he trundled her off down the path in her wheelchair, she pushing her cane

like a musket ahead to blast any Fates or Furies they might
meet out of the way.

"Careful, don't run me into the flowers, thank God we'd
sense not to go to Paris after all. You'd've had me in that nasty
traffic. You're not disappointed?"

"No, Mother."

"We'll see Paris next year."

Next year...next year...no year at all, I heard someone murmur. Myself, gripping the windowsill. For almost seventy years
I had heard her promise this to the boy, boy-man, man, man-
grasshopper and the now livid male praying mantis that he was,
pushing his eternally cold and fur-wrapped woman past the
hotel verandas where, in another age, paper fans had fluttered
like Oriental butterflies in the hands of basking ladies.

"There, Mother, inside the cottage..." his faint voice fading
still more, forever young when he was old, forever old when he
was very young.

How old is she now? I wondered. Ninety-eight, yes, ninety-
nine wicked years old. She seemed like a horror film repeated
each year because the hotel entertainment fund could not afford
to buy a new one to run in the moth-flaked evenings.

So, through all the repetitions of arrivals and departures, my
mind ran back to when the foundations of the Green Bay Hotel
were freshly poured and the parasols were new leaf green and
lemon gold, that summer of 1890 when I first saw Roger, who
was five, but whose eyes already were old and wise and tired.

He stood on the pavilion grass looking at the sun and the
bright pennants as I came up to him.

"Hello," I said.

He simply looked at me.

I hesitated, tagged him and ran.

He did not move.

I came back and tagged him again.

He looked at the place where I had touched him, on the shoulder, and was about to run after me when her voice came from a distance.

"Roger, don't dirty your clothes!"

And he walked slowly away toward his cottage, not looking back.

That was the day I started to hate him.

Parasols have come and gone in a thousand summer colors, whole flights of butterfly fans have blown away on August winds, the pavilion has burned and been built again in the selfsame size and shape, the lake has dried like a plum in its basin, and my hatred, like these things, came and went, grew very large, stopped still for love, returned, then diminished with the years.

I remember when he was seven, them driving by in their horse carriage, his hair long, brushing his poutish, shrugging shoulders. They were holding hands and she was saying, "If you're very good this summer, next year we'll go to London. Or the year after that, at the latest."

And my watching their faces, comparing their eyes, their ears, their mouths, so when he came in for a soda pop one noon that summer I walked straight up to him and cried, "She's not your mother!"

"What!" He looked around in panic, as if she might be near.

"She's not your aunt or your grandma, either!" I cried. "She's a witch that stole you when you were a baby. You don't know who your mama is or your pa. You don't look anything like her. She's holding you for a million ransom which comes due when you're twenty-one from some duke or king!"

"Don't say that!" he shouted, jumping up.

"Why not?" I said angrily. "Why do you come around here? You can't play this, can't play that, can't do nothing, what good are you? She says, she does. I know *her*! She hangs upside down from the ceiling in her black clothes in her bedroom at midnight!"

"Don't say that!" His face was frightened and pale.

"Why not say it?"

"Because," he bleated, "it's true."

And he was out the door and running.

I didn't see him again until the next summer. And then only once, briefly, when I took some clean linen down to their cottage.

The summer when we were both twelve was the summer that for a time I didn't hate him.

He called my name outside the pavilion screen door and when I looked out he said, very quietly, "Anna Marie, when I am twenty and you are twenty, I'm going to marry you."

"Who's going to let you?" I asked.

"I'm going to let you," he said. "You just remember, Anna Marie. You wait for me. Promise?"

I could only nod. "But what about—"

"She'll be dead by then," he said, very gravely. "She's old. She's *old*."

And then he turned and went away.

The next summer they did not come to the resort at all. I heard she was sick. I prayed every night that she would die.

But two years later they were back, and the year after the year after that until Roger was nineteen and I was nineteen, and then at last we had reached and touched twenty, and for one of the few times in all the years, they came into the pavilion together, she in her wheelchair now, deeper in her furs than ever before, her face a gathering of white dust and folded parchment.

She eyed me as I set her ice cream sundae down before her, and eyed Roger as he said, "Mother, I want you to meet—"

"I do not meet girls who wait on public tables," she said. "I acknowledge they exist, work, and are paid. But I immediately forget their names."

She touched and nibbled her ice cream, touched and nibbled her ice cream, while Roger sat not touching his at all.

They left a day earlier than usual that year. I saw Roger as he paid the bill, in the hotel lobby. He shook my hand to say goodbye and I could not help but say, "You've forgotten."

He took a half step back, then turned around, patting his coat pockets.

"Luggage, bills paid, wallet, no, I seem to have everything," he said.

"A long time ago," I said, "you made a promise."

He was silent.

"Roger," I said, "I'm twenty now. And so are you."

He seized my hand again, swiftly, as if he were falling over the side of a ship and it was me going away, leaving him to drown forever beyond help.

"One more year, Anna! Two, three, at the most!"

"Oh, no," I said, forlornly.

"Four years at the outside! The doctors say—"

"The doctors don't know what I know, Roger. She'll live forever. She'll bury you and me and drink wine at our funerals."

"She's a sick woman, Anna! My God, she *can't* survive!"

"She will, because we give her strength. She knows we want her dead. That really gives her the power to go on."

"I can't talk this way, I can't!" Seizing his luggage, he started down the hall.

"I won't wait, Roger," I said.

He turned at the door and looked at me so helplessly, so palely, like a moth pinned to the wall, that I could not say it again.

The door slammed shut.

The summer was over.

The next year Roger came directly to the soda fountain, where he said, "Is it true? Who is he?"

"Paul," I said. "You know Paul. He'll manage the hotel someday. We'll marry this fall."

"That doesn't give me much time," said Roger.

"It's too late," I said. "I've already promised."

"Promised, hell! You don't love him!"

"I think I do."

"Think, hell! Thinking's one thing, knowing's another. You *know* you love me!"

"Do I, Roger?"

"Stop relishing the damn business so much! You know you do! Oh, Anna, you'll be miserable!"

"I'm miserable now," I said.

"Oh, Anna, Anna, wait!"

"I have waited, most of my life. But I know what will happen."

"Anna!" He blurted it out as if it had come to him suddenly. "What if—what if she died *this* summer?"

"She won't."

"But if she did, if she took a turn for the worse, I mean, in the next two months—" He searched my face. He shortened it. "The next month, Anna, two weeks, listen, if she died in two short weeks, would you wait that long, would you marry me then?!"

I began to cry. "Oh, Roger, we've never even kissed. This is ridiculous."

"Answer me, if she died one week, seven days from now…" He grabbed my arms.

"But how can you be sure?"

"I'll *make* myself sure! I swear she'll be dead a week from now, or I'll never bother you again with this!"

And he flung the screen doors wide, hurrying off into the day that was suddenly too bright.

"Roger, don't—" I cried.

But my mind thought, Roger *do*, do something, anything, to start it all or end it all.

That night in bed I thought, What ways are there for murder that no one could know? Is Roger, a hundred yards away this moment, thinking the same? Will he search the woods tomorrow for toadstools resembling mushrooms, or drive the car too fast and fling her door wide on a curve? I saw the wax-dummy witch fly through the air in a lovely soaring arc, to break like ridiculous peanut brittle on an oak, an elm, a maple. I sat up in bed. I laughed until I wept. I wept until I laughed again. No, no, I thought, he'll find a better way. A night burglar will shock her heart into her throat. Once in her throat, he will not let it go down again, she'll choke on her own panic.

And then the oldest, the darkest, most childish thought of all. There's only one way to finish a woman whose mouth is the color of blood. Being what she is, no relative, not an aunt or a great-grandmother, surprise her with a stake driven through her heart!

I heard her scream. It was so loud, all the night birds jumped from the trees to cover the stars.

I lay back down. Dear Christian Anna Marie, I thought, what's this? Do you want to kill? Yes, for why not kill a killer, a woman who strangled her child in his crib and has not loosened the throttling cord since? He is so pale, poor man, because he has not breathed free air, all of his life.

And then, unbidden, the lines of an old poem stood up in my head. Where I had read them or who had put them down, or if I had written them myself, within my head over the years, I could not say. But the lines were there and I read them in the dark:

Some live like Lazarus
In a tomb of life
And come forth curious late to twilight hospitals
And mortuary rooms.

The lines vanished. For a while I could recall no more, and then, unable to fend it off, for it came of itself, a last fragment appeared in the dark:

Better cold skies seen bitter to the North
Than stillborn stay, all blind and gone to ghost.
If Rio is lost, well, love the Arctic Coast!
O ancient Lazarus
Come ye forth.

There the poem stopped and let me be. At last I slept, restless, hoping for the dawn, and good and final news.

The next day I saw him pushing her along the pier and thought, Yes, that's it! She'll vanish and be found a week from now, on the shore, like a sea monster floating, all face and no body.

That day passed. Well, surely, I thought, tomorrow...

The second day of the week, the third, the fourth and then the fifth and sixth passed, and on the seventh day one of the maids came running up the path, shrieking.

"Oh, it's terrible, terrible!"

"Mrs. Harrison?" I cried. I felt a terrible and quite uncontrollable smile on my face.

"No, no, her *son*! He's hung himself!"

"Hung himself?" I said ridiculously, and found myself, stunned, explaining to her. "Oh, no, it wasn't *him* was going to die, it was—" I babbled. I stopped, for the maid was clutching, pulling my arm.

"We cut him down, oh, God, he's still alive, quick!"

Still alive? He still breathed, yes, and walked around through the other years, yes, but alive? No.

It was she who gained strength and lived through his attempt to escape her. She never forgave his trying to run off.

"What do you mean by that, what do you mean?" I remember her screaming at him as he lay feeling his throat, in the cottage, his eyes shut, wilted, and I hurried in the door. "What do you mean doing that, what, what?"

And looking at him there I knew he had tried to run away from both of us, we were both impossible to him. I did not forgive him that either, for a while. But I did feel my old hatred of him become something else, a kind of dull pain, as I turned and went back for a doctor.

"What do you mean, you silly boy?" she cried.

I married Paul that autumn.

After that, the years poured through the glass swiftly. Once each year, Roger led himself into the pavilion to sit eating mint ice with his limp empty-gloved hands, but he never called me by my name again, nor did he mention the old promise.

Here and there in the hundreds of months that passed I thought, For his own sake now, for no one else, sometime, somehow he must simply up and destroy the dragon with the hideous bellows face and the rust-scaled hands. For Roger and only for Roger, Roger must do it.

Surely *this* year, I thought, when he was fifty, fifty-one, fifty-two. Between seasons I caught myself examining occasional Chicago papers, hoping to find a picture of her lying slit like a monstrous yellow chicken. But no, but no, but no....

I'd almost forgotten them when they returned this morning. He's very old now, more like a doddering husband than a son. Baked gray clay he is, with milky blue eyes, a toothless mouth, and manicured fingernails which seem stronger because the flesh has baked away.

At noon today, after a moment of standing out, a lone gray wingless hawk staring at a sky in which he had never soared or flown, he came inside and spoke to me, his voice rising.

"Why didn't you tell me?"

"Tell you what?" I said, scooping out his ice cream before he asked for it.

"One of the maids just mentioned, your husband died five years ago! You should have told me!"

"Well, now you know," I said.

He sat down slowly. "Lord," he said, tasting the ice cream and savoring it, eyes shut, "this is bitter." Then, a long time later, he said, "Anna, I never asked. Were there ever any children?"

"No," I said. "And I don't know why. I guess I'll never know why."

I left him sitting there and went to wash the dishes.

At nine tonight I heard someone laughing by the lake. I hadn't heard Roger laugh since he was a child, so I didn't think it was him until the doors burst wide and he entered, flinging his arms about, unable to control his almost weeping hilarity.

"Roger!" I asked. "What's wrong?"

"Nothing! Oh, nothing!" he cried. "Everything's lovely! A root beer, Anna! Take one yourself! Drink with me!"

We drank together, he laughed, winked, then got immensely calm. Still smiling, though, he looked suddenly, beautifully young.

"Anna," he whispered intensely, leaning forward, "guess what? I'm flying to China tomorrow! Then India! Then London, Madrid, Paris, Berlin, Rome, Mexico City!"

"*You* are, Roger?"

"I am," he said. "I, I, I, not we, we, we, but I, Roger Bidwell Harrison, I, I, *I*!"

I stared at him and he gazed quietly back at me, and I must have gasped. For then I knew what he had finally done tonight, this hour, within the last few minutes.

Oh, no, my lips must have murmured.

Oh, but yes, yes, his eyes upon me replied, incredible miracle of miracles, after all these waiting years. Tonight at last. Tonight.

I let him talk. After Rome it was Vienna and Stockholm, he'd saved thousands of schedules, flight charts and hotel bulletins for forty years; he knew the moons and tides, the goings and comings of everything on the sea and in the sky.

"But best of all," he said at last, "Anna, Anna, will you come along with me? I've lots of money put away, don't let me run on! Anna, tell me, *will* you?"

I came around the counter slowly and saw myself in the mirror, a woman in her seventieth year going to a party half a century late.

I sat down beside him and shook my head.

"Oh, but, Anna, why not, there's no reason why!"

"There is a reason," I said. "You."

"Me, but I don't count!"

"That's just it, Roger, you do."

"Anna, we could have a wonderful time—"

"I daresay. But, Roger, you've *been* married for seventy years. Now, for the first time, you're not married. You don't want to turn around and get married again right off, do you?"

"*Don't* I?" he asked, blinking.

"You don't, you really don't. You deserve a little while, at least, off by yourself, to see the world, to know who Roger Harrison is. A little while away from women. Then, when you've gone around the world and come back, is time to think of other things."

"If you *say* so—"

"No. It mustn't be anything I say or know or tell you to do. Right now it must be you telling yourself what to know and see and do. Go have a grand time. If you can, be happy."

"Will you be here waiting for me when I come back?"

"I haven't it in me any more to wait, but I'll be here."

He moved toward the door, then stopped and looked at me as if surprised by some new question that had come into his mind.

"Anna," he said, "if all this had happened forty, fifty years ago, would you have gone away with me then? Would you really have married me?"

I did not answer.

"Anna?" he asked.

After a long while I said, "There are some questions that should never be asked."

Because, I went on, thinking, there can be no answers. Looking down the years toward the lake, I could not remember, so I could not say, whether we could have ever been happy. Perhaps even as a child, sensing the impossible in Roger, I had clenched the impossible, and therefore the rare, to my heart, simply because it was impossible and rare. He was a sprig of farewell summer pressed in an old book, to be taken out, turned over, admired, once a year, but more than that? Who could say? Surely not I, so long, so late in the day. Life is questions, not answers.

Roger had come very close to read my face, my mind, while I thought all this. What he saw there made him look away, close his eyes, then take my hand and press it to his cheek.

"I'll be back. I swear I will!"

Outside the door he stood bewildered for a moment in the moonlight, looking at the world and all its directions, east, west, north, south, like a child out of school for his first summer not knowing which way to go first, just breathing, just listening, just seeing.

"Don't hurry!" I said fervently. "Oh, God, whatever you do, please, enjoy yourself, don't hurry!"

I saw him run off toward the limousine near the cottage where I am supposed to rap in the morning and where I will get no answer. But I know that I will not go to the cottage and that I'll keep the maids from going there because the old lady has given orders not to be bothered. That will give Roger the chance, the start he needs. In a week or two or three, I might call the police. Then if they met Roger coming back on the boat from all those wild places, it won't matter.

Police? Perhaps not even them. Perhaps she died of a heart attack and poor Roger only thinks he killed her and now proudly sails off into the world, his pride not allowing him to know that only her own self-made death released him.

But then again, if at last all the murder he put away for seventy years forced him tonight to lay hands on and kill the hideous turkey, I could not find it in my heart to weep for her but only for the great time it has taken to act out the sentence.

The road is silent. An hour has passed since the limousine roared away down the road.

Now I have just put out the lights and stand alone in the pavilion looking out at the shining lake where in another century, under another sun, a small boy with an old face was first touched to play tag with me and now, very late, has tagged me back, has kissed my hand and run away, and this time myself, stunned, not following.

Many things I do not know, tonight.

But one thing I'm sure of.

I do not hate Roger Harrison any more.

The Utterly Perfect Murder

It was such an utterly perfect, such an incredibly delightful idea for murder, that I was half out of my mind all across America.

The idea had come to me for some reason on my forty-eighth birthday. Why it hadn't come to me when I was thirty or forty, I cannot say. Perhaps those were good years and I sailed through them unaware of time and clocks and the gathering of frost at my temples or the look of the lion about my eyes....

Anyway, on my forty-eighth birthday, lying in bed that night beside my wife, with my children sleeping through all the other quiet moonlit rooms of my house, I thought:

I will arise and go now and kill Ralph Underhill.

Ralph Underhill! I cried, who in God's name is *he*?

Thirty-six years later, kill him? For *what*?

Why, I thought, for what he did to me when I was twelve.

My wife woke, an hour later, hearing a noise.

"Doug?" she called. "What are you doing?"

"Packing," I said. "For a journey."

"Oh," she murmured, and rolled over and went to sleep.

"'Board! All aboard!" The porter's cries went down the train platform.

The train shuddered and banged.

"See you!" I cried, leaping up the steps.

"Someday," called my wife, "I wish you'd *fly*!"

Fly? I thought, and spoil thinking about murder all across the plains? Spoil oiling the pistol and loading it and thinking of

Ralph Underhill's face when I show up thirty-six years late to settle old scores? Fly? Why, I would rather pack cross-country on foot, pausing by night to build fires and fry my bile and sour spit and eat again my old, mummified but still-living antagonisms and touch those bruises which have never healed. Fly?!

The train moved. My wife was gone.

I rode off into the Past.

Crossing Kansas the second night, we hit a beaut of a thunderstorm. I stayed up until four in the morning, listening to the rave of winds and thunders. At the height of the storm, I saw my face, a darkroom negative-print on the cold window glass, and thought:

Where is that fool going?

To kill Ralph Underhill!

Why? Because!

Remember how he hit my arm? Bruises. I was covered with bruises, both arms; dark blue, mottled black, strange yellow bruises. Hit and run, that was Ralph, hit and run—

And yet...you loved him?

Yes, as boys love boys when boys are eight, ten, twelve, and the world is innocent and boys are evil beyond evil because they know not what they do, but do it anyway. So, on some secret level, I *had* to be hurt. We dear fine friends needed each other. I to be hit. He to strike. My scars were the emblem and symbol of our love.

What else makes you want to murder Ralph so late in time?

The train whistle shrieked. Night country rolled by.

And I recalled one spring when I came to school in a new tweed knicker suit and Ralph knocking me down, rolling me in snow and fresh brown mud. And Ralph laughing and me going home, shame-faced, covered with slime, afraid of a beating, to put on fresh dry clothes.

Yes! And what *else*?

Remember those toy clay statues you longed to collect from the Tarzan radio show? Statues of Tarzan and Kala the Ape and Numa the Lion, for just twenty-five cents?! Yes, yes! Beautiful! Even now, in memory, O the sound of the Ape Man swinging through green jungles far away, ululating! But who had twenty-five cents in the middle of the Great Depression? No one.

Except Ralph Underhill.

And one day Ralph asked you if you wanted one of the statues. Wanted! you cried. Yes! Yes!

That was the same week your brother in a strange seizure of love mixed with contempt gave you his old, but expensive, baseball-catcher's mitt.

"Well," said Ralph, "I'll give you my extra Tarzan statue if you'll give me that catcher's mitt."

Fool! I thought. The statue's worth twenty-five cents. The glove cost two dollars. No fair! Don't!

But I raced back to Ralph's house with the glove and gave it to him and he, smiling a worse contempt than my brother's, handed me the Tarzan statue and, bursting with joy, I ran home.

My brother didn't find out about his catcher's mitt and the statue for two weeks, and when he did he ditched me when we hiked out in farm country and left me lost because I was such a sap. "Tarzan statues! Baseball mitts!" he cried. "That's the last thing I *ever* give you!"

And somewhere on a country road I just lay down and wept and wanted to die but didn't know how to give up the final vomit that was my miserable ghost.

The thunder murmured.

The rain fell on the cold Pullman-car windows.

What *else*? Is that the list?

No. One final thing, more terrible than all the rest.

In all the years you went to Ralph's house to toss up small bits of gravel on his Fourth of July six-in-the-morning fresh dewy window or to call him forth for the arrival of dawn circuses in the cold fresh blue railroad stations in late June or late August, in all those years, never once did Ralph run to your house.

Never once in all the years did he, or anyone else, prove their friendship by coming by. The door never knocked. The window of your bedroom never faintly clattered and belled with a high-tossed confetti of small dusts and rocks.

And you always knew that the day you stopped going to Ralph's house, calling up in the morn, that would be the day your friendship ended.

You tested it once. You stayed away for a whole week. Ralph never called. It was as if you had died, and no one came to your funeral.

When you saw Ralph at school, there was no surprise, no query, not even the faintest lint of curiosity to be picked off your coat. Where *were* you, Doug? I need someone to beat. Where you *been*, Doug, I got no one to *pinch*!

Add all the sins up. But especially think on the last:

He never came to my house. He never sang up to my early-morning bed or tossed a wedding rice of gravel on the clear panes to call me down to joy and summer days.

And for this last thing, Ralph Underhill, I thought, sitting in the train at four in the morning, as the storm faded, and I found tears in my eyes, for this last and final thing, for that I shall kill you tomorrow night.

Murder, I thought, after thirty-six years. Why, God, you're madder than Ahab.

The train wailed. We ran cross-country like a mechanical Greek Fate carried by a black metal Roman Fury.

o

They say you can't go home again.

That is a lie.

If you are lucky and time it right, you arrive at sunset when the old town is filled with yellow light.

I got off the train and walked up through Green Town and looked at the courthouse, burning with sunset light. Every tree was hung with gold doubloons of color. Every roof and coping and bit of gingerbread was purest brass and ancient gold.

I sat in the courthouse square with dogs and old men until the sun had set and Green Town was dark. I wanted to savor Ralph Underhill's death.

No one in history had ever done a crime like this.

I would stay, kill, depart, a stranger among strangers.

How would anyone dare to say, finding Ralph Underhill's body on his doorstep, that a boy aged twelve, arriving on a kind of Time Machine train, traveled out of hideous self-contempt, had gunned down the Past? It was beyond all reason. I was safe in my pure insanity.

Finally, at eight-thirty on this cool October night, I walked across town, past the ravine.

I never doubted Ralph would still be there.

People do, after all, move away....

I turned down Park Street and walked two hundred yards to a single streetlamp and looked across. Ralph Underhill's white two-story Victorian house waited for me.

And I could feel him *in* it.

He was there, forty-eight years old, even as I felt myself here, forty-eight, and full of an old and tired and self-devouring spirit.

I stepped out of the light, opened my suitcase, put the pistol in my right-hand coat pocket, shut the case, and hid it in the bushes where, later, I would grab it and walk down into the ravine and across town to the train.

I walked across the street and stood before his house and it was the same house I had stood before thirty-six years ago. There were the windows upon which I had hurled those spring bouquets of rock in love and total giving. There were the sidewalks, spotted with firecracker burn marks from ancient July Fourths when Ralph and I had just blown up the whole damned world, shrieking celebrations.

I walked up on the porch and saw on the mailbox in small letters: UNDERHILL.

What if his wife answers?

No, I thought, he himself, with absolute Greek-tragic perfection, will open the door and take the wound and almost gladly die for old crimes and minor sins somehow grown to crimes.

I rang the bell.

Will he know me, I wondered, after all this time? In the instant before the first shot, *tell* him your name. He must know who it is.

Silence.

I rang the bell again.

The doorknob rattled.

I touched the pistol in my pocket, my heart hammering, but did not take it out.

The door opened.

Ralph Underhill stood there.

He blinked, gazing out at me.

"Ralph?" I said.

"Yes—?" he said.

We stood there, riven, for what could not have been more than five seconds. But, O Christ, many things happened in those five swift seconds.

I saw Ralph Underhill.

I saw him clearly.

And I had not seen him since I was twelve.

Then, he had towered over me to pummel and beat and scream.

Now he was a little old man.

I am five foot eleven.

But Ralph Underhill had not grown much from his twelfth year on.

The man who stood before me was no more than five feet two inches tall.

I *towered* over him.

I gasped. I stared. I saw more.

I was forty-eight years old.

But Ralph Underhill, forty-eight, had lost most of his hair, and what remained was threadbare gray, black and white. He looked sixty or sixty-five.

I was in good health.

Ralph Underhill was waxen pale. There was a knowledge of sickness in his face. He had traveled in some sunless land. He had a ravaged and sunken look. His breath smelled of funeral flowers.

All this, perceived, was like the storm of the night before, gathering all its lightnings and thunders into one bright concussion. We stood in the explosion.

So this is what I came for? I thought. This, then, is the truth. This dreadful instant in time. Not to pull out the weapon. *Not* to kill. No, no. But simply—

To see Ralph Underhill as he *is* in this hour.

That's all.

Just to be here, stand here, and look at him as he has become.

Ralph Underhill lifted one hand in a kind of gesturing wonder. His lips trembled. His eyes flew up and down my body, his mind measured this giant who shadowed his door. At last his voice, so small, so frail, blurted out:

"Doug—?"

I recoiled.

"Doug?" he gasped. "Is that *you*?"

I hadn't expected that. People don't remember! They can't! Across the years? Why would he know, bother, summon up, recognize, call?

I had a wild thought that what had happened to Ralph Underhill was that after I left town, half of his life had collapsed. I had been the center of his world, someone to attack, beat, pummel, bruise. His whole life had cracked by my simple act of walking away thirty-six years ago.

Nonsense! Yet, some small crazed mouse of wisdom scuttered about my brain and screeched what it knew: You needed Ralph, but, *more*! he needed *you*! And you did the only unforgivable, the wounding, thing! You vanished.

"Doug?" he said again, for I was silent there on the porch with my hands at my sides. "Is that you?"

This was the moment I had come for.

At some secret blood level, I had always known I would not use the weapon. I had brought it with me, yes, but Time had gotten here before me, and age, and smaller, more terrible deaths....

Bang.

Six shots through the heart.

But I didn't use the pistol. I only whispered the sound of the shots with my mouth. With each whisper, Ralph Underhill's face aged another ten years. By the time I reached the last shot he was one hundred and ten years old.

"Bang," I whispered. "Bang. Bang. Bang. Bang. Bang."

His body shook with the impact.

"You're dead. Oh, God, Ralph, you're dead."

I turned and walked down the steps and reached the street before he called:

"Doug, is that *you*?"

I did not answer, walking.

"Answer me," he cried, weakly. "Doug! Doug Spaulding, is that you? Who is that? Who are you?"

I got my suitcase and walked down into the cricket night and darkness of the ravine and across the bridge and up the stairs, going away.

"Who is that?" I heard his voice wail a last time.

A long way off, I looked back.

All the lights were on all over Ralph Underhill's house. It was as if he had gone around and put them all on after I left.

On the other side of the ravine I stopped on the lawn in front of the house where I had been born.

Then I picked up a few bits of gravel and did the thing that had never been done, ever in my life.

I tossed the few bits of gravel up to tap that window where I had lain every morning of my first twelve years. I called my own name. I called me down in friendship to play in some long summer that no longer was.

I stood waiting just long enough for my other young self to come down to join me.

Then swiftly, fleeing ahead of the dawn, we ran out of Green Town and back, thank you, dear Christ, back toward Now and Today for the rest of my life.

Hammett? Chandler? Not to Worry!

Introduction to *A Memory of Murder*
by Ray Bradbury

When my first detective mystery stories began to appear in *Dime Detective*, *Dime Mystery Magazine*, *Detective Tales*, and *Black Mask* in the early '40s, there was no immediate trepidation over in the Hammett–Chandler–Cain camp. The fact is, it didn't develop later either. I was never a threat. I couldn't, in the immortal words of Brando, have been a contender.

I was a survivor, however, and one of my heroes was Leigh Brackett, who met me every Sunday noon at Muscle Beach in Santa Monica, California, there to read my drear imitations of her Stark on Mars stories or my carbon copies of her first-rate detective tales, which were beginning to appear in all the above mentioned magazines. I would lie on the beach and weep with envy at how easily her characters slid forth, adventured, died, or lived to grieve a death. How she managed to plow through my early agonized contrivances I cannot say. The word friendship arises here to oil the machinery.

Leigh Brackett knew that heart, soul, and guts, I wanted to be a writer. I still had not found my proper voice, though I was beginning to find some of my truths in the weird tale, and an occasional science fiction yarn that wasn't too embarrassing. Leigh was my loving teacher, and I had yet to work free from her influence, both creative and constricting.

Most of the stories in this collection were written to please

Leigh, to get an occasional "Well done!" or, once in a while, "This is your best yet!"

Starting back in the year when I left Los Angeles High School, I put myself on a regimen of writing one story a week for the rest of my life. I knew that without quantity there could never be any quality. I sensed that my stories at that time were so bad that only practice could clean the junk out of my head and let the good stuff flow. In the meantime, I tried to cram as much literary experience as I could—good, bad, indifferent, or excellent—into my eyeballs so that eventually it would jump out of my fingertips.

So every Monday I wrote a first draft of any story that leaped into my head. On Tuesday I wrote a second draft. On Wednesday, Thursday, and Friday, third, fourth, and fifth versions followed. On Saturday the final draft went into the mail. On Sunday I collapsed for a day on the beach with Leigh, and on Monday I was back starting a new story. So it has gone for some forty-four years. I am still writing a story a week, or its equivalent. These days I do seven or eight poems a week, or a one-act play, or three chapters of a new novel, or an essay. But the same number of pages come out now as came years ago: somewhere between eighteen and thirty-two pages a week.

I hasten to add that all this was not mechanical. I didn't hold myself to account. I didn't have to. I loved what I was doing, even as a mother loves her homely or ugly babies. You may or may not like my children, but at the time I wrote them, I was plowing my typewriter and reaping the paragraphs. God protects young writers so they do not know, at the time, how badly off center they are performing. That's what quantity production is all about. The good stories you write later are an umbrella over the bad stuff you discover you left behind you in the years. It all equals out. And, if you love writing, it is all a lark.

It follows that detective fiction, as well as the fantasy, science, and weird genres, was a lark of mine. My talent developed faster in the latter fields because it was intuitive. My weird, my fantastic, my science fiction concepts came as lightning bolts and knocked me head first into my machine. The detective tales, because they required hard thinking, prevented my flow, damaged my ability to use my intuition to the full. They were, as a result, quite often walking wounded. Today, many years later, with a greater knowledge of the field and having learned lessons from Ross Macdonald meanwhile, I feel I might be able to do better. I feel it enough, I might add, that I recently finished—and Knopf will soon publish—my first mystery suspense novel, *Death Is a Lonely Business*.

Now, as to the stories in this collection. First, the titles. I would like to have changed some of them from their pulp versions, simply because I did not like the titles the editors of those magazines hung on my stories without asking permission. After all, "Hell's Half Hour" and "Corpse Carnival" are not exactly sterling examples of title-making. I was astonished when the editors let "The Trunk Lady" and "The Long Night," my titles, slip through.

What you have here in this collection, then, is a record of the way I wrote and tried to survive through the early '40s, with Leigh Brackett trying to help around the edges. I floundered, I thrashed, sometimes I lost, sometimes I won. But I was trying. Perhaps this collection is only of historical interest to those with an immense curiosity about my work in a field unfamiliar to many, but I can name my favorites, "The Long Night" and "The Trunk Lady," and add that "The Small Assassin" seems to me to be one of the best stories in any field that I have ever written. It was so successful, in fact, that it appears to have influenced a dozen novels and films written and produced in the last ten years.

As for the other stories, you must read and judge. But I hope you will judge kindly, and let me off easy. I was, after all, in my early twenties and still had a long way to go, with Hammett and Chandler and Cain way over there on the horizon, standing tall, and me on the beach, sweating it out and taking advice from Leigh Brackett. I hope that her dear ghost will not mind that this book and its stories are dedicated to her with love.

RAY BRADBURY

Additional Copyright Information

Don't Let the Mystery End Here. Try More Great Books From HARD CASE CRIME!

Hard Case Crime brings you gripping, award-winning crime fiction by best-selling authors and the hottest new writers in the field:

The Cocktail Waitress

by JAMES M. CAIN

"AN ENDING YOU'LL NEVER FORGET"—STEPHEN KING

The day Joan Medford buried her first husband, she met two men: the older man whose touch repelled her but whose money was an irresistible temptation, and the young schemer she'd come to crave like life itself...

The Twenty-Year Death

by ARIEL S. WINTER

"EXTRAORDINARY"—NEW YORK TIMES

A masterful first novel written in the styles of three giants of the mystery genre. Stephen King says it's "bold, innovative, and thrilling...crackles with suspense and will keep you up late."

Charlesgate Confidential

by SCOTT VON DOVIAK

"TERRIFIC"—STEPHEN KING

An unsolved heist of priceless art from a Boston museum sends deadly repercussions echoing from 1946 to the present day. The *Wall Street Journal* calls this first novel "impressive, inventive, and immensely enjoyable."